THE
REPORT
TO THE
JUDICIARY

Also by
The Honorable Eugene Sullivan

The Majority Rules

THE
REPORT
TO THE
JUDICIARY

Best wishes
EUGENE SULLIVAN
Eugene Sullivan

FORGE®

A TOM DOHERTY ASSOCIATES BOOK
New York

THE REPORT TO THE JUDICIARY

A Forge Book
Published by Tom Doherty Associates, LLC
175 Fifth Avenue
New York, NY 10010

www.tor-forge.com

Forge® is a registered trademark of Tom Doherty Associates, LLC.

Library of Congress Cataloging-in-Publication Data

Sullivan, Eugene (Eugene R.)
    The report to the judiciary / Eugene Sullivan.—1st hardcover ed.
        p. cm.
    "A Tom Doherty Associates Book."
    ISBN-13: 978-0-7653-1388-1
    ISBN-10: 0-7653-1388-X
    1. Judges—Fiction. 2. United States. Supreme Court—Fiction. 3. Washington (D.C.)—Fiction. 4. Political fiction. I. Title.
    PS3619.U424R47   2008
    813'.6—dc22

                                                          2008004504

First Edition: May 2008

Printed in the United States of America

0 9 8 7 6 5 4 3 2 1

To Lis again . . . and forever.

ACKNOWLEDGMENTS

The Book

One could say there are three themes in this novel: modern racism, real-time history, and the future.

The racism in this novel can be traced back centuries, to William Shakespeare's *Othello*. Unfortunately, this stain on the universal human character seems to be timeless and still exists today. I have tried to alert people to this by making it an integral part of the story of *The Report to the Judiciary*.

The setting of the novel is a contemporary, controversial nomination to the U.S. Supreme Court. In this theme, you will see the constitutional process of a President nominating a person to a lifetime appointment on the highest court in our Nation. If you examine the Supreme Court nominations of the past century, history will show the nomination process has become harder and more brutal. In *The Report to the Judiciary* you will see that a nomination to high office in the U.S. Government today has the potential to be a high-tech, dirty "mugging" of a worthy candidate's character and record.

The last theme you may observe in *The Report to the Judiciary* is one of the future—our increasing use of spy satellites to observe our daily lives and to protect us from not just our military enemies, but also from terrorists and criminals. Properly supervised, this can be a good thing.

My Thanks

Certainly the birth of a novel benefits from many backers. I thank Lis, my "forever" love, and also my children, Kim and Gene, for their inspiration and help in writing this book. I thank Brian Thomsen, my outstanding editor, for his brilliant idea to bring *Othello* to Washington, D.C. Thanks also to my super agent, Frank Weimann of The Literary Group in NYC, for his sage guidance.

I honor the help of Judges Stanley Sporkin and Louis Freeh for their support in my writings. Our consulting group, Freeh Group International, is a real family.

For technical help, I relied on former FBI (and now corporate) superstars Hollis Helms, Barry McManus, and Rod Smith of Abraxas Corporation. I also received tech help from one of Delta Force's heroes, Lee Van Arsdale, now CEO of Triple Canopy, a tier-one security company.

Thanks also to Lynn Everett and Chief Judge Robinson Everett for their valuable help in editing the manuscript.

Finally, I treasure the inspiration and the courage of my brother, Dr. William K. Sullivan, which helped me finish the book.

O, beware, my lord, of jealousy!
It is the green-eyed monster which doth mock
The meat it feeds on.

—Shakespeare, *Othello,* Act 3

THE
REPORT
TO THE
JUDICIARY

NOVEMBER 18, 2008

1

EVERYBODY THOUGHT THE CHIEF JUSTICE HAD BEEN shot by a silenced weapon. There was no sound of gunfire in the courtroom, what other explanation existed for the scene that started a panic run for the exits?

The Chief Justice of the U.S. Supreme Court, his face contorted in agony, suddenly snapped his head back and jumped up from his high-back leather chair, grabbing his head with both hands. Then he fell forward, hitting his forehead with a sickening thud on the mahogany bench, and landed in a fetal position on the dark burgundy carpet of the courtroom. The sound of this startling sight was amplified by the open mike on the bench in front of the now empty Chief Justice's chair.

The attorney arguing her case at the podium stopped in midsentence, her mouth a red circle and her eyes wide with shock . . . and fear. Even though the case being argued was a rather dry and boring import-tax-rate case, the courtroom was nearly three-quarters full—a crowd relatively in excess of one hundred people, a large number at risk, if a terrorist shooter was in the room.

For just a moment, the courtroom was completely silent.

Everyone seemed frozen by what they had just witnessed.

A full second passed

... and then there was a sudden movement from behind the bench.

Associate Justice Oscar Moorman leaped up from his dark leather chair several seats from the center of the bench and quickly moved to the fallen Chief Justice.

His eyes studied the stricken justice closely.

Moorman bent over and calmly spoke into the Chief Justice's mike: "Marshal, clear the courtroom. We have a medical emergency here. Is there a doctor in the courtroom? I repeat . . . we need a doctor now!"

His voice over the courtroom PA system was even and controlled with a firm air of authority. However, inside Justice Moorman was not calm. His mind was racing.

God, was the Chief Justice shot?

I thought I saw his head jerk back as if shot.

Is there a gunman here in the courtroom?

Moorman knew that the fact that he heard no shot fired didn't necessarily mean the Chief wasn't shot by a gun. A silenced weapon might have been used.

The U.S. Supreme Court was a very prime target for terrorists.

A successful attack on the heart of the American justice system would shock the world and show that America was vulnerable at its highest level. Moreover, any attack during an oral argument would be instantly seen by millions in real time since all hearings were televised live nationwide on the quasi-public network C-SPAN ever since the last term of the Supreme Court. (It was last September when the young Chief Justice Simmons had convinced the slimmest of a majority of the justices—five to four—to allow television coverage via C-SPAN for all Supreme Court arguments.) Now there were four cameras in the courtroom, all discreetly operated via remote from the C-SPAN control room four blocks away. One camera in the rear of the courtroom, two on the sides, and one positioned immediately behind the bench to have a frontal shot of the attorney who was

arguing the case at the podium. The Court had insisted that the tele-
vising operation be performed by unmanned cameras so that the TV
presence would be as unobtrusive as possible and not distract from
the oral arguments. Seeing the Supreme Court on TV now had become as boring to most Americans as the debates occurring on the
floor of the U.S. Congress—the staple of C-SPAN programming.

The possibility that there was a terrorist attack in progress was
foremost on Justice Moorman's mind when he attended his fallen
leader. He as a rational man naturally wanted to get out of the danger
area—the courtroom . . . Nevertheless he didn't. Moorman stayed
and saw no one except the Supreme Court Marshal, John Abbot, who
rushed up to him.

The Marshal said curtly, "Doesn't appear to be a doctor here in
the courtroom, sir." The Marshal's hard brown eyes looked directly
into Moorman's. Moorman stood still and returned the stare of the
Marshal.

"Medical team been called." Moorman didn't waiver from looking for a doctor to emerge from the crowd in the courtroom.

No one came forward.

The Marshal whispered softly, "No doc, Mr. Justice. Up to you
now. . . . Do your thing. I hear you were good at this once."

Moorman murmured, "John, it's been too long. I've forgotten so
much."

Last man I treated died—that was Justice Moorman's thought as
he realized he was the only person who could give medical attention
to the fallen Chief Justice. Moorman remembered the stench of the
drainage ditch, the heat, and the slick blood . . . so much blood.
Moorman closed his eyes, shook his head, and tightened his jaws almost until he could feel his teeth crack.

God, please help me do this right, mouthed Moorman to himself.

The Supreme Court justice dropped down and started to give
basic medical treatment to the man twitching on the floor, treatment Moorman had learned long ago before he went to war . . . to
Vietnam.

Once Moorman was down on the floor next to the Chief Justice, the Marshal rushed off back to the phones at his station at the end of the long courtroom bench.

Communication was important in a crisis, and the Marshal was tethered to the phones and electronic equipment at his position.

Moorman found that Chief Justice Simmons had now moved on his side into a fetal position, his body and legs shaking in spasms. His eyelids were fluttering with the whites of the eyes mostly visible.

Moorman rolled the Chief Justice over on his back, and as he did so, the Chief Justice's legs straightened out but continued shaking. Moorman tore open the Chief's robe to examine him.

Moorman quickly needed the answer to a key question—was he shot or was he suffering from a purely medical condition.

First, he looked closely at the face of the twitching man. Out of the corner of his eyes, Moorman had seen the head of Simmons snap back just before he jumped up.

No blood there.

Moorman closely examined the front of the fallen man for any blood spotting on the white shirt that he was wearing.

No blood.

Once that was completed, Moorman gently probed with his hand under Simmons's body, checking for a possible wound in the back of his head and torso.

His hand came back without any blood on it.

Moorman was puzzled. There was no sign of a wound anywhere.

The sounds of screams from the courtroom pulled him back to the reality of the situation . . . and to his duty as a judge. He needed to stop the chaos in the courtroom. It was possible that he could have missed a small wound. It could have been an ultra-thin dart gun that leaves a nonbleeder wound. He had heard of such things from a friend in the Pentagon who was ex-Delta. Who knew what triggered the seizure? He wasn't sure about the "shot" part, but he knew one thing for sure—someone needed to calm the rising panic in the courtroom. Moorman was the only one who had physically examined the Chief and he did have a little prior medical training. It was up to him. Although he was not the next-ranking justice, he knew sometimes circumstances picked a person to act and do what was necessary.

No visible wound, no bleeding. My best guess now is that the Chief is having a seizure brought on by some medical condition. I'll go with that now. It will help calm the courtroom. Christ, I'm sure everyone thinks the Chief was shot . . . and that they're next. Fear had to be controlled.

Moorman rose from behind the bench. Six feet and powerfully built with short cropped hair, Moorman projected a commanding presence in his black robe at the center of the tall bench. He grabbed the Chief Justice's mike.

Again his calm deep voice floated over the courtroom.

"Attention. The Chief Justice is ill. There is no danger to anyone. Please be calm. There is no danger here. Please leave the courtroom quietly."

God, I hope I'm right.

As soon as he was finished with his "best guess" announcement, Moorman dropped down to help Simmons again. The man was in full seizure. His head was bouncing off the carpet. Moorman looked around and grabbed the thick seat cushion the smallish Chief Justice used to boost his height. Moorman used it as a pillow so the Chief Justice wouldn't hurt his head as it hit the carpet with each violent contortion of his body in seizure. Also Moorman checked the airway of the Chief to make sure it was clear and pulled out his thick Mont Blanc pen to hold it in the mouth of the Chief to prevent him from biting his tongue. As he was holding the pen in place with his right hand, the strong smell of urine hit the nostrils of Moorman. With his other hand, Moorman felt the inside leg of the Chief Justice.

Wet pants! Damn! Definite signs of a grand mal seizure, thought Moorman.

It had been a long time since Oscar Moorman had given any medical treatment. The last time was in 1975. He was a nineteen-year-old Navy medical corpsman stationed with a Marine infantry company helping secure the main airport of Saigon while U.S Air Force planes were frantically evacuating the embassy staff and U.S. citizens in the final days of the Vietnam War. The last casualty Moorman treated was a Marine captain shot in the chest . . . and he died after Moorman had worked on him alone in a ditch under sniper fire, keeping him alive for almost twenty minutes—twenty long minutes—before he died. For his actions that day so long ago, Oscar Moorman was awarded the Silver Star, the third-highest Navy decoration for valor in combat.

All of the other justices had initially rushed from the courtroom via the exit behind the bench. Several had ducked down and crawled through the heavy burgundy curtains behind the bench to the safety of the small anteroom, which contained the rear door of the courtroom. One justice, running away, tripped over the thick cables leading to the sole C-SPAN camera mounted behind the bench and crashed to the floor before scampering out of the courtroom through the curtains.

Now two justices cautiously returned to the courtroom, Justices Vincent Bianco and Carolyn Ryland. They crawled back from behind the curtains and were both watching Moorman work on Simmons. Ryland was bent over, crouching behind the nearest chair. Bianco was on his hands and knees next to Moorman. The Supreme Court bench was probably the safest place to be if there was gunfire in the courtroom. Years ago, a thick wall of Kevlar had been fastened to the length of the dark mahogany bench. The bench was bulletproof up to the heaviest caliber of assault rifles.

Justice Vincent Bianco, a short squat man with a raspy voice, thinning black clearly dyed hair, and closely set brown eyes, urgently asked, "Was the Chief shot?"

Moorman briefly glanced to his side and caught the fear in Bianco's eyes.

"I don't know. I don't think so, Vince. It looks like he's having a seizure. But the Marshal may know for sure if there was a shooter in the courtroom using a silenced gun and some kind of chemical agent bullet. Remember his station has a high-tech monitor that can sniff gunfire smells . . . goddamn, Vince, I need to know that . . . Go get the Marshal back up here."

Bianco recoiled from the request as if it was a snake. He didn't move off his knees.

"So there could be terrorists in the courtroom?" Bianco asked in a hushed voice.

"Yeah, there could be terrorists. I announced that there was no danger because I wanted to stop the panic in the courtroom." Moorman whispered back, conscious that there probably were open mikes on the bench.

Apparently that was all Bianco needed to know.

He crouched down farther, actually hugging the carpet hard. Moorman thought if Bianco could have chewed his way through the floor to the basement below he would have done it right at that moment. All the while, Bianco was staring vacantly into Moorman's eyes.

Moorman knew from the look on his face that Bianco was going nowhere. The terrified justice was definitely not going to move over to the exposed end of the bench to get the Marshal. He thought of asking Carolyn Ryland, the other justice, but decided to fall back on one of his old principles—when there's an emergency situation and you want something done, *do it yourself.*

So Moorman, without moving from cradling the shaking judge, yelled at the top of his lungs, "Marshal, Get back here. I need you. ASAP!" His strong voice didn't need the open bench mikes and operating PA system to be heard throughout the courtroom.

Within twenty seconds, U.S. Supreme Court Marshal John Abbot slid to a kneel beside Moorman. Abbot was alert and composed—ready for orders.

Moorman said in one breath. "I see no wounds on the Chief Justice. I'm thinking a medical seizure. Talk to me, John. Did the gunsniffing monitor at your station register any gunfire?"

"Negative, Your Honor. Just checked my gear again. Absolutely no sign of any gunfire discharge. Looks like no terrorists here. Court-room is being cleared. Your announcement helped on the panic. Lat-est on medical care—we can't locate the nurse. My office thinks she may have wandered upstairs to the Court library. My people will find her though. Also the doctor from the U.S Capitol is on his way. ETA five minutes." Moorman liked that directness about him. Moorman had been the head of the three-justice search committee two years ago when the prior Marshal retired. He liked the quiet and efficient ex-military officer from the start of the interview. Moorman had been the key vote to hire him. And John Abbot knew it and appreci-ated it. Abbot, an ex-SEAL, would walk through a brick wall for Moorman.

"Got to get the nurse now, John, find her!" ordered Moorman.

The Marshal moved away quickly to the phone on his desk at the end of the bench. Moorman could hear Abbot shouting into the phone at the Marshal's station.

Those first two minutes while Justice Moorman was administer-ing emergency aid to the Chief Justice, the courtroom had been in controlled chaos. The Marshal of the Supreme Court had twelve Supreme Court plainclothes policemen in the courtroom, all armed with holstered 9mm Sigs concealed under their blue blazers. Ten of them were methodically clearing the public, the press, and the staff from the room. Two were positioned at each end of the bench with orders to shoot anyone who advanced upon the justices. The Marshal had practiced this emergency procedure several times a year with his police force and now the training showed. Moorman's announce-ment and the professional manner of the police calmed things down.

Right at the beginning of the incident, Marshal John Abbot, a re-tired highly decorated Navy SEAL, had followed procedure and placed a call from the landline on his desk to his office alerting his staff to the situation in the courtroom and requesting the on-duty nurse in the Marshal's office. In addition to the nurse and, according to the plan of a medical emergency at the Court, the duty doctor from the U.S. Capitol with a full emergency medical team just across

First Street from the Supreme Court was summoned. The uniformed Supreme Court police would empty the courtroom and temporarily hold everyone in the public area of the massive marble foyer right outside the courtroom until they received a release order. A key provision of the emergency plan was a lockdown—the Supreme Court was now a sealed fortress. Only the medical team from the U.S. Capitol would be let in. No one was going out until the emergency was over.

Now that the courtroom was almost cleared, the Marshal stayed next to Moorman behind the long bench. Justices Bianco and Ryland had been joined by three other justices. Things were calming down. The Marshal quickly briefed the justices that it was a medical emergency not a terrorist attack. Bianco looked especially relieved when Moorman glanced over at him.

Then everything went south . . . very quickly.

Moorman faced another crisis.

He was the first to notice. The Chief Justice in his arms had stopped shaking . . . and breathing.

Moorman quickly bent his head over to check the Chief's airway, and he put his finger on his neck to check for a pulse. The practiced actions of his past EMT life were returning.

"No pulse. No breathing. Get the defibrillator from the emergency gurney behind the curtains!" Moorman barked to the Marshal.

Moorman ripped open the shirt of the Chief Justice. The ivory buttons of the Chief's white buttoned-down Brooks Brothers shirt bounced noiselessly on the carpet. Moorman's dark ebony hands as they searched for the sternum were a sharp contrast to the pale thin hairless chest of Chief Justice William Simmons as Moorman started CPR. First, Moorman gave the one hard pound to the heart area. The thump startled the justices watching Moorman. Then fifteen pumps with his hands just below the sternum. Then two breaths mouth to mouth. Fifteen and two. Fifteen and two.

When the Marshal had the portable defib set up, Moorman used it. The mechanical voice from the machine talking him through the steps. The display on the machine continued to show a flat line for Simmons.

It was now over five minutes since Simmons had stopped breathing. The defib hadn't restarted the heart. Still a flat line. Moorman looked up, his face grim and tired, and asked, "John, please get me a flashlight from the kit on the gurney. And check on the nurse and doctor again."

There was no urgency to his voice in that last request.

This man is dead. No pulse, no breathing, and I bet his eyes won't respond to the flashlight, thought Moorman.

When the flashlight was handed to Moorman by the Marshal, there was no reaction to the light. Simmons' pupils remained fully dilated in his electric blue eyes.

Still Moorman worked on the man for another minute until the nurse and doctor arrived at almost the same time.

After the doctor examined the Chief Justice, he and the nurse used the defibrillator several times before the mechanical voice said, "Do not shock again." There was a smell of burnt flesh from the defib paddles.

The doctor pronounced the Chief Justice of the United States dead.

◆

As the other justices gathered around the body, Justice Moorman took off his own robe and covered the face and body of Simmons with it. As he got up, Moorman thought back to his shining the flashlight into the Chief's eyes.

The eyes sometimes tell you the story.

After he was standing there looking down at the covered body, the courtroom was suddenly relatively quiet for the first time since the Chief Justice fell down. It was quiet enough for Moorman to hear his own heavy breathing. It was then that Moorman heard an unusual sound.

A whirring of a mechanical device.

He turned around and saw it.

The C-SPAN camera mounted behind the bench, not ten feet from the fallen justice, was making the whirring sound as it was being remotely operated by the control room at the main offices of C-SPAN on North Capitol Street in Washington. The lens was moving in and out obviously focusing and the entire camera moved slightly side to side for different views as Moorman stared at it. He saw there was a red light at the top. It was lit. The camera was live and transmitting.

This glass eye was still telling the whole story of the terrible event—to everybody watching—to everybody watching the C-SPAN feed now broadcasting to all major TV networks.

With a shoulder push worthy of an NFL linebacker, the six-foot, powerfully built Moorman knocked over the heavy camera; his hard hit ripped out the power cord.

The camera showed the ornate ceiling of the courtroom to its viewers for a moment before it went black.

The red light went out showing the eye was dead.

MSNBC transcript of Hardball *for the evening of November 18, 2008.*

MATTHEWS: "Good evening. It has been an amazing day at the Supreme Court. The young fit Chief Justice William Simmons has died of a brain aneurysm during a session of the Court. The whole incident was dramatically captured on film. We will start by showing a C-SPAN clip of the scene at the Supreme Court to recap what many of you have been seeing all day. We also have in our studio in Washington retired Federal Judge Stan Sporkin and, by remote, we'll be talking with political analyst Maggie Concannon out in Los Angeles. Two items for tonight's discussion—the startling event at the Supreme Court and whether the president has the clout to get a new justice confirmed before he leaves office in about two months.

I'm Chris Matthews and let's play *Hardball!*

[Twenty-second clip of the video released to the networks by C-SPAN, ending with Justice Moorman's touching act of covering Simmons' body with his robe.]

MATTHEWS: Dramatic shots! The official word was that Chief Justice Simmons died from a brain aneurysm—a condition that couldn't be foreseen. Simmons was only fifty four years-old and was in excellent health. Daily jogged two miles—top shape for his age. Terrible loss. Judge Stan Sporkin is a retired federal judge and a very close friend of Chief Justice Simmons.

Judge Sporkin, welcome to *Hardball* and what can you tell us about the late Chief Justice?

SPORKIN: Good evening, Chris. What can I say? I have known Bill Simmons for years. He was one of my first law clerks and one of the brightest clerks I ever had. He was not only smart, but he had compassion and a true love of the law. I thought he was an excellent pick for the Supreme Court . . . and I guessed that he had many years ahead of him on the bench. Tremendous loss today. My heart goes out to Marilyn, his wife, and their two daughters.

MATTHEWS: Any hint of medical problems?

SPORKIN: Absolutely none. I heard that the doctors say no one could predict a thing like this aneurysm. Very strange—he was a daily runner and was in excellent health. No way to see this coming.

MATTHEWS: Judge, let's talk about the Supreme Court. That was fantastic footage of the crisis in the courtroom. What if that had been a terrorist attack instead of a medical emergency? Are they ready for an attack up there?

SPORKIN: Who knows for sure, but I think so. The Supreme Court realized that it is high on all target lists, especially for Muslim terrorists. Few people know that there is a lesser known, but a very good reason why a radical suicide-bent Muslim would want to strike the Supreme Court.

During the 1990s there was a controversial news story that quickly became national news. The story alerted America to the fact that the ornate decorative carved figures of lawgivers on the white frieze high up on the walls of the Supreme Court courtroom included not only Moses and other famous historical makers of the law . . . but there was a carving of Mohammed! Mohammed is on the north frieze, a stone bas-relief where Mohammed in his role as lawgiver is shown holding a book and a scimitar. He is between Charlemagne and Justinian, other noted historical figures of the law.

Many Muslim groups protested that it was a terrible insult to the Muslim faith to include the face of "He" who was to have no earthly representation of his face. The protests then were brushed aside in the 1990s by Chief Justice Rehnquist and the other sitting justices at the time and the carving of Mohammed remains in place today. The Supreme Court carving escaped any notice in the "Danish cartoon" firestorm of 2006. However, according to intelligence reports of some radical sects of Muslims throughout the world, there are terrorists who have vowed to destroy this institution that they feel has mocked and offended Mohammed the Messenger.

MATTHEWS: Fascinating stuff. How about the medical response?

SPORKIN: They need to work on that. It was way too slow for the medical team to arrive. The Court was lucky it had a former Navy medic as a justice. That Oscar Moorman was just terrific! He really took charge.

MATTHEWS: Yes, he was great and I want to get back to that super display of leadership. However, I was just reading the official write-up of the Silver Star Moorman won in Vietnam. He is the real deal. A combat hero. Braved enemy sniper fire to run across the Saigon Airport main runway to the aid of a Marine who was shot. Nearly saved the Marine captain by performing a tracheotomy with a Swiss Army knife—doing the makeshift operation under intense sniper fire. Did this despite being wounded by shrapnel from an enemy grenade. Silver Star and a Purple Heart! How about that, Your Honor?

SPORKIN: Moorman's amazing. I completely agree with you, Chris. He's a real war hero and he hasn't lost it—has the right stuff. He did a hell of a job today taking charge and helping Simmons until the medical team arrived.

MATTHEWS: That brings me to the next point. Justice Moorman really showed all of America that he is a "take charge" kind of a guy. How about him for chief justice, Judge Sporkin? And I want to bring in Maggie Concannon on this also for the political angle. But first you, Your Honor, would he be a good chief justice?

SPORKIN: Absolutely. You saw how he took control of the Court today. He's a real leader. Also, intellectually Moorman has grown over the years since he has been on the Court. His decisions are sound, moderate, and are written in plain English so ordinary people and judges like me can understand them. His recent switch on affirmative action will make him very acceptable to liberals and the minorities. I like him for the top spot. Maybe I'm prejudiced because he voted on my side in the Microsoft case.

MATTHEWS (*LAUGHTER*): OK, OK, Your Honor. Thank you. By the way, I sided with your view on the Microsoft case when you were sitting on the U.S. District Court in D.C.

SPORKIN (*LAUGHING AND NODDING*): Too bad you weren't sitting with the Court of Appeals!

MATTHEWS: OK, OK. Now let's look at the political landscape for a possible Supreme Court nomination for the chief judgeship. Maggie Concannon is with us today from Los Angeles. She is a top political analyst. Maggie, there is a vacancy on the Supreme

Court. Will President Ramsey be able to fill that vacancy and possibly name a new chief justice in the short time left on his term—in about two months?

CONCANNON: Chris, first, thanks for having me on your show. To answer your question on whether there is a chance that Ramsey will be able to nominate . . . and get confirmation on anyone for the vacancy before he finishes his term on January 20. The answer— Two words—Im-possible! . . . President Ramsey is such a lame duck that he can barely quack.

MATTHEWS: Ouch! I see you've taken off the gloves. And viewers, in case you haven't guessed it Maggie is a hard-core Democrat.

CONCANNON: Listen, Chris. Even the Republicans I have been talking to today see absolutely no chance Ramsey will get to fill that lifetime slot on the Court. Let's face facts. The Democrats have just won the presidency so the president-elect will probably make the nomination for the vacancy his top priority. And don't forget the Republicans and their present weakness from the November election. Although they presently have a slim majority in the Senate, that majority includes many enemies of the president. Ramsey, with his Middle East policy and the failures of his economic and immigration policies, has alienated many in his party. By the way, as you know Ramsey just hit a new low in public approval. No help for him there. Simply put, there's no way Ramsey will get to fill that vacancy on the Supreme Court.

MATTHEWS: How about naming a new chief justice from someone within the present court? Switching a sitting justice to be chief justice won't add a new justice to the Court. That should be a lot easier than taking a lifetime slot that will be filled by the Democrats once they take the White House. I should add . . . That view is the heavy buzz going around political and legal Washington this afternoon.

CONCANNON: Well, that's a different question. President Ramsey may be able to work out a deal with the Senate to successfully nominate one of the present justices to be chief justice and give the Court leadership at this critical time. Some big cases are on its calendar in the next few months. Picking a chief justice from within the Court is a definite possibility. That is . . . if Ramsey smartens up and picks someone very confirmable.

MATTHEWS: All right. Let's get down to it. Maggie, who would you pick?

CONCANNON: Well, the real mystery is who would President Ramsey pick. But if I had to guess, I think President Ramsey would go with Justice Vincent Bianco. Great credentials—Harvard College, Yale Law, a former Deputy Attorney General of the U.S. Department of Justice. Moreover, as a judge, he has a sterling record on the Court . . . He's the heavyweight intellect in the center, a real legal scholar. The moderate center of the Republican party and a lot of Democrats love him . . . and there is another plus that would weigh heavily with our religious President—Bianco is a born-again Christian, the anointed darling of the religious right. I think Ramsey might pick Bianco. The only possible downside is his age. He's just about to turn seventy, I think. However, his age might actually be a plus—the Democrats might be OK with the selection of a Justice in his seventies rather than one in his fifties—with these lifetime appointments, longevity is a factor. Nevertheless, Bianco's in excellent health and would have a lot of support from a lot of factions—a critical factor for a lame-duck nomination.

MATTHEWS: How about the star of the day, Justice Oscar Moorman, as chief justice?

CONCANNON: I don't know. He was impressive on TV. Good record in the military—a Vietnam War hero, the Silver Star and Purple Heart you mentioned—and, quite frankly, one of the most recognized and respected African-Americans in America today. However, years ago, he did have a rough set of hearings to get on the Court. As you remember, he was a longtime Washington bachelor after his divorce and his reputation as a womanizer was a big issue then at his Senate confirmation hearings to get on the Supreme Court. But he is married now and has gotten some recent good press for working with high-profile African-American causes. The American public, especially African-Americans, respect and admire his generosity and his hard work outside the Supreme Court as a volunteer in charitable work, primarily helping raise awareness for HIV/AIDS children in Africa. While most justices fly around the world being treated as judicial royalty and collecting speaking fees at legal conferences during the summer, Moorman spends most of his summers working as an unpaid low-level medical helper in refugee centers in some of the poorest parts of the African continent. The UN even made him an honorary UNICEF ambassador for his work in Africa. You know he attends benefits and has helped raise millions for the UN program for African children infected by the AIDS virus. Moreover, Moorman is a moderate Republican and a protégé of Bianco. They share many views and often vote together. Around legal circles, they call them the "Center Twins" of the Court.

Yes, I would say that for the nomination as chief justice, Moorman could be a *dark horse* . . . God, I can't believe I just said that!

MATTHEWS (*LAUGHTER*): Absolutely no comment on that! Thank you both, Judge Sporkin and Maggie Concannon. With that we'll wrap up. I'm Chris Matthews. Thank you for watching *Hardball.*

❖ 3 ❖

AT THE VIRGINIA HOME OF JUSTICE MOORMAN JUST outside Washington, Oscar and his wife had just watched the finish of MSNBC's *Hardball*. Debby was in a silk robe ready for bed and Moorman was dressed in a T-shirt and sweatpants. He had just returned from a short run and had joined Debby, who'd been watching the TV program.

Debby Moorman was excited as she muted the TV with the remote and turned to her husband. "O, you were magnificent today. I'm so proud of you. And just think . . . you're being considered for the chief justice's position. Wow, I can't believe it. You as Chief Justice!" She gently touched his face, then her soft fingers dropped and traced the jagged scars on his arms—shrapnel scars from an enemy grenade. (While treating the dying Marine long ago in that ditch at the Saigon Airport, a grenade was thrown nearby. Corpsman Moorman had used his body to protect the Marine and received multiple wounds to his arms and back.)

Her touching the scars on his arms was one of Debby's habits. She said it made her feel closer to him to feel them—the memories of his pain in war.

Moorman closed his eyes to her gentle touching as she traced the scars. He answered his young wife in a soft voice. "Baby, I don't think I'm really being considered. Don't believe those 'talking heads' on TV." Then he opened his eyes and looked directly into hers. Seeing she was still serious about him taking a shot at the Center Seat, he suggested, "If anyone on the Court has a shot at being nominated by the president as Chief Justice, it's Vince. He's very plugged into this White House. Remember how the President pays attention to the 'born-again' crowd since he's one himself—just like Vince."

Debby just smiled, undeterred. "But, O darling, remember Daddy called today and said that already two members of the Judiciary Committee seemed very strongly leaning toward you. They asked him to check to see if you were interested in the Chief's job. Daddy said he could help with the Chair of the Senate Judiciary Committee, Senator Powers. He's very friendly with her. All I have to do is call Daddy and he'll put a quiet campaign into motion to push the president into nominating you as chief justice. . . . Shall I call Daddy and tell him you'll do it?"

Moorman looked at his wife and slowly shook his head at her suggestion.

Deborah Sloane Moorman was Moorman's wife of only two short years. It was his second marriage and her first. Debby was in her mid-thirties, five-six with long, dark brown hair. Bright, pretty face with freckles she hated, but that O found sexy. She had a wide mouth with full lips and large brown eyes. Her skin was almost milk white.

They first met when she had been a junior reporter for the DC-based *Legal Times* newspaper on an assignment to interview Moorman in his chambers three years ago. At the interview, Moorman was stunned with her energy and charm. After his first wife broke his heart, leaving him shortly after he came to Washington to work long hours as an antitrust lawyer in the Justice Department, he thought he would never be in love . . . or get married again. But he was wrong about both. He fell in love with Debby during the interview and they were married within a year.

During that interview with Debby, he was shy and reserved—a clear break in behavior from a man known for aggressively pursuing many women around Washington. Too many. When he was nominated for the Supreme Court from his position as a U.S. Appeals Court judge on the D.C. Circuit Court, there were some embarrassing moments during his Senate confirmation hearings when it came to light that Moorman had dated a couple of women who had worked as strippers in a Washington topless club. It also was a big blow to the nomination when it came to light that he, a federal judge, had also dated for six months a woman who had been arrested once for prostitution and once for drug use. Although charges in court were dropped and she was never convicted of anything, Moorman's dating of such a woman was smeared over his nomination. All in all, his love life as a bachelor after his failed first marriage had been reckless and made his nomination to the Supreme Court a hard sell, even though the Republicans then had a six-vote majority in the U.S. Senate.

Nevertheless, when it came time to vote, the Senate, mostly males with public false shock about a single man chasing the women of Washington, approved his nomination, and Moorman was elevated to sit on the U.S. Supreme Court.

At the end of that *Legal Times* interview in his chambers, it was Debby who asked him out to dinner. He was caught so off guard that he almost didn't accept. When he considered the dinner proposal, delivered as she uncrossed her long legs and started to rise up after the interview, he started to stammer an excuse. There were three facts that made him hesitate: (1) she was white and the only child of the senior U.S. Senator from Connecticut; (2) she was twenty years his junior; and (3) the main reason—he instinctively knew that if he went out with her, he would never get her out of his heart. For Moorman, love at first sight went from a myth to a reality during the span of that fateful interview. And he was a smart enough judge to recognize that . . . but her dinner invitation made with a self-assured smile was irresistible. As Victor Hugo observed in *Les Misérables,* the first symptom of true love in a man is timidity; in a woman, it is boldness.

At the end of the long moment following the invitation, Moorman did accept. . . . That dinner was followed by a series of dates. And the black justice fell deeper in love with Debby the more he knew her.

In many ways he believed she was his opposite. He sensed she was drawn to him because of his life . . . as a man scarred in war and as a black man scarred in peace growing up in America. He was a policeman's son who grew up in a Bronx four-story walk-up and worked his way through CCNY and Fordham Law. She was born to "old money," raised on a New Canaan, Connecticut, horse farm and was Ivy League to the max—including the blue-blooded Lawrenceville prep school, Yale undergrad, Columbia grad school in fine arts, lazy summers on the Cape, and a father who was a U.S. Senator—a very wealthy one who dearly loved his only child.

As if reaching a mountaintop, Moorman felt that when he married his Debby he'd finally arrived and fit into the last stage of his achievements—"tier-one class," a place he'd never been before. A long way from the Bronx. A world of pedigree, privilege, and private jets.

And he was happy there. He was happier than ever before in his life. Life with Debby and as a Justice on the Supreme Court was just fine with Moorman . . . as perfect a dream as it got. He was quite satisfied to be one of nine justices on the highest Court in the land. He didn't need anything further. He didn't need a final promotion to be the "One"—the owner of the Center Seat.

Moreover, to Oscar Moorman, another confirmation hearing before the Senate was one of the last things he wanted. Way too much sunshine . . . and possible pain there. The Senate confirmation process would be brutal for any major nomination of a lame-duck president. Confirmation by the Senate would be especially tough for Moorman . . . because of the sex angle—dating many women, especially the strippers and a possible prostitute.

His womanizing before he met Debby would likely be recycled again if he was nominated for chief justice. His past life and loves would be spotlighted—if not on the Senate floor, at least in the many newspapers and tabloids that seemed to sell papers based on celebrity sex. For today's media machine, the sex angle—if available—is demanded because it sold. For Moorman, the "chief" word in front of his current title "justice" was not worth the risk to his present stability and happiness.

Moorman felt that the legendary Supreme Court Justice Oliver Wendell Holmes got it right when he said, "I wouldn't do much more than walk across the street to be called Chief Justice instead of Justice," and Holmes had uttered this famous quote in the days before bare-knuckle partisan confirmation fights in the Senate and sex muckraking in the media.

Today with the media focus and the Senate's microexamination of one's life, even Holmes would be afraid to be nominated for the Chief's job. Moorman recalled that Holmes was a justice noted for his undisguised appreciation of good-looking women and rumored to be "especially fond" of a beautiful Irish noblewoman he met several summers in London when he was traveling without his wife. In today's world, Holmes probably wouldn't even stand exposed on a public sidewalk for ten minutes to be Chief Justice, thought Moorman.

So he turned to his wife and gave her a short kiss and whispered, "Debby, we are very lucky. I love you and I want nothing more in life than what I have now with you. If your dad calls again, please tell him I'm not interested in being the Chief Justice."

Debby smiled mischievously and said in a sweet voice, "Well, don't dismiss anything at this stage, O. An opportunity to be Chief could come your way. Why don't we wait and just see what comes up?" She playfully pulled her husband over her on the large sofa and gave him a deep kiss as she slipped her hand down inside his sweatpants.

Duke Law School, Durham, North Carolina—Press announcement for immediate release (November 24, 2008).

Today Professor Robinson O. Everett, a retired Federal Judge and the founding director of the Center of Law, Ethics, and National Security (LENS) at Duke Law School will host Supreme Court Justices Vincent Bianco and Oscar Moorman at a special law conference of the Duke Law School covering the topic of "Judicial Independence and Ethical Problems of Elected Judges in America."

The late Chief Justice of the United States William Simmons, a Duke Law graduate, was initially scheduled to chair this event. At Professor Everett's suggestion, Justices Bianco and Moorman graciously have agreed to come to the Duke Law School to preside over this conference to fulfill the promise of the late Chief Justice.

Professor Everett announced that Duke Law School and LENS will establish this conference as an annual event focused on ethics in the legal profession. The conference will be named the Chief Justice Simmons Memorial Conference.

The faculty and students of the Law School welcome Justices Bianco and Moorman to the Duke University community. Due to the large registration for the conference, the site of the conference has been moved to the Asian Continental Hotel in downtown Durham, North Carolina.

All inquiries on the conference will be referred to the Duke University Press Office on West Campus to the attention of Ms. Sissy Boyer, 919-555-1340.

THE LARGE ELEGANT CONFERENCE AUDITORIUM OF THE Asian Continental Hotel was almost at its max capacity of four hundred attendees. Students, lawyers, Duke Law faculty, members of the public, and news reporters crowded into the conference room. In reality, most were there to see in person the two men that were, according to heavy rumors coming out of the White House, under consideration to be nominated as Chief Justice by President Ramsey.

There was a small VIP room to the side of the stage in the auditorium used as a waiting room for speakers. It had a large one-way glass mirrored window where the people in the room could look out on the stage and audience without being seen. There were currently three men in the room looking at the jammed auditorium. They were a diverse group in appearance and manner. An older white man, whose six-foot-six-inch ample frame loomed over the other two, seemed jolly and excited. The man on the older man's right was an athletically fit six-foot black man who looked relaxed and confident. The last man, a five-foot-six-inch squat, swarthy white man, was looking as he felt—wound tight and impatient. Justice Bianco wanted to get away from the conference and head up to his hotel room to make some calls in his campaign to be chief justice.

"Your Honors, I never expected such a turnout for this conference. Really, as I explained last night at dinner, when my former student,

Bill Simmons, died, I thought the conference was finished. I considered canceling it. But then when you both volunteered to come down to Duke and lead the sessions, the conference was saved," said Professor Robinson Everett. The tall, bearlike older man was beaming. According to feedback Professor Everett learned during lunch, the morning session of the conference had been an unqualified huge success with the attendees. The afternoon session promised to equal the morning triumph. Justice Moorman was known to be good with audiences. He was naturally cheerful, witty, and down-to-earth.

Professor Everett went on to say, "I can't thank you both enough for coming to Duke."

The other two men in the VIP waiting room smiled at the statement by the former federal judge, now a tenured professor on the Duke Law faculty, as they looked through the one-way mirrored window in the waiting room out at the packed auditorium that people were still crowding into.

Justice Vince Bianco gave a solemn nod to the professor and replied, "I think Bill Simmons would have wanted the conference to go on. The Lord provides in times of crisis. O and I are happy to be here, Robbie."

Justice Oscar Moorman, his eyes fixed on the crowd outside the glass, whistled. "Great attendance, Robbie! Are all your conferences so popular?"

Bianco thought, *O's always been naïve. It's really my possible nomination to be Chief Justice that's causing these numbers.*

Professor Everett shook his head and smiled, "Heavens, no! You're both responsible for this turnout. Vince, your morning presentation was fascinating. I didn't know that eighty percent of all the judges in America were elected in one form or another. And the fact that a recent confidential survey done by *BusinessWeek* showed that forty-six percent of the judges surveyed admitted that campaign contributions played a role in some of their decisions. Amazing and intriguing . . . and just the right setup for Oscar's afternoon session on the ethical problems of elected judges."

Justice Moorman responded, "Yes, I have some good examples of judges getting in trouble due to the pressures from campaigning and raising money. Oh, by the way, please thank your wife, Lynn, again for the wonderful dinner last night. It is such a pleasure to see her and I'm pleased to hear that she likes her new job as a fiction editor. She's a wonderful lady. You're a lucky man, Robbie."

Kindness and thoughtfulness, observed Bianco. *Moorman has always been good at this kind of thing. It helps him make up for his lack of intellect . . . and blue-collar education.*

Everett smiled broadly at the compliment to his wife. "Last night was a wonderful evening. Well, I guess I'll get out there and introduce you. I'll be on your panel with Professor Pam Young to comment on the points you make. Remember tonight we three are having dinner with Coach Mike Krzyzewski. He wants to tell you a bit about his Center on Leadership and Ethics at the Duke Business School. We're thinking of merging on a law-business ethics program. I think it will be a fun night. Our dinner is at a fine old Durham restaurant, the Magnolia Grill. By the way, Coach K is bringing a couple of autographed basketballs from last year's NCAA championship team—a little reward for you great guys for coming to the rescue of Duke and the conference. I'll pick you both up from the hotel lobby at seven P.M. . . . Well, it's almost one o'clock now; I guess we better start the afternoon session before the crowd gets rowdy," Everett said in a soft Southern drawl.

As Professor Everett and Justice Moorman headed for the door and the short corridor leading to the stage, Bianco stayed behind, staring out the window and called at their retreating backs, "I'll low-key it and watch from in here for an hour or so. Then I have to go up to my room and make a few phone calls back to my chambers. There's an opinion that I want to get out," Bianco lied convincingly.

A grinning Everett looked back and waved. "There's a switch on the wall for the audio. It adjusts for volume, Your Honor. See you at seven."

Bianco saw the switch and left the audio off. He had no intention of listening to the afternoon session.

As soon as it looked like Professor Everett had started the introductions for Justice Moorman and Professor Young, Bianco quickly left the room and walked to one of the auditorium exits that led to the hotel lobby and the main bank of elevators. Along the way, Bianco was lost in focused thought. In particular, there was a story in the local paper that mentioned the "race card" being a factor in the possible Chief Justice nomination.

I have to work the phones and gear up more support to get President Ramsey off his ass. I have favors owed. Now is the time to call in all chits. The President has to make the decision to nominate me ASAP. Unless I put pressure on him, that idiot might name Moorman in a vain attempt to better his poor record over the two terms of disaster after disaster. I am sure that Ramsey might be enticed to be the first president to name a black as chief justice. Ramsey is stupid enough to think that might help his pathetic legacy.

Bianco was nervous as he waited for the elevator. His time to be named Chief Justice was now. He was about to turn seventy years old—aging with far too much velocity. That milestone birthday was in January. With a Democrat coming in as president in January 2009, this shot with the Republican President Ramsey was probably his very last chance to be named chief justice. Soon he would be considered too old. No one in the last century had been appointed chief justice who was over seventy. In fact, Justice Oliver Wendell Holmes was considered by many as being too old when he was appointed to the Supreme Court at sixty-one in 1902. Holmes, however, showed those critics. Though never becoming chief justice, he was one of the most active leaders on the Court for over thirty years, retiring only when he was well into his nineties.

Bianco got off the hotel elevator on the top floor—the Executive Floor—and walked down the deep plush–carpeted hallway to his corner suite. As he approached his room, he saw the maid coming out of the opposite suite—the suite where Moorman was staying. She was about to close the door . . . an act she would never complete.

Bianco always tried to seize fortune when it was presented. God was giving him an opportunity. On impulse, he took it—Bianco decided to do a dirty trick . . . to his friend and competitor for the center seat.

Bianco confidently and dismissively said to the maid before she closed the door, "Good timing. I'm going in for a nap. Thanks." With that, Bianco blew by the hotel maid and was in Moorman's room. As soon as he closed the door on the smiling maid, Bianco looked through the suitcase that was open on the dresser. Bianco inspected it with care, especially the shaving kit to see what pills or drugs Oscar had. Disappointed at the innocent medicine he found—just aspirin and over-the-counter decongestion medication—Bianco set to work on the original dirty trick that he had in the hallway.

Well, if Oscar gets the nomination, how is it going to look if the word gets out that the nominated Chief Justice watches dirty movies?

Bianco crossed the room and looked at the menu card for the in-room movies for an X-rated movie he could order. He knew that the hotel had immoral movies because he had been repulsed by the movie selections last night when he tried to find a movie to watch after returning from the dinner with Professor Everett and his wife.

Yes, here's a perfect fit—a ninety-minute dirty movie about a man with two prostitutes . . . how fitting for Moorman . . . and the ninety-minute movie will be over before Moorman's afternoon session is finished. The best thing about adding this charge to Moorman's room account is that Moorman most likely will probably never be given a hotel bill since Duke Law School is paying for all expenses at the hotel.

With that thought and the realization that he would have something unpleasant on his friend, Bianco grinned and punched in the numbers on the remote. The X-rated film started. Bianco waited for over five minutes of the movie until bare tits were showing. Satisfied that it was a suitably disgusting porno film, he quickly left the room.

I love the predictability of these international chain hotels. Immorality is a staple you can count on worldwide in some hotels.

After looking down the deserted corridor to see if the maid was still around, Bianco crossed over the corridor to enter his suite. He still had a smile on his face as he used the hotel phone to make his first call of the day in his campaign to be named as chief justice. That first call went to the very politically-connected director of the National Christian Center for Morality ("NCCM") in Washington. Bianco reminded the director of his record of supporting NCCM's agenda over the years as the reason for the director to immediately call the White House to lobby for his nomination.

Bianco gave no thought backward to what he had just done to Moorman's electronic hotel record as he proclaimed his bedrock Christian life as his main qualification to move the NCCM leader to use the leverage of the one million–plus NCCM membership to push the White House to nominate him. Hypocrisy was not going to stand in Bianco's way to be the chief justice. In fact, it never occurred to him. He was moving toward an end sanctioned, in his mind, by God. The means of travel were ordained by his self-interested political instincts and by his faith that God wanted him to lead the nation from the position of chief justice.

Bianco made several more calls after that initial call. The calls were made to two congressmen and several lobbyists who were members of his small Catholic charismatic church. All were very supportive of advancing Bianco's cause of doing God's work from a higher position.

After the calls, Bianco got on his knees with his hands folded in prayer and his elbows on the king-size bed. He started to softly recite out loud his personal mantra. Over and over, he uttered, "*Solo Christo . . . Solo Christo . . .* ("Christ Alone").

His mantra was his time-worn gateway into his deepest private prayer. He had learned to use his special prayer form when beseeching God for guidance in a time of doubt. Soon Justice Bianco was in a trancelike state, he felt he had touched God—his maximum pleasure on earth.

THE COLD LATE NOVEMBER RAIN LASHED THE AIRPORT
tarmac as Senator Irma Powers (R-Va.) walked toward the sleek
black Gulfstream V jet. The jet had a big scarlet red "C" with a cross
inside it on the tail—the logo of Carpa Pharmaceuticals Corporation, a large global drug company based in Richmond, Virginia. An
attendant from the General Aviation Terminal, the passenger terminal
for private and corporate jets at Reagan National, held a large black
golf umbrella over her head as she walked with her briefcase in one
hand and the other clutching her brown leather Gucci purse. The
umbrella wasn't doing much good since the rain was gusting from
the sides.

Senator Powers was irritated . . . and not just by the fact that her
dress was wet and her shoes were already soaked from stepping in a
large puddle on the pathway leading to the aircraft.

*Christ, the Carpa CEO would have to paint all the jets in the Carpa
fleet that distinctive color,* thought Powers. *Why couldn't the Carpa
jets be like most of the large corporation jets, painted nondescript white
and with no corporate markings? Any reporter up at this early hour
could ID this plane from a mile away.*

It was not that Senator Powers would not report this corporate
perk next May in her yearly ethics disclosure report for the U.S. Senate, it was because Powers didn't want to be so visually connected to
the powerful international company at this point in time of increased scrutiny of lobbyists and the Senate, especially since several
months ago she had introduced some helpful legislation that was

passed and gave the mega company an enormous benefit in federal tax relief.

Her irritation with the showy Carpa corporate jet had never deterred her frequent use of such luxury transportation. Senate rules allowed her to fly on these great comfortable jets with the taxpayers footing the bill by paying Carpa only the fare of a first-class air ticket . . . and her staff usually found the price for a heavily discounted fare even for first class. Such perks were common in the life of a senator who set his or her own rules.

At the bottom of the fold-out chrome and wooden steps of the big jet, a man in uniform stood in the rain with a big golf umbrella. She recognized him as the copilot from some of her previous trips.

"Good to see you again, Senator. Mr. Fay is already aboard. As soon as we break through this weather cover, we'll have a smooth flight to West Palm Beach," said the copilot as he helped her up the stairs to the aircraft cabin. Powers felt the welcome heat of the cabin as she got in out of the rain. Down the aisle of the cabin, well furnished in shiny dark wood paneling and light beige leather seats, she saw Don Fay, Carpa's CEO, drinking from a champagne flute and chatting with a very pretty flight attendant.

"Madam Chair, welcome to your chariot to Florida!" roared Fay in an overdone manner when he saw her enter the plane.

"Good to see you, Don," replied Powers as she approached the vacant plush leather captain's chair opposite Fay across a shiny dark wooden oval table. Powers noticed with approval that Fay at least remembered to see her seat was facing forward. She had told him the first time they traveled together to a function that she was prone to motion sickness and liked to face the cockpit. He had remembered ever since. That was one of the very few things she liked about him.

When Senator Powers was seated, the flight attendant introduced herself and softly asked her what she wanted for breakfast.

"Just wheat toast, no butter, and black coffee, thank you," replied Powers as she inspected the young woman's uniform—a short, tight skirt and a white silk blouse, undone one button too many to show her ample cleavage.

"Cindy, I'll have some of that delicious corn beef hash you make and a side of bacon with a toasted bagel . . . and another glass of DP." Fay winked at the young lady as he finished ordering. Then he turned to Powers and said, "She just opened a nice bottle of Dom Perignon, Senator. Why don't you join me?"

"No thanks, I'll stick with the coffee," said Powers in an icy voice.

As Cindy turned to walk to the galley in the rear of the aircraft, Powers observed that Don Fay took his eyes from her and watched the firm ass of the flight attendant as she walked away.

Men are such pigs! All of them just follow that little stick between their legs, she thought.

That thought reminded Senator Powers of her husband.

Jim Powers had been living apart from her most of the time, ever since she'd been elected a U.S. Senator following the end of his one term as the Governor of Virginia. His unfaithfulness had surfaced early in their marriage; however, Irma Powers had managed to swallow most of the embarrassments and had been a significant help in her husband's political career as he moved along the path from a state senator all the way to the Governor's Mansion in Richmond. Now he was with a major law firm in Richmond as a showpiece and client magnet. He had never lost his wandering eye, but was more discreet now in deference to his wife's status as a U.S. Senator from Virginia.

Irma Powers was a distinguished-looking woman, but she had never been pretty and age had definitely not improved her looks. Of medium height, a stocky build, and a thick neck, when she was dressed in slacks and had a dress shirt on, she was often mistaken for a man from a distance.

Her mind, however, was a beautiful thing. Blessed with true social cunning, an almost photographic memory, and an extraordinary array of deft political skills rare even in Washington, Senator Powers was a Republican star on the rise in Washington. Now the Chair of the Senate Judiciary Committee, there were many political professionals who believed that she would become the first female President of the United States.

That was her all-consuming goal . . . and the reason for her relationship with the CEO of the largest corporation in Virginia, the global drug giant—Carpa Pharmaceuticals Corporation. In her view, Don Fay could be a major help to her on the road to the White House.

She was not naïve; she knew there were tolls along the road. She knew that this unexpected lucrative fund-raising trip Carpa had quickly arranged in West Palm Beach had a price to it. She was curious to know the reason why Fay had set up this trip. It was odd timing for a fund-raiser—just before Thanksgiving and on extremely short notice. Powers' antennas were up and sending her a powerful message—Carpa had an urgent favor to ask her. What was it? Why had it come up so quickly? On this, the politically savvy Powers was stumped.

The smooth liftoff of the G5 from the runway of Ronald Reagan National Airport was followed by some bumpy moments until the sleek big jet powered its way through the foul weather and found the sun and smooth air at ten thousand feet. Soon the jet climbed to its cruising altitude and was heading south toward Florida at thirty-eight thousand feet. Although Powers was anxious to learn the real price for this trip, it would have to wait until after breakfast by the shapely Cindy.

Breakfast was served promptly once the ride smoothed out and, over breakfast, Don Fay went generally through the fund-raising agenda he had arranged for Senator Powers in Florida.

After Cindy had cleared the breakfast plates from the small conference table serving as a breakfast nook and was busy in the rear galley, Fay bluntly outlined the cash benefit from the three events he had set up—a tidy and welcome sum which was expected to fill Senator Powers' campaign coffers with over three million dollars by the end of the day.

"It's very nice of you to do this for me, Don. And very unexpected as well. My Chief of Staff, Donna, told me that this trip came out of the blue, an unanticipated bonus that puts me well ahead of my regular fund-raising schedule. Thank you again." Powers knew that her statement of thanks would probably produce the "ask" portion of the traditional political dance done in Washington.

And she was right.

Don Fay smiled a reptilian grin and leaned forward. He was so close that Powers smelled the alcohol on his breath.

"There is a favor I want you to do for us at Carpa. It's very important to our company and it concerns the possible nomination of a certain justice to be the chief justice," said Fay.

Senator Irma Powers recoiled back from this statement into the deep rich leather of her seat as if a dangerous snake coiled to strike was facing her instead of a slick CEO.

"No, no! Don, you know I don't discuss official business at set locations. As the Chair of the Senate Judiciary Committee, any possible nomination would come before my committee, so I can't discuss any advance suggestions."

Don Fay shook his head. "Goddamn, Irma. There are no bugs here. Cindy is not back in the kitchen recording any conversations. You're a real paranoiac. Those rumors of your *all-girl* senior staff are really too much. I hear you don't even let the Senate cleaning staff into your personal office—your girls do the cleaning themselves." Fay was angry now.

Powers' face winced at the rebuke.

He's so much like my husband—reckless and hurtful.

"We'll talk about Carpa's needs later. My door is always open to constituents' suggestions," Senator Powers said with a firm voice, knowing that, if this conversation was being recorded, her words would pass muster at any ethics hearing. Then, not wanting to irritate Fay, one of her biggest donors, she softened her approach, "Don, why don't we talk about this when we get to West Palm Beach?"

Don Fay nodded with pursed lips. He looked out the large oval window by his seat on the cloud tops beneath the jet and, after a minute of obvious thinking on what Powers said, shouted into the intercom by his seat, "Cindy, get me another glass of DP . . . no, no make it a bloody mary. A stiff one with Grey Goose."

The rest of the trip passed in silence as Senator Powers pulled out papers from her briefcase and started to read briefing papers. Fay, meanwhile, used the plane's satellite phone to keep up with the flow of business from his office.

As the plane pulled up to the tarmac ramp at the private jet section of the exclusive Palm Beach airport, Irma Powers told Fay, "Have the pilot keep the starboard engine running at low power. We'll discuss the Carpa needs outside."

Fay and Powers exited the aircraft and stood a bit away on the left side at the tail of the G5 where the low rumble of the running engine prevented anyone overhearing their conversation.

Satisfied with the extremely slim possibility of anyone listening, Powers was straight to the point. "What does Carpa want?"

Fay was equally blunt. "Carpa has a patent case coming up before the Supreme Court on the January calendar. It's a 'make or break' patent case for Carpa. If we win, Carpa gets three more years on the patent of its most profitable drug, the painkiller Varakain. This fucking patent case is literally worth more than four billion dollars in profits alone to us. Our company's General Counsel has done a very careful analysis of our chances at the Supreme Court. In his view, with Oscar Moorman as Chief Justice, his vote and leadership will almost guarantee a win. Moorman has been very influential on the rest of the Court in patent cases . . . out of the last eight patent cases while he's been on the Court, he's written the majority opinion in all eight. As you know he has a premed undergrad degree and a strong patent and antitrust background. We know his record is very pro-patent, especially for drug patents. As Chief Justice, his vote for us will carry more weight—especially with two of the weaker justices—that dumb bitch Ryland and the almost senile Farnsworth. . . . Irma, we . . . I would really appreciate it if you got the President to nominate him . . . and get him confirmed. If you do this, I'll promise you

that Carpa will be the lead donor on both your 2010 Senate reelection campaign and . . . also for your rumored 2012 presidential bid.
Get us Moorman. Get us a win at the Supreme Court!" As he finished
his say, the CEO stared into Powers' eyes.

Powers' quick mind examined the request . . . and the great opportunity for her. Fay was right about her wanting to run for president in 2012. Carpa would be a key in raising money for the expensive
race. With Carpa as a lead donor, she could raise the serious money
she would need to launch a first-rate presidential bid. The converse
was also true; if Carpa, the biggest employer in her state—outside of
the Federal government—didn't back her bid, then few corporations
would jump on her presidential campaign bandwagon.

*I've got to do this for Carpa! I need them. Obviously they need me
now.*

Senator Powers hesitated while she carefully examined the politics of the situation and then said, "Are you positive Moorman will go
your way?"

"Nothing's positive," said Fay and shrugged his shoulders.

Immediately after he said that, Fay added, "It might help if you
could sound out Moorman on the case?"

Senator Powers weighed this risky move. Then she firmly said,
"It's possible that, in my capacity as the Chair of the Senate Judiciary
Committee, which would recommend his confirmation to the full
Senate, it might be appropriate if I conduct a short discreet interview
of Justice Moorman before I push the President to nominate him.
Naturally, I suppose that I could ask him a question or two on his
patent positions."

"Good. That would be excellent . . . excellent." Fay's wide mouth
spread in a large grin.

Senator Powers then said in a firm voice, "OK, I'll try to get
Moorman in as Chief Justice. However, let's get some rules straight.
You and I must never have any direct communications on this subject. While the nomination is pending, there must be absolutely no
e-mails to me. No telephone calls. None! To communicate with me,

you should immediately hire my husband, Jim, and his Richmond law firm on a temporary basis while this nomination thing is in progress. I'll naturally write a memo to my Chief of Staff, Donna, when I return from this trip and recuse myself immediately from any Carpa matters while Jim is working for Carpa. On the Moorman nomination, I'll communicate everything on any developments to you through Jim—and, now this is very important, you'll use *only* him to communicate with me on this nomination. I repeat—we work on this only through Jim."

"Smart lady. All you say to him will be covered by the husband-wife privilege . . . and all he and I talk about is covered by the attorney-client privilege—a virtual bulletproof communication system. Brilliant!" murmured Fay as he smirked.

"Well, now, Oscar Moorman . . . I think he will be a fine chief justice . . . a fine chief justice," pronounced the Chair of the Senate Judiciary Committee slipping into her deep Virginia drawl.

Getting Moorman as Chief Justice will put Carpa in my debt . . . and make a fat fee for my Jim . . . and me. A Washington home run. Everybody wins.

With the high-pitched jet engine still running and covering the frank remarks being exchanged, Don Fay grinned and observed, "I knew I could count on you, Madam Chair. Now let's go shake down some of these rich friends of mine down here in West Palm Beach and get some money for your next Senate win . . . you know, I was just thinking, all major corporations should have a Senator in their corner."

Most do, replied Senator Powers to herself.

7

AS SENATOR IRMA POWERS LOOKED OUT THE TALL WINdow behind her desk in her large first-floor office of the U.S. Senate Russell Office Building, she saw the rush-hour traffic clogging Constitution Avenue. She always had been an early riser, but today was going to be a big day. It would also be a long day with much to do. So she was in very early today—before six o'clock—even though she returned to her Capitol Hill townhouse very late last night on the Carpa jet. She was glad the return trip was solo. Fay had stayed in Florida to get in a day of golf. She was tired, but pleased with the knowledge that her ten hours among the rich favor seekers of Palm Beach had grossed over three million for her Senate campaign.

Now it was nine o'clock and Powers had already done an important breakfast, conducted a special meeting of her senior staff, and made a dozen telephone calls—a long one to President Ramsey and other calls to Senators who were vital to a confirmation vote for a Chief Justice nomination. Getting in touch with key Senators was difficult because many had already taken off for the long Thanksgiving holiday weekend. But phones and Blackberrys were inescapable cords back to the Senate.

Powers was in full throttle, lining up her committee to move on a possible nomination for the appointment of Oscar Moorman as Chief Justice of the United States.

Her breakfast was a solo breakfast with Senator Sloane, the senior Senator from Connecticut . . . and the father-in-law of Oscar Moorman. The Sloane meeting had been the key to her follow-up actions that day.

It was an interesting breakfast. Powers and Sloane were the only customers in the exclusive Senate Dining Room at that hour so no one heard Senator Sloane state that Moorman did not want to be Chief Justice. That bad news rocked Powers. She almost dropped her coffee cup.

Damn, Carpa's plan is dead. They aren't going to like it . . . and they will doubt my ability to deliver.

However, it proved a temporary blow. Senator Sloane followed the bad with the good. The good news elicited, after she prodded her colleague from Connecticut, was that Moorman's wife, Debby, wanted very much to be "Mrs. Chief Justice." Senator Sloane further opined that he thought that Moorman would take the nomination . . . just to please his wife. Moorman would do anything to please her, assured Sloane.

Thank God for women. We still run the world and always will . . . as long as we don't tell the men.

Nevertheless, that breakfast meeting put Powers on alert that she had to convince two men to nominate Oscar Moorman as Chief Justice—President Ramsey and Moorman himself.

One of the things that she had to promise Senator Sloane was to keep him *fully* informed—she told him that she would give him copies of all the very restricted reports of her Special Counsel. Sloane wanted to have the inside information on what was surfacing in the confidential investigation being conducted prior to and during the confirmation hearing. He was a father looking out for his only child. Powers understood and had no problem with that—an easy "do" for Debby Moorman's dad.

After breakfast and back in her spacious high-ceiling private office in the Russell Senate Office Building, she worked the phones. Most of her calls to fellow senators went well. She had been in the Senate for over a decade now and her favor bank was nearly full; there were many favors she had accumulated over the years and now

was the time to collect. Most of the senators she called were cooperative and she was able to strike what is called a perfect Senate deal—
both senators needed and got something from the other.

Now finished with most of the calls she felt were necessary to get
the pulse of the confirmation, Powers reflected on the job ahead for
her today with regard to further work in lining up the Moorman
nomination.

She had already had a short talk with Jim, her husband, in Richmond, setting up the temporary communication system that would
be used for the period the Moorman nomination was in play. As soon
as the nomination process was finished, the financial tie of Carpa to
Jim and his Richmond law firm would be cut. Senator Powers had to
have full access to the largest corporation in her state once the confirmation was over.

Yet, while the confirmation process was proceeding, Carpa would
use Jim Powers to do meaningless legal reviews of pending litigation
matters. With that attorney-client relationship in place, Senator Powers would have an unbreakable communication system in her efforts
to maneuver Oscar Moorman into the job of Chief Justice. Moreover, during that time Carpa would pay the generous legal retainer of
four hundred and fifty thousand to Jim's firm for an estimated two
months' work. Of that almost half million in legal fees, 75 percent of
that would be paid personally to Senator Powers' husband. A sweet
deal for the Powers husband-and-wife team.

The money aspect was very attractive—the legal fees to her husband, the promise of Carpa money for her Senate race in 2010, and
the possible Presidential race in 2012. Yet the downside was the big
risk Irma Powers was taking in helping Carpa literally install Moorman as Chief Justice just to win Carpa's big patent case. Powers *was*
using her official duties to help Carpa. And she was being paid for her
actions with present and future money. *Bribery,* plain and simple. She
knew she was in a very dangerous area.

Powers thought of a saying by Ralph Waldo Emerson—"In skating over thin ice, our safety is in speed."

So Senator Powers wasted no time. She picked up the phone to punch in the numbers of the direct private line of Justice Oscar Moorman at his chambers in the Supreme Court, located just one block down First Street from the Russell Senate Office Building.

The Supreme Court was not in session that day so he should be at his desk and not in the courtroom.

And he was. Moorman was a hard worker, usually in by 8 A.M. and often stayed until 7 P.M.

Justice Oscar Moorman answered his phone on the second ring. "Oscar Moorman, here."

"Mr. Justice, this is Irma Powers. Can we meet today? It's important."

NATURALLY WITH THE MEDIA FRENZY OVER THE POSsible immediate nomination of a chief justice by President Ramsey, the Chair of the Judiciary Committee couldn't just walk over to the Supreme Court to chat with a justice when the media spotlight was focused on a possible new chief justice. At such a time, Senator Powers would be under heightened observation by the press. Conversely a Supreme Court justice couldn't just show up at her Senate office. Although most news stories now were saying that President Ramsey didn't have the votes in the Senate to name a chief justice this late in his presidency, some reports were saying that the appointment of Justice Vincent Bianco was imminent. A few African-American newspapers did however mention Moorman as a good nominee. All in all, it was bad form for the Chair of the Senate Judiciary Committee to meet privately with any member of the Supreme Court while there was speculation that the President might make a nomination.

It was a given that any meeting of Senator Powers and Justice Moorman had to be a secret. And keeping secrets was something very hard to do in Washington.

Senator Powers, however, was not only smart, but creative. Her request to Moorman for the meeting included a plan for secrecy.

Under the first part of the plan, Moorman was to leave the Supreme Court building without being followed by the press. This was accomplished by his walking out of an unexpected place—the underground parking exit of the Court. The weather cooperated with a cold snap and was covering Washington with a convenient soft winter drizzle. So Moorman, with his umbrella held low and tight to his head, and his Burberry raincoat with the collar turned up, was hard to identify for anybody watching the parking entrance to the Court. As far as he knew, no one noticed him as he walked south the three blocks under the dark overcast sky to Union Station, the main train station in Washington. As Senator Powers had requested, it was precisely noon when he arrived at the station. It was a good time to do the secret meeting since the terminal and especially the food court on the lower level were both packed with midday travelers and the lunch crowd from the nearby federal buildings.

Although the purpose of the meeting was not revealed to him, Moorman assumed Powers wanted his views and some personal reassurances about Justice Bianco and his possible nomination. He was happy to do this because Vince Bianco was his best friend at the Court. Moorman would do anything to help Bianco become the chief justice.

I wonder what information she wants that we couldn't discuss on the phone? thought Moorman.

It was common knowledge in Washington that Senator Powers was a very good friend of Justice Vince Bianco. Moorman personally was aware that Bianco had regularly attended prayer breakfasts with Senator Powers and that she thought highly of his brilliant and ambitious friend.

As he stepped down the last of the marble stairs from the ground floor of the station into the basement food court, Moorman started to look for the pretty Chief of Staff of Senator Powers, the person who would lead him to the Senator.

Donna Pitt was an old friend of Moorman's. She had worked for Powers for almost ten years. Her hard work and deep loyalty to her boss had paid off. Donna was now the top aide to the Chair of the Senate Judiciary Committee. Moorman had first met Donna when he was an appeals court judge before his elevation to the Supreme Court. At that time she was an analyst for the Senate Judiciary Committee, working for Powers as a committee staffer, and he was the judicial representative from his court for several meetings with Senate and House staffers to get the appropriations to expand the federal courthouse in D.C.

That was during his bachelor days.

Donna attended night law school at George Washington University while she worked days as a staffer for Powers on the Senate Judiciary Committee. Moorman, always on the lookout for an attractive woman, even considered asking out the one-time model, but he never did. Although she was cordial to him, he had gotten negative sexual vibes from Donna Pitt. He didn't know whether it was the "black and white" thing or whether she just didn't like him. She was now in her forties, still single, and quite attractive.

In her call to him that morning, Senator Powers had told Moorman that Donna would be waiting for him in front of the Cinnabon kiosk at the food court.

And she was.

"Hi, Donna. Good to see you again. Where do I meet up with your boss?" Moorman gave her a slight hug and friendly air kiss on the cheek as expected for old friends.

He saw Donna was nervous, her eyes darting around the packed room.

"I'll take you to her. Just follow me . . . at a distance. Say fifty feet. And I'll lead you to the Senator."

"Gee, spy stuff, right here in D.C.," joked Moorman.

Donna's beautiful face hardened. "O, please cooperate. Senator Powers is very tight ass about this meeting."

O nodded and let the stylish woman lead him through the station. They went out the rear exit into the huge multitiered parking structure attached to the train station.

As Moorman rode up the escalators to the second parking level and watched Donna Pitt walk toward the first row of parked cars, Moorman was thinking, *No way—a "Deep Throat"-style parking lot rendezvous and in daylight no less! What a sensational story this would make in the newspapers if the meeting were observed.*

Moorman was mad at allowing himself to be put into such a "made for prime time news" situation. He saw that Donna had stopped and was pointing to a dark blue Volvo station wagon parked right next to the escalators and under a video surveillance camera. Since the car had no tinted windows, he could clearly see that there was someone sitting in the backseat.

This is a bone-headed meeting place. Too much traffic from the escalators and in full camera view. The Senator and Donna may be smart about a lot of things, but this is a bad place to have a meeting.

One of the rules he lived by was that if you make a mistake and get on the wrong path—that's one mistake. If you know it is the wrong path, but continue down the track, it is not one mistake, but two back-to-back mistakes. And Oscar Moorman tried *never* to do doubles.

Moorman walked up to Donna and shook his head.

"I . . . and perhaps anybody who walks by . . . can clearly see your Senator in the backseat of that Volvo. I'm leaving. If the senator wants to talk, make it a quick pickup from the street near here. I'll be standing at the corner of Massachusetts and New Jersey Avenue in ten minutes. That's two blocks from here."

Donna was flustered. "But the Senator is in my car waiting to discuss your appointment as Chief Justice."

Oscar Moorman was stunned.

So it's not Vince, but me!

"That's even more reason to abort this meeting place. You've parked right under a surveillance camera and right by the main path to the train station. Way too much exposure by pedestrians. It's a terrible place. You do have a choice—pick me up in ten minutes on Mass Avenue or forget about a meeting today."

With that, Justice Moorman turned and started to retrace his steps back to the parking lot escalators. When he came to the ground level, Moorman headed for the station exit closest to Massachusetts Avenue.

He wasn't sorry he aborted the meeting. Moorman learned long ago to trust his instincts, instincts that saved his life in Vietnam . . . and later helped his career. His test was simple.

When something didn't feel right, it usually wasn't.

JUSTICE MOORMAN WAS ON THE STREET CORNER AS the blue Volvo wagon slowly came down Massachusetts Avenue ten minutes later.

Donna was driving. When she stopped, Moorman got in the empty front passenger side and turned to face the person in the backseat—Senator Irma Powers.

Powers grinned and confessed, "Your Honor, good call about the meeting place. This is better; we'll drive around and talk. Much better!"

She added, "By the way, no one is following us or saw me in the garage."

After Moorman nodded, Powers got right to the point.

Donna drove the car around some of the sparsely populated streets near the Mall, where there were few pedestrians and tourists due to the rainy weather.

Powers started the substantive conversation with an attention getter.

"Do you want to be Chief Justice of the United States?"

"Not particularly." Moorman's voice was firm and confident.

Although he knew his wife, Debby, wanted very badly for him to become the Chief, he still was afraid that he would be attacked once again in a brutal confirmation battle.

Unfazed, Senator Powers came back. "Let me rephrase the question. *Will* you do it? I know about your reservations. You had a tough go in your initial hearings to get on the Court. The womanizing thing in your personal life must have been tough. But I'm in charge of the Judiciary Committee now, and I can assure you that your confirmation hearing will be an easy ride, full of softball questions. No repeat of the womanizing angle. I promise I can control that. The Court needs a real leader. I've talked to the President and Justice Bianco will never get the nod. The President agrees with me. You're the only other justice in the very small stable of two moderate Republicans that could get enough Republican and Democratic votes to be confirmed at this late stage in the Ramsey Administration. Will you do it? Will you help the Court and our nation?"

That new approach made Moorman pause.

So politics has determined it's him or no Chief Justice until the Democrats take over on January 20.

Powers didn't wait for an answer—she quickly followed up with reassurances of the votes she had already lined up for Moorman. She said she had key Republicans and Democrats committed. The list was impressive. She also threw in the fact that it was time for an African-American to be the first Chief Justice.

Powers went further and suggested in a kind voice, "You can't ignore the country and the good you can do as the Chief Justice. If you don't take it, who knows who will be appointed by the new president? Besides this may be the last time for a long while to have a Republican appointed as the Chief Justice."

"Clever, Senator. A political-party appeal and a 'Better the devil you know' argument?" Moorman observed with a smile.

The smile signaled a crack in the dam for Moorman's resolve not to be Chief Justice.

She's right. The new Democratic president-elect is a weak, rather stupid man who may well make a bad choice for the Chief Justice. Besides, Debby really wants for me to be Chief Justice.

As the Volvo cruised around the streets of downtown Washington, Powers continued to gently argue persuasively for Oscar Moorman to do his duty and take the helm of the Supreme Court. She also pounded home how easy the confirmation would be with her in charge. She would protect him, she said again.

During the ride, Moorman weakened. The head of the Judicial Branch of the United States was being offered to him.

A great general doesn't desire a bigger tent; what he wants is the top command, remembered Moorman.

And so did Moorman want to command the nation's judiciary.

That did it. He waved the white flag and tentatively agreed to accept the nomination if President Ramsey offered it to him. "Senator, if the President offers me the CJ job, I'll take it."

The expression on Senator Powers told all. She was beaming like a child on Christmas.

At that point, Senator Powers cheerfully told Donna to pull over and park. They were now driving up the Mall on one of the side streets leading toward the U.S. Capitol building. Donna saw there were some empty spaces ahead on the long Mall near the Air and Space Museum, a street nearly deserted now in the dead of winter and the clearly over tourist season.

"Donna, could you get out and let Justice Moorman and I talk privately?" said Senator Powers. Donna wrapped her scarf around her raincoat collar and popped her umbrella as she got out of the vehicle.

It was still drizzling lightly. She moved over to one of the mall benches and sat down, hunching over in the chill and watching her car being used as a conference room.

"Oscar, here is the vetting part I have to do. I'm putting my career on the line to do this and I must be sure about some things."

"I understand," said Moorman flatly, not really understanding and wondering what he was going to be quizzed on. His record was pretty much in the open with three years on the U.S. Court of Appeals and now eight years on the Supreme Court, after a bruising "tell all" series of confirmation hearings to get on the top Court.

Senator Powers started with a question that is usually the final "catch-all" question asked in any preconfirmation interview by a Senate investigator, "Please don't take offense. But is there anything in your background that is not public knowledge, but could prove to be embarrassing in a confirmation hearing?"

Moorman sighed and answered, "No. That tank is empty. The last confirmation hearing pretty much aired all the dirt about my bachelor days and running with the ladies. I did some stupid things then, but I'm happily married now and can't think of anything that could be used this time around that's not in the public record."

He added hesitantly, "Not that it's any of your business, but since I married Debby I've been faithful. No affairs."

Powers stared deeply into his eyes and replied, "Okay, I'll take that. But realize, Oscar, everything is my business if it could damage the confirmation."

Powers continued, "That brings me to the public record—your voting record on the Court. As you are aware, when you were nominated to the Supreme Court eight years ago, you clearly stated in your confirmation hearing that you were opposed to affirmative action. The conservatives *loved* that. An African-American against affirmative action. But *then*, when the first affirmative action case came up four years into your term on the Court, you voted *for* government set-aside contracts on highway construction projects. In fact, you were the swing vote and wrote the opinion—which, by the way, I happen to agree with. Nevertheless, people are going to wonder whether you deceived the Senate by your apparent change of position on a very touchy subject. Why did you vote for affirmative action after you stated in sworn testimony that you were against it?"

Moorman shook his head and said in a firm voice, "First, I didn't lie to get the conservative vote. I was against affirmative action at the time of my hearing. However, I changed my mind several years later."

"Why?" Powers pursued the reason.

"Time had passed. When that affirmative action case came up, I was smarter about race in our country. Moreover, I had a personal experience that woke me up—convinced me we were not a colorless society yet. Minorities still needed to get a little help to get the playing field evened out. That's all I'm going to say."

Powers didn't respond right away. She just stared into Moorman's eyes. Eyes that didn't blink, but told her not to ask more.

"Okay, I guess people change their minds. I know I have shifted my positions when I learned new facts. But, Oscar, be ready for the media and some senators to hit you about that. I can't help you on your voting record. It's fair game. However, I don't think that will be a major problem. Overall you have a very good voting record."

Powers then added, "By the way, your pro-patent record hasn't changed, has it? I mean, you still favor the extension of patent rights under the recent intellectual property legislation . . . like you did in last year's case?"

Moorman was at first taken aback at that seamless add-on question. That week he had been reading the bench memos prepared by his clerks in preparation for the next month's scheduled cases. He quickly put the significance of the question into context and realized that Powers' question was very relevant to one of the Supreme Court's pending major cases, the case involving Carpa Pharmaceuticals—a drug company in Senator Powers' state. Carpa had a case on the January schedule. A big patent case that Carpa would want justices to be pro-patent in their approach to the major issue in the case— whether the drug patent should be extended three years under recent legislation that provided discretion in this area. Carpa had lost in the U.S. Court of Appeals below and the Supreme Court had taken the case to review. Moorman knew that case could be worth several billions of dollars if the patent coverage was extended as a pro-patent justice was likely to do. Most of the other justices would probably follow his lead on the case as they had last year, since he was the only justice with patent and antitrust experience. That would be especially true if he were made Chief Justice.

Here was a defining moment. Here is where Moorman had to make a decision. Was he going to please Senator Powers, who obviously wanted him to affirm his very consistent position in favor of extending patents?

Or would he take the ethical and much tougher course and refuse to comment on a case coming up before the Court?

He looked at Powers, who was actually leaning forward in the backseat in anticipation of his answer, her eyes large with anticipation The question was obviously very important to her; it clearly was not the "by the way" casual question that she attempted to make it appear to be.

It was the time that Moorman realized that Powers' support, like most things that advanced people in Washington, might have a price. This could be the time where an ambitious justice seeking the top slot was expected to take the easy road and say, "Yes, I'm still pro-patent." After all, that was actually his well-documented position . . . and obviously it was what Senator Powers (and her constituent, the big drug company—Carpa) wanted him to say.

Realizing that his nomination hung in the balance with his answer to this question, Moorman hesitated a bit to understand the consequences and finally answered, "Senator, that is an inappropriate question since there is a patent case pending on the January calendar. A case where my views on patents are very relevant. That area is out of bounds. I won't answer that. Not now . . . and not in any hearing before your Committee."

As he said the unexpected, Moorman felt proud of himself.

I'm not for sale. If this dooms my chance at the nomination, so be it.

Senator Powers, in the backseat, shot up straight as if slapped. Her quick mind processed the answer and she grinned in a calculating manner. "Quite right, I didn't know that about a case being on the Court's oral argument calendar. I apologize. I shouldn't ask a question that would prejudge a case."

That's a lie. She's too smart not to know that the largest corporation and donor in her state—Virginia—has a major patent case pending in my Court.

"Well, then I guess the last thing we have to discuss is your *guardian angel*."

Moorman shook his head and repeated, "Guardian angel? What do you mean?"

Senator Powers gave a wink and smiled, "Really the title will be the Special Counsel to the Senate Judiciary Committee. He'll be the lead investigator and lawyer for the committee during the confirmation. However, as a practical matter, he'll be the key person to shepherd your nomination through the hearing process. He'll also act as your adviser and help with any road bumps that may come up. I suggest that you pick a prominent D.C. attorney who is knowledgeable about the confirmation process . . . also it should be someone you trust. This is the person who will investigate your background and any allegations that may be made against you during the hearings. His reports will be given to the committee members and used to justify the vote of the committee. I call him your guardian angel because he'll be the one watching over you in the process."

Moorman, who had been turned around to his left side looking back at Senator Powers during this whole interview, adjusted his position and faced front. Through the windshield, he stared down the Mall and looked at the U.S. Capitol; his mind racing through the possibilities of who would be a good choice. He was silent for a full two minutes. Then he turned back to Powers and said, "I want Judge Tim Quinn. He knows the process and he's a man I can count on."

"Quinn. Good choice. A former Federal judge. Very credible. He's now back at his old firm, a D.C. legal powerhouse. Very politically wired. He certainly knows Washington and is respected for his integrity. I didn't know he was a close friend of yours."

"He's a friend, not a close one. We see each other from time to time working out at the University Club. We're both members there. I do know his rep and I like him. He's my choice. A man I respect and, moreover, he has excellent connections in this town."

Powers nodded and said, "Okay, Good choice. Former Federal Judge. He's got the Washington juice and savvy that may come in handy. I'll call him and see if he'll do it. If he accepts, I'll have him appointed as the temporary special counsel to the Senate Judiciary Committee, reporting directly to me. However, his main job will be to oversee all investigations during the confirmation hearings ... and to look out for you and your nomination."

"Well, let's hope he has an easy time with that," said Oscar Moorman.

"Don't worry; your confirmation will be a piece of cake. You will make a fine Chief Justice," replied Powers in a confident voice.

After that, a smiling Powers quickly hit the button lowering the back window and called to Donna, "We're through, Donna. Let's get back to the Hill. We can drop Justice Moorman at his Court."

As Donna was getting back into the station wagon, Moorman addressed Powers in a formal tone, "Madam Chair, I think I'll get out here and walk back."

Powers shrugged. "Fine. I'll talk to the President ASAP and tell him that I'm completely committed to your nomination ... and have the votes to do it."

Moorman got out and watched the Volvo disappear into the traffic. It was no longer raining but he was bone-cold. Moorman pulled out a black wool knit cap from his raincoat pocket and put it on. He stuck his hands in his pockets and started walking toward the Capitol and to his Court just behind it.

On the long hike back to the Court, Moorman made a cell phone call home to his wife, Debby. When he told her he might get the nomination, she was ecstatic with joy.

Nevertheless, as he hung up, he looked up at the gloomy sky and wondered if he'd made the right decision to give his approval to be nominated as the Chief Justice.

Piece of cake, Senator Powers had said . . . I wonder. Nothing's easy in Washington politics, especially for a black man.

❖ 10 ❖

WHEN SENATOR POWERS GOT BACK TO HER OFFICE ON Capitol Hill, she made an immediate call to President Ramsey on the secure phone furnished to key members of Congress by the White House Communications Agency. One of the Agency's jobs was to protect sensitive communications by the President. Her call was certainly that—the appointment of the next Chief Justice of the U.S. Supreme Court.

The Chair of the Senate Judiciary Committee clearly merited a new STU-3 encrypted satellite phone, especially now. The call with the President lasted over twenty minutes and ended with the following wrap-up dialogue:

"He'll make a fine Chief Justice, Mr. President. The first black to lead one of the three branches of our government—a historic appointment for your great conservative legacy . . . and moreover I'll appreciate this favor forever," said Powers.

"I know you will, Irma. That's how Washington works. The favor bank has permanent records. When you win the Presidency in 2012,

I might drop by the White House to call in a chit or two," said the President with an easy laugh.

After they hung up, Senator Powers started making calls from her Senate phone. She would be on the phone with many of her fellow senators most of the afternoon, lining up votes for the next Chief Justice of the United States. The outlook for confirmation was good. Powers was exceptional at picking up votes when it counted—she knew how to trade favors for votes. Moorman was going to be an expensive vote for her, lots of favors would be promised . . . but the rewards from Carpa would be worth it.

Late in the afternoon, she called Tim Quinn, hopefully the guardian angel who would see Moorman through the minefields of the confirmation process.

Quinn took the call from the senator and didn't seem surprised at all by the Special Counsel job offer.

Powers was suspicious and asked why.

"Justice Moorman already called me and explained the situation. I already told him I'd do it. He's a good man and I think it will be an interesting assignment."

"Good. Then your answer is yes."

"A yes, but with two conditions. First, I want to pick my own personal staff—just a deputy counsel and a head investigator. Don't worry. They won't cost your budget anything because they are already on the government payroll. The deputy counsel is Vicky Hauser, a Justice Department attorney, and the investigator is Bill Sharkey, an FBI special agent—both can be temporarily detailed to the Senate Judiciary staff from the Department of Justice—I already checked and both agreed to do it. Administratively all it will take is a letter of request from you to the Attorney General. I've prepared a draft of the letter and will e-mail it to your Chief of Staff, Donna Pitt, if you like."

"OK, Judge Quinn, I agree to your first condition and I must say I'm impressed. You appear to be as good as your reputation," responded Senator Powers.

"Don't be fooled. I'm overrated, but don't tell my paying clients. They think I'm worth the thousand dollars an hour I usually charge."

"What is the second condition?" asked Powers pointedly.

"I'm my own boss. I investigate whatever I think is relevant to the confirmation. And when I communicate with the committee I'll send you . . . *and all* the members of the Judiciary Committee a written report on everything that is referred to my staff during the hearing process. However, no one on the Judiciary Committee, including you, can tell me what to put in my reports. I'll call the issues I investigate as I see them. No politics or spin. Moorman gets treated fairly and accurately."

"I wouldn't have it any other way," said Senator Powers, wishing the opposite.

This could be trouble, she thought.

She wished Moorman hadn't picked Quinn to do the lead investigative work on the confirmation. She wanted someone she could influence as the senior investigator. She had a lot riding on this. Control was the way Powers usually did business.

Quinn was a good judge—and good judges usually are way too independent, thought Senator Powers.

❖ 11 ❖

A "BLUE PORTAL" EXERCISE WAS SCHEDULED FOR SUNday morning during President Ramsey's attendance at the Holy Eucharist service at St. John's Church right across the park in front of the White House. Presidents have been attending church services at St. John's ever since the 1800s.

Blue Portal was the present Secret Service maneuver for the temporary disappearance of a president during an official event. For instance, President Clinton did a "Blue Portal" from a White House dinner to have a FBI lab scientist (observed by an FBI agent and one of Ken Starr's lawyers) take his DNA sample for use in matching it with stains found on Monica Lewinsky's cocktail dress. Clinton, it is said, excused himself from the dinner for a call of nature and met with the FBI team to secretly give the DNA sample.

Today the Blue Portal began ten minutes after the church service started. The President was seated on the right side of the church and when the service goers were filing up the aisles for communion, the President, accompanied by three Secret Service agents, slipped down the side aisle and into the sacristy at the rear of the church. The foursome quickly went through the sacristy and out the back of the church into the covered, enclosed walkway that connected the church to the parish house where two clergymen lived. Three agents were stationed in the walkway and nodded as the President and his party swept by at a brisk pace.

Once in the parish house, the four went to the stairway to the basement where another pair of agents guarded that point. Quickly down the stairs and through an old lighted tunnel that ran beneath the driveway next to the parish house, the Presidential Blue Portal team reached the secret basement entrance of the huge Department of Veterans Affairs federal building that stood next to the St. John's church property.

The President now was one block away from the entrance to the church. Only the assigned Blue Portal Secret Service agents and the President knew his destination.

As the President and the security team reached the basement of the VA building, they moved quickly to the private elevator of the VA Secretary.

In less than two minutes, the president entered the large office of the Secretary of Veterans Affairs on the ninth floor. When he came in, Justice Oscar Moorman got up from a leather sofa to greet him. The chief Secret Service agent politely reminded the President that the Blue Portal event in the VA Secretary's office was scheduled for only ten minutes and closed the door.

"Well, we have ten minutes alone. Sorry it can't be longer. This nomination thing is on a fast track," the President announced as he shook Moorman's hand with a double-fisted politician's grip.

"I know you have had a talk with Senator Irma Powers. Damn fine lady and crackerjack senator. She has been carrying water for this Administration for eight tough years. She has recommended you to take over the Supreme Court. She says only you have the votes to be confirmed. Irma's one of the best vote counters on the Hill so I trust her on this one. This would be one of the final things I might be able to do as President. I think you will make a fine Chief Justice. What do you say? Will you accept my nomination?"

Both men were standing by the large window at the south end of the office. That window had one of the best views of the White House in town. Before answering, Justice Moorman looked out at the White House gleaming in the bright sunlight.

I can't refuse the President of the United States.

Yet he had to ask. Moorman looked back and eyed the President.

"Mr. President, are you picking me because I'm black?"

The President smiled his frat boy smile and answered, "Hell, Judge, I'm picking you because you're my only option. Irma Powers told me that Bianco has too much religious baggage to make it through a quick confirmation. Bottom line, I would pick you even if you were green."

Moorman's white teeth appeared and, with a deep laugh, he said, "You know in Vietnam when I served as a Navy medic with the Fifth Marines, I *was* called a 'dark green' Marine!"

The president laughed and said with a smile, "We better keep this green thing just between us. I don't want that in any press releases . . . or in any quotation books. Even though that was a great comeback!"

Moorman grinned in return and then held out his hand. "Okay, Mr. President, I'll be your Chief Justice nominee, if you want me."

The President nodded and sealed the deal with the handshake.

"Good man, Oscar. You got it. Now let's keep this meeting confidential, at least until we get you over to the White House tomorrow for the announcement."

The President then exhaled to signal the end of the business and said, "Well, I'm glad that's over. Now let's sit down and shoot the shit until the Secret Service comes and arrests me for playing hooky from my Sunday service."

✦ 12 ✦

CNN.com—*Breaking News (Internet)—Justice Oscar D. Moorman nominated for Chief Justice of the U.S. Supreme Court.*

WASHINGTON, D.C., DECEMBER 3, 2008—Today at ten o'clock, President Thomas Ramsey in a surprise move nominated Associate Justice Oscar D. Moorman as the Chief Justice of the U.S. Supreme Court. His nomination letter was sent to the Senate immediately after the announcement. There was a brief ceremony in the East Room of the White House where the President introduced Justice Moorman and his wife, Deborah Sloane Moorman. The President and Justice Moorman did not take any questions from the press corps after the announcement.

Justice Moorman was born on December 28, 1954, in New York City, New York. He served in the U.S. Navy as a medical corpsman from 1974 until 1977. On April 29, 1975, Moorman won the Silver Star for gallantry in action and the Purple Heart during combat operations at the Saigon Airport in South Vietnam while assigned to a

Marine battalion during Operation Frequent Wind, the evacuation of U.S. personnel from the Saigon area at the end of the Vietnam War.

Following his service in the military, Justice Moorman graduated from City College of New York with a premed degree in biology. He received his J.D. degree from Fordham Law School.

After law school, Moorman was an attorney in the Anti-Trust Division of the U.S. Department of Justice in Washington from 1983 until 1988. From 1988 to 1990, he was in private practice as an assistant general counsel with Salton Drug Company, specializing in intellectual property and antitrust matters. In 1990, he was appointed a Federal judge on the U.S. Court of Appeals for the District of Columbia Circuit. In 2000, Moorman was named an associate justice of the Supreme Court.

Justice Moorman is married to Deborah Sloane Moorman. Mrs. Moorman is the daughter of Senator Courtney Sloane (D-Conn.). This was a second marriage for Justice Moorman and the first for his wife. Justice Moorman's first marriage ended in divorce. The Moormans have no children.

Reached at her office on Capitol Hill to comment on the announcement, Senator Irma Powers, the Chair of the U.S. Senate Judiciary Committee, indicated that Justice Moorman's confirmation might be heard on an expedited basis. "In light of the importance of filling the leadership role tragically left vacant by the untimely death of Chief Justice William Simmons, I expect that Justice Moorman's hearings will be a top priority and will begin in mid-December."

· 13 ·

carrying a paper shopping bag, walked down the deserted long white marble hallway toward the chambers of Oscar Moorman. It had been a tough day for Bianco. The surprise White House announcement that morning had rocked Bianco and sent him into a deep depression.

Immediately after hearing the news on the TV in his chambers that morning, Bianco had closed the door to his inner office and told his secretaries not to disturb him with any calls or visitors. Inside his office, Bianco quietly prayed for guidance. He thought the Lord had been so clear in his prior communication to him—he was to become the next Chief Justice and would lead the Court and America in a new direction. A direction that restored morality and Christian ideals to America, no more abortions, no gay marriages, no gays allowed in the military, smut banned from TV and radio . . . a new morality for America.

After his private moment Bianco came out of his prayer flushed in the face and exhausted, but with a new interpretation of what he must do. God had spoken to him once again. With this new guidance, he reassessed the situation and interpreted the Moorman nomination as a temporary obstacle God had sent him to prove that he was worthy to be the next Chief Justice.

Then he began to plan. What someone might view as personal ambition had been changed into God's will. Bianco was following the path envisioned by his Savior. Christian principles and the loyalties of a friend had been transformed into a new course of practical guidance: the ends would justify the means. Bianco would destroy Moorman's confirmation somehow. Then God would find a way for Bianco to take his place as the nominee . . . or perhaps President Ramsey would install Bianco as Chief Justice by a recess appointment. Either way, Bianco believed that he would become Chief Justice. It was God's will.

Focusing on making the confirmation of Moorman a political train wreck, Bianco knew that the President's power in the Senate was fragile and weak at this time. He also knew that Moorman in the past had been an easy target for political and moral assaults based on his wanton womanizing. Therefore, the confirmation was not a sure thing. In Washington, the saying is especially true that "no deal is done, until it's done."

Being nominated and becoming Chief Justice were two separate things. Perhaps he could help Moorman fail in the confirmation process. Surely that's God's will?

Now was the time to learn his friend's weaknesses. Weaknesses that could be used to kill the confirmation. Moorman certainly wasn't perfect. He barely got on the Supreme Court due to his immoral and reckless behavior with women. People don't change. There must be some secret that could be learned from Moorman—some dark and unknown secret from his past that could derail the nomination.

So just before three o'clock, Bianco called Justice Moorman and asked if he could visit him in his chambers later to congratulate him. Of course, Moorman wanted to see his friend and mentor. Bianco had timed his planned visit at the end of the day so that they could have a celebratory drink and a relaxed time where Moorman might let down his guard.

Now as Bianco walked into Moorman's chambers, it was after six. Moorman's secretaries had departed so Bianco crossed the empty reception area and knocked on the door of the inner office. Moorman rose to warmly greet his old friend as Bianco walked into his chambers.

"Vince, thanks for coming by. Sorry I couldn't tell you about meeting with the President and the nomination before the official announcement. I gave my word to the President."

Bianco hugged Moorman and shook his head.

"O, my friend, no need to explain. I completely understand. Look I've brought us some good wine to toast the Moorman Court."

Bianco put the shopping bag he was carrying on O's desk and pulled out three bottles.

"Wow, Chalk Hill Chardonnay. Two bottles and already cold. This is great wine. And a bottle of Jack Daniel's. What a choice? We better do the wine."

"Yeah, wine is fine. I didn't know if you wanted wine or something a little stronger so I compromised and brought both. By the way, the wine is a favorite of mine that I thought you might like. I visited the Chalk Hill vineyard in the Sonoma Valley last year when I was at the ABA convention in San Fran. Beautiful place and they make super wine. Let's celebrate."

"Well, let's open the wine. Let me get a corkscrew and glasses. I have them in my bathroom," said Moorman as he disappeared into the small private bathroom next to his inner office.

As the two justices got comfortable in two dark leather wing chairs facing each other, Bianco raised his glass and toasted, "Here's to the next Chief Justice. I'm happy for you, O."

"Buddy, I was really surprised. I thought for sure it would be you, Vince. You would make a great Chief."

Nodding, Bianco ignored the compliment and replied, "No, O. You're the one for the job. You'll be fine."

Then there was silence in the chambers as the two justices took deep pulls on the cold wine and drank in silence until Moorman opened the conversation to tell his friend the details about the way he was selected.

Outside Bianco was the very picture of deep interest and friendly support as he listened to the particulars of the odd meeting with Senator Powers in her Chief of Staff's old Volvo and the secret "Blue Portal" meeting with the President, but inside Bianco was in a deep jealous rage.

As O related the details of both meetings, Bianco was very interested in the Powers question on the upcoming patent case, apparently involving the Carpa drug company. He agreed with Moorman that it was an improper question and was most likely based in Powers' vested interest in servicing a major Virginia donor,

So Senator Powers wanted to know if Moorman would do his usual pro-patent thing with the Carpa case. That's a good-to-know item. And I guess it explains why his supposed friend Powers was apparently backing O. She's obviously looking out for one of her big political donors— no surprise around D.C. Friendship is always trumped by self-interest! However, maybe I could use that Carpa thing as some leverage with Senator Powers if Oscar fails?

Moorman was drinking the wine quickly and appeared to Bianco's studied observation uncharacteristically both nervous and happy.

"How does Debby like the idea of you being Chief Justice?" probed Vince, knowing the ambition of Moorman's wife.

"Funny you should ask, buddy. She's the main reason I accepted. I think it is something about showing her Senator dad that she did well in marrying me."

Bianco chose to ignore the comment. He let it hang and reached over to refill O's empty glass. Moorman was drinking at a three-to-one pace ahead of Bianco.

I'm not interested in why you want to be Chief . . . I'm interested in stopping you.

They were well into the second bottle before it warmed to room temperature. Pretty fast pace drinking. O looked sleepy and was clearly feeling the effects of the alcohol.

"Hey, buddy. You're not driving tonight, are you? We wouldn't want the next CJ to be pulled over for DWI, would we?"

"No, Vince. Debby is picking me up at seven. We're going to dinner at the University Club to celebrate. But you're right. Didn't sleep much last night. The wine is good, but damn it went right to my head. I feel a little dizzy."

"Good wine—'that men should put an enemy into their mouths to steal away their brains . . .' I forget the rest of the saying." Bianco had an almost photographic memory that allowed him often to quote to the circumstances of most social or legal situations. It was a familiar trait that Moorman admired in his friend.

"Good quote, buddy! Where's that from?"

Bianco turned pale. He had without thinking quoted from Shakespeare's *Othello*—a play where a white man *betrays* his black comrade over a promotion.

Whoa. Think before you speak. Othello is too close to home here.

Bianco recovered quickly and lied, "I think it's from Jonathan Swift, the Irish poet. He also was a clergyman who tended to the two Irish scourges, poverty and drink."

Moorman was silent for a while, then he remarked, "Deep down, Vince, I've always been jealous of your classical education at Harvard. As you know, I took premed at City College of New York on the GI Bill after Vietnam. Worked as a waiter in the cafeteria to get student aid. Always busy. Never had much time to read much literature."

Yes, your blue collar shows in a lot of areas. How could the President pick you over me? You don't even belong on this Court. Bianco had to hide his looking down on Moorman's education.

The wine was finished, but Bianco talked Moorman into a couple of shots of the Jack Daniel's. O was definitely drunk now to the point of slurring words.

Bianco knew Debby would be coming by to pick up O soon. Now was the time to drill for dirt, so he asked, "The hearings are coming up in a couple of weeks. Aren't you worried about the confirmation? Anything negative the Senate will focus on?"

"Yeah, I guess the fucking Democrats are going to rehash my dating history. I took a hell of a beating last time on that. I had trouble sleeping last night thinking about the confirmation hearing."

"I don't know, buddy. The dating thing was unfair, but that's water long gone under the bridge. And now that you're remarried, your dating history really is yesterday's news. . . . Things are good with you and Debby? Aren't they?" asked Bianco, hoping things weren't.

Moorman's eyes were drooping. "No problem there. Couldn't be better. We're very happy and deeply in love. Maybe too much. . . . You know . . . I mean, I already said, I'm doing this CJ thing for her. To make her happy and proud of me."

"O, I know you too well. Something's bothering you. What are you worried about? You said you couldn't sleep last night," Bianco probed further.

Then he decided to throw a "Hail Mary" question. "O, old buddy, does anyone have anything on you? Anything that could really bite you?"

Moorman rolled his eyes and with a slight slur said, "Maybe, could be something. . . . I am worried about how big this nomination is making news in the international press, especially in England. Lots of coverage about me. With pictures and everything."

"So what? Who cares about what the English think about you?"

Moorman leaned closer. Bianco could see his eyes were a bit unfocused. Then Moorman whispered in a low voice, "In England about five years ago—now this was a couple of years before I met Debby. Well . . . this is hard to say, Vince."

"Go on, O. I'm your friend. You can tell me anything." Bianco's grin was genuine and evil. He had a feeling that he was about to learn something to bring down Moorman's nomination.

And he was.

Moorman paused, took a deep breath and exhaled. He then continued, "Well, this could be a land mine for my confirmation. . . . There was a girl, a young woman I met at a reception in London. . . . She was in the law delegation that handled my visit. We both had a lot to drink . . . I went home with her. And I think I might have raped her . . . not really rape. Just forcing myself on her after she said no."

Bianco nearly fell off his chair, but recovered and asked, "Tell me about it, buddy. You can confide in me."

<h1 align="center">⟡ 14 ⟡</h1>

CNN.com—*Breaking News (Internet)—Former Federal Appeals Court Judge Timothy Quinn named Special Counsel to U.S. Senate Judiciary Committee for confirmation hearing of Justice Oscar Moorman.*

WASHINGTON, D.C., THURSDAY, DECEMBER 4, 2008—Senator Irma Powers, Chair of the U.S. Senate Judiciary Committee, announced that the Honorable Timothy Quinn was named as Special Counsel to the Senate Judiciary Committee for the imminent confirmation hearings of Associate Justice Oscar D. Moorman, who has been nominated by the President as the Chief Justice of the United States.

Timothy Quinn is a partner of the Washington, D.C., law firm of Wellington & Stone. Quinn served for over five years on the United States Court of Appeals for the District of Columbia circuit. His prior government positions include service as the General Counsel for the National Reconnaissance Office and as a prosecutor in the Department of Justice. Quinn is a decorated Vietnam veteran and was a Ranger instructor in the U.S. Army. He is a graduate of the United States Military Academy at West Point and Columbia Law School. He has two grown children: Anne, a photo editor in New York, and Paul, an attorney in Chicago. Judge Quinn's wife, Katy Johansen Quinn, was tragically killed in an automobile accident last year.

Serving as staff with Judge Quinn in the Special Counsel's Office will be Ms. Victoria Hauser, a senior Justice Department attorney on temporary assignment to the U.S. Senate, and FBI Special Agent William Sharkey, also on temporary detail to the Senate from the Washington Field Office (WFO) of the Federal Bureau of Investigation.

Senator Powers, in making the announcement of Judge Quinn's appointment, stated: "The Moorman confirmation hearings are on a fast track due to the time pressures of the end of the Congressional session. I am pleased that Judge Quinn has agreed to accept this advisory role during these very important hearings. On that point, the hearings are scheduled to proceed on December 18."

Asked about the likelihood of confirmation of Justice Moorman, Senator Powers replied, "Excellent. Justice Moorman is extremely well qualified to become the chief justice, the first African-American to head the Court in America's history. President Ramsey has made a very good choice and the Senate is prepared to swiftly exercise its constitutional duty in the confirmation process."

15

A TRIM, DISTINGUISHED-LOOKING MAN IN A DARK BLUE suit stood before the receptionist in the office of Senator Powers and said, "Could you please notify the Senator that Tim Quinn is here to see her? I'm about five minutes early for my appointment."

Quinn had a face that had obvious mileage on it. He wasn't what normally passes for handsome. There were deep crow's-feet at the corners of piercing blue-gray eyes, a broken nose that leaned slightly to the left, and a small crescent-shaped scar on one of his cheekbones. He had short hair in a distinctive military cut with mixed gray and dark brown hair with the gray obviously winning the battle. His erect posture made him seem taller that his measured five foot, eleven inches. But it was his smile that made most people remember him at a first meeting. He looked like he was having fun at life. They didn't know it, but a lot of people were tricked by the smile. He smiled equally at enemies, friends, and fools. It was an old trait. When things got tough, he never showed fear, anxiety, or sorrow. He was prone to grin in pressure situations—like before a boxing match at West Point or later before combat missions in Vietnam. Mainly, Tim's smile was his Irish mask that hid his true feelings.

Today and for most of the last year, his face hid his sorrow. Last year he lost his wife . . . his Katy. His sweetheart died instantly in a one-car accident on the snowy George Washington Memorial Parkway next to the Potomac River last December just before Christmas. Shortly after that he resigned from the U.S. Court of Appeals for the D.C. Circuit and returned to his old law firm to seek the busy hectic life of a high-speed Washington attorney. A life filled with daily challenges and not much time for inner thoughts about how much he missed Katy. He was here today because he thought the Special Counsel position was a challenge to keep him on the fast track of doing difficult and worthy things that his wife Katy would approve of. Even in death, he sought to impress his Katy and make her proud of him. It was a way to cope.

Quinn had waited less than a minute before Senator Powers came bursting into the reception room to personally lead him through the maze of cubicles to her office—a nice touch, Quinn thought.

As Quinn and Powers got settled in deep comfortable chairs in the informal greeting area of Powers' spacious office next to the tall windows looking out onto Constitution Avenue, she spoke, "Thank you again for taking this assignment, Judge Quinn. Are your offices okay? I told my staff on the committee to put you, Ms. Hauser, and

Agent Sharkey in the suite of offices right next to the Senate Judiciary Committee hearing room in the Dirksen Building."

"Thanks, Senator. Everything is fine. My senior staff—Vicky Hauser from Justice and Special Agent Sharkey from the WFO—are up and running. Thanks to your efforts, I also have the Senate Judiciary Committee professional staff working to review all the legal opinions and speeches of Justice Moorman to alert us to any possible contentious issues that may arise during the hearings. Personally, I am concerned with Moorman's switch on affirmative action. I think that's a major area where the conservatives will attack him. Also there is an abnormality in Moorman's Navy records that I'm studying. Well, that's the situation report for now."

"Good, good, Judge! Now on the general investigation, as you know, the FBI is concurrently doing a standard full field investigation on him—which we will get progress reports on—but I think nothing negative will show up from that on our man. Moorman has not raised any red flags on anything he's done since he got onto the Supreme Court. The raking he got on his dating habits at his first confirmation obviously scared him straight. Also his marriage seems very stable from all reports. And I would know. I'm a close personal friend of Senator Sloane, Moorman's father-in-law. Sloane swears that the marriage is rock solid. . . . FYI, there *is* a small side issue that the rumor mill surfaced and that you should know about— Moorman's wife has an alcohol problem—not major—I'm told."

Quinn replied. "I'll look into it. That should be out-of-bounds for the hearings. This is a hearing on him, not his wife."

Powers nodded approval and seemed to be speaking to herself when she said, "Everything will be fine. There should be no problems with this confirmation. You should have an easy job."

Quinn said nothing, but thought, *Confirming the first black man to be the Chief Justice of the United States will be anything but easy.*

Quinn had no idea how right he was. Just a couple of blocks down First Street—at the Supreme Court—was a man making a phone call that would trigger a ton of dirt being dumped on the nominee.

✦ 16 ✦

JUSTICE VINCENT BIANCO KNEW THAT TIME WAS against him. The Moorman hearings were set for December 18. The new president—a Democrat—would be inaugurated next month on Tuesday, January 20, 2009. Bianco had to move fast and effectively if he wanted to derail Moorman and make a bid to get himself eased in as Chief Justice before President Ramsey left office. And he was keenly aware it was also important to move covertly. It would be fatal to his bid to be Chief Justice if it was seen that he had anything to do with the destruction of the nomination of his friend. Washington tolerated many sins, but being a traitor was not one of them.

To deliver his secret blows to the Republican nominee Moorman, Bianco decided to go to the most powerful member of the obvious opposition to the president's naming of a chief justice—the Democratic Minority Leader of the Senate, Senator Dalton. The Minority Leader was scheduled to become the Majority Leader of the Senate in January due to the "sea-change" November elections, which elected not only a Democrat as president-elect, but also changed the controlling party in the Senate . . . and nearly missed taking over the House of Representatives, where the Republicans still held a very slim majority in the new Congress that convened in January.

In Bianco's mind, Senator Thomas J. Dalton (D-Ala.), the man who would soon become the Majority Leader, was the key to destroying the Moorman confirmation.

It seemed strange for a Republican to go to a Democrat for a favor. However, this was political Washington, which lived by the saying—"Enemy of my enemy is my friend."

As Bianco dialed the direct line to Senator Dalton, he was apprehensive about how he would approach Dalton and keep the contact secret. He shouldn't have worried, since Dalton was cunning and a master at stealth meetings.

"Senator, this is Vince Bianco. I have some urgent and important information that you should be made aware of with regard to Oscar Moorman."

"Mr. Justice, thank you for calling, but I can assure you that the Moorman propaganda machine is pumping out sufficient favorable material on your friend. There is no need to waste your time—and mine—to lobby me to vote for him. I am committed to leading the opposition to this ill-advised and ill-timed nomination. The next chief justice should be picked by a Democratic president. The people of America have spoken at the polls."

"Senator, I'm afraid that you have the wrong idea here . . . I have some important information—*negative* information. Damaging information that would clearly disqualify Moorman from being confirmed as Chief Justice. . . . We need to meet soon—perhaps today?"

Dalton was silent. Then he responded to this strange request. "I'm at a loss to understand what you are proposing . . . and why."

"All the more reason to meet, Senator. However, there are two ground rules. The meeting must between just the two of us and it must be in a place where we can't be observed. Not your office or my chambers or any public place. Do you have any suggestions?"

There wasn't any hesitation by Dalton. He was being offered a possible political WMD for the confirmation fight. "Let's meet at three o'clock today. In a discreet meeting place where we can be alone; leave that to me. I'll have a Senate 'staff pass' hand-delivered to your chambers within the hour. It will let you come through all Capitol checkpoints without signing in and with no escort. No records of your visit. Just be at the Capitol Rotunda, directly under the dome at three today and someone from my staff will take you to my hideaway office. I must say I'm intrigued by your call and look forward to our little chat."

The exclusive "no-escort-required" Senate pass was delivered to the Supreme Court by courier as promised.

However, little gets unnoticed in Washington. The meeting between a Republican Supreme Court Justice and the U.S. Senate Minority Leader was not to be as secret as Senator Dalton and Justice Bianco anticipated.

⟡ 17 ⟡

ABSOLUTELY NO PACKAGE GETS DELIVERED TO A U.S. Supreme Court justice without being X-rayed, sniffed for chemical weapons and explosive devices, and opened by the Supreme Court police. The SOP guidelines set by the Supreme Court Marshal also require that a duty supervisor personally double-check the screening of any package.

That is how Supreme Court Marshal John Abbot was alerted to the thick envelope from the Senate Minority Leader's office, which contained a magnetic swipe pass and metal neck chain. According to Marshal Abbot's security instructions, all suspicious and unusual packages destined to be given to any justice should be reported to him before delivery. A magnetic pass from an unlikely source—the Senate—was definitely unusual. The fact that a Democratic Senator was sending such an item to a solid Republican-appointed Supreme Court justice also rang a political alarm bell with the alert supervisor.

When Abbot got the call from the duty supervisor, he walked from his first-floor office to the side entrance in the basement floor of the Supreme Court, where he was shown the already opened envelope. The Senate staffer had already departed after being reassured by the police supervisor that the envelope would be immediately delivered to the chambers of Associate Justice Vincent Bianco. Abbot, a quick study, immediately understood the significance of the "no-escort-required" pass being transferred from the head of the confirmation opposition to the obvious runner-up to the Chief Justice nomination. Politics existed everywhere in Washington.

"Go ahead and deliver the envelope to Bianco's chambers," ordered the Marshal to the security checkpoint supervisor. Once the supervisor had departed, Abbot headed back upstairs via the central marble staircase and was soon in his office.

Abbot sat behind the antique desk positioned next to a floor-to-ceiling window so that he could look out onto one of the two inner white marble courtyards of this historic 1934 building. He was troubled by the implications of what he had just done. He was a servant of the Court, loyal to all justices. He reasoned through the apparent political intrigue and arrived at the conclusion that another justice needed to be aware of the situation. Abbot picked up the phone and called the chambers of that justice and asked to see him. The secretary on the line after checking with her boss told him to come to the chambers.

As Abbot walked out of his office, he looked at the small photos of his predecessors in office on the wall by his door. The Supreme Court Marshals dated back to the first named Supreme Court. They were lined up by dates of service and many photos were photos of portraits; underneath each one was a small brass nameplate with full name and dates of service. The most recent photos ended with that of Marshal John Abbot.

Abbot's photo wasn't hard to spot from a distance.

His face was the only one on the wall that was black.

Soon John Abbot was in the reception area of the chambers of Justice Moorman.

Moorman's chief secretary announced over the intercom that

Marshal Abbot was in the reception area to see the Justice. Moorman said to send him right in.

As he walked into the inner office of Oscar Moorman, the Justice got up and motioned the Marshal to the leather sofa. Moorman took the chair opposite to the sofa so he could face the Marshal.

When they were both seated, Moorman asked, "How have you been, John?"

"Fine, Mr. Justice. I want to report an unusual delivery that just occurred. A top-level Senate pass is now being delivered to Justice Bianco. It was hand-delivered to the Court ten minutes ago. I am familiar with the pass since the Chief of the Capitol Police and I have periodic meetings on security procedures, including the types of passes used in our building and in all the Senate and House buildings. This pass will allow Justice Bianco access to any portion of the Senate, including the Senate floor . . . without any escort or without any signing-in requirement. The pass was apparently issued by Senator Dalton, the Democratic Minority Leader of the Senate. There was no note, but the envelope showed Dalton's office as the sender. I just wanted you to know this."

Moorman stroked his chin with his hand and didn't say anything for a full minute.

This is definitely curious. A probable visit to the head Senate Democrat. Especially coincidental after Vince visited me this morning and asked some follow-up questions to my stupid confiding to Vince that I probably forced sex on that English barrister in London. Senator Dalton, as the top Democrat, will be the leader of the opposition against my confirmation. Fucking strange that Vince would get a special pass from him today . . . of all days.

Moorman's face was a mask.

"Thanks for this info, John. I'm sure that Justice Bianco has a good reason to receive this type of pass. The timing is curious. You were sharp to pick up on it. I expect nothing less from a SEAL— always on the alert," remarked Moorman with a grin.

The Marshal smiled, nodded, and stood up.

"Well, Your Honor, I just wanted you to know that piece of info. By the way, Mr. Justice, a lot of people in the Court are pulling for you to become Chief. Good luck."

Moorman sincerely said, "Thanks, John. Nice of you to say . . . and again thanks for the info on the pass. . . . Ahh, probably wouldn't be wise to mention this to anybody else. It might be misunderstood. Lot of gossip around the Court these days!"

"Roger that, Sir." The Marshal turned and left.

Moorman returned to his desk and just sat there for a while staring blankly . He knew that Bianco had been a friend and mentor over his years on the Court, but he also knew Bianco's burning ambition to be Chief Justice . . . and his expectation that this nomination would be his. Must have been a big disappointment to him not to get the nomination for the Center Seat.

Moorman's final thought . . . and a wise one was—*Better watch Vince. It is probably true what they say around political Washington— that you should keep your friends close, and your enemies closer! Bianco probably was a little of both.*

18

AT THREE O'CLOCK SHARP, JUSTICE BIANCO WAS directly under the dome of the U.S. Capitol. The Rotunda was jammed with tour groups and the Justice was starting to worry about being recognized by someone in the crowd when an older well-dressed lady with a Senate staff badge hanging around her neck approached him and said, "Mr. Justice, I'm Judy Carver—the private secretary for Minority Leader Dalton, please follow me."

The Capitol Rotunda with its large dome is a beautiful piece of architecture and is known to tourists for its massive historical paintings on the walls and the attached hall of white marble statues of famous Americans. Moreover, the Rotunda is the traditional hallowed place where the caskets of national figures like former presidents lie in state so the public can pay their respects before their funerals. Not just presidents rate this space—several generals, justices of the Supreme Court, and more recently, the civil rights pioneer Rosa Parks were accorded this special honor.

Only a few people knew that the rooms above and around the Rotunda are the places for the ultimate perks for senior senators—a group of small private hideaway offices. Senator Dalton, the senior Democratic leader, rated a nice little nest in the dome office area where he could escape the fishbowl atmosphere of his busy Senate office in the Russell Senate Office Building. There were only two people on Dalton's staff who knew the location of his hideaway—his Chief of Staff and his private secretary of twenty years, the lady leading Justice Bianco to the unmarked office near the top of the dome.

Bianco was left outside the office by the Senator's secretary, who quickly vanished back down the labyrinth of narrow corridors that they had traveled to the secret office of Senator Dalton.

"The Senator is inside and waiting for you," were her last words before her disappearance. Apparently even she was not allowed into this special place.

Knowing that he was taking a big step—a crossing of a personal Rubicon—by betraying his friendship with Moorman and loyalty to the Republican party, Bianco hesitated before knocking on the door of the hideaway.

As soon as he rapped on the solid oak door, a voice bellowed, "Come in."

Two things struck Bianco about the hideaway—the room was tiny and there was only one window—an amazing window—a large oval almost as big as the room. The view down the Mall toward the Washington Monument was breathtakingly beautiful. The window made the small room seem much bigger and almost as if you were sitting on the side of the Capitol building.

There were two large wing chairs, a large well-worn brown leather sofa (big enough for a six-footer to take a nap), and a small desk with a flat-screen TV on the wall.

Senator Thomas Dalton was sitting on one of the wing chairs smoking a long cigar and he had a tumbler of whiskey on the coffee table in front of him.

"Want a drink or a cigar, Mr. Justice?"

"No thanks, Senator. I'm fine."

"Please call me 'TJ.' Now what is on that brilliant mind that I hear you have?"

"Hypothetically, I want to make a deal, TJ. I'll give you the ammo to sink Moorman's nomination if you pressure President Ramsey into giving me a recess appointment as the Chief Justice. Moreover, after I serve for a decent interval and well before the end of the next session of Congress, I want you to support my Senate confirmation as the Chief Justice."

Dalton whistled. "My, my! This is surely something. I can see why you wanted to meet one-on-one. Now, what makes you think you can trust me? I could take what ever smut you think you have and still renege on our deal."

"I've thought about that . . . Senator, and think that you and your party could lose a lot if you did that. I'll be on the Supreme Court for the rest of my life and you *definitely* don't want me as your enemy. You would be surprised at the way I could hurt you and your party with judicial rulings and . . . with speeches outside Court."

The older man laughed and said, "You know, Judge . . . you have the makings of a fine senator. You may be in the wrong branch of government! . . . Okay, hypothetically, it's a deal. If—and only *if*—you help me sink Moorman, I'll put my oar in the water with that punk Ramsey before he leaves town on January 20. He's a political animal and he'll want favors from the Democrats right up to the end of his Administration and most likely well into the new Democratic

Administration. . . . Moreover, on your second point, I'll help you get confirmed near the end of your recess appointment. That is . . . if Ramsey gives the recess to you. Hell, that will make me look good and nonpartisan, helping getting you, a Republican, confirmed. You certainly have the ability to be a good Chief Justice. Personally I always thought you had the brain power to run circles around those other political hacks and pompous asses on the Court."

Bianco smiled at the deal . . . and the compliment.

Dalton took a pull on his whiskey and leaned forward to shake Bianco's hand to seal the deal.

"Now let's hear what you've got on that bastard."

"There are two items that could be used . . ."

Bianco started small—he related the fact that there was a dirty movie charged on Moorman's hotel bill at the Duke Law conference. Dalton was impressed, but he knew that watching dirty movies in a hotel room wasn't a killer blow in these days of bare tits at the Super Bowl and rampant pornography on the Internet.

After they discussed how the Durham hotel bill would be prima facie proof for the X-rated movie smear on Moorman, Bianco brought out the heavy artillery—he revealed the details of the date rape situation in England that Moorman had confessed to Bianco last night at their Supreme Court "wine plus Jack Daniel's" celebration. The effect of this information on Dalton was immediate.

"I'll be goddamned! I knew that Moorman was a fucking-ass bandit, but this is something else—a very, very big deal. So he really raped a young barrister or student in London after a reception a few years ago. Wow. This is dynamite! This shit will blow that black son of a bitch right into an impeachment hearing unless he is extradited to England first for a criminal trial. Now let's go back over the details."

The devil was always in the details—it was here where the glow wore off the party to a certain degree. Bianco could only reveal what Moorman had shared with him—the place, an approximate time, and the general circumstances (in London five years ago after some summer law program reception where a wine-lubricated Moorman had accompanied an "English girl" home and given her an unwanted tumble between the sheets). Bianco said he couldn't confirm it, but Moorman mentioned the "girl" was a young barrister. Bianco reported Moorman didn't give the name or any description of the girl other than that she was English and that he was worried that the heavy press coverage about his nomination might bring the woman forward to reveal his having sex with her.

Bianco told Senator Dalton that he was prevented from getting more details from Moorman because Moorman's wife, Debby, showed up last night right when Moorman was unloading on him about the incident. Bianco also told the Senator that this morning when he tried to get the name of the woman or more specifics on the incident, the now sober Moorman was not forthcoming and clammed up on further details. However, Bianco reported that Moorman still was fearful that the extensive international press coverage in England about his nomination might trigger the "girl" to come forward to formally claim "date rape." Celebrities are always a target . . . and Moorman was becoming a hot international celebrity due to the extensive press coverage.

Dalton and Bianco strategized for a good twenty minutes about how more details of the incident could be gained.

At the end of the meeting, Dalton summed up the meeting with an optimistic tone, "You've given me some good stuff on Moorman. I'll find a way to locate that English bitch and make her tell her story about how he raped her. After that, the press will eat Moorman alive . . . and you may get your shot at the Center Seat."

· 19 ·

AS SOON AS BIANCO LEFT THE SENATE HIDEAWAY, SEN-
ator Dalton returned to his Senate office and placed a call on his private line to an unlisted phone number in the outskirts of Montgomery,
Alabama.

"Yeah?" said a gruff, gravel voice.

"It's me—TJ. I've got something for you. Remember that person
you were complaining about to me yesterday when you heard the
news on the TV about his . . . possible promotion?"

"You mean that black son of a bitch Moorman?"

Senator Dalton winced at the mention of the name on an unse-
cured phone, but considered the source and respectfully replied, "Yes,
sir, that's the person I'm talking about. Well, there might be a way to
stop the confirmation . . . something fatally damaging to the hearings.
I can't talk about it on the phone, but wanted you to know that I have
just received some direct information from a high-level source . . . really damaging information . . . perhaps we could talk about it and you
might give me some advice on using this info. . . . I might need a little
help in airing it in the media."

There was a long pause on the phone; then the rough voice demanded, "TJ, get your ass down here and tell me what the fuck is going on."

Without any further word, the phone went dead in Dalton's hand.
No good-bye. Nothing but a click.

*Christ, I hate that prick! But he has had my balls in his pocket for a
long time.*

Dalton then punched in the speed dial number to his Chief of Staff.

"Dorothy, please get me on a plane to Montgomery tonight and an early morning flight back to D.C. tomorrow. Use one of those first-class upgrade certificates the airlines send me. Also get me a rental car—a Lincoln Town Car if they have it—and a room at the Holiday Inn downtown for one night. I'll be available all the time on my cell. And don't alert my Montgomery office or tell anyone in the D.C. office . . . or put it on my daily schedule. This is an 'off-the-record' trip. I don't want anyone to meet me at the airport or prepare any special welcome at the hotel. This is an official trip but I don't want anybody to know I'm coming. Confidential Senate business— an investigation matter. Understand?"

"Yes, sir. Reportable official visit but no advance notice to anyone."

⬦ 20 ⬦

IN TEN MINUTES, I'LL BE WITH THE BILLIONAIRE. GOD, I *regret the day I took that first fucking stock tip from him. He's made me rich, but he's owned me ever since.*

Senator Dalton had just passed the gatehouse security checkpoint of the billionaire's estate and was driving his rental car up the long private road leading to the main house. In theory, the house, the outbuildings, barns, and fenced land were classified for tax purposes as a cattle farm. But the herd of cattle was mainly for show. This place really was the world headquarters of the billionaire for the unusual array of diverse global companies he owned in the U.S. and

Europe—investment companies, newspapers, TV and radio stations, construction companies, medical clinics, trucking companies, and car rental franchises. He was very hands-on in all his business enterprises. He had no children and no present wife—married only to his work, his grudges, and his prejudices. His first and only wife committed suicide after two years of marriage. He had been a widower for almost twenty-five years now. With no hobbies or any children, making money and exercising stringent control of his businesses was his life.

Although Montgomery was having a cold snap for this time of year—temperatures in the lower forties—the billionaire was outside on the flagstone patio behind his huge French château–style home sitting beneath a large restaurant-type heating lamp at a table reading from a stack of newspapers. The billionaire owned papers ranging from small-town weeklies to daily newspapers in major cities and national tabloids. He never read books, just newspapers—*his* papers.

As the Senator came onto the patio, the billionaire said, "Sit down, TJ. What news do you bring from that town of fucking political whores you live in?" The billionaire spoke without looking up. It was a sign of disrespect. The Senator was used to such treatment from the wealthy man who made him millions on tips in advance stock deals and land transactions in his state of Alabama.

"I've got some dirt on Moorman." The Senator said flatly.

That got his attention. The billionaire looked up and his thin wrinkled tan face broke into a toothy grin.

"Some minor dirt . . . and some big-time mud," added the Senator with a slight smile, the smile of a schoolboy bringing home a report card with all "A"s to a strict parent.

"Well, now, let's hear the mud first, Mr. Minority Leader," said the rich man with a slow thick Southern drawl.

The Senator quickly outlined his unusual visit from Justice Bianco and the date rape incident in England as related by Bianco. The billionaire listened intently.

At the end of the story, the billionaire gave his view. "Good stuff . . . but only if we can actually prove date rape. If we get the proof—let's just say we can get an interview from this here English girl to say she was raped by that black bastard—well, you don't have to be a rocket scientist to know that such a statement will definitely kill the nomination. If we get this out quickly there may not even be a hearing; he'll withdraw and may very well find his black ass in an English prison with some not so nice people. Now that would be an interesting endgame. . . . But looking at this from a realistic viewpoint, a pretty vague story about a rape without even the name of the girl— or any witnesses showing he was even with the girl—may get some initial interest, but without more specific information is not a story with legs. What I mean is that it's really not going anywhere without more concrete details. Bottom line, the story is thin, very thin. No name of the victim, no evidence of a crime. This is not a story that any major newspaper would run with. It's not really confirmed news yet. . . . and I *know* news. Nevertheless I'll put some people on it . . . hummm . . . maybe, just maybe I'll also put it on the Internet with the bloggers—their standards are a lot lower than a newspaper. Hell, they don't have any standards. They'll go with a story with no proof at all sometimes. I think I'll have the blog come from England— might as well play it there. It plays to Moorman's fear that the news of his nomination in England will trigger the surfacing of the girl. Yes, this story definitely should come from England."

The billionaire smiled broadly at his tactics and added, "What else have you got on my boy? What's the lesser info—the dirt."

The Senator related what Bianco told him about Moorman during a recent trip to the Duke Law conference—that Moorman mentioned to Bianco he saw an X-rated movie on his hotel TV. A soft porno movie.

"Now, why would Moorman tell Bianco about watching a dirty movie? Sounds fucking strange to me."

"I don't know why he would confess it to Bianco. But Bianco says it's true. And he also says the hotel bill in Durham will definitely prove it. I can put a Senate investigator on that . . . if you like," said the Senator.

"No, I'll have one of my investigative reporters get a copy of the bill. People will wonder how the Senate investigator knew about the hotel bill. That would put your fine Senate fingerprints on this whole thing. No, better, I get it done. An investigative reporter is the bottom-feeder type that looks in garbage cans and government trip expenses. Better this story about a Supreme Court justice looking at dirty movies on the taxpayer's dime starts in the media. . . . Actually it's really a good start on smearing Moorman. The American people won't like that the recently nominated Chief Justice is a dirty old man watching porno movies in a hotel room—real bad judgment for a Chief Justice-to-be!

"Anything else for me?"

"No," replied the Senator, anxious to end the meeting.

The billionaire stood and walked the Senator to the door of his mansion. There was no socializing. No dinner invite. No invitation to spend the night. The Senator would leave the luxury home with nine empty luxury guest suites and drive to Birmingham for a single nonsmoking room in a midprice hotel that was covered by the government per diem.

The longtime relationship between the Senator and the wealthy man had never been on a personal friendship basis. It had been business from the start when, years ago, the billionaire started giving stock tips to the newly elected Senator from his home state. Those tips had made the Senator a millionaire several times over. The investment advice to buy stock in companies was always solid. There never were any sensational tips that made a "stock killing" overnight. However, there were never any losers; all were "solid gold" tips that gradually and quietly built up the Senator's stock portfolio and his private fortune. The Senator in turn did favors in legislation and a little arm-twisting in various agencies of the government that helped the billionaire and his businesses.

That was the deal—just business. The Senator gave government favors to the billionaire and the billionaire kept giving discreet and very valuable "insider" stock tips to the Senator.

As the Senator went out the large oak front door, he turned and asked, "I'm curious. What have you got against Moorman anyway?"

The billionaire's face went into a grimace. Then he coldly said, "Well, now, Mr. Senator, it's really none of your damn business. But I'll just say this. It will be a long cold day in hell when a fucking black man is made the Chief Justice of the United States. Moreover it's personal. Let's just say he fucked one of my companies once a long time ago when he was in the Department of Justice Anti-Trust Division. He was the lead attorney on a case that disapproved a merger. Goddamn black bastard cost me a lot of money and heartache . . . and now I get to do the same to him. Payback time. Have a good trip back to D.C., TJ."

That was it. The end of the visit. No handshake. The billionaire just made a dismissive wave directing the U.S. Senator toward his car parked in the graveled circular driveway.

The door shut with a heavy thud and the front porch light went out. Alone in the dark, the Minority Leader of the U.S. Senate crunched his way on the gravel toward his rental car.

❖ 21 ❖

THE NEW SPECIAL COUNSEL TO THE SENATE JUDICIARY Committee, Tim Quinn, was sitting in his office in the Dirksen Senate Office Building. The room was a long rectangular conference room with tall windows overlooking Constitution Avenue. There were obvious signs that the room had functioned as the Committee's private conference room for the senators before Senator Powers had ordered it converted into Quinn's office. Tim made his "desk" one end of the long mahogany conference table that dominated the beautiful room, with its high ceiling and a large crystal chandelier centered in the middle of the table. In a few minutes, he would be meeting with his two-person personal senior staff. Vicky Hauser, a prosecutor from the Justice Department, and FBI Special Agent Bill Sharkey.

Quinn was pleased that Hauser and Sharkey had agreed to the special detail as his personal staff for the confirmation hearing. In his mind, he couldn't have done better.

He had significant history with these two. For one thing, they were the legal team of federal prosecutor and FBI investigator that Tim had trusted to help him expose a sensitive case-fixing scheme at his Federal Court of Appeals some years ago when he first became a federal judge. Tim had risked his career at first and later his life to get the evidence to Vicky and Sharkey. And they came through for him—they expertly put together an airtight criminal case that resulted in a plea-bargain conviction of a top D.C. lawyer, a former president of the D.C. Bar. The criminal case and the exposure of the dirty lawyer's payments to a judge on Tim's court also indirectly led to the suicide of the federal judge who was involved in the case-fixing scheme Tim uncovered. The judge was never arrested—he chose to end his life rather that face prison for bribery.

Victoria Hauser was a top prosecutor in the Public Integrity Section of the U.S. Justice Department—tall, blonde, and most people considered her good-looking except for a facial scar. She was in her early forties, and still single. Vicky Hauser was a bulldog in an investigation. Quinn was lucky that she had agreed to help him in this important assignment. She was not only good. Tim trusted her.

Special Agent Bill Sharkey was an FBI legend close to mandatory retirement—a heavyset, balding "Old School" agent with hooded eyelids that fooled people into thinking he was almost asleep. Looks aside, he was a rule-bending and imaginative investigator who solved many cases on instincts not taught at the FBI Academy—he thought like a criminal. He had been Vicky's lead investigator for years.

But even the sharp, alert Sharkey didn't know that Tim and Vicky had a secret back story: They were past lovers long ago in law school and, more recently, partners in Tim's one-time adultery.

Quinn had known Vicky since his student days at Columbia Law. They worked together on the law review and eventually became lovers. After law school, they had dated in a commuter mode—him in D.C. and she working in New York City—until the strain of distance broke up the relationship. After the breakup, Tim married Katy Johansen, a Danish exchange student he met at a Georgetown party. Happily married for years, Tim eventually took a risk and had a brief affair with Vicky. For a short time, Tim believed he could love two women. But he couldn't leave Katy and the marriage. When Katy eventually learned of the affair it had been long over. Nevertheless, Katy's realization of Tim's unfaithfulness nearly destroyed the marriage. After a short, painful separation, Tim and Katy reconciled. Although Katy forgave Tim, the guilt of his adultery was always there for him.

Tim's Catholic guilt had intensified this past year following Katy's death. As a consequence, until the present Senate appointment of Vicky to his staff, Tim had not seen Vicky socially in the year after Katy's funeral. The Moorman confirmation had been Tim's excuse to see her again—he used his professional need to reestablish contact with her.

There had been an indirect contact with Vicky this past year, but Tim doubted Vicky even suspected it.

Shortly after Katy's accident, Vicky was seriously injured. The deranged wife of someone Vicky prosecuted—a government employee who had embezzled several millions from Social Security funds—attacked Vicky at her apartment. The wife had thrown sulfuric acid at Vicky's face when Vicky answered the door of her apartment. Fortunately Vicky had turned and only the side of her face near her ear and her neck were burned by the acid. Nevertheless, it was a disfiguring injury that plastic surgery had only partially been able to repair.

When Tim learned of Vicky's injury, he'd sent a beautiful flower arrangement to the hospital—anonymously. He was not yet ready to bring any woman into his personal life. The Moorman job he'd accepted, he considered a professional one—and he wanted the best people he knew.

I hope it was not a mistake to bring her into my life again.

Tim put his reflections aside. He had a big job to do in guiding Justice Moorman through the confirmation hearing, but he had two tier-one professionals—Hauser and Sharkey—people he could trust to help him.

There was a knock on the tall door of the high-ceilinged office. "Enter," shouted Quinn, and Vicky and Sharkey walked in.

"Hi, gang. Is the case review double checking finished?"

"Absolutely. The professional staff here on the judiciary committee is not only sharp but quick. The second review of Moorman's cases on the U.S. Court of Appeals and the Supreme Court is finished and, as we thought before, showed no surprise land mines. That is . . . except for the big, obvious case where Moorman reversed his affirmative action position. Well, that's where we stand, Judge," reported Vicky.

Tim shook his head and said, "Vicky, I'm not a judge anymore. Let's use 'Tim,' okay?"

Vicky shrugged her shoulders and looked at Sharkey, who grinned slightly.

Vicky went on, "OK, *Tim*. Now how do we get around the issue of the Democrats beating up on Moorman for saying in his confirmation hearing that he was 'against affirmative action' and then voting for affirmative action in that government case which authorized minorities to get a percentage of federal government highway construction contracts? He's going to be accused of perjury by the Dems over one of *their* issues."

"I know. I know. We'll have to have Moorman give a reason for the switch."

Vicky volunteered, "Passage of time? He can say he thought about it over time and changed his position."

"No, in his confirmation hearings, Moorman went out of his way to make it clear that he had given it a lot of thought over the years of his legal career and thought affirmative action wasn't necessary—that minorities shouldn't have a head start in anything based on race. The conservatives ate that up with a spoon. Nope, we can't say he thought about it some more and reversed his decades-old belief . . . something must have happened to him to change his mind. But what?" Tim mused out loud.

The gruff voice of Bill Sharkey spoke. "Why don't you ask him?"

Tim and Vicky looked at each other.

Then Tim said, "The direct approach. Not a bad idea!"

Vicky questioned the move. "Are you supposed to be talking to Moorman? I mean . . . we're now senior staff of the Senate Judiciary Committee. Can we just do it? Do we have to get Senator Powers' permission?"

Tim rubbed his hair with a hand, a sign he was getting a tension headache.

After a while, Tim responded, "Well, I think we can do anything reasonable to answer any question that may come up in the hearing. I'm sure there's some Senate protocol that might say we can't interview the nominee without approval of the full committee, but I'm not going to ask anyone. I'll just do it. Better to ask forgiveness than permission. I'll call Moorman tomorrow and ask if he'll see me. Good idea, Bill."

Tim continued, "Well, since I'll hopefully be seeing Moorman and asking him to explain his flip on affirmative action, is there anything else I should ask him?"

Bill Sharkey answered, "*Judge*—and, for the record, FBI agents call all judges and ex-judges 'Judge' so don't get on me about that—there is something in Moorman's military record that never came up at his prior hearings—not at his initial hearings to be a judge on the U.S. Court of Appeals nor at his Supreme Court confirmation hearings. I don't know how they missed it, but I looked at all the records of all those hearings and it ain't there."

"What isn't there?" asked Tim.

"There's no mention that Moorman was tried and convicted by a special court-martial for disobedience of a direct order."

"Christ!" Tim's headache suddenly got worse.

◆ **22** ◆

TIM QUINN WAS IMPRESSED BY THE LOOK OF JUSTICE Moorman's office as soon as he walked into it. The room projected the warmth of an old-fashioned English club with a dark leather sofa, a deep plush green rug, a pair of comfortable wing chairs, and dark wood blinds on the tall windows of the room. It was interesting to Quinn that the room was devoid of the typical Washington, D.C., "I love me" wall coverings of plaques and photos of famous people shaking hands with the owner of the office. Instead the walls only had a few tasteful African paintings and a large beautiful oil portrait of someone Quinn instantly recognized—Henry O. Flipper, the first black graduate of West Point.

Oscar Moorman came around from behind his desk to greet Quinn.

"Welcome, Judge Quinn."

"Thanks for seeing me so soon, Mr. Justice."

They shook hands. Moorman had a strong, firm handshake, Quinn observed.

Moorman led Quinn over to the twin wing chairs that faced each other over a small antique butler's table.

On seeing Quinn staring at the Flipper portrait, he added, "I know you see an old friend of yours. Flipper has been a hero of mine since childhood and the National Portrait Gallery was very generous to loan me the painting for my chambers."

Moorman smiled with a flash of white teeth and added a deep chuckle before he said, "I know the role you had in the movement to remove the stain on Flipper's name. Thank you for it."

Quinn was stunned.

Very few people knew Quinn had performed a quiet early role in the Flipper case.

Flipper had graduated from West Point in 1877 and served well in the cavalry as the only black officer in the entire Army until he was dismissed from the Army in 1881 following an extremely flawed and obviously racially motivated court-martial that convicted Flipper following the disappearance of a small amount of Army funds under Flipper's control.

At the strong request of a friend, Minton Francis, the eighth African-American graduate of West Point (class of 1944), Quinn had looked into the court-martial and had voluntarily undertaken the twin tasks of getting the Army and court records of Flipper from the National Archives and of reviewing the records for constitutional and legal flaws. He had found plenty, but could do nothing, since he was an active Federal judge. So Quinn quietly turned over the records and his findings to another West Pointer, Tom Carhart, who used the material in his Ph.D. thesis at Princeton. Quinn wanted someone to pull together the racially motivated and flawed evidence into a clear story of how Flipper was judicially railroaded into a felony conviction by an Army court-martial.

Tom Carhart was a good choice by Quinn. He did a fine job of analyzing the flawed court-martial. Once Carhart put the story of the injustice done to Flipper into the form of a compelling narrative as part of his Ph.D. thesis, Quinn urged him to turn the entire expanded package over to another West Pointer, a politically connected attorney in Washington who got the materials to the White House, where a presidential pardon finally cleared Flipper's name in the late 1990s.

Quinn expressed his shock at Moorman's knowledge of his role.

"Well, thank you. I was happy to have a small part in the Flipper case. I'm surprised you knew about that. It really was Minton Francis that got the whole effort started. Who told you about my role?"

"Minton did. You see, I've been checking up on you just as you have been looking at me and my past. Now, what brings you over to see me?"

"Your Honor, in my role as Special Counsel for the Senate Judiciary Committee, I've found two items that may arise in the hearings. I think there will be questions on both . . . tough questions. Maybe you could explain what really happened and then I could take some of the heat from the committee off your back."

"Why don't you call me 'O'? . . . And I'll call you Tim. We really have too much in common to be so formal—hell, we belong to the same club—moreover, we both served in Vietnam and were judges on the same court—although at different times. Well, Tim, let's get to it. What's troubling you about my past? Why did you ask to see me?"

Tim nodded and started, "Okay, O. The two things are your court-martial and your reversal on your affirmative action position. Both are issues that may generate a lot of questions—tough questions at your hearings, especially by Southern conservatives."

Moorman smiled and replied, "I guess I'll go through that court-martial question first. It's come up before. It was raised in both my prior confirmation hearings, you know."

"No, that's strange. The FBI agent on my staff—a good and careful man—told me that there was no prior mention of it in either of the sets of hearings—the confirmation for you to be on the Court of Appeals and the one for the Supreme Court. Special Agent Bill Sharkey told me he looked through the records of both confirmations."

"Well, that's not surprising. That subject was examined by the Senate Judiciary Committee in closed sessions . . . without a recorder present. No transcript made. Really it was considered too sensitive for the public to hear. . . . Actually it must have been like something Flipper experienced in the Army. The court-martial came up when I'd just qualified as a medical corpsman and was on a temporary training exercise in New York City with twenty or so medics from the Army—we would ride in pairs at night in emergency medical vehicles in some of the toughest sections of the Bronx and Brooklyn. We all stayed in the barracks at Fort Hamilton, New York—right at the bottom of Brooklyn. Since we were all probably headed to Vietnam, some Pentagon big shot set up the exercise to give us real-life training in treating gunshot wounds. Actually it was a good idea; it's surprising how many gunshot wounds are treated in a typical night in a major city like New York, especially on a Saturday night. Well, the officer in charge of our little group was a 'cracker' lieutenant from Kentucky and he set up a little trick for me—the only black medic in this special unit. He called for a two-mile run in fatigues and boots one morning on one of the few free days we had. One of his redneck buddies put dog shit in my boots just before the run. Luckily I smelled it before I put my feet in them and so I reported to the run formation in my socks, no boots. The lieutenant ordered me to put on my boots. I refused the order. By the way, the lieutenant was used to getting his way since his daddy was a four-star general . . . and so bottom line I was court-martialed. End of story."

Tim nodded, "Explains a lot, especially the sentence. I don't think I ever saw a sentence of one-hour confinement before."

Moorman agreed with a smile that was more sad than funny, "The JAG judge who heard my explanation at the trial was a brand-new captain afraid of dismissing the charge because of the four-star daddy, but in the end he did have the balls to do almost the right thing. It was an unusually light sentence. For one hour in the courtroom following the sentence, I just read the novel I had in the duffle bag of gear I had packed, expecting to go immediately to prison."

Tim lifted his reading glasses to his forehead and rubbed his eyes. Then he wrote a few sentences in the notebook where he had the court-martial records filed.

After he was finished, he looked at Moorman.

"I'll brief the committee on this and I don't think that they will want to go into this area. It would be bad for the military . . . and for any senator who questions you on this. Now, tell me please why you 'flipped-flopped' on your affirmative action position?"

Moorman leaned back into his chair, looked straight into the eyes of Tim Quinn, and stated, "Well, time and circumstances change. I changed my perceptive on affirmative action when I was a witness to someone being allowed to be in pain just because she was black. That incident happened the year before the government 'set-asides' for minority contractors case on affirmative action came to our Court."

And then the person nominated to become the next Chief Justice of the United States started to talk about an incident in a hospital very near Washington where racial hatred changed his mind on whether America was ready to stop helping minorities by affirmative action.

Moorman never mentioned names, but the story involved Moorman's ex-wife, who was dying of cancer, and was denied pain medication in a local hospital. After being alerted to the situation by a friend, Moorman personally witnessed that racial prejudice not medical procedures caused his ex-wife to suffer for over eight hours without the doctor-prescribed dose of morphine. Moorman, a former medic and knowledgeable about medical procedures, went over the white head nurse's head and called the medical director of the hospital directly to straighten out the situation.

However, it was a sad story and made Quinn feel ashamed that it happened in Washington in the last few years . . . right before the affirmative action case came to the Supreme Court.

No wonder Moorman changed his mind, concluded Judge Quinn. *I guess America hasn't progressed as far on race as we think. Racism exists today even in hospitals for a dying black woman.*

❖ 23 ❖

E-MAIL   (Committee Senator—Eyes Only)
FROM   TIM QUINN, SPECIAL COUNSEL
DATE   TUESDAY, DECEMBER 9, 2008
TO   MEMBERS OF U.S. SENATE JUDICIARY
            COMMITTEE
SUBJECT   CONFIDENTIAL—REPORT TO THE
            JUDICIARY COMMITTEE #1

The second review of the judicial cases (both at the U.S. Court of Appeals and at the Supreme Court) of nominee Justice Moorman has been completed by the Committee staff and approved by me. The summary review of all opinions and with their case citations is attached to the hard copy of this report, which will be hand-delivered to each Senator.

The review basically shows that Justice Moorman's judicial opinions are in the range of what most legal scholars classify as "moderate conservative" and are viewed as being in the mainstream of legal thought. It is anticipated that the majority of legal scholars will find little to attack from a professional basis. Ideology attacks are always possible, but will be viewed as such and should pose no significant obstacle to the nomination.

The one noteworthy exception is the Supreme Court opinion (Wenicke v. United States) that deals with affirmative action. As you all know, Moorman stated under oath in his prior Supreme Court Justice confirmation hearing that he was opposed to affirmative action. Yet in the <u>Wenicke</u> case, Justice Moorman, in writing the majority opinion for the Supreme Court, clearly accepted the principle that a reasonable program of affirmative action in Federal government contract "set-asides" was acceptable. Of political relevance in the upcoming confirmation hearings of Justice Moorman is the obvious question of whether Justice Moorman misled the Senate in his views on affirmative action in his prior hearings.

In my role as Special Counsel, I have interviewed Justice Moorman about this subject and he has convinced me that his vote in the Wenicke case reflected a change of position as a result of an experience with racial injustice in the year preceding the <u>Wenicke</u> decision. Moorman explained to me that he witnessed personally an incident in a hospital where he saw medical attention (administration of pain medication) being deliberately withheld from a close African-American friend of his by the head nurse in a surgery ward of a local hospital. It was Moorman's considered opinion that the withholding of medicine was based not on medical necessity, but on race prejudice. Moorman would not reveal to me the exact circumstances (name of the patient, hospital, or even the location of the area around Washington where the incident occurred). Nevertheless it was apparent to me that this life experience of Moorman was a valid, reasonable, and sufficient reason why he did change his position on an issue such as affirmative action.

I recommend to the committee that any questions in this area of racial prejudice be very circumspect. In my opinion, Justice Moorman did have a sufficient reason to change his judicial position on this issue of affirmative action. I would be happy to discuss this matter with any Senator who so desires.

One final point that bears mention is Moorman's military

record. His complete Department of Navy record is in my possession and there is evidence of a special court-martial conviction of Moorman for disobedience of an order. I have interviewed Justice Moorman on the circumstances of that conviction and am satisfied that the minor conviction with a "de minimis" and unusual sentence of one-hour confinement was a result of a blatant racial incident. I recommend that this matter be "off-limits" for questioning in any public session of the confirmation hearing. Moorman has not released his military records to the public and any inquiry by this Committee on this matter, if any, should be in closed session. If any Senator so desires, I will orally brief him or her on the specifics of the racial incident. I am reluctant to put such specifics in writing in case this report is compromised by an unauthorized or inadvertent disclosure.

As a final point, I and Ms. Victoria Hauser, my Deputy Special Counsel, are available to meet with any Senator to discuss the conduct of the investigation to date of the confirmation of Justice Moorman to be the Chief Justice.

Timothy R. Quinn
Special Counsel
U.S. Senate Judiciary Committee

After he e-mailed the Report to the Committee Senators, Quinn seemed pleased that the investigation for the confirmation hearing of Moorman was on track. Working off the large conference table in his office, he and Vicky Hauser put together the individual packages for each Senator containing a hard copy of his "Report to the Judiciary Committee #1" and the bulky attachment of the opinion summary book containing research material plus all the legal opinions that Justice Moorman participated in while a judge on the U.S. Court of Appeals and while on the Supreme Court.

The Report would be shortly hand-delivered in sealed boxes to each individual senator. No aide could sign the receipt for the "Committee Senator—Eyes Only" package. Only a senator could accept the package. Everything that needed to be done for a quick confirmation appeared manageable to Quinn.

Tim Quinn was in for a surprise.

The gloves were coming off in the media world and Moorman's name was headed for a beating.

24

SENATOR IRMA POWERS WAS STEAMING AS SHE READ the hard copy of Quinn's report.

Damn. This is exactly what I was afraid of—Judge Quinn running loose. He should never have gone over to interview Moorman without my approval.

Powers' hand reached for the phone on her desk. But then she hesitated. She didn't know Quinn well. But she knew enough about him to know that he might quit if she exerted any restraints on his investigation. She remembered that Quinn wasn't someone who needed this job. He would quit in a Washington heartbeat if she made him get preapproval to interview the subject of an investigation he was running.

Her hand slid off the phone.

Her quick mind turned positive.

I'll make a copy of the report and deliver it to Senator Sloane.

I promised I would give him a bootleg copy of all the Special Counsel Reports.

And Powers knew exactly what he would do with that copy. Senator Sloane would get the report to his daughter, Mrs. Deborah Sloane Moorman.

Washington really had no secrets.

25

CNN.com—Breaking News (Internet)—Supreme Court Justice Moorman reported to have watched X-rated movies in hotel room while on official speaking trip.

WASHINGTON, D.C., WEDNESDAY, DECEMBER 10, 2008—Several national tabloids and a local North Carolina TV station have reported this afternoon that Associate Justice Oscar Moorman, the President's nominee for Chief Justice, watched a soft porn film in his hotel room during a recent speaking engagement at Duke University. According to the news report, the film was listed as a Pay per View selection in his hotel room. The TV station allegedly mentioned it had a copy of a hotel bill that purports to be the room charges for Justice Moorman's stay at the Asian Continental Hotel in downtown Durham, North Carolina. The TV station broadcast also stated that it had a copy of an internal hotel record showing that the movie watched by the Supreme Court Justice was classified as an X-rated film involving prostitution and nudity.

There has been a general denial issued by the White House Press Office. The press officer at the Supreme Court and the chambers of Justice Moorman have refused to comment on the allegation.

Senator Powers, the Chair of the Senate Judiciary Committee, when reached at her Capitol Hill office, stated, "This is an outrageous smear of a fine judicial nominee and I am quite certain that these unsubstantiated reports will prove to be entirely without any basis. I suspect this is a politically motivated hoax."

◆ 26 ◆

IT WAS SEVEN-THIRTY IN THE EVENING AND SEVERAL hours after the "hotel movie" story broke on the national news. Tim Quinn had just gotten off the phone with Senator Powers. Vicky Hauser and Bill Sharkey were in Quinn's office listening to Quinn try to reassure Powers that there was no way Moorman would make such an obvious mistake of judgment while he was being considered for the nomination as Chief Justice. When the call ended, Tim's face was grim as he reported to his senior staff,

"Powers is worried about the story. In the Washington media, you are guilty until proven innocent. What should we do?"

Vicky replied, "We better nail down this rumor quickly. I think Bill and I need to get down to the hotel in Durham with a congressional subpoena and secure the hotel records to determine the truth of the matter."

Quinn said, "Why don't I find out the truth right now?"

"How?" Vicky was puzzled.

"I'll call Justice Moorman at his home. If this is a setup, I'd like to hear what Moorman says."

Vicky and Bill Sharkey nodded approval.

Quinn looked in his wallet and retrieved the business card Moorman had given him when Quinn interviewed him at the Supreme

Court. Moorman had scribbled his unlisted home number on the back and told Quinn to call him any time he needed to get in touch with him urgently.

Well, now's that time. This could be a huge blow to the confirmation.

Quinn quickly punched in the numbers and Moorman answered. Quinn had deliberately put the call on the speakerphone. Long ago he was taught that when you are conducting an investigation, you should always try to have a witness when the questioning was critical. And the answer to the question could determine whether the confirmation stalled in a mud-slinging contest about an X-rated film.

"Mr. Justice, I'm sorry to have to call you at your home. Moreover, I have you on speakerphone. Listening with me in my office are my deputy, Ms. Victoria Hauser, and my chief investigator, Special Agent Sharkey of the FBI. We need to ask you about the hotel movie thing."

There was a long pause before Moorman answered. "I see. So this is an official inquiry by the Special Counsel."

"I'm afraid so, Mr. Justice. You realize that you don't have to answer any questions now? I am trying to sort out this movie business that's in the news and you could save us a lot of time and trouble by telling us whether you watched an X-rated movie at that hotel. Did you watch such a movie, Your Honor?"

The voice over the speakerphone came back without any hesitation. It was firm and strong. "I did not watch anything but the local news when I was in my hotel room during the trip to Duke. This story is either a mistake in the hotel bill . . . or someone is trying to smear me. My wife has taken this false story hard, very hard. She's . . . understandably upset. Her friend, Justice Bianco's wife, Lucy, is over here now with her." Moorman's voice got softer and carried some pain at this point when he was talking about the effect this incident was having on his wife.

"Thank you, Mr. Justice. That is all we needed to hear. We'll investigate and find out how this movie rental got on your bill. Good evening."

"Please straighten this out soon, Judge Quinn. I would appreciate it."

When the call ended, Quinn said, "I believe him. We will now assume the report is false. Now how do we prove it . . . fast . . . before the rumor becomes reality?"

Sharkey spoke up, "The answer to proving it is in Durham. We have a problem. I checked the airlines schedule and the last direct plane to Durham from D.C. leaves in thirty minutes. If we miss that, we have a five-or-so-hour drive down there."

Tim Quinn smiled and said, "There is another airline that we can use. That one flies *whenever* we want it."

Bill Sharkey looked skeptical. "I don't understand, Judge."

"Senator Powers is also on the Senate Armed Services Committee and I bet she can get the Air Force to fly us down to Durham this evening on a military executive jet. By law, the military is supposed to provide travel support to the Congress when necessary. And now it's necessary for us to get to North Carolina to put out this fire before it gets out of control."

Quinn called Senator Powers and in less than ten minutes an Air Force colonel from the Eighty-ninth Airlift Wing stationed at Andrews Air Force Base just outside of Washington called Tim to say that a C-21 Lear jet would be made immediately available for the flight to Durham from Andrews AFB—the home of Air Force One.

◆ 27 ◆

QUINN, VICKY, AND SHARKEY WERE BUSY DISCUSSING
how they would proceed on the short hop from Andrews Air Force
Base to the Raleigh-Durham airport. The sleek six-passenger jet had
two satellite phones onboard and Quinn and his team used them to
get logistics set up for their visit to Durham. Bill Sharkey called the
Resident Agent of the FBI field office in Durham. The RA agreed to
assign two agents to help in the investigation. From the plane, Quinn
had set up two meetings.

Quinn would meet personally with Professor Robinson Everett,
the Duke Law professor who was the chairman of the legal conference that Justice Moorman had attended. Professor Everett was a retired federal judge and the chair of the conference Moorman
attended at Duke Law where the alleged movie incident occurred.
Quinn hoped that Judge Everett would be a big help in finding out
the times that Moorman was busy with conference duties and had
witnesses to his activities. Quinn didn't know how precise the hotel
records were with regard to showing the times the alleged movie was
played in Moorman's room. Maybe Quinn could show that Moorman was somewhere else when the X-rated movie was played. An alibi defense was what Quinn hoped to find by getting the schedule
information from Professor Everett.

The key meeting was really in Vicky's and Bill Sharkey's hands.
They would meet with the general manager of the Asian Continental
Hotel, where Moorman stayed during the conference.

It was imperative to discover the authenticity of the movie charge.

Was it a mistake?

Were the records of Moorman's room charges tampered with?

Once the Air Force Lear jet rolled to a stop on the tarmac outside the Durham civilian terminal, there were two Bureau cars that appeared next to the plane. Quinn introduced himself to one of the FBI agents and left in one of the Ford Crown Vics to meet Professor Everett at his home. Vicky and Sharkey went in the other car with the second FBI agent. It was now just after 9:30 P.M.

It was close to ten o'clock by the time the Bureau car stopped in front of the professor's home. Quinn had never met the former judge, but he sounded very cooperative over the phone. Quinn told the FBI agent to wait in the car. There was no need for him now. It was best to keep the initial meeting with Everett low-key.

Quinn knocked on the front door and a smiling bear of a man with sparkling, intelligent eyes opened it with a welcoming grin. Quinn started with an apology.

"Your Honor, thank you for seeing me so late. The matter with Justice Moorman is very urgent."

Professor Everett was pure Southern gracious. "Not at all, Judge Quinn. Please come in. I have some sweet tea set out for us. I have heard the rumors of the outrageous slur against Justice Moorman. Terrible . . . I can't believe it."

"I am sure it is a mistake or a false charge, but I need your help in proving it," Quinn said in a low voice.

"Well, I'll do all I can. I've already started. After your call, I drove over to the Law School and got the tapes of the conference as you requested," said the professor.

"That's a good start." Tim smiled.

✦ 28 ✦

VICKY HAUSER USED HER PROSECUTOR'S RADAR AND quickly sized up Mr. Amoko, the general manager of the Asian Continental Hotel, as she and Sharkey sat down in chrome and leather chairs in front of the long glass table the manager used as his desk in his sleek, ultra-modern office. Its glass wall overlooked the spacious atrium of the luxury hotel.

He's scared to death that his hotel will get very bad publicity about its adult movie selection here in the "Bible Belt," observed Vicky.

The manager explained that he had recently arrived in the States from Japan to run this hotel in America for a year—part of his hotel chain's training program to give all its Asian managers overseas experience in Europe or America. Vicky could see that he was falling over himself to cooperate and make this incident go away. Clearly, the manager was seeing this unwanted publicity firestorm as a career ender for him.

With that pressure, Vicky didn't even have to show him the Congressional subpoena that she had in her handbag. It would make lawful the seizure of any evidence she thought relevant to the room charges on Justice Moorman's bill.

Sharkey took over the quizzing of the Japanese manager initially and asked about security video tapes for the inside of the hotel.

The answer came back quickly.

And it was what Vicky and Sharkey wanted to hear.

"We have the very latest in video surveillance equipment for the hotel. All entrances, lobbies, and elevators are covered 24/7. By the way, we archive all video for three months, so the video for the Duke Law conference is still here. I had the CDs brought up so you could see them if you liked. I can play any of the CDs on my TV here."

Satisfied about the video coverage, Vicky wanted to see the Moorman room charges.

The manager was sharp. He already had copies of the bill and the underlying computer description of the charges. As he handed the copies to Vicky and Sharkey, he nervously explained, "As you can see, the bill the customer received in this case just lists 'pay TV' as a room charge. There is no identification of what pay TV event was seen on the customer's bill. However, the second page I've given you is the computer printout, which shows that it was a movie that was charged to the Moorman room. It also tells what movie was seen and when it was shown."

"Did you say these documents will show the times the movie was played?" Vicky was excited. She saw the possibility of the alibi defense that she and Tim Quinn talked about.

With the times, we might be able to show that Moorman was somewhere else.

"Of course, look at the bottom of the second page. Those are the start and end times of the movie, *Room Service Sex and the Businessman.*" When he said the name of the movie, the Japanese manager blushed. He seemed ashamed that his fine hotel would have such porn on its menu.

"Our home office in Tokyo is reviewing all the movie selections for its hotels in America," the manager added.

Vicky was focused in on the exact times the movie played in Moorman's room. She could see an abnormality already—the time the movie was played was not at night. It was almost in the middle of the day. A time where Moorman might be attending one of the conference events with plenty of witnesses.

"I have to call someone. Bill, why don't you start looking through the elevator video that Mr. Amoko has gotten for us. Concentrate on when Moorman left and returned to his floor and the times around the start of the movie."

Sharkey nodded and went over to the TV and its DVD recorder with the first CD that manager gave him.

After studying the computer printout showing the times the movie played in Justice Moorman's room, Vicky stepped into the hall outside Mr. Amoko's office and called Tim Quinn.

"Tim, it's Vicky. I have the start and finish time of the movie in Moorman's room. The movie ran from 1:12 P.M. until 2:43 P.M."

QUINN MET WITH VICKY AND SHARKEY AT 2 A.M. IN Quinn's room. They all had rooms at the Asian Continental Hotel. The mini bar had yielded a nice glass of California white wine for Vicky and two Coronas for Tim and Bill Sharkey.

Tim was relaxed. They had won a battle in the last few hours that Tim had seriously doubted they would be able to win.

We have the evidence to sink the Moorman dirty movie rumor.

It was a combination of luck and initiative. Making the decision to get down to North Carolina and face the problem head-on was typical Quinn. His favorite animal was the buffalo—one of the few animals that faces into a storm. And he did just that in Durham . . . and came out a winner.

"Congratulations, Your Honor," said Bill Sharkey, toasting Quinn with his longneck beer. "That time-coded conference video you got from Duke Law School showing Professor Everett and Justice

Moorman on the stage of the conference from 1 P.M. until 3 P.M. was the smoking gun that proved Moorman couldn't have watched that movie in his room."

"Well, the elevator video you found was helpful as well. Pity it only showed inside the elevator and not down the hallways on the floor. Nevertheless, it showed that Moorman left his floor at 8:15 A.M. and didn't return until after 5 P.M.," Quinn replied.

Vicky added a question. "Well, we showed Moorman didn't watch the movie, but really we don't know if someone else entered his room to start the movie . . . or whether the hotel computer was manipulated to show the movie on Moorman's bill. What really did happen here? Mistake or smear?"

Sharkey spoke up, "It might be unusually coincidental that the movie had something to do with strippers and prostitutes. Remember Moorman's womanizing from the first confirmation hearing had some allegations of strippers . . . and that Moorman had dated a woman with a couple of convictions for prostitution. Damn coincidental."

Quinn got serious. "Well, computer mistake, prank, smear, political dirty trick . . . we may never know . . . and it doesn't matter. All we needed to prove was that Moorman *didn't watch* the movie. And we did that! Senator Powers was especially happy with the news. She wasn't even mad I woke her up. And the White House Counsel was extremely happy that we have the evidence to back up a full denial of the story."

The old-school agent didn't give up on his view. "There's something strange about this whole incident. I think Moorman is a target . . . and that this is not the last shot, but the first at him."

❖ 30 ❖

E-MAIL   (Committee Senator—Eyes Only)
FROM   TIM QUINN, SPECIAL COUNSEL
DATE   FRIDAY, DECEMBER 12, 2008
TO   MEMBERS OF U.S. SENATE JUDICIARY
          COMMITTEE
SUBJECT   CONFIDENTIAL—REPORT TO THE SENATE
          JUDICIARY COMMITTEE #2

I have conducted an investigation of the recent rumors in the press that Justice Moorman watched an X-rated movie in a hotel room while he was attending a legal conference at Duke Law School.

My investigation conclusively proves that such rumors are false and without any merit. Hotel records of the Asian Continental Hotel in Durham were either altered or showed a mistake in the room charges. The Duke Conference time-coded videos, authenticated by the conference Executive Director, show Justice Moorman sitting on an academic panel at the times when the movie was allegedly played on Moorman's TV.

Affidavits from Professor Robinson Everett, from the General Manager of the hotel, and from the Executive Director of the Conference are attached to this Report to the Judiciary Committee and explain the facts surrounding the mistaken

room charge of a movie on Justice Moorman's hotel bill.
Video footage from the hotel security system and from the
official video recordings from the conference conclusively
show that Justice Moorman was not in his room at the time
the movie in question was alleged to be shown in his hotel
room. Copies of hotel security video and Conference video
will be attached to the hard copy of this Report and will be
delivered to all Committee Senators as attachments to this
report.

   As a final point, I and Ms. Victoria Hauser, my Deputy
Special Counsel, are available to meet with any senator to discuss the conduct of this special investigation into the false rumors of inappropriate conduct by Justice Moorman with
respect to this incident.

> *Timothy R. Quinn*
> *Special Counsel*
> *U.S. Senate Judiciary Committee*

Tim Quinn thought the firestorm was over and that the Justice
Moorman confirmation hearing set for the very next week could
proceed without any further controversy.

   He was wrong.

◆ 31 ◆

EnglishInjustice.blogspot.com—Friday, December 12, 2008
(The Blog of England, which keeps a watchful eye on the justice system and on judges in the U.K.)

Posting by "Devil Barrister"—Well, I just learned some absolutely delicious gossip while having lunch in the Middle Temple today. The table talk with one of my fellow barristers focused on the state of judicial affairs in America. Well, it appears that the "Honourable" (and I use that term with some doubt now) Justice Oscar Moorman, the black judge who may be the next Chief Justice of the United States, might have a skeleton in his closet, a female one, I might add.

My "wagging tongue" meal mate told me that, a few years ago, the American judge Moorman went bonkers during a summer legal conference in London. At an evening reception, he got very drunk and took one of our pretty female barristers home to her flat for a romp between the sheets. My lunch mate didn't know who the lady was, but he did reveal that Moorman definitely forced himself on her.

What do they call it in America? I think it is called date rape there. Here we call it just plain rape. "No" means "bloody no!" in England.

I hope the young lady comes forth and tells her story before this man is confirmed as Chief Justice. In my view, judges, whether English or American, should not be above the law. Bloody colonials should be more selective of their judges, especially their Chief Justice.

I can't wait to hear the details. To my fellow lady barrister, please come out, dear one, and give us and America the truth before the Black Yank is made Chief Justice.

(Posted by "Devil Barrister" at 2205 hrs., December 12, 2008)
————Webmaster's note—*2 comments (omitted due to the obscene nature of the language)—zero back links*

32

CNN.com—*Breaking News (Internet)—Justice Moorman is attacked by a new sex rumor coming from an English blog site.*

WASHINGTON, D.C., SATURDAY, DECEMBER 13, 2008–After the quick dispelling of the hoax regarding Justice Oscar Moorman allegedly watching an X-rated movie, there is a disturbing report coming from an Internet site in England that accuses Justice Moorman of nonconsensual sex with an unnamed English barrister. The blog site posted this anonymous report of apparent sexual misconduct by Moorman. The sexual encounter apparently occurred at an unspecified social event several years ago. The rumor surfaced yesterday on the blog site in England and quickly spread throughout Internet Web sites in Europe and America.

Due to the vague and factually deficient nature of the allegations on the blog report (there was no name or description of the alleged victim, no date or description of the supposed assault, and no supporting details), newspapers in England apparently treated the report as an unfounded rumor and so far have not published any accounts of the alleged misconduct.

Sir Richard Foster, a prominent London barrister who specializes in libel cases stated, "No proper newspaper would publish this sheer accusation. Libel laws in England are quite strict and any paper that reported this unsupported accusation would be treading very close to the libel threshold indeed and may find itself possibly facing a punishing law suit for damages. I have previously stated that I am not impressed with the low criteria for Internet blog publishing of anonymous accusations. From my perspective this blog posting may very well be racially motivated."

In an interview in Atlanta today, Mr. Jesse Turner, a spokesperson for the NAACP, declared, "Justice Moorman is being targeted by lies and racial hate once again. There are those out there who will stop at nothing to prevent an African-American from assuming the position as Chief Justice of the United States. There has already been one proven hoax of a false accusation against this fine jurist. This new, unsubstantiated report out of England with no specifics is probably just another hoax, a cruel one at that."

The White House Press Office issued a firm general denial of the story when asked about it during today's press briefing following the President's regular Saturday radio broadcast.

· 33 ·

THIS COULD BE THE START OF THE DEATH SPIRAL OF *Moorman's nomination*, thought the smiling Justice Vincent Bianco as he watched the CNN.com story appear on his computer. He had been checking the major news sources periodically for several days to see which one would pick up the English blog story first.

He knew that "watching an X-rated movie" smear would probably not kill the nomination of Moorman even if it had not been disproved. America's morals had fallen so low that watching filth was not a disqualifier for high office. However, Bianco hoped that the X-rated movie story would be such a glancing hit on the sexual reputation of Moorman that it would set the stage for the killing blow of the "date rape" allegation. Now that the date rape rumor was out, it was his fervent hope that the English woman would appear and give testimony to what Moorman did to her.

Bianco also hoped that Moorman would not trace the story back to him. He had reflected on it and now wondered whether he should have asked those follow-up questions the next morning after Moorman had revealed the incident involving date rape.

No good to second guess now. I like that the rumor looks like it started in England with the blog. Oscar will probably think the extensive coverage of his nomination in the foreign press triggered the surfacing of his rape, either from the girl or perhaps from one of her friends who knew about it.

Bianco wondered why the blog story mentioned that the rape victim was a woman barrister. Moorman's "drink-filled" confession to him had been unclear as to whether it had been a barrister or a student. He had hoped that the rape victim would turn out to be a young student. He had leaked the possibility to Senator Dalton of the victim possibly being a student *or* a young barrister. Perhaps Senator Dalton had found out more information that pinpointed the victim as a barrister.

It made no difference really—rape was rape.

◆ 34 ◆

THE DATE RAPE STORY HAD HIT THE MOORMAN HOME hard that Saturday.

It was late morning at the Moorman four-bedroom colonial in McLean, Virginia. The home was on a wooded cul-de-sac just off Georgetown Pike near I-495, the Interstate beltway that encircles Washington. It was a modest home compared with the new megahomes that were going up in the surrounding subdivisions. In fact, Moorman's home was dwarfed by huge "McMansions" on both sides. Ten thousand square feet was the apparent midsized home for the twin-income professionals now standard in the more affluent sections of the Washington suburbs.

Debby and Oscar were in the great room off the kitchen reading—she, the *Washington Post* and he, one of the Court files for the next week's oral arguments.

Debby answered the phone. Moorman knew from the greeting he heard that it was Lucy Bianco, one of Debby's closest friends. It was apparent from the conversation that his worst fear about the confirmation process was somehow being relayed to his wife. The words "rape" and "English barrister" repeated by his wife stunned him so much that he had a hard time breathing while the conversation continued. Mercifully the phone conversation didn't last long. When she hung up, Debby looked at him with moist, ready to cry eyes, but didn't speak.

"What's wrong, Baby?"

When she didn't answer, Moorman knew his marriage was on the line.

Then he saw Debby take one of the pill cases from her purse. From the yellow color of the two pills she had in her hand, Moorman knew she was taking Valium. He saw her wash the tranquilizer down with coffee from her mug. She didn't say anything for a few moments, then it came out in a rush—she erupted and confronted Moorman with pieces of the accusation she learned from her friend on the phone, specifics from the English blog and the reports on Internet news sites about the allegations of Moorman and date rape.

Moorman listened, appearing calmer than he was.

"Wait, wait—Honey, let's see what the hell they are saying on CNN."

Moorman sat next to her on the sofa and turned on his laptop computer. He and his wife read the CNN.com story together.

Moorman knew as he read the story that he was faced with an immediate dilemma. The tough choice of confessing a sexual encounter with another woman to his wife . . . or lying about it.

I never should have tried for Chief Justice. Damn, my life is blowing up.

Debby started crying after reading the news story. He tried to comfort her by holding her, but she pulled away. She went into the kitchen and came back with a bloody mary.

"Good idea. I'll join you." Moorman didn't want a drink, but he didn't want her to drink alone. Her drinking had been markedly earlier each day since he was nominated. It was becoming a problem. The stresses of his confirmation seemed to be slipping sideways to land squarely on her.

Moorman started to mix himself a bloody mary in the kitchen. He could see Debby, sitting on the sofa in the great room, taking deep pulls on her drink.

God, I hate it when she does that—taking Valium with a drink to get numb quicker. She has a problem.

"Honey, you really should watch mixing alcohol with your medicines," Moorman suggested gently as he finished making his drink.

Debby was ignoring him and focusing on her drink.

Moorman came back into the room and sat beside her.

When she didn't say anything, he started to tell her that this was another hoax, but she waved him off. She had stopped crying and turned to stare at him coldly, the mascara leaving small black streaks under her eyes. Looking at her face showing a combination of anguish and anger, it was then he decided he had to tell her the truth—the full truth.

She was headed for a meltdown with stress.

He loved her. She had beauty, brains, and breeding. But her character was her flaw. She was weak and would crack under pressure . . . that's why she depended on pills and booze.

If this story about the Englishwoman was coming out, he wanted to get in front of it—at least to his wife. He needed to prepare her for what might be in the newspapers or what she might see on TV if she was alone.

Shaking his head, Moorman spoke in a soft voice, "Baby, this is what happened. God, I'm ashamed of myself. . . . It was in the summer several years before we met. I think it was during my second year on the Court. I was at a reception at Gray's Inn in London during a couple-days-long joint English-American legal program . . . there was an English barrister, a prosecutor at the Old Bailey. We were friends—we had been on the same panel discussion at the beginning of the first day and we sort of hung out together during the first three days. We went to dinner with a small group that first evening. I sat next to her. . . . I liked her. She was pretty and had a clever, dry wit. . . . Well, there was a reception after the third day of the conference. I was drinking too much that night. She was very friendly and, right before the reception ended, she asked me if I wanted to have a nightcap—at her home. I accepted. We were discreet and left separately. We took separate cabs to her home. I was pretty smashed. . . . When we got to her flat, we drank cognac . . . I remember kissing her . . . and I also remember being dizzy and throwing up in her toilet, but not much else . . . until the next morning when I woke up wearing only my boxers and a huge headache. She was quite different that morning after."

Moorman stopped. Debby was paying attention, absorbing the confession with silence and vacant eyes. Moorman thought it was the effect of the tranquilizer and the alcohol until she spoke. Her voice carried with it the stone-cold anger of a jealous woman.

"Did you have sex with her?"

"I don't know . . . maybe. I don't remember anything specific. I was very drunk. Most of the evening was a blur."

"Come on, O. *Did* you have sex with her?"

"God, Debby! I already said I don't know. . . . I think so. God, I may have because I woke in her bed. As to whether the sex was consensual, God . . . I may have forced it because she was distant and angry in the morning . . . she was already dressed and asked me to leave as soon as I woke up. It was unreal. I had a splitting headache and she couldn't wait for me to leave. She said nothing. I tried to apologize for whatever I did, but she just repeated for me to leave. So I got my clothes on and left."

Moorman waited a bit then continued his story under the cold stare of Debby.

"I am sure I must have done something wrong. This lady was very much together. A prosecutor in England's top criminal trial court . . . very squared-away lawyer. . . . I will say before I met you, I had been . . . reckless. When I was young, a couple of times, if I had been drinking a lot and my date said a weak 'no' . . . well, I didn't stop right away. I'd push for the finish line. . . . I might have done something stupid like that with the lady barrister . . . didn't stop after the 'no' . . . she was on the small side and I was much bigger and stronger. . . . It was the coldness and eagerness to get rid of me the next morning that makes me think that I might have forced her to have sex. . . . Also when the conference resumed later that morning, she was there, but didn't even speak to me. It was as if I ceased to exist for her. She obviously wanted to forget the entire prior evening. . . . Now this report comes out of England. I don't think this is coming from her now, but maybe a long time ago she told someone about me . . . and that evening." Moorman ended his story.

Debby was more focused now. She had the factual basis for the news report. She seemed to be calculating the future.

"So now this English lawyer will go to the newspapers and your confirmation is finished," pronounced Debby with a dead voice and an air of practical resignation.

"Not necessarily, Baby. Like I said, I don't think this report is coming from her . . . or that she will confirm my one-night stand with her," corrected Moorman.

"Why not?"

"Well . . . when the X-rated movie hoax came up and my name got splattered across the national and international media, I got worried that the focus on my sexual life might trigger a rumor of this incident surfacing in England so I did some Google research on the status of the lady lawyer in England. I never knew what happened to the woman after that conference, never saw or heard from her. Well, I researched the barristers. It wasn't hard. She's done well in the law. Lots of Google hits on her name. . . . Bottom line, because I know the situation now, I don't think she may want this encounter to come out in public anymore than I do. Especially now."

Debby was incredulous. Her brown eyes opened wide with surprise at the statement.

"Why on earth wouldn't she want this to come out? She would be an instant celebrity . . . TV shows, articles in magazines . . . maybe she would be paid for her story!"

"Well, I'm pretty sure she wouldn't want any of that. In fact, I think any publicity at all would be extremely bad for her career. You see, according to the news reports I found on the Internet, shortly after my . . . evening with her, she was appointed an English judge. She's now the number-two ranking judge at the Old Bailey, England's top trial court . . . and, according to one of the newspaper articles I read, the woman is a cinch to be promoted to be a justice on the Royal Court of Appeal in London the next vacancy that occurs. That would be almost like being appointed to our U.S. Supreme Court. She would receive a title—she would become a 'lady'—the female equivalent of a lord in England. So being involved with this date rape allegation . . . specifically her *not reporting* the rape is the type of news that may kill her judicial career. Someone who doesn't report a crime is definitely not the type of judge you want on your top appeals court. Moreover, she would have to recuse herself from any case involving rape or violence against a woman. No, I don't think she will come out to the press with this."

Debby was speechless and seemed lost in thoughts—angry ones.

The silence was broken by the chirping of Moorman's cell phone—an unlisted number. The phone call interrupted a very tense moment with his wife. Moorman, grateful for the timely distraction, flipped it open.

It was Tim Quinn, calling to inform him about the increasing attention of the media with regard to the blog.

"Mr. Justice, just wanted to alert you to the story and to see if you thought we should meet to discuss it. We were able to put out the Duke firestorm only because we faced the story right away."

"Tim, I'm glad you called. Yes, I agree we may very well have another 'news frenzy' on our hands . . ."

I may need Quinn's help on this. I can't stop the press. They will eventually get somewhere on this story, reasoned Moorman.

In a low-pitched voice, a voice of resignation to the inevitable task of facing the rising storm, Moorman agreed to meet Quinn. "Yes. We should talk . . . and it might be a good idea if we met tonight. Somewhere quiet?"

✦ 35 ✦

at the University Club that evening as it would be almost deserted, according to Quinn.

Good choice for the meet, thought Moorman.

Moorman didn't want to be seen in a high-visibility public place and risk being photographed with Tim—Special Counsel to the Senate Judiciary Committee—during this time of heightened press coverage. He also instinctively knew that it wasn't wise for Tim to come to Moorman's home in case an alert member of the press had camped on the street watching for some interesting photo opportunity of the Justice being visited by the Senate Special counsel at his home on a weekend following this new rumor—not a good thing for Moorman.

A private club on a slow evening seemed to be a good idea, and Moorman needed to see Tim, as he could be the key to solving the problem with this new allegation.

After setting up the meeting, Moorman tried to calm Debby. The tranquilizer and alcohol made her tired and she wound up taking a nap most of the afternoon. Moorman played out many damage-control scenarios in his mind and thought about the legal aspects of the date rape situation he was facing. He finally came up with a plan of action by the time Debby woke up.

They had an early dinner. He was worried as Debby drank three glasses of wine to his one during the quiet meal. She was gulping not sipping.

"Honey, we should slow down on the wine," he suggested quietly.

"I can't help it, O. I'm so worried. The wine calms me down. . . . What if that Englishwoman doesn't care about the publicity and goes public? Your nomination—we'll be ruined. God, I can't bear waiting for the next shoe to drop."

"Don't worry. I think I have a plan to quickly check out where we stand . . . and possibily end this date rape thing."

"What is it?"

"I need to see Judge Tim Quinn, Special Counsel, tonight and talk about it. I need to get his advice. I'll tell you what we come up with to-morrow. You really should get to sleep early tonight."

After dinner, Debby decided to go to bed. When Moorman had made sure she was all right, he kissed his sleeping wife and left to meet Quinn at the University Club in downtown Washington.

Oscar Moorman drove his red Corvette down the George Washington Memorial Parkway in Virginia, a four-lane divided highway, that paralleled the Potomac River and led to the downtown bridges of Washington.

He, as usual, kept the powerful turbocharged sports car well within the fifty-mile-per-hour limit. The parkway was a well-known speed trap and Moorman wasn't looking for anymore trouble on his plate.

As he drove alone, Moorman reviewed his precarious legal situation. He was about to meet with the head investigator of the Senate Judiciary Committee, a man who was supposed to help him win confirmation but could possibly help English authorities convict him of a sex crime. That worst-case scenario would happen only if Moorman made any incriminating statements to Quinn about his suspicions of forcing the barrister to have sex.

Well, now Moorman had decided to face the ghost he had lived with for years. Sometimes the best way out of a problem was straight through it. With Quinn's help, he could . . . no, he was being forced to discover the truth. Was he a rapist? If Quinn helped him, he would finally know the truth he had wondered about for years.

He was afraid.

They say the truth will set you free. Well, Moorman wondered if the truth would possibly do the reverse—possibly put him in an English jail. He would have to watch his words in asking for Quinn's help. His statements to Quinn might come back to haunt him as incriminating admissions in an English courtroom. In a worst-case scenario, if the English judge went public with a story that Moorman had raped her, Moorman might be extradited to England to stand trial. A U.S. Supreme Court Justice in the dock of an English courtroom. Few people in American history could match such a fall from grace.

MOORMAN DROVE BY LAFAYETTE SQUARE PARK AND slowly made the turn onto Sixteenth Street. He was now three short blocks from the University Club. On an impulse, he pulled the Corvette to the curb and stopped in front of St. John's Church at the corner of Sixteenth and H Street. He got out of the car and walked to the edge of the park. He was not far from where this confirmation nightmare had started. There he stood watching the brightly lit White House across the deserted park.

The view of the White House was different than the one he remembered from the secret meeting with President Ramsey. At that meeting, he was looking down at the White House from the top floor of the Veterans Administration building. The White House he saw that day was a warm, sunny place, full of the hope for the chance to lead the Nation's judiciary.

The White House he stared at now was cold and ominous—a

view from the ground on a cold night with low intermittent rumbles of thunder from afar promising rain or maybe snow. As he stood at the edge of the park, the doubts of running for the Center Seat returned. Was the reward worth the risk?

I initially did it for Debby. Ironic now I may lose my happiness and peace with her because of it. The stress on Debby was changing her. It wasn't her fault. She was his love, but he knew she wasn't strong.

He thought about his new wife. She was for him something unexpected—love at first sight. For many years he enjoyed playing the eligible bachelor. The higher he progressed in government, the more attention he got from women—many women wanted to be near the power he gained on the Federal bench. It wasn't until he met Debby at that interview at the Supreme Court that he knew this was the only woman he wanted to wake up next to for the rest of his life. He believed in the old saying explaining love—love is not reason but emotion. He loved her because she was she and he was he.

Their love, however, was being threatened by the present stress. He had never seen this side of her—the lows of depression, the mood swings, and now the crutches of the stress . . . the pills and the drinking. One of the reasons Moorman wanted Judge Quinn to push forward and get the date rape resolved was to bring peace to Debby.

But there was also the other reason to go forward and win the Center Seat.

I want it for me. I want the Center Seat. It's time for an African-American to be at the top of the judiciary. If I can just get through this English threat, I can do this. I can win the Center Seat.

He remained there fixed in his thoughts for a few minutes looking at the brilliantly lit home of the President from across the dark empty park with its newly installed chain-link security fence around it. At night, the park was closed to visitors. The security protection for the White House pushed out several blocks at night. He looked back toward his parked car and saw that there was movement under the front overhang of St. John's Church. He realized there was no danger—just a few homeless people that crouched in the shadows of the church's columns for the night. On cold winter nights, it wasn't uncommon to see the homeless huddling on the heating grates, which were thankfully located under the roof overhang. The church pastor refused to let the police chase away these people. "We give sanctuary to all who come," he was quoted as saying when interviewed about the incongruity of the President and the homeless being neighbors separated only by the small park.

Suddenly Moorman's attention to the church was averted by a sound to his right. There was a noisy crowd of four young males coming down H Street toward him. Their loud, probably alcohol-fueled voices would have frightened a typical lone pedestrian standing in their unsteady path. Moorman, however, was not overly concerned. He knew that unseen eyes and cameras were watching the males . . . and him. The White House has multiple rings of security around it. He was in the night zone of protection. If there was any threat from the approaching quartet of youths, several uniformed Secret Service police would immediately be on the scene. Nevertheless, he moved back toward his car.

As he got into his red Corvette, he knew that he would not be safe for long. Moorman was about to do a very dangerous thing, seeking the truth about an event long ago. But it was a risk he had to take now.

Although he had reluctantly entered the nomination for the "Center Seat," he was committed and was going to see it through. There were apparently forces at work to prevent him from becoming the first black Chief Justice. Race was probably at the heart of the game here. . . . And Moorman wasn't going to let the racists win.

◆ 37 ◆

"GOOD EVENING, JUSTICE MOORMAN. YOU HAVE JUDGE Quinn waiting for you inside. He's in the Franklin Room."

"Thanks, Jack," said Moorman with a friendly wink and gave the valet a five-dollar bill folded in a small square, passing the bill surreptitiously during a handshake. He always did this for the man who parked his car. Tipping wasn't allowed by club rules, but Moorman didn't always play by the rules.

Moorman left his overcoat in the car and buttoned his shirt collar as he stood under the glass canopy of the club's entrance. Then he straightened his tie before he pushed open the heavy glass-and-wrought-iron door of the exclusive club.

Moorman knew Quinn was an active member here. He had also heard that Quinn frequently took his meals here, especially now that he was alone, a widower.

He walked down the lobby with its dark oak-paneled walls and its floor-to-ceiling oak columns. The plush burgundy-patterned carpet was illuminated by soft recessed lighting.

He thought of Quinn's beautiful late wife, Katy. He had seen Quinn with his striking wife often at dinners in this old building. He thought there must be a lot of memories for Quinn to absorb here. Maybe that's why Quinn liked to come to the club with its memory echoes from his life with Katy. Some people avoided familiar places with memories of a loved one. A positive man like Quinn was strong enough to get past the dark sorrow of such places and push into the sunlight of good memories.

I surely need a positive man in my corner for this fight now. And I think my man is Quinn, thought Moorman.

As he walked through the plush but empty lobby, Moorman nodded to himself about the meeting place. Quinn had picked it correctly; the club was almost deserted on Saturday night. Moorman smiled and said hi to the porter on duty at the reception desk then turned right at the end of the long lobby. That's when he saw Quinn through the glass doors in the room at the end of the hall. Quinn was sitting alone in the Franklin Room—a small cozy room just off the lobby, connected to the club library by a set of glass doors, recently modified to make them airtight to prevent smoke from entering the library. The Franklin Room was the last of the shrinking spaces in the club where a member could enjoy a cigar. It was an attractive and warm "clubby" room with rich dark green bamboo and red-flowered wallpaper. The walls were lined with several antique bookcases and had leaded-glass windows. There were several leather sofas and chunky club chairs in conversational clusters where small groups could relax with their drinks and cigars. Tonight the room was empty—save for Quinn and Moorman.

Quinn was sitting in a leather wing chair by the flaming gas fireplace puffing on a cigar stub. Quinn seemed lost in thought and obviously didn't see Moorman as he entered the room.

Moorman announced himself. "Tim, you picked a good spot—by the fire and in the club's last outpost for us cigar smokers. I appreciated your call this morning and your concern for my situation. Thank you."

"No problem, Your Honor. I was coming to the club for a late workout anyway. I thought it would be a good place for us to meet. I checked with the desk and no events were scheduled for this evening."

Moorman closed the door to the lobby before he crossed the room to Quinn. On the other wall—that facing the next-door library—the glass doors were in their usual closed position. The room was now sealed from eavesdroppers.

"Good, good, our meeting gave me an excuse to take a nice drive with my new Corvette. Debby talked me into getting one—always wanted a 'vet . . . Seriously, I've got some things on my mind. Senator Powers said you were going to be my 'guardian angel.' Well, I could use some advice from up there now." Moorman motioned upward with a thumb and a subdued smile.

Moorman and Tim Quinn shook hands before the two men settled into wing chairs in front of the inviting fire.

Moorman noticed Tim was nearly done with his cigar.

"Tim, I knew you were a cigar man so I brought us both a couple of cigars."

He reached into his inner coat pocket and pulled out two cigars.

Tim took one, examining it closely.

"Damn, a Cuban cigar. Mr. Justice, you are a man of surprises!"

"Tim, please call me 'O.' And actually, to be precise, the cigar's a Habana Monte Christo No. 4. There are some smart people who rank it as the finest cigar in the world. And I agree with them. I hope you like it. By the way, for the record, it's a crime to import them, not smoke them."

"I'm aware of the distinction," retorted Quinn with a grin. "But still, to have a *Supreme* Court Justice be caught smoking a Cuban cigar would make front-page news," commented Quinn as he took the already cut cigar and the proffered light from Moorman. He started taking short puffs to get the Monte Christo fired up. Quinn appeared relaxed to Moorman.

He won't like the bomb I'm about to drop on him, thought Moorman as he lit up his cigar and watched Quinn.

The two men seated in opposing leather wing chairs before the fire were quiet briefly as they got their cigars going. Soon they were enveloped in a small cloud of smoke.

Then Moorman's eyes hardened and his mood turned serious. He concentrated on the purpose of the meeting. The social foreplay was over. He remarked softly as he rolled his cigar between his fingers, "You know, I'd rather get media coverage for smoking a Monte

Christo than what, unfortunately, may be front page on many papers tomorrow. This growing date rape allegation is far more serious than smoking a Cuban cigar."

"Wait a minute, O, my read is that this date rape blog thing is bullshit—just political smoke . . . or maybe it's just plain hate hype for a black man seeking the Center Seat on the Court."

Tim stopped and looked directly at Moorman. "Are you telling me the date rape story has legs?"

"It might," parried Moorman. "First I need to set up some ground rules. I need to end this rumor quickly. I think you can do it by questioning someone. Just one person—that should end this story. That's why I came tonight. I want to give you a name—the name of a lady, but I need assurances that you will keep the name confidential—at least for now. This witness may clear me—or at least reveal that whatever I did will not come out. Tim, I need your discretion and understanding on this."

Quinn seemed perplexed. Moorman knew he would be. Quinn was in a difficult position. Quinn had a duty to the Senate Judiciary Committee, and part of that duty was to get facts for the Committee to move along the confirmation process.

Quinn leaned forward and spoke in a low voice, "O, you know I work for the Senate Committee and I have to report the results of any investigation. It's my duty."

"I know. And I want you to investigate this rape allegation— immediately. I'll help you and give you the right person to talk to, but—I want you to do the investigation without revealing the name I'm about to give you to the public—or to the Senate Committee— for now."

Moorman paused and breathed out with a deep sigh. "I'll give you the name of the alleged rape victim in the story. This name—this woman could say some damaging things about me—or she could clear me. I really, truly don't know what she will say if she allows herself to be interviewed. The reason for that is that I was smashed that night in London—and can't remember if I had sex with her. It's crazy, but I can't remember. . . . Just know this, if the interview comes out badly for me, I'll probably withdraw my name from the nomination. However, I want you to keep the lady's name confidential for now. Any publicity about her—whether we had consensual sex or not—may hurt her just as much as it could hurt me. She is a prominent person. A very public figure. Her name must be a secret before the interview and afterward if she says that we never had sex. On the other hand, if she accuses me of date rape, then I realize you must tell the Committee. That is . . . if I don't withdraw from the confirmation. That's the deal. That's all I'm asking here. A little decency for her . . . and a little truth for me. Please!"

Moorman tried not to show his inner anguish as he made this request.

He waited for Quinn to mull the favor over.

He knew Quinn was a courageous man. Quinn had proved that on the same battlefield that Moorman had—a Bronze Star, an Air Medal, and two Purple Hearts in Vietnam. Moorman also knew Quinn also had a track record of doing the right thing as a lawyer and as a judge, whatever the cost. On the bench, Quinn had risked his career and cooperated in a Federal investigation to get evidence on a crooked judge. A man with courage and a strong sense of fairness.

Moorman was counting on both those qualities now.

Quinn looked serious as he rolled the long cigar in his fingers. Then he smiled and said, "Fuck it. What are they going to do? Send me to Vietnam again? Okay, Mr. Justice, I'll do it your way. Who's the lady? I promise I'll keep the name secret . . . for now."

Moorman quietly said, "As I said, the key to this date rape rumor is interviewing one person. She's a judge in England. She has the answer to this rumor about me. Her name is Morgana Temple. She's presently the number-two judge at the Old Bailey court in London."

There, I've said it. No incriminating words—or any confession, yet I've given the name of the person who could destroy me—or save me. The press might very well hunt her down anyway. There's probably a conference program on file at the Gray's Inn with both our names on the same panel for the conference. She was the only lady barrister on a panel and the media will surely focus on her. I'd rather Quinn or his Deputy—that prosecutor Vicky Hauser—be the first to find out the truth. It's time to get this ghost off my back.

TIM QUINN STAYED ROOTED IN HIS CHAIR IN THE Franklin Room after Justice Moorman departed. Moorman left immediately after giving Tim the name of Judge Morgana Temple, Q.C. Her official title was the Common Sergeant of London, but her function was the number-two judge at the Old Bailey, probably the most famous trial court in the world.

Tim knew a lot about "the Bailey." He actually sat there for one day as an observer judge on a murder case and was a good friend of several judges on the court, including the head of the Court, the Recorder of London, Sir Brian Fairmont, who functioned as the chief judge of the Old Bailey.

This job Senator Powers talked me into is turning out to be quite a delicate and busy investigation. This date rape thing could ruin Moorman at the confirmation hearings. And could possibly lead to an English prosecution of Moorman, a sitting American justice.

If the new allegation of date rape was true, then Moorman had just handed Tim the name of the person who might not only sink the confirmation, but might become the main prosecution witness in an English rape trial.

Quinn was bothered by the revelation of the name of the alleged unknown victim. If the allegation was false, why didn't Moorman deny it?

Moorman doesn't know what she will say! The blog mentioned that the American justice was smashed. Oscar Moorman was probably so drunk that night in England he doesn't know if he raped the woman or not.

Quinn had had a similar case before. Some years ago when he was in private practice before going on the bench, he had handled the defense of a young college football player accused of date rape. His college client's version of the sexual conduct that had happened that night was sketchy—too much alcohol had prevented a clearer memory of the sexual encounter. Was the sex consensual? The college man really didn't know. He had blacked out and had no memory of sex. Therefore the trial testimony of the woman was the key to the college case. Quinn only hoped that Moorman's fate would be different from his client—he had been convicted.

Quinn knew that speed would be important now. He was still alone in the Franklin Room so he used his cell phone to call Vicky Hauser on her cell.

It was now 10:30 P.M. He hoped he could reach her.

Vicky answered on the second ring.

"Vicky, Tim here. Sorry to call so late. My meet with Justice Moorman just ended. Can you talk? Are you alone?" Tim immediately regretted inquiring if she was alone. It was none of his business. And in light of the fact that they had been lovers in law school long ago, and had had a brief affair during his marriage not so long ago, it was a stupid thing to ask. He had no right to ask who she was seeing or sleeping with now.

Tim did care about the answer to that question. He had hidden his feelings for Vicky when he and his wife reconciled, long after his wife learned about the affair with Vicky. That was years ago—far back in the rearview mirror, but he remembered that at a point during the difficult reconciliation period to save his marriage, he felt he actually could love two women at the same time. But practicality and custom led to his choosing Katy, his wife.

After Tim's wife died in a car accident, he forced himself to ignore

Vicky out of remorse, grief, and love for Katy. However, the Senate Counsel job offer gave him a professional reason to see Vicky again. He thought he did love her, however, he was careful never to show it—with one exception.

AT THE OTHER END OF THE PHONE CALL TIM MADE, Vicky Hauser saw the caller ID and smiled. It was late on a Saturday night. Maybe Tim's calling her this late signaled it would be personal . . . not business. Tim was often in her thoughts these days, and she wished she was in his.

The flowers Tim had sent during her recovery from the acid attack that marred her face had given Vicky hope—hope that she and Tim might become lovers again—that's why she agreed to the temporary assignment to the Senate. She wanted to be near Tim—if only professionally. Maybe the office relationship would drift to a personal one? That was the dream she had . . . and it definitely was possible. At Columbia, their love affair had not been casual, but caring and deep. The strong type of love that they both thought might lead to marriage. But the relationship had ended. Perhaps not forever.

"Sure, Tim. I can talk. I'm home and yes, I'm alone," Vicky's voice was warm and suggestive.

God, maybe he is lonely and wants to stop by to see me? Ever since he asked me to be on his Senate Counsel's staff, I've been waiting for this. I understand why he didn't call me right after his wife's death. But now, it's been a long time since his Katy died.

Then the "get together" bubble burst—Tim told her about his

meeting with Moorman. This call definitely went south from the hope of a personal call to business—serious business.

The disappointment in Vicky's voice never came out because of the shock of the news that Moorman had revealed the name of a witness to corroborate the sex rumor out of England.

"No way! You're kidding me. Right?" Vicky's voice was in complete disbelief after Tim relayed the startling news about the justice.

Bill Sharkey, Tim, and Vicky had had a conference call earlier that day. They had discussed the increasing number of news reports based on the English blog story. All three—Bill, Tim and Vicky–had agreed that it probably was just another hoax smear of Justice Moorman and shouldn't be taken seriously. In their collective view, it was a nothing story . . . or so Vicky thought until now.

"Vicky, I'm telling you the story may be true." Tim hesitated for effect and repeated the meat of the call, "Why else would Moorman give me the *name* of the lady involved in the incident. And he wants us to interview her . . . in London. She apparently is an English judge now."

Vicky was silent on the phone for a few seconds as she thought this through. Then she accepted the possibility of the likely endgame. Long ago she learned as a young prosecutor that smart people do dumb things in the criminal law area—IQ had no relation to "I did." Criminals often gave up valuable information voluntarily that later was used to hang them . . . literally and figuratively.

Vicky saw the immediate issue. "Well now, the date rape allegation seems to have gotten real. There really is no other way to look at it when Moorman gave you the name of the alleged victim. We have a duty to treat this as a significant matter to be investigated—perhaps a criminal matter, not just a confirmation issue," concluded Vicky.

Then she added in a softer voice, "I must say, I'm stunned. I dismissed this blog report as pure Washington political gossip. . . . But Moorman giving you the name makes this the real deal—definitely a matter to be fully investigated."

Tim took charge. "Right. Vicky, I want you to be lead on this. I'll stay behind in Washington to hold the fort and handle anything else.

It would only lend credence to the rumor if I were to be seen jetting off to London in light of this English blog story. You're going to be the lead on this. Take Sharkey. Also, with the hearings coming up next week, I don't need to remind you that speed and discretion are important."

Vicky stayed silent.

She remembered that trait of his—Tim was in his aggressive "I'm in charge" mode, and she understood it. Tim had been conditioned to be a leader at West Point, then later with the Rangers, and still later in combat in Vietnam. And Tim led from the front, never requiring his troops to do that which he wouldn't do first. He was a hard charger of a leader, but he was a good leader, giving support and credit to his people. She liked that about him. He was decisive, but unselfish. Momentarily she drifted off into her longing for the past. She wanted so much to go back in time and have him love her again, the way he had when they were in Columbia Law together.

Tim's voice, calm and unemotional, brought her back to the urgency of the situation. "Okay, you and Bill Sharkey will have to go over to London ASAP and discreetly interview this Judge Morgana Temple. You should leave for England tomorrow. The last flights have probably left for tonight. Better go commercial. Low-key is good here. If I commandeered another Air Force jet the way I did for the Duke hoax thing, it probably would be leaked to the news media. However, please get business-class tickets and charge them to your personal credit cards. I'll make sure the Senate reimburses you both. You two need to arrive in London as fresh as you can. Bottom line, I would like you to try to see Judge Temple and interview her on Monday."

"I still can't believe that Moorman would give you the name of the woman. Is he nuts? Does he want us to verify his rape?" remarked Vicky. She still was trying to make sense of Moorman's move.

"I don't think he's crazy. He's probably been deeply troubled by whatever he did that night. Besides, he knows that the media will not let up on a sex story like this. This incident with Judge Temple will come out. I think he wants to get ahead of the story. His not being able to remember due to alcohol has been haunting him. Well, that's what I think. It's truth time for him. I guess he hopes he's innocent. My view is that he's right—it's best to get in front of a story that the media will uncover anyway. Well, whatever. Go and find out what Judge Temple has to say about our Justice Moorman. I'll send in a report to the Judiciary Committee telling the Senators that you and Bill are on this mission. By the way, for now I'm going to keep the English judge's name secret."

"I have no problem with that. People have a right to privacy. Especially rape victims."

"*Alleged* rape victims," corrected Tim. "Oh, Vicky, can you call Sharkey and tell him he's going on a trip? By the way, your flight probably won't leave until late afternoon—most of the flights to Europe leave later in the day—so maybe you and Sharkey could meet me at our offices in the Senate at ten tomorrow morning? I want to go over the approach to Judge Temple. It's very possible that she may not want to talk to you about this. In that case, I may be able to help. I know her chief judge and a few of the judges on her court. So if you run into any reluctance with her talking to you, I may be able to give you the name of a friendly judge to help her see that cooperation is best for all of us."

Vicky replied, "You know, you have a good point about Judge Temple not wanting to talk about this incident. I mean, if she didn't report the rape when it happened, she might not want to report the rape now. I saw some stats that here in America fifty-eight percent of rapes go unreported. I would guess that it's actually a higher percentage."

"*Alleged* rape. *Alleged*. We don't know if there really was a rape," corrected Tim.

To Vicky, Tim's words sounded more like wishful thinking than belief. She suspected that Tim was getting too close to Moorman and wondered whether that was a good thing. Normally it's not good to get friendly with the subject of an investigation.

After the call with Tim, Vicky called Bill Sharkey and alerted him to the trip the next day.

Then she went into her bathroom to get ready for bed. Tomorrow would come soon enough and she wanted to be up early to pack before the meeting with Tim and Bill Sharkey.

Before she washed her face, she pulled her shoulder-length blond hair back from her right side and stared at the patch of disfigured flesh left from the acid attack.

I wonder if Tim still thinks I'm beautiful?

E-MAIL	(Committee Senator—Eyes Only)
FROM	TIM QUINN, SPECIAL COUNSEL
DATE	SUNDAY, DECEMBER 14, 2008
TO	MEMBERS OF U.S. SENATE JUDICIARY COMMITTEE
SUBJECT	CONFIDENTIAL—REPORT TO THE JUDICIARY COMMITTEE #3

As the Committee knows, Justice Oscar Moorman has been the subject of a recent series of news reports about the rumor of a date rape in England some years ago. The media's source is an English blog site that outlines a forcible sexual assault upon an English barrister by Justice Moorman during a legal conference in London (blog report is attached to this e-mail).

Although there are official records which indicate that Justice Moorman did attend a conference during the summer of 2001, I wish to indicate to the Committee the fact that there has been no firm proof that any such assault took place.

Nevertheless the alleged incident must be investigated. I am aware that the opening day of the confirmation hearing has been now scheduled for this coming Wednesday, December 17.

I have just received highly credible information pertaining to the identity of the alleged rape victim in London. Accordingly, I am sending my Deputy Special Counsel, Ms. Victoria Hauser, to England this afternoon together with Mr. William Sharkey, the Chief Investigator on my staff. They will attempt to interview the alleged victim tomorrow, December 15, and immediately report the results to me.

It is my hope that Ms. Hauser and Mr. Sharkey will be successful and that a factual basis will soon exist for the Committee to evaluate this recent allegation against Justice Moorman. With this information, the Committee can either allow the confirmation hearings to proceed as scheduled or terminate the hearings.

Timothy R. Quinn
Special Counsel
U.S. Senate Judiciary Committee

SUNDAY WAS A DISASTER FOR SENATOR IRMA POWERS. She received the "Report to the Judiciary Committee" e-mail from Tim Quinn at eight o'clock that morning. She immediately called Quinn on his cell.

"Judge Quinn, I just read your report and am very disappointed that you didn't call me with this information sooner. I'd also like to know the name of this alleged rape victim and how you learned about her." She made no attempt to hide the agitation in her voice.

"Madam Chair, our deal was that I would have direct access to the Committee with all my reports. So there is no requirement that you be notified ahead of the other Senators on the Committee. On the identity of the alleged victim and the source of the information, I'm afraid that that information will have to be confidential for now."

I never should have picked Quinn for this assignment.

"What . . . Quinn, I'm the Chair and I demand to know the identity of this woman."

"Sorry, Senator, until my people interview her to see if there is any substance to this alleged sexual assault, I'm keeping her identity secret to protect her privacy. And that's final."

It was here that Quinn was almost fired.

He was saved only by the operation of the excellent political common sense of Senator Powers. And the U.S. Senate is a noted place where common sense is not common. In fact, some wise veteran political reporters have often joked that a historical landmark should be erected over the Senate doors saying, "All ye that enter here, check your brains in the coatroom."

Nevertheless, Senator Powers was operating on all cylinders that morning and thought before she spoke.

If I fire him now, just days before the confirmation hearings, the Democratic opposition to Moorman will use that as a reason to delay the hearings. I burned up a lot of favors to get these hearings scheduled before the holiday adjournment of the Senate. The favor bank is on empty. I'll never get another hearing date from the damn Democrats if the hearings are postponed. Then I will lose Moorman's chance to be confirmed.

With iron will, Senator Powers kept her temper in check.

"Well, I guess the Committee will have to wait until the results of this new investigation. Judge Quinn, as you know, an investigation at such a sensitive time needs to be handled very delicately. I hope your

Ms. Hauser and Agent Sharkey will be discreet in their travel plans and will not be staying or interviewing this mystery witness at the American Embassy in London. It's a real sieve and I'm sure that the media will be looking for the lady mentioned in this rumor. By the way, when are Hauser and Sharkey leaving?"

"Don't worry, Senator. There will be no alerting the Embassy. My people will be staying at the London Marriott at Grosvenor Square. They'll be leaving this afternoon on the five-thirty United flight to Heathrow. They're pros. They'll be low profile."

"Good. Keep me informed." Powers hung up on Quinn without a good-bye. She scored a point in rudeness over Quinn—a small win for her.

After the call, she sat alone at her kitchen table and thought about her next move. Politics was like chess. You didn't win without planning your next move. Failing to prepare is the next bus stop before arriving at failure.

I have to get this information on the interview in London to the Carpa Pharmaceuticals CEO. Maybe he can get some money to the rape victim to shut her up. Getting Moorman to be Chief Justice may be worth billions to Carpa. Paying some quiet money now makes a lot of sense.

Her mind decided; she executed her plan.

Senator Powers called her husband, Jim, at their home in Richmond. Time to put him to work as the secure conduit of information to the Carpa CEO—Don Fay.

Fay's a clever fellow. With this info, he'll be able get someone to follow the Senate investigators to find the rape victim . . . and to pay off the English slut. Money can perform wonders for NBA players and large corporations in the witness-influencing world. These types of women are whores anyway. All that separates them is the amount and the place of payment. What difference does it make if the money is on the nightstand in the morning or in a Swiss bank four years later?

✦ 42 ✦

ON SUNDAY MIDMORNING, DON FAY WAS ABOUT TO swing his driver on the elevated fourth tee at the Burning Tree Country Club just outside of Washington. It was his favorite hole on the club course—a 430-yard dogleg to the left, almost all downhill. He was taking a practice swing when he felt the vibrating of his Black-Berry in his back pocket. It was a phone call, not an e-mail. He pulled it out and looked at the number calling. Shaking his head, he realized this was a call he had to take.

Fay, a tall man with a slim physique and gracious manners, politely excused himself from his three companions, three regional vice presidents of Carpa Pharmaceuticals, and walked off the tee to take the call with a degree of privacy.

As he listened to Jim Powers, the ex-governor and present spouse of Senator Irma Powers, he knew that his day on the beautiful golf course was ruined.

"Okay, I get the picture, Jim. The Moorman nomination is in trouble. Thanks for the info. Keep me posted on any further developments."

Fay went back to his threesome and told them the news that they should continue on without him. Before he left, he put a ball down on the tee. No matter how pressing an issue on the front burner, Fay was definitely not leaving without hitting a ball on this hole.

Fay took his time in addressing the Nike ball and swung with his usual smooth power. The ball quickly shot high down the sloping fairway, but then it seemed to hit a gust of wind and hooked to the right . . . into the tall pine trees and the deep saw grass, where finding the ball would be difficult, if not impossible.

Fay didn't bother to hide his disappointment as he pounded the ground in anger once with his expensive Big Bertha driver.

"Gentleman, apparently this isn't my day. By the way, that call I took reminded me of a long-standing commitment I'd forgotten so I've got to get back to Richmond right away. I'll take one of the carts and send it back from the clubhouse."

When his partner for the day took his golf bag from the cart, Fay pressed on the accelerator of the cart hard. The wheels spun and threw gravel from the path as the cart headed back to the clubhouse.

Soon Fay was off-loading his golf bag into the trunk of his dark blue Mercedes S500. Before he left the parking lot, Fay reached into the glove compartment and pulled out one of the two cell phones there. These were his disposable phones—throwaway phones that he used to mask calls that he wanted to be hard to trace. He powered up the cell phone.

When he saw sufficient bars of reception, he punched in a number and heard the familiar raspy hello.

"Meet me at my office in two hours. By the way, I'll need some more of these one-time phones."

"Well, sounds like you have a problem for me."

"Nothing on the phone. And why the fuck else would I be calling you on a Sunday? Just be at my office."

Fay didn't even bother to hang up. He just ripped the battery out of the phone and tossed it down the storm drain next to his car. GPS made these phones easy to trace unless you disconnected the battery. The rest of the phone would be thrown into the thick brush at the entrance to the club as Fay started his hour-plus drive back to Richmond to meet with the man who might solve his and Carpa's problem.

Long ago Fay became careful of communicating when he was handling the dark side of his business. He had developed some general rules when he was operating in this definitely black area—way outside the line of the law.

—Don't e-mail.

—Don't talk on the phone if you can talk in person.

—Don't talk if you can nod.

✦ 43 ✦

CNN.com—*Breaking News (Internet)—Suspected terrorist bombing in London*

LONDON, ENGLAND, SUNDAY, DECEMBER 14, 2008—There was an explosion in the Mayfair section of London this afternoon just before the shops closed. The blast was in front of the McDonald's restaurant on busy Oxford Street near the entrance to the Marble Arch underground station. It has been reported that there were at least eight fatalities and scores of injured have been transported to local hospitals.

A source close to the Metropolitan Police has reported that the source of the explosion was a young man with a backpack—an apparent suicide bomber. The bomber stood outside the windows of the crowded restaurant to utilize the glass fragments to increase the lethal effects of the explosive device.

BBC has reported that shortly after the blast, a male voice made a brief call to the BBC-TV station in London and claimed responsibility on behalf of al-Qaeda.

The spokesperson for New Scotland Yard has declined to comment

on this possible al-Qaeda attack other than to say that an active investigation is underway and all CCTV cameras in operation around the
Oxford Street site of the bombing were being reviewed.

England's vast network of surveillance cameras ("closed-circuit
television," also known as CCTV) has been relied upon by police authorities as a major factor in solving many crimes in the United Kingdom in recent years. In the U.K., CCTV cameras are omnipresent.
They are in all public subway, train, and bus stations. They cover most
public streets in central London and most major cities. These cameras
are monitored 24/7 by the police. The twin terrorist bombings in
London in 2005 were solved in large measure from evidence gained
by the City of London's CCTV network.

In a breaking development, CNN's White House correspondent
Nina Tratora reports that President Ramsey telephoned British
Prime Minister Darby Morton and promised to immediately make
available "substantial U.S. intelligence assets" to prevent further terrorist attacks in the United Kingdom.

IT WAS ALMOST NOON SUNDAY. VICKY HAUSER WAS IN
the spacious office of the Special Counsel next to the Senate Judiciary
Committee room in the Dirksen Senate Office Building. Tim Quinn
and Bill Sharkey had just left to go down the hall to get coffee from
the Senators' Lounge. Vicky was thinking back to last night. She remembered that she was initially pleased when she saw that it was Tim
Quinn on the caller ID screen of her cell phone last night. At that
moment, she had thought that perhaps the late call on a Saturday

night from Tim would be personal—a signal that Tim was coming out of his year of mourning following the death of his wife, Katy.

She briefly entertained the depressing thought that Tim might never know that she had decided that she could love only one man in her life—Tim Quinn. She had been a fool to let her early career lead to the destruction of her relationship with him. In law school at Columbia they had lived together and carried on a bi-city (New York and Washington) relationship for two years before she broke it off.

Tim had moved on and found his Katy in Washington. Vicky remained in New York for a while and later moved to Washington to give everything to her brilliant career.

The call last night unfortunately had been all business.

Vicky refused to give up on her dream that someday Tim would call to start up what they had so long ago. Someday . . . maybe after this confirmation job is finished.

Her dreams disappeared when Tim and Bill returned to the office and the three of them resumed the discussion of the strategy for Vicky's and Bill's trip this afternoon to London.

"God, Vicky, I just don't know. I hate to send you to London now. This terrorist bomb thing in London could be the start of a new offensive by al-Qaeda in London. You know these bombings usually come in multiples. Maybe you should interview Judge Temple about whatever thing she had with Justice Moorman by phone?"

Vicky was actually pleased with Tim's concern about her safety, especially since she knew Tim was too good a lawyer to actually believe that such an important interview could be taken by phone.

"Tim, you know that it's always better to interview a witness in person—especially a potential rape victim. Help me on this, Bill." Vicky looked over at the sleepy-eyed FBI Special Agent.

Bill Sharkey shrugged his shoulders and responded in his usual curt fashion, "Phone interviews are always the last choice. Got to eyeball the witness—FBI basic course 101. Don't worry, Judge. We'll be fine. I'm sure places like the Old Bailey and American hotels will be well secured by the London bobbies."

"All right. Go on to London. But let's think about this a bit—really about the approach to Temple. Will Judge Temple even talk to you two about Moorman? Moorman told me that Temple is a hotshot judge and might be under consideration for a slot on the Royal Court of Appeal. She might not want to get involved in this Moorman thing. English judges are quite reluctant to having their names in the news, especially if they are up for a promotion. The real question is whether she will talk to you at all."

Vicky nodded. "Yes, she might not even want to meet with me when I tell her that I want to interview her about the date rape rumor. Refusal to even meet with me is a very likely scenario here."

Tim flipped open his Rolodex, wrote down something on a piece of paper, and handed it to Vicky, saying, "Several years ago when I was sitting on the Court of Appeals here in D.C., I attended an international judicial conference in Copenhagen and made friends with a very nice judge from England. He's a very good guy and an excellent judge . . . and I think he's still the chief judge of the Old Bailey. They call that position "the Recorder of London." Anyway, I got to visit him in London the next year and actually got to sit with him for a day as an observer judge at the Old Bailey on a murder trial. Bottom line: he's a good friend and here's his name and direct phone number. If Judge Temple balks at talking to you, tell her that you will have me call her chief judge, Sir Brian Fairmont, and ask her to cooperate in our investigation. . . . Oh, and, if you have to, make sure to emphasize to her that her chief judge and I are old friends."

Vicky shook her head and smiled. "Tim, you never cease to surprise me with your network. The possibility of going to her boss may well be the stick that may make her cooperate. One other thing we should be aware of is that she may only consent to talk with me . . . alone."

Tim replied, "Right, this is such a sensitive subject that she'll likely just talk to you. Female to female. Bill probably will be cut out of the interview. Now that I think on this—she may not allow any tape-recording of the interview. . . . Nevertheless, it would be good to have a record of what she says." Quinn left the unsaid question just hang in the air. What he was asking Vicky and Bill to do was to figure out a way to tape Judge Temple's interview . . . without her permission.

Bill Sharkey picked up the hint. "Judge, I'll bring along some of my audio toys from the FBI lab. Some of their new stuff. We'll try to get the lady judge's story on tape for you and the Committee."

Quinn nodded with a serious face.

Well, thought Vicky, the pressure was on her now—not only to interview the woman judge, but to get a tape of the interview—secretly if possible.

What Judge Temple said about this date rape allegation was going to be very important. And Vicky knew that Tim didn't want to rely on a hearsay statement from her if he had to make a formal recommendation to the Committee on the "up or down" vote for Moorman to be Chief Justice.

✦ 45 ✦

THERE ARE SOME LAWSUITS THAT ARE WORTH A *murder,* decided Don Fay.

As he sped down I-95 toward Richmond and his office at Carpa's main corporate headquarters, Fay played out the situation in his mind. Here was his company on the verge of maneuvering Justice Moorman into the Center Seat on the Supreme Court. Senator Irma Powers had brilliantly moved the nomination from the lame-duck White House of President Ramsey to the Senate Judiciary Committee where she had greased the nomination for confirmation this week before the holiday recess of Congress.

With Moorman as the new Chief Justice, he would have the influence to sway the Court to allow Carpa to prevail in the drug patent case coming up for argument next month in the Supreme Court. Everything has been set. Powers had assured Fay that Moorman will play ball on this case.

But now a rumor appeared from a blog site in England that could derail the fragile nomination of Moorman already weakened by the Duke "dirty movie" hoax.

Fucking media will have a field day with this date rape allegation. And what if some hungry reporter actually chases down the English bitch who may substantiate the charge of rape. Thank God, Powers' husband has given me the way to find the woman in England.

Without stopping at his home to change from his golf clothes, Fay went directly to Carpa's headquarters to meet with the man who would help Fay silence the mystery woman in England.

As Fay approached the drug giant Carpa world headquarters in a beautiful ten-story glass and shiny steel building next to the James River just outside the city limits of Richmond, Virginia, Fay mentally went over exactly what information and orders he would tell his security chief, Victor Dagnar.

Fay, on the drive down from Washington, had decided that he would give the man only what he needed to know to do the job in London. Fay would keep the source of his information and his relationship with Senator Powers and her husband secret from this dangerous man who worked for him. Fay didn't like or trust Dagnar.

Fay's office was on the top floor of the building and his office décor reflected his personality. Cold and detached. His corner office had two walls of tinted glass overlooking the James River, and the dominant furnishings were a long dark teak desk, several black leather sofas and chairs, and a thick light-gray rug. The twelve-foot ceilings and large mirrors on the two inner walls made the office seem larger than it was.

When Fay walked through his reception area and into his private office, a small, bent over but powerful-looking man rose from one of the long sofas and said in a raspy low voice, "Mr. Fay, what's the problem?"

Fay jumped from the shock. He had thought his office would be vacant.

What's the little gnome doing in my office? How did he get by the security systems? . . . Wait a minute! . . . Dagnar was the head of security and an electronic genius and personally installed all the security for my office.

"Ah, Victor, I want you to take care of a matter for me." Fay quickly recovered his composure and projected his usual air of superiority.

Don Fay waved Dagnar over to the far corner of his office, where four low square leather and chrome chairs faced each other in a loose square with a small table in the middle. The table was bare except for a heavy steel desk lamp on it.

Dagnar hesitated to follow Fay over to the two chairs in the corner.

With a twisted smile on his face, Dagnar shook his head and uttered, "I'm disappointed. You still don't trust me, do you?"

"Get used to disappointment, Victor" was the curt reply, as Fay settled into one of the chairs.

Fay thought he noticed a temporary injury in Victor Dagnar's eyes.

Dagnar is an ugly, mean man who probably has few friends. His social life has probably been filled with rejection and disappointment. No need to hurt him. Especially now that I need him for this job.

"No offense meant, Victor. Come over here and we can get started. This is sensitive stuff. We'll need privacy."

After the two men took the seats facing each other, Fay reached over and turned on the desk lamp on the table between them. Not only did the frosted lightbulb go on, but there was an immediate high-pitched hum emanating from the light and filling the room. The sound was that of a white noise producer embedded in the base of the light. The white noise device would cancel out any voice frequency on a tape recorder anywhere within ten feet of the light. It also would neutralize any acoustical listening device that might be aimed at the windows of Fay's office. The white noise, in effect, made a "cone of silence" for Fay in his office.

Whatever was said here could never be played back in any court of law.

Fay got right to the point with his chief of security.

"There is a woman in England that must be silenced—permanently. It must be made to look like an accident. I don't have her name, but she is to be interviewed by a Senate attorney—a federal prosecutor on detail to the Senate—and an FBI special agent tomorrow or the next day in London. I know you probably know of the rumor that Justice Moorman date raped an English lady some years ago."

Dagnar said, "Sure, interesting story. All over the news. Mostly denials."

Fay then continued, "Well, I have a solid lead that will take you to the English woman that Justice Moorman slept with . . . maybe raped . . . it doesn't matter. This woman even talking about sex with him could kill Moorman's confirmation. And that would be bad for us. Carpa has a huge stake in Moorman getting to be Chief Justice. We want him. Our legal department and outside counsel tell us that Carpa will probably win our big patent case involving our drug, Varakain, *if* Moorman gets to be Chief. He could be the key to our winning that big patent case scheduled for January. A win in the Supreme Court would be worth at least four billion in profits for our company. I don't need to say it, but this is a big case for us, very big. The Board of Directors of Carpa is putting a lot of pressure on me to get a win. . . . And I've more or less promised them that we *would* prevail. Anyway, you can see this English thing would harm our chances for the win. . . . So I want you to follow the prosecutor and FBI agent in London, and they will most likely lead you to this English woman. When they lead you to her, do her—I mean *do* her. Silence her—forever. Make it look like an accident if you can. . . . Here are the names of the prosecutor and the agent."

After Fay gave Dagnar a small piece of paper, he continued, "The

Senate investigating team—this Hauser lady and Agent Sharkey—will be leaving this afternoon on a commercial plane, a United flight out of Dulles that arrives at Heathrow at 6.30 A.M. tomorrow morning. One of our Carpa G5 jets will be at the Richmond airport ready for you to take off at six tonight. With our corporate jet, you should beat the commercial jet to London by at least three hours if you leave by six. If you miss the interviewing team at the airport, they will be staying at the Marriott on Grosvenor Square near the American Embassy. You still have that Scotland Yard inspector on our payroll, don't you?"

Dagnar nodded.

"Well, call him this afternoon and use him in London to track this interviewing team and to help you on the job. You will have full access to Carpa's London office and our manufacturing plant out near Heathrow Airport. As a cover, make your trip look like you are on a surprise security check of the London operations . . . and keep the Scotland Yard man in the dark if you can. If you can't, make sure there are no loose ends. Well, Victor, I've just hit the highlights—what are your questions?"

"Why not pay off the Englishwoman?"

Fay rubbed his face with one of his hands and offered his answer in a thoughtful way. "I considered that . . . briefly, but rejected it. Payoffs are so temporary . . . and sometimes lead to blackmail. Elimination of a witness is a more—shall we say—permanent solution. . . . Now you've done some good things recently for Carpa in the industrial spying area. We both know you're no virgin in this elimination area. This job should be an easy 'do' for a man of your considerable talents. . . . You're not losing your edge for crossing the line, are you? . . . Do we have a problem here?" Fay was frowning with concern.

Dagnar smiled with his twisted face and calmly replied, "No, no. Permanent is okay with me. . . . I *would* like to know how good this info is. How do you know all this? I mean—about the identity of the Senate investigators and where they're going to stay—how do you know the details?"

"Why—from our good friend in the Senate—Senator Powers. We do her favors—gifts, an annual stipend of 400K to an untraceable bank account she and her husband set up, campaign contributions, help on this and that—and she gives us some help. This morning she phoned her husband—the lawyer with the firm we use in Richmond as a cut-out means of passing info—well, she gave him all these details and he passed them to me at her request—all protected by attorney-client privilege. You may know that Powers is helping us big time on the Moorman nomination and she wants us to stop the woman from blabbing to the press and killing the confirmation. Powers is a little naïve and thinks hush money is the way to go. Well, anyway, back to the real issue and bottom line, can you do it? I mean—follow these investigators and get to the woman . . . with a permanent solution."

He's asking too many questions . . . and I'm answering them. Damn it! Why can't I keep my mouth shut? . . . Well, I guess I want someone to know I have a senator in my pocket—pure ego. I've got to watch that.

Dagnar just grinned and coldly asked, "No problem here, boss. I do have a few requests for the logistics. But first, since this— elimination operation—is such a big thing for the company, are we talking bonus?"

Fucking guy is holding me up for this hit. I shouldn't have mentioned the fucking four billion, thought Fay.

✦ 46 ✦

VICTOR DAGNAR, THE CHIEF OF SECURITY FOR CARPA
Pharmaceuticals, was an ugly man by any standard. He was short,
balding, and had a genetically deformed spine that made his right
shoulder hunch up almost to the bottom of his right ear and made
his head tilt slightly downward. Naturally the twisted spine made his
torso shorter than normal and caused him to walk with a noticeable
limp. Genetics was not kind to his face either. He had a hawk nose
with a weak chin on his downward sloping face. Being picked on in
school for his looks as a sort of a freak made him a lifetime fanatic at
weightlifting. His long arms became very strong and were effective at
deterring bullies.

Nature does have a sense of compensation. What was lacking in
the body was made up in the mind. Victor Dagnar was absolutely
brilliant.

His exceptional mind was his ticket to scholarships to a top high
school and college. He was not only smart, but ambitious and ruth-
less. Carpa recruiters picked him as a research chemist, but with his
chemical and computer skills, he soon found his niche in the Carpa
Security Department as an industrial spy, stealing secrets from other
drug companies and research hospitals.

His big break at Carpa came in his fifth year, when Dagnar murdered a security guard who found him late at night stealing files from
the research laboratory of a rival drug company in Germany. He
made a good escape from the scene and managed to bring with him
research notes on a new pain killer drug that was worth millions to

Carpa when it beat its rival to market with the drug. No charges were ever brought against Dagnar. The German police investigation concluded that the unsolved crime was a random murder committed by an unknown drug addict during a burglary to steal drugs.

The German incident, however, caught the eye of Donald Fay, a fast-track senior vice president, and when Fay took over Carpa as the CEO, Victor Dagnar was promoted to be the head of Carpa security. It proved a wise choice for Fay. There were several times in the past decade that Dagnar had proved his worth to Fay and Carpa by several significant examples of corporate devotion. One involved the "accidental" death of a potential whistle-blower in Carpa—the ending of a nagging problem for Carpa management. Another was the hit-and-run death of a key expert witness in a negligence trial brought against Carpa that ended in a favorable settlement for Carpa—a result welcomed by Fay and confirming his reliance on Dagnar's talent. The loss of the expert seriously weakened the case for the plaintiff and efficiently lubricated the settlement.

Dagnar had one more killing during his tenure at Carpa. Fay didn't know it because it was done for a personal not a corporate reason. A year ago, Dagnar had strangled a prostitute he had picked up at a security convention in New York City. That woman was drunk and made the mistake of making fun of both his sexual performance and the appearance of his body while rendering services to Dagnar. The murder was never solved or even officially noticed. Dagnar had broken several hotel video cameras and buried the body in the industrial swamps of nearby New Jersey. The prostitute was a ghost who had disappeared from the earth—unmissed except by her regulars, who kept quiet about their loss.

A clever and resourceful man who was willing to kill for his company, Dagnar earned a salary that equaled or exceeded that of most of the senior vice presidents of Carpa, an unusual compensation package for a head of security. And Dagnar knew he was worth it. Dagnar figured that not many Fortune 100 companies could boast of having an in-house assassin . . . not that any would admit it.

After the detailed briefing of the need and timing for the English lady to die, Dagnar returned to his office in Carpa headquarters and packed a large canvas equipment bag to take to England.

Even before the ending of the briefing by Fay, Dagnar had decided that the English lady should probably die by using drugs. For this job, he liked the irony of using drugs to kill, not save. And he had the best tools of his trade at his disposal. Carpa had always given its security head a generous budget to do his dark work.

After packing his professional gear, he went to his home to pack his clothes for his short trip. Dagnar lived alone in a townhouse in the downtown historic district of Richmond. He had been married twice but had no children. His former wives enjoyed the money he made, but eventually could not take his alcohol addiction, which led to violent mood swings and the abusive traits of Victor Dagnar.

Victor Dagnar had escaped the poverty and career failures of his alcoholic father, but not his nature.

47

VICKY HAUSER AND BILL SHARKEY SETTLED INTO THE business-class section of the United flight bound for London.

Vicky had spent the afternoon after the meeting with Tim Quinn at their Senate offices packing for a three- or four-day trip and doing a Google search of the woman to be interviewed, Judge Morgana Temple, Q.C.

Vicky found that Temple was an interesting woman. Her education was impressive. She did very well in university. She was an upper-second-class honors graduate of the small and select law program at the prestigious London School of Economics. The LSE law program was not a factory producing nearly a thousand law graduates per year like Georgetown or Harvard. LSE graduated less than one hundred per year—top legal minds drawn from all over the world. Vicky was a little surprised that LSE, not Cambridge or Oxford, was ranked as the number-one law program in England, largely because of the talent of the faculty and the rigorous law courses.

After graduating from LSE, Morgana Temple enrolled in the College of Law in London, a one-year program leading to the exam to become a barrister. Once qualified as a barrister, she became a member of a small law firm in Gray's Inn. Her talents for research and writing soon were recognized, as she was selected as the youngest member of the elite Government Treasury Counsel section, trying major criminal cases for the prosecution at the Central Criminal Court, the legendary Old Bailey. Her excellent trial work at the Old Bailey led to her receiving an appointment as one of the twelve regular trial judges at the Bailey—the top rung in the English trial court system.

According to the news reports, Vicky found that Temple was not married and was known as a talented, hardworking judge who might wind up on the Royal Court of Appeal.

Vicky shared her research on Judge Temple's background with Bill Sharkey as they munched on the evening meal served onboard, before they both tried to get a few hours sleep on the flight.

"This Judge Temple doesn't sound like the 'roll in the hay' gal in the news stories about Justice Moorman," commented Sharkey, adjusting his pillow and blanket before attempting to go to sleep.

Vicky knitted her brow at Sharkey's somewhat overly broad comment. "Well, rape victims can be all types. Most victims go on with their lives. Rape doesn't change the woman's postrape behavior in most cases."

Sharkey asked, "What's the plan to talk to her?"

Vicky replied, "Well, we arrive at Heathrow at 6:30 A.M. so I suggest we taxi into London, check into the hotel, and call the Old

Bailey to try to arrange a meeting with Judge Temple . . . hopefully tomorrow—that is, if she'll speak with us."

"She sounds like you. A fast-track woman prosecutor type. Probably best if you make the initial call to her. You can do the woman bonding thing. I'm not too smooth with women lawyers." Sharkey turned over and closed his eyes.

Vicky smiled and said, "What a surprise!"

DAGNAR'S PLANE SMOOTHLY TOUCHED DOWN ON A wet runway at London's Heathrow Airport a little after 4 A.M. The rain beat on the skin of the jet as it pulled up to the tarmac of the executive aircraft terminal, on the other side of the runway from Terminal Three—the main commercial passenger terminal for international flights.

Standing in a long khaki raincoat next to the parking space for the black Carpa jet was a short, portly, red-faced detective inspector from Scotland Yard. His name was Reggie Whiteside. His current police duty assignment was impressive. He was one of only five officers assigned to Scotland Yard's liaison office at the British Parliament. He was a gregarious, affable, and creative "fixer of problems" for the legislators, but his midlevel title was unfortunately a terminal one, since Reggie was definitely lower class, and his type rarely fit into the upper reaches of the Oxford-Cambridge types that dominated the top tier of Scotland Yard leadership positions. Promotion-wise, his detective inspector position was as far up the ladder in the Yard as he realistically expected. At fifty years old, he had a good steady government job, but low pay and a very modest pension. His credit card history frequently showed slow payments and, with a free-spending wife and four children, he came up clearly on Carpa's radar screen as an easy target to be recruited by the big bucks of Carpa security people. . . . And he was.

The Yard naturally didn't know that one of their top and very connected detective inspectors had been on the secret payroll of Carpa for over five years. He was a big help to the drug company in its aggressive industrial spying program. In fact, Reggie was well worth the three-hundred-thousand euros—plus bonuses—that Carpa deposited in the Swiss account of Whiteside each year. Dagnar made sure that the money Reggie Whiteside got was absolutely untraceable.

Dagnar smiled as he looked out the oval window of the jet where he was seated.

Glad I woke up Reggie and told him to meet the plane. He's a very useful fellow. Nice to have a policeman watching over you in another country—especially if you will be breaking laws!

Having Detective Inspector Whiteside meet the G5 jet was a smart move for Dagnar that morning. Even though London was under increased security due to the recent terrorist bombing, a detective inspector from Scotland Yard meeting the Carpa jet at the executive jet ramp of Heathrow almost certainly guaranteed that no customs inspector would look into the suitcase or the big canvas bag of equipment that Dagnar had the copilot off-load from the plane. Although Dagnar hadn't much time between the CEO, Don Fay, giving him the mission and the Carpa jet taking off from the Richmond Airport, Dagnar had used the time wisely and had packed not only clothes for a short stay but some useful and nasty toys for the job he had to do in London—things that might not pass muster by inspectors, especially now during the raised security alert status due to the recent terrorist attack in downtown London.

As Victor Dagnar emerged from the jet and stepped into the

London rain with a golf umbrella, held above him by the pilot, he shouted, "Reggie, good to see you again!"

"Good morning, Governor," replied the smiling man from Scotland Yard.

VICKY HAUSER FELT LIKE SHE KNEW SHE LOOKED TIRED and in need of a shower as she and Sharkey waited for their bags after passing through customs at Heathrow. She was alert enough to notice something unusual—she had sensed that the uniformed processing official took a little longer studying her passport and the U.K. entrance form that she filled out on the plane before landing. She thought the official's questions about where she was staying were odd and mentioned it to Sharkey as they waited for their checked baggage.

"I've been to London before and never had the passport control officer ask about my hotel. It was clearly filled in on the form," Vicky remarked. It was a pointed statement meant to get a reaction from Sharkey, who had a fine-tuned nose for smelling out the unusual.

Sharkey, red-eyed from too little sleep, shrugged his shoulders and grunted. "Must be the Saturday bombing here in London that makes them double-check what's on the forms. It's odd, though. I was asked the same question—about where I was staying—even though I clearly put 'Marriott' on the form. Maybe the Brits are just jumpy from the terrorist attack. Funny, they quizzed us and let the fucking twenty-year-old towel head just ahead of us in the line pass through without a blink of an eye. The fucking PC syndrome about profiling must be spreading from our country over to here."

Vicky bit her lip on Sharkey's remark and abruptly changed the subject. "Bill, keep your eyes peeled for my red suitcase with the yellow scarf on the handle. I'm going over to the money exchange and get some English pounds for the taxi ride into town."

Soon, with both their bags in tow, they made their way into the taxi line at the airport and got into a traditional London black cab.

"Marriott Hotel on Grovesnor Square—near the American Embassy," Vicky said to the cabdriver. Their taxi headed off through the morning rush hour and the misting rain toward the central area of London.

Fifty yards behind them was a dark blue ten-year-old Jaguar convertible keeping pace and matching them turn for turn.

IT WAS THREE O'CLOCK IN THE MORNING IN WASHINGTON.

Justice Moorman was in his small study off the hallway down from the master bedroom of his home.

He couldn't sleep.

Not sleeping was understandable; this was going to be the "Mother of All Weeks" for Moorman. First, he was extremely worried about what would happen in London with the interview of Judge Temple. That interview could possibly happen within hours. Quinn had promised that he would call ASAP after any news from Vicky Hauser.

Also on his troubled mind was the fact that his confirmation hearings before the Senate Judiciary Committee were scheduled for Wednesday and Thursday. As if that wasn't enough action for Moorman that week, on Friday, the Supreme Court was having its final oral argument day of the calendar year. Three cases were on the docket for that day starting at 10 A.M. Yes, this would be quite a week.

He and Debby went to bed at 11 P.M. and he had tried to sleep, but his mind was over in London where he knew that Vicky Hauser and Bill Sharkey were just getting off the plane and starting the quest to discover the secret from that night with Morgana Temple.

Moorman thought perhaps he had made a mistake in telling Debby what was happening with Quinn sending his two investigators to London. He knew she would find out anyway about the London trip. Her father, Senator Sloane, was getting Judge Quinn's Judiciary Committee reports from Senator Powers and feeding each one to his daughter, either by telephoning her or by faxing her Quinn's reports.

Still he wished that there was a way to keep Debby from hearing about the blow-by-blow account of the investigation. Despite being the daughter of a politician, she had never inherited the rhino skin of her father. Debby was obsessed and frightened of what would be discovered over in England . . . and of the impact on the confirmation hearing that was due to start that Wednesday in the Senate Judiciary Committee.

To top off his worries, Tim Quinn had called before dinner and informed Moorman that the *Washington Post* was going to run a story about the mystery woman from the English blog. Quinn had talked to the reporter—a slimy weasel who was heavily fishing for some lead. Quinn relayed his conclusion to Moorman that the *Washington Post* had nothing more than the speculation from the blog.

The Washington Post *and all the newspapers—all the trash fit to print,* silently cursed Moorman.

Nevertheless, O felt he should tell Debby about the coming story in the *Post.* Predictably in O's view, the news had caused Debby to drink more and more . . . and maybe to pop more pills to go with the drinks at dinner.

Debby was sleeping very hard now. Before he left the bed to go to his study, Oscar Moorman several times checked her to see if she was okay because her breathing was so shallow.

Now in the study, Moorman was wondering whether he should just withdraw from the nomination.

I never should have put Debby into this media meat grinder. My nomination may ruin her . . . and maybe me as well.

Moorman was somewhat cheered by something that Quinn said in his conversation earlier. Quinn told Moorman about his friendship with Morgana Temple's chief judge at the Old Bailey. Maybe he could help with Morgana. Maybe Morgana would tell Vicky Hauser that there was no rape—just consensual sex. . . . Maybe Morgana would just not talk about that night. She had a lot to lose if she really wanted that future appellate appointment.

So many maybes—damn, bottom line—if I did force her to have sex, she may keep quiet about it. She and I both lose if she accuses me.

That thought when it appeared in his mind caused Moorman to be ashamed for just thinking about it.

God, what am I thinking? More important, how can I be a Supreme Court Justice of the most powerful country in the world and be so stupid as to get into this situation?

The answer was brutally simple—because judges are all just ordinary men and women, all just human. And Moorman felt very human just now.

· 51 ·

AS JUSTICE MOORMAN WAS EXAMINING HIS FATE IN THE early hours of Washington, Vicky and Sharkey were checking into the Marriott in central London.

"Bill, give me an hour to shower and dress and come to my room about nine-thirty. We want to call Judge Temple before she goes on the bench. Judge Quinn says that the Old Bailey trials usually start at ten."

"Okay, counselor. I'll be there. I think I'll clean up and have some room service breakfast. I need some grease and eggs. I hear the English do a proper breakfast complete with fried toast."

Vicky shook her head and said, "I have a feeling your diet is going to have a setback over here."

Sharkey mugged a smile and retorted, "What diet? See you in your room at nine-thirty."

An hour later, after a shower and a change to fresh clothes, Vicky dialed the telephone number of the main operator of the Old Bailey. Sharkey was slumped in a chair across the room; he gave her a smile and a nod of encouragement.

After explaining to the operator that she was an attorney from the United States Department of Justice, Vicky was switched through to a telephone in the chambers of Justice Morgana Temple, the Common Sergeant of London—the number two ranking judge of the court.

Soon Vicky heard a crisp, confident female voice on the line.

"Judge Temple, here."

"Your Honor. My name is Victoria Hauser. I'm an American

prosecutor temporarily assigned to the United States Senate as an investigator. I wonder if I could have a word with you in person sometime today. I just flew in from Washington this morning and urgently need to ask you a few questions. I am sorry I couldn't call in advance."

There was a long pause—dead silence.

Vicky felt she had to play the only card she had. "My boss, the Senate Counsel, is Judge Tim Quinn. He's a friend of your chief judge, the Recorder of London. Perhaps Judge Quinn should call Sir Brian Fairmont and ask for your cooperation in our official investigation?"

Judge Temple replied quickly and in an angry tone. "There's no need to bother Sir Brian. He's terribly busy. I'll meet with you, but—"

After a hesitation of a few seconds, Judge Temple continued with a softer, more vulnerable voice. This voice had fear in it. "What sorts of questions?"

Vicky wanted to spare the judge any suspense so she went right to the point. "They pertain to your meeting with the American Justice Oscar Moorman some years ago at a legal conference here in London."

❖ 52 ❖

VICKY GAVE SHARKEY A THUMBS-UP SIGN. SHE WAS not one to let a partner wonder about an important fact any longer than necessary. Sharkey had often told her over the years they worked criminal cases that she was the first prosecutor . . . or woman . . . who let him know where he stood all the time. Most prosecutors had a sense of superiority over their investigators and liked to keep them out of the loop most of the time. Vicky wasn't like that. Not with Bill.

She made an effort to treat him like an equal partner on the prosecution team.

"Well, Judge Temple agreed to see us. . . . I mean, she agreed to see me . . . just me . . . alone . . . at noon today. I'm to meet her at the main public entrance to the Old Bailey. For your information, we caught some luck. Judge Temple is not in trial today. She will be in her chambers all day and has a dinner function tonight. Some formal function at the Guildhall for the visiting Secretary of Justice from Hong Kong. However, she's in what she called a judge's reading period—looking over court motions and preparing for her next trial, ironically a rape trial, which starts on Thursday morning."

"Well, that's something. The Senate confirmation starts in two days. Maybe we can get her to give us her story today," Sharkey observed thoughtfully. "How did she sound?" he added.

"Surprised, but not stunned. Also suspicious and angry at one point. She didn't like my name-dropping of Sir Brian. Apparently, she was keenly aware of the English blog and several tabloid stories. She mentioned that there was some coverage in the British press over the weekend about the 'date rape' allegation and Justice Moorman. This is just a guess, but it seemed to me that my direct question about her and Moorman hit her hard—probably it was the first indication that anybody connected her to the story. You know the English tabloids go on about a mystery woman who could torpedo Moorman's hearing . . . and possible set up a rape charge over here in England. Very juicy stuff. . . . I felt very clearly that she's very uncomfortable about being dragged into this mess . . . maybe even afraid."

Sharkey was listening intently and thoughtfully rubbed his face. "So she wants to meet on her turf . . . at her Court. Well, that sounds reasonable, but it's a big problem for me to get a secret tape recording of her when you two girls talk."

Vicky ignored the "girls" term—Sharkey was old-school FBI and would never be trained on the "PC" aspect of gender. However, Vicky was puzzled about the taping of the upcoming interview with Judge Temple. "Why are you worried about the taping?"

"Well, you don't think she is going to give you permission to tape-record her statement about Moorman, do you?" Sharkey asked.

Vicky frowned and replied, "Probably not. By her tone, I'm sure she will be very guarded about speaking to me about Moorman. Moreover, her upcoming possible judicial promotion will make her very reluctant to get dragged into a sex scandal."

"Precisely. So we can forget about a voluntary taping of your interview. So all that's left is a secret taping possibility. But now that's probably off the table." Sharkey then added, "It's really a shame you'll be meeting at the court because I had some cool toys for you from the FBI lab." With a flourish, Sharkey pulled out of his suit pocket two large chunky gold-plated earrings and a small slender box.

"Latest FBI gadget in miniature transmitters! These earrings will transmit to this small micro–tape recorder that I can slip into your purse lining. I thought we could record Judge Temple without her knowledge with this little system . . . However, since you are meeting her at the Old Bailey, these probably won't work. These earrings are wireless to a small box receiver you must put into your purse or wear. It's the size of a pack of cigarettes—too big to escape going through an X-ray machine. You can be sure the Old Bailey will certainly be on full alert with the latest bombing. You'll never be able to go through the Bailey's sophisticated court security system with this. It will pick up the microchips in the earrings and in the box receiver even if the device is turned off. Too bad. . . . But I can give you Plan B—the straightforward approach. Don't worry, I might have a Plan C."

"What's Plan C?"

"Better you don't know. It might make you nervous when you're talking with Judge Temple. Well, here's Plan B—the direct approach, Counselor. As we've been discussing, it will probably fail, but we need to try."

Sharkey paused and reached into a canvas bag next to his chair and pulled out a small machine.

In a flat voice, Sharkey explained, "Here's Plan B—a standard compact tape recorder. Just openly bring it into the court with you in your purse and ask her if you can tape her statement. All she can say is 'no.'"

Vicky made a frown while shaking her head and dryly observed, "The 'no' word is probably what got Moorman into this whole mess in the first place."

❖ 53 ❖

VICKY HAUSER AND BILL SHARKEY LEFT THE MARRIOTT hotel at 11:30 A.M. for the taxi ride across town to the Old Bailey, the Central Criminal Court of England.

As their black cab left the front entrance of the hotel, the faded blue Jag driven by Reggie Whiteside pulled out from the curb and followed from a safe distance.

Victor Dagnar and Reggie said little as they watched the taxi expertly weave through the traffic in an eastward direction. As usual, the weekday traffic was very heavy in this central part of London.

During the ride, Dagnar took out a silver flask and took several deep pulls.

"A little hair of the dog to get me started," Dagnar announced to Reggie.

The bent Scotland Yard man said nothing; he was intent on keeping close to the speeding taxi several cars in front of them.

Dagnar broke the silence first, "If we lose them, will you be able to discreetly use police assets to get the destination of the cab?"

"Bloody right, no problem. If I have to, I'll just call Met Police Central Operations and they can contact the taxi company. As you can see, that cab has a radio antenna. And I've got the license number. All the London taxicabs have to record the drop points. But don't worry, Mr. Dagnar, I won't lose them."

Reggie waited a beat and then added a treat for his off-the-book employer. "Besides, I think I know where they are headed. The lady lawyer—Ms. Hauser made one call this morning—a four-minute call to the Central Criminal Court—the Old Bailey. The cab is headed dead-on the exact crosstown way I would use to get there. Traveling to the Bailey like a bloody judicial homing pigeon, it is. Yes, the Old Bailey it is. Aye, that's my guess, Mate. I'd put five quid on it."

Dagnar digested this new information and then asked the obvious. "How did you know about the call?"

This apparently was where Reggie wanted to show off. "Right. Well, you knew I was eight years in counterintelligence before I got this posh assignment as Parliament liaison, didn't you?"

Get to the fucking answer, you pompous English asshole!

"While you was waiting outside the hotel in me car. Remember I went inside . . . and myself was scoping out the lobby. Well, I flashed my ID to the hotel operator and chatted her up. She gave me the number of the Old Bailey, she did, as the only outside call made from the rooms for the Hauser lady. The bloke Sharkey only called room service. Well, I say that operator bird has true respect for the law. Anyway, it's the Old Bailey that they're going to."

Dagnar hid his annoyance at Reggie's uneducated cockney English, and nodded in fake approval, adding, "Good job, Reggie. You're really something."

That is why we pay you, dickhead—to be a crooked cop and find out things like that.

Then Dagnar glanced over at the policeman to see if his false compliment had registered. It obviously had—Reggie had a big grin on his face.

Dagnar briefly wondered whether the reason for his smile was the rare compliment Dagnar just paid him or whether it was the fifty-thousand-euro bonus he had earlier promised Reggie for this job. Money was a big motivator for the Scotland Yard man.

Actually I don't really care what makes Reggie do his thing as long as we succeed.

"Taxi's making a left onto High Holborn Street, still headed east—like I said, just the route I'd take to the Bailey. It's only four blocks away," said the still smiling detective inspector.

When the taxi turned onto Old Bailey Street, the Jag followed a full twenty yards behind and slowed down, almost immediately pulling to the curb and into the small parking lot of the Rochester House, a commercial building opposite the main entrance of the Old Bailey. Reggie quickly got out his New Scotland Yard ID sign and slapped it on the dash to allow the car to park in such a high-security zone. They were now in an excellent position with a clear view of the entrance. They could clearly observe that a hundred feet down the street the taxi was stopped just past the main public entrance of the Central Criminal Court (CCC) of London, known worldwide as the Old Bailey.

Dagnar and Reggie Whiteside intently stared through the windshield of the Jaguar and saw a small cover drama going on down the street with the stopped taxi.

Reggie and Dagnar first saw Sharkey exit the black cab and walk directly up to the glassed-in bulletin board on the outside wall of the courthouse, staring unconvincingly at the public notice board with the listing of the cases to be heard at the Bailey that day. The board also showed the assigned courtroom and the judge for that day's listed cases. It was a good place to spend time without raising suspicion. There were small clusters of people also looking over the daily schedule of the many courtrooms inside the Old Bailey.

Immediately after Sharkey took his place staring at the bulletin board, Vicky got out of the cab, turned left, and quickly walked to the public entrance of the courthouse. Vicky was carrying an open umbrella from the hotel even though it wasn't raining—an obvious signal marking her to whoever was meeting her.

Vicky only waited for less than a minute outside the entrance when an attractive lady, looking perhaps in her early forties, emerged from the Old Bailey building and shook her hand in a hasty greeting.

"Bloody hell!" shouted Reggie. "The Yank lady is meeting Judge Morgana Temple, one of the top Bailey judges! So she's the mystery woman you've been talking about—the mysterious English bird your black American judge shagged over here in London according to the rumors in the tabloids."

Dagnar was controlled and focused as he stared at the two women now entering the Old Bailey Courthouse. "Reggie, do you have your Scotland Yard wireless laptop here in the car?"

When Reggie looked at Dagnar with a puzzled look, Dagnar repeated, "Your Parliament laptop, you have it now, don't you? Well, get on it. I want to know the background of this lady judge . . . and where she lives. You can discreetly do that without leaving any computer tracks at New Scotland Yard Headquarters or at Parliament, can't you?"

"Yes, bloody right, Mr. Dagnar. My Parliament job gives me untraceable access in and out of the Scotland Yard central computer system. It contains the personnel records of all high-ranking government officials. No traces anywhere. The MPs are always doing research on this bloke or that one and cleverly insisted the Scotland Yard system erase our MP tracking records as soon as I, an authorized user designated by Parliament, pull out of the system. I must say our bloody legislators are a little craftier that your Yank congressmen and senators, who are always getting their tits and dicks caught in the keyboards of their e-mails and computers with their dealings with bloody lobbyists."

Reggie was in full swing as he typed into his wireless laptop.

"Here's a nice piece of information for you, Gov," added Reggie. "She's going to be out to dinner tonight. A right fancy one at the Guildhall, where she will be one of the two official hosts for a foreign big shot—the Secretary of Justice from Hong Kong. As a co-host judge, she'll most likely be there at least until ten tonight. Also, she lives at Number 12 Burlington Square, right nice place in central London. Oh, and there's an IRA trial going on today."

"Good, good stuff," said Dagnar. "Keep getting more data on her.

While you're pulling up everything on Judge Temple, I'll keep an eye on the entrance to see how long Vicky Hauser visits with Temple."

As Victor Dagnar stared at the main door of the Old Bailey, his quick mind was already planning the chess moves he needed to make to satisfy the CEO of Carpa's orders.

Above the idling Jag was the steep slate roof of the Old Bailey Courthouse with its famous ten-foot-high bright gold statue of Lady Justice with a scale in one hand and a sword in the other. The only difference between the Lady Justice statues commonly seen in American courthouses and the well-known statue on top of the Old Bailey was that the English one had no blindfold on her eyes. And rumor had it that the scales she held were tilted—one scale was just over one foot lower than the other. An interesting piece of trivia Reggie prattled on about to Dagnar while he pounded on his laptop and Dagnar continued to stare at the entrance. Dagnar wasn't interested in the off-balance of the scales. He knew justice wasn't always fair anywhere in the courts of the world. He was more interested in the sword Lady Justice held. The sword she held was more threatening to Dagnar.

Dagnar was increasingly uncomfortable sitting in the car across from the most famous court in England. He knew England was full of eyes. There were public closed-circuit cameras, called CCTV cameras, all over England, especially in London—all monitored 24/7 by experienced police specialists and probably sophisticated facial recognition software. One newspaper reported that there was one public CCTV camera for each fourteen U.K. citizens. The same news story said that a survey showed that a typical Londoner was reported to be caught on CCTV over three hundred times a day. The police in London were closely watching all high-security sites, especially now, two days after the Oxford Street suicide terrorist bombing.

Dagnar knew he was in a danger zone as he stared at the entrance. He instinctively pulled his blue baseball cap lower over his eyes.

· 54 ·

THE FROSTY UNFRIENDLY GREETING JUDGE TEMPLE gave Vicky outside the Old Bailey was matched by the rough treatment of the court security personnel inside the entrance of the court.

Vicky was treated in a cold, efficient manner by the female security officer who pawed thoroughly through her purse, removing the obvious tape recorder Bill Sharkey had given her.

In a sharp voice, Vicky was lectured by the female guard. "No cameras or tape recording devices of any kind are allowed in the Central Criminal Court. This tape recorder will be returned to you after your visit. Here's your claim check." The officer tonelessly recited the stock instruction, handing Vicky a small ticket as she put the purse on the conveyer belt of a large elaborate X-ray machine and pushed the start button of the machine. Vicky's purse quickly disappeared from sight.

"Now please remove all metal objects and your shoes and step into the personal detector," ordered the security officer.

Vicky removed all her metal accessories and her cell phone, placing them on a plastic tray by the X-ray machine, before walking into a large metal detector, which also had a sniffing device that puffed air from all sides as Vicky stood in the middle of the huge machine with her feet on shoe outlines painted in the plastic floor. There were no alarms that went off. Nevertheless, after she was motioned out of the machine, Vicky was also checked by an electronic wand and physically patted down by the female officer.

Looks like I'm getting the "full monty."

As Vicky was going through the most extensive security inspection she ever had—including on an official visit to the White House during a code orange security alert—Judge Temple was watching the ordeal from the far lobby of the court entrance. She had no expression on her face as she watched the thorough search of Vicky. To Vicky, Temple seemed to be measuring her as an adversary . . . not an ally. It was not a friendly face on the judge. Vicky was sure of that.

The first few questions Vicky had prepared for the Judge would reveal Temple's "friend or foe" attitude.

Minus the confiscated tape recorder, Vicky walked over to Judge Temple when the security inspection was completed, her high heels clacking on the speckled well-worn marble floor of the old building.

"Your people do a very complete search," remarked Vicky with a face and a voice tone that showed irritation.

"They have to be . . . especially for an American lawyer who is on the team for a barrister who represents the IRA terrorist. You must know we have a very well-publicized IRA terrorist trial in session right now. Our security personnel can't be too careful in that situation, now can they?" remarked Judge Temple matter-of-factly.

Vicky's eyes glared. "Is that what you told them? That I represent an IRA terrorist? Is that what triggered that special detailed search?" Vicky's face flashed red with anger as she asked. Vicky had noticed that she was the only one of the visitors getting a very full search.

"Well . . . yes, you might say I mentioned it to them. I wanted you to be thoroughly checked out. Now, what were you going to do with the tape recorder they found? Do you think I'd allow you to tape me—perhaps telling sex stories involving Justice Moorman? Stories that would be leaked to the U.S. media by your slimy politicians?"

Vicky was stunned by the hostile attitude of Judge Temple and was speechless.

Without waiting for a reply, Judge Temple asked to see Vicky's

United States Department of Justice credentials. Satisfied with the authenticity of Vicky's ID, Temple said, "Follow me. We're going to a pub." Then she turned and walked briskly toward the security exit of the court with Vicky trying to catch up.

And the two women left the Old Bailey.

✧ 55 ✧

"CHRIST, THE TWO BITCHES ARE LEAVING ALREADY," yelled Dagnar at Reggie Whiteside, who had his head buried in his laptop and was scribbling notes on a small pocket notebook.

Reggie looked up and took in the scene. "Bloody hell!"

Dagnar ordered him out of the car and to follow the women.

"Impossible! Judge Temple will recognize me in a London minute. I'm one of the escorts for the Members of Parliament who regularly visit the Old Bailey for lunches and receptions. You've got to do it—and bloody quickly. We'll lose visual at the end of the street."

"Fuck!" Dagnar cursed and got out, certain that he was being observed by the damn CCTV cameras ringing the Old Bailey; so he pulled the baseball cap he had been wearing farther down over his face.

After he took a few steps, he turned and shouted back to Reggie, "Stay with the goddamn car and keep your cell phone clear. I'll call you when I need you!" With that angry burst at Reggie, Dagnar quickly accelerated his walk, knowing his limp was a distinctive trait for the watching cameras.

As Dagnar walked in pursuit of the two females, he noticed that the FBI Special Agent accompanying Vicky Hauser, Bill Sharkey, was still in his "overwatch" position pretending to be studying the glassed-in shadow box of the court's daily calendar on the wall of the courthouse. Dagnar noticed there was no sign of recognition from Vicky to Sharkey as she and Judge Temple passed him. However, as soon as the two women went by him, Sharkey turned away from the bulletin board and started to follow Vicky Hauser and Judge Temple at a distance of fifteen yards. As he started to move, Dagnar was ten yards behind him and closing.

The strange parade marching down Old Bailey Street didn't last long, because near the end of the street, Vicky Hauser and Judge Temple abruptly turned into the doorway of an Irish pub. Sharkey followed the two ladies into the pub.

Dagnar thought that the pub was an odd place for an English judge to frequent when there was an IRA trial in progress right down the street at the Bailey.

And a damn strange place to conduct a U.S. Senate investigation!

AS JUDGE TEMPLE CAME INTO THE PUB, SHE IMMEDI-ately headed for a small two-seat table under the television in the rear of the main bar area. She leaned over to Vicky and whispered, "An Irish pub is a place I most likely won't run into my colleagues from the bench." She motioned with her head back to the Bailey, then continued, "at least not today, with an IRA trial in progress. Don't take it personally, Ms. Hauser, but the last thing I need is to be seen with an American Senate investigator right now with that Justice Moorman story floating around in the newspapers and in the blogs over here.

By the way, the reason we are not meeting in my chambers at the Bailey is that we judges have such small rooms—each right next to the other—that privacy is a problem, especially in sensitive matters. My fellow judges would be curious about who you were. And I don't like to lie."

Vicky said, "I understand," as they took seats opposite each other over the tiny round table. The television was blaring overhead with a rugby game.

Vicky looked up at the TV and had to raise her voice, "Good choice of tables. The telly, as you call it over here, is a good safeguard from someone overhearing our conversation. You must have been a sharp prosecutor before you joined the bench—good tradecraft!"

Judge Temple smiled slightly for the first time since Vicky met her. The compliment about picking a safe place to have a covert conversation even in a public place apparently scored. Any prosecutor worth her salt picks up good police—or criminal—tricks.

"Yes, I learned a few things prosecuting cases at the Bailey. By the way, the loud rugby game overhead is a repeat of yesterday's game—the Sunday game in Dublin—Ireland playing the All Blacks from New Zealand. Not to spoil it for you, but I read in this morning's paper that Ireland lost. Odd people—the Irish. They seem to like to replay their defeats and wallow in their sadness. No wonder we Brits never understood them."

So she is human after all. I may have a chance to get her to open up to me. Especially with the opening statement to her that I planned.

Vicky looked around and noticed that the pub was filling up with the lunch crowd. Vicky also saw Sharkey enter the pub and take a table across the room—in a direct line of sight to the table where the two women sat.

A waiter appeared at their side and Judge Temple ordered. "We don't have much time. We'll just have tea." Temple looked at Vicky and offered the question, "Unless you want something to eat?"

Vicky shook her head. "No. Just plain tea for me will be just fine."

When the waiter left, Temple explained, "I said I'll give you some time . . . but just a little. I really don't want to get involved with this Moorman thing."

With the loud TV above them, Vicky studied Judge Temple and was about to deliver her opening statement to her. On the long airplane ride over to England, she had thought a long time about how she would get the judge to open up about what had happened that evening with Moorman. Rape victims make a decision early on to report the crime. After that moment of decision, rape victims rarely go public—this would be especially true in this situation, years after and with an eager press ready to smear all parties.

Once Vicky had decided about the approach she would take with Judge Temple, she shared it with no one—not with Sharkey, and she would never want Tim to know either. It was one of her special dark private things, a secret from her past—something she'd told nobody before. There was no need to reveal a very low point of her life to anyone. That is—until now.

Before she started to talk to Judge Temple with her planned opening, Vicky glanced across the room and saw that Bill, sitting at a table in the front of the barroom, had a pint of beer before him and had opened a large hardcover book—one of those big large-print ones. The cover was clear and familiar—*The Da Vinci Code*. Bill also had small earphones from an iPod in his ears and was fiddling with the controls of the device. Odd behavior for a man who was supposed to be helping her. She had expected him to try to sit closer—maybe the next table—to try to overhear the conversation she was about to initiate. It would be good if Sharkey could corroborate what Judge Temple might say.

Christ, what is Bill Sharkey doing? Reading a book and listening to music while having a beer? Why doesn't he move closer so he can possibly tape this or at least attempt to overhear it? That is, if he could over this loud TV.

Nevertheless the strange scene with Bill didn't distract Vicky. It was a special trait of Vicky's—when she had a task before her, she was all focus.

The waiter brought the tea and Judge Temple pulled out a small pillbox from her purse and took a pill, using the tea to swallow it.

"This is a very stressful time for me. I'm prone to migraines. My doctor gave me something for them."

Vicky didn't know what to say. It was obvious that Judge Temple was letting her guard down a little, confessing that intimate detail.

Christ, if that pill is for stress, give me two, Judge, thought Vicky.

Without thinking about it, Vicky adjusted her hair on the right side of her face to make sure it was forward enough to hide the scars left from the acid attack—it was a recent habit triggered by stress. What Vicky was about to do was going to be tough—to make a reluctant witness talk and tell the truth. Two very different and difficult things for a prosecutor to do.

Vicky glanced again briefly at Sharkey, then leaned forward toward Judge Temple, and began her attempt to get the Judge's story.

"Judge, Justice Moorman gave us your name. He thinks he *may* have raped you. He apparently doesn't remember because of drinking too much that night five years ago at the legal conference. That's why I'm here."

Vicky could see the shock on Judge Morgana Temple's face. Temple's mouth fell open and she took in a shallow breath of air.

I've got her attention. Now is the time to get her to talk about it.

Vicky continued, but in a soft tone, speaking only loud enough to be heard over the TV overhead.

"As I said on the phone, I work for the Senate Committee investigating him for his confirmation. I need to know about that night— about you and Justice Moorman. But before I ask you about Moorman, I want to tell you something. As a woman, I know it is hard to share what happened if you are forced to have sex. Some stats I've seen in America indicate that almost sixty percent of the rapes in America go unreported. I suspect that the number is actually higher. At least that's what I think. And I want you to know that I have personal knowledge about rape. I was raped my first year in law school by one of my law professors at Columbia. And I didn't report it. I was alone in his office discussing a paper I was going to turn in and the next thing I knew he grabbed me from the chair and pushed me onto a sofa. So—." Then Vicky stopped dead.

Vicky had no idea she would react this way as she related the fact that she too was raped. Her encounter with the degrading act of rape had been long buried. She was almost experiencing an "out-of-body" moment when she heard her voice crack as she described her own rape and her act of not reporting it—a further shame in her life. She never attended any more classes after that semester yet the professor had given her an "A." The professor had paid off his sexual guilt by sacrificing his academic honor. That assumed he had ever had any of either.

Focus! Damn it. You made the decision to use it—the key to establishing the ultimate bond with a rape victim—to admit that you were both sisters in rape and didn't report it. Why does that so-long-ago thing still paralyze you?

Vicky, during her involuntary pause, saw the expression change on the face of the tough judge. Judge Temple visibly softened. So Vicky plowed ahead with what she had determined to say.

"But that was long ago. I just wanted you to know that I've been there." Vicky stopped again and composed herself.

Damn it. Control yourself—control your feelings. Don't stop now. The connection is made—use it.

However, she was freezing up . . . her mind was being pulled back to the fat ugly professor and what he did to her . . . and the guilt in not reporting it. She felt her eyes begin to tear up. She was determined not to cry, although she felt a strong urge to do just that.

Pull yourself together, girl.

Vicky stopped once more to control her emotions. She closed her eyes and bit her lower lip. The pain helped bring her mind to finishing her talk with Judge Temple.

Then Vicky recovered and continued in a voice that was still cracking with emotion. "Judge, as I explained on the phone, I've been detailed as an investigator by the American Senate to determine if you were raped by Justice Oscar Moorman. It is very important to know what happened that night with you and Moorman. Moorman may be the next Chief Justice of the United States. If he raped you, I . . . all the American people must know."

There she was back in the groove. She was the interrogating prosecutor—seeking the truth from a crucial witness.

The time it took Vicky to say those opening remarks couldn't have lasted for more than one minute. But it was a powerful minute that obviously registered strongly with Judge Temple.

When Vicky finished, Temple pulled back from Vicky and studied her for a short time. Suddenly she leaned in, reached over the table, put both her hands on Vicky's, and squeezed them.

Then the English Judge started to talk. She kept one of her hands over her mouth. Vicky wondered whether it was a habit or whether she was doing it to defeat any lip reader who might be watching. Maybe one of the big tabloids had figured out that Judge Temple was the mystery woman in the alleged Moorman affair. If that was the case, a lip reader hired by a reporter following Temple was not out of the question.

Nevertheless, the witness was telling her story. Vicky's gamble of telling her secret maybe was the key to unlock Temple's vault, but Vicky had paid the price by reliving that terrible time of violence long ago.

57

OUTSIDE THE PUB, DAGNAR LOOKED THROUGH THE large front window. He observed Vicky Hauser and Judge Temple together at a back table. In addition he saw the other investigator, the FBI agent, sitting at a separate table toward the front of the pub.

Dagnar debated whether he should enter the pub. In light of what he was thinking of doing to Judge Temple later, he made his mind up not to risk being seen by Temple in the small pub. He was too distinctive-looking a man. People tended to remember him. He stood out in a crowd—one of his shortcomings that his brilliant mind couldn't conquer. His short twisted body with its sharp hawk nose and distinctive face didn't blend well, and he knew it.

Dagnar didn't have long to wait in the cold outside the pub where he was playing a role—he occasionally looked at his wristwatch and pretended to be waiting for a lunch partner. Less than ten minutes later, Judge Temple emerged from the pub and walked briskly back up the street to the Old Bailey. Dagnar followed from a safe distance to ensure that the Old Bailey courthouse was her destination.

It was.

Dagnar smiled.

Things are looking good. There's no way that Judge Temple was co-operating with these two Senate investigators. Way too short a time for a proper interview. I'm sure Judge Temple didn't tell that prosecutor bitch Hauser anything. Temple just gave her the brush-off. This is a good development. Temple's not talking! Makes sense for a woman who didn't report the rape years ago. Why would she now—a respected judge—want to be pulled into a media sex circus in America? God, I love apathy—people who won't get involved! Well, my boss, Fay, will be pleased to hear this.

Dagnar called Reggie Whiteside on his cell. "Meeting's over. I'm halfway down the street from the Old Bailey. Come pick me up. We've work to do."

While he was waiting for Reggie and the Jag, Dagnar thumbed out a Blackberry message to Don Fay, Carpa's CEO. The message was short and cryptic, but to the point. Fay had said he wanted to know everything that was happening in London. The text message sent to Fay was:

"Identified problem. She's apparently not giving her story to the two visitors. Situation appears contained for now. I expect to have final resolution later tonight."

Dagnar was smiling as he got into Whiteside's Jag. To him, it was a win-win situation for Carpa—Judge Temple obviously was not talking to the Senate investigators about her date rape, at least for now, and, more important, Dagnar had successfully identified the "date rape" lady of the media—she was no longer a mystery lady. She was now a target.

❖ 58 ❖

JUDGE TEMPLE HAD JUST LEFT. THE PUB NOW WAS crowded with the lunch traffic from the offices in the area. Vicky left some pounds on the table and got up to walk over to Bill Sharkey's table at the front of the pub. She moved slowly and confidently, pursing her lips to prevent a triumphant grin. She felt very good, but she didn't want to show it yet to Sharkey.

Vicky had gotten the details of that night from the lips of Judge Temple. Tim Quinn would be pleased that she had solved the date rape issue so quickly. The road to the confirmation of Moorman was now clear of issues to be resolved. His Senate confirmation hearings were just two days away.

"Well, I got the whole story right from Temple." Vicky paused for effect and then announced, "Moorman's in the clear. No rape! She completely clears Moorman of any rape allegation. And I believe her."

"I know," said the sleepy-eyed Sharkey with a deadpan face.

A surprised Vicky asked, "How could you?"

"I told you the FBI has some magic stuff. I got almost all what you ladies talked about on tape."

Stunned, Vicky said, "What, all of it? Including what I said to Judge Temple at the beginning. . . . What I started with?"

Sharkey's face was somber and he nodded. Then he broke into a wide smile and said, "Everything. I got everything except for your order to the waiter. . . . I didn't get that. It took me time using the frequency controller to skip through the frequencies to negate the ambient noise of that fucking loud rugby game on the TV above you before I got the clear audio of your conversation. By the way, it was either luck or very clever of Temple to pick that table. She made it tough to record the conversation."

Vicky was openmouthed and speechless. Her eyes wide with surprise.

Then Sharkey opened the volume he had been reading from—it wasn't a book. It was hollowed-out and inside was a metal frame with dials, read-out meters, and the plug-in connections for the earbuds— it was a high-quality electronic listening and recording device. Sharkey removed the stiff front cover of the book in the front to show a compact parabolic dish, which Sharkey had obviously aimed at the table where Vicky and Judge Temple were sitting. Sharkey wasn't done with his show. He punched in a button and out popped a small CD disk that he held up and said, "Here's the audio of your conversation with Temple."

"Why didn't you tell me you were going to do this, Bill?"

"Two reasons: One—I thought you knowing it might make your conversation sound like an interview. And more important, two—I thought that if Temple asked whether you were taping the conversation, she would see you were lying. So I thought it would be better if you didn't know about it. No offense, Counselor, but you don't lie convincingly. By the way, if you hadn't come out of the Old Bailey with Temple, I was going to try to get in on my FBI badge and attempt to record you and Temple wherever I could find you inside the building. That definitely would have been a long shot. My little bag of audio equipment might not have made it past the lobby even with my FBI badge and inherent personal charm. So I'm glad you gals decided to talk in a public place outside the Bailey."

Vicky was anxious to hear what the tape recorder had captured, but she had a nagging problem. "Bill, this is tough to say, but I really don't want Tim—I mean Judge Quinn—and the entire Senate to hear details of my rape at Columbia. It was long ago and it is . . . private. I just used it to try to get Temple to talk about her own situation."

Sharkey studied the face of the woman he'd worked with for over seven years. He could see the obvious discomfort of having the Columbia rape scene available as a public document in the hands of a leaky Senate committee. He hesitated a bit, then exhaled, and said, "Counselor, my beer seems to be pretty low. Must be a crack in the bottom of the glass. Why don't you go over to the bar and get me another pint of Harp in a good glass?"

Sharkey added with a tight smile, "And take your time. I'm going to adjust the recording a bit—to get the audio a little better."

When Vicky came back five minutes later with a pint of beer and a glass of red wine for herself, Sharkey announced, "Gee, while I was fine-tuning the CD, I seem to have erased the first part of the conversation—the part about you saying something about you and Columbia. Well, no matter—all that was relevant was what Judge Temple said about her night with Justice Moorman."

Vicky's grin was wide. She impulsively reached over the small table to give Sharkey a kiss on his cheek and whispered as she did it, "You're something else."

Sharkey laughed and said, "Watch out or I'll report you for sexual harassment! I'm happily married to the Bureau."

Then he got out an extra set of earbuds and said, "Why don't we listen to the recording of what Temple said before we call Judge Quinn with the good news?"

✦ 59 ✦

THERE IN THE BUSTLE OF THE NOONDAY LUNCH RUSH
of the crowded Irish pub, Vicky inserted the earbuds Sharkey offered
her. Sharkey had a spare set for himself. He plugged in the wires to
his clever FBI toy—the book/recording device—and fiddled with the
volume controls until Vicky heard the crystal clear voice of Judge
Morgana Temple:

> *Well, let me tell you about my night with Justice Oscar Moorman.
> It was quite a night. Often I think back on it and wonder if I did
> the right thing that night—and, more important, the following
> morning.*
>
> *First, let me explain that I was single—and still am. And Oscar
> was then a bachelor—a very eligible and good-looking man. Well . . .
> Oscar and I spent the first two days at the conference almost con-
> stantly together—absolutely delightful times. We were on the same
> panel during the entire three-day conference. He was funny, atten-
> tive to me, and very earthy. Not at all stuffy or stiff like so many
> judges, here and in America. He had the most wondrous deep laugh
> and was very witty. I liked him from the very first time he made me
> laugh—which was about two minutes from the moment I met him.*
>
> *The main thing—there was a reception at Gray's Inn of Court
> on the evening of that second day. Oscar and I had perhaps too
> much wine at the reception. I invited him back to my flat at the end
> of the reception. I instinctively knew it wouldn't do to be seen leav-
> ing with him, so we decided to take separate cabs. We were to have a*

nightcap together—and I thought it would be nice for him to spend the night with me. I guess I really did communicate that message of a drink and sleeping with him clearly to him before we left to get separate cabs. Mind you, he was a little drunk, but seemed very willing at the suggestion—yes, very willing.

However, when I got into the brisk cool air of the night to catch a taxi, I sobered up quite a bit and realized that bedding down a sitting U.S. Supreme Court Justice at this particular time in my life was a very, very bad idea. You see, I had just been selected as a circuit judge. It was all very hush-hush—the public announcement of the Queen's appointment of me to the bench was two weeks away. Only the Lord Chancellor and a very few people in Her Majesty's Court Service knew that I had been selected to become a judge. I realized that if I was seen in a current relationship with such a high judicial official from America . . . well, my appointment might be seen as attained less on merit that on connections with a Justice of England's favorite ally. Yes—it was during the taxi ride that I decided on a plan to sabotage any sexual affair.

To this day, I am quite ashamed of misleading Oscar both in proposing the trip to my flat and what I later did there.

I was the ultimate tease in the little drama I concocted for the liaison at my flat.

Well, enough for my judgment of myself—back to the story. At that time, while I was living on a Treasury Counsel's salary, I had a cozy, but very small flat in Knightsbridge near Harrods. Oscar and I arrived within a few minutes of each other. I let him into my home.

My flat was really just a small studio and the bed was a prominent piece of furniture. Oscar Moorman, a little unsteady on his feet already, headed directly to my bed and plopped down. I pulled up a chair opposite him and then went into the kitchenette to prepare our nightcaps—vodka for him and . . . water for me.

After several rounds of drinks—Oscar, poor dear, tried to be manly and keep up with my quickly downing tap water with his

drinking of one-hundred-proof Russian vodka. The contest of match-
ing nightcaps didn't last long. Justice Moorman's eyes started to roll
back in his head. Then I came over and started to kiss him. He revived
briefly with the physical contact and gamely started to unzip my
dress. However, soon he fell back on my bed—completely passed out.

The rest of my plan was to undress him—which I did—he was a
beautiful man by the way. Kept himself in good shape even at his
age. After I tucked him in, I actually ironed his shirt and suit, be-
cause I knew our legal panel had an early breakfast the next morn-
ing and I didn't want him to look like he had slept in his clothes.

Well then, the rest of the story is simple. He awoke the next morn-
ing when my alarm went off and I played the "taken advantage of"
bitch. I wanted him to think he had forced himself on me and that I
was very angry that he did—that was my plan—the ultimate in re-
jection for an honest man—a plan that would not only discourage
him from pursuing me, but would make him fear me because of a
"date rape" situation. I played the angry "deflowered" woman so
well that he practically ran out of my flat the next morning—and
until my host committee put him on the plane back to the States
from Heathrow.

So you see, there was no date rape . . . just a little playacting to
discourage a very nice man who came into my life at a very wrong
time.

Within two weeks, I received my appointment and was sworn in
as the first woman judge to sit on the Old Bailey.

I often think of Justice Moorman and my choice at ending a pos-
sible promising relationship with a solid, bright man—fun to be
with—a real man.

Well, I obviously chose career over a man. Maybe I made the
wrong choice. Now I may be appointed as a Justice on the Royal
Court of Appeal . . . and I am still single. As a smart woman like you
can guess, the emergence of even a hint of a sex scandal now would
just about doom my chances at being on the Royal Court of Appeal—
England is still an "old boy and no controversy" institution. especially

in the Lord Chancellor's office, where the judicial appointment deci-
sions are made.

There you have it. The real story—that is what really happened
to Justice Moorman that night so long ago. I am cooperating with
you now to help that nice man through this "date rape" firestorm. . . .
And in the hope that you might be able to close your investigation
once you know the truth. Also, I have the selfish reason that you may
be able to make all this "mystery woman" speculation eventually die
out. The unwanted publicity of me being in this date rape contro-
versy would all but destroy my chance at an appeal court appoint-
ment. Thus, I very well can assure you that I will not be going public
with a breath of this—I won't be telling anyone else about Justice
Moorman or that visit to my flat . . . and furthermore, if asked about
our little chat now I will absolutely deny speaking to you about Jus-
tice Moorman.

Good-bye, Ms. Hauser, and good luck to you.

Vicky heard her own voice clearly and remembered she had asked
Judge Temple a last question as Temple got up to leave the table.

Judge, I have to ask. One question: Is there any chance that Moor-
man might have been with another woman during his visit to En-
gland for the conference?

Vicky smiled as the audio continued.

Good heavens, no! In my view, there was absolutely no possible op-
portunity for Moorman to have a liaison with another woman. The
poor man's schedule was punishingly full—no free time at all, except
for the night he spent with me after the early ending of the Gray's Inn
reception. And I would very well know since I was on the Moorman
host committee of three barristers. We were practically glued to him
from his arrival at Heathrow until his departure from the U.K. The
conference was on a very tight schedule—starting early and working

late. The night I spent with Moorman would have been the only op-portunity for him to "get lucky"—as you Americans say. And as I have strongly assured you . . . he bloody wasn't.

After the audio ended, Vicky asked Bill Sharkey, "What do you think? Does this do it? Can we end this investigation?"

Sharkey's head went up and down quickly. "It does it for me. I was watching Judge Temple closely for 'Deception Detection' body signals during her talk with you. You know I teach 'Deception Detection' at the FBI Academy. Well, the judge passed with flying colors—she dis-played all the signals of a person telling the truth—no deception. She was telling the truth as far as I'm concerned. I'd say we're finished here. Good job on the interview."

"Thanks, Bill. Okay, let's call Judge Quinn and give him the good news. No date rape . . . not even any sex. Bill, it's good that you got that audio of the conversation. However, I'll recommend to Judge Quinn that we keep that CD and Judge Temple's name out of the re-port. Let's go outside to make the call, Bill. There may be someone in here with a listening toy similar to yours."

Bill Sharkey replied, "Nah, no way. I would have spotted any tail on us."

Nevertheless he looked around very closely as they got up to leave the smoky pub. A full 360-degree observation. He was a true FBI pro—never underestimate the opposition.

60

IT WAS EARLY MONDAY MORNING, DECEMBER 15, IN Washington, D.C. Justice Moorman naturally was completely unaware of all the London events—Dagnar's shadowing of the two Senate investigators, the Vicky Hauser and Judge Morgana Temple interview in the Irish pub, and the surreptitious recording of Judge Temple's description of her night with Justice Moorman.

Justice Oscar Moorman was deeply disturbed by two national news stories hitting the media world in America that early Monday morning.

Moorman like many Americans had moved to the Internet to get the news. Newspapers and the evening TV news programs were increasingly losing audiences to the instant news carried almost real time on the Web. Moorman, with his confirmation hearing so close, was constantly checking the news reports on his computer in his Supreme Court chambers.

❖

The first news report was in video form and was very troubling to Moorman on a personal level. It seemed that the reporter was speaking directly to him and accusing him by implication of a crime. Hearing his name being used that way rocked him to his core:

CNN.com—*Breaking News (Internet)—Justice Oscar Moorman under cloud of suspicion on eve of confirmation hearings.*

(*Atlanta, Georgia, Monday, December 15, 2008*) With the first day of his Senate confirmation hearing to become the first African-American Chief Justice just two days away, Justice Oscar Moorman's sex life has become increasingly the subject of speculation as a result of last week's English blog story of a unresolved rumor involving a possible date rape by Moorman in England some five years ago. Specifically, there was an allegation that Justice Moorman forced a female English barrister to have sex after a night of drinking. The story contained no details supporting the charge except for the vague accusation that the alleged incident of sexual misconduct occurred during a legal conference in London some years ago.

News archives and Moorman's financial disclosure report filed in 2004 have confirmed that Justice Moorman was in fact in London during the summer of 2004 attending a legal education symposium for several days at Gray's Inn, one of the four Inns of Court that frequently sponsor educational training involving bench and bar. In an interview with the chair of the conference, Lord Justice Neil Boal, Q.C., he dismissed the date rape allegations and stated his belief that there was absolutely no evidence to confirm that Justice Moorman was involved in such misconduct.

Lord Stoneman, Head Bencher at Gray's Inn, has called the allegation, "Pure rubbish! An absolute total invention—perhaps politically and even racially motivated to thwart the elevation of a fine jurist to the Supreme Court. In my view, Justice Moorman conducted himself in the most exemplary manner while he was attending this prestigious annual summer program of education for our students and barristers of Gray's Inn."

Reaction to the story of the popular Supreme Court Justice has focused on the critical element that the story is almost completely devoid of facts. Accordingly legal authorities, community leaders, and law school scholars almost uniformly have been supportive of the well-respected Justice Moorman and point out the danger of attacking public figures with unsubstantiated allegations.

Reverend Tobias Jefferson, a prominent civil rights leader, has termed the preconfirmation attack as racially motivated. "Justice Moorman is a fine judge and would be a great Chief Justice—the first African-American to lead our judiciary. Naturally, there are racial groups in America who would use any means to slander and politically lynch Justice Moorman to prevent him from being appointed as the first black Chief Justice of the Supreme Court. Moorman is a well-respected champion of justice and role model for all African-Americans and there are plenty of hate-filled racists who would stop at nothing to slur this fine judge."

Notwithstanding the paucity of supporting facts and the strong preconfirmation support for the popular jurist, a senior ranking source in the U.S. Senate has confirmed that Judge Timothy Quinn, the Special Counsel of the Senate Judiciary Committee, recently dispatched two members of his staff to London to investigate the troubling rumor. Judge Quinn, a former Federal judge, had declined to comment on this report.

In the view of many, the allegation, even unsupported, remains such a serious one for the Senate Judiciary Committee charged with investigating the possible next Chief Justice, it cannot be ignored. The Senators, in the performance of their duties, should ask critical questions about this issue during the confirmation hearings of Justice Moorman:

Is this English rumor of date rape true?

Most senators contacted for this story failed to comment on the date rape issue. One of Justice Moorman's strongest supporters, Senate Judiciary Committee Chair Senator Irma Powers, stated:

"No victim or any witnesses have come forward with the slightest bit of evidence of any inappropriate behavior by Justice Moorman. Accordingly, until evidence is received, the Committee will treat these unfounded rumors as just that—pure rumors. And as Chair of the Committee, it will be my duty to disallow any questioning that is racially based and has absolutely no foundation. To do otherwise would be unjust and undermine the dignity and the purpose of the hearings. Not only is the impeccable integrity of Justice Moorman at stake but the integrity of the U.S. Senate is at risk as well. I will simply not allow this to be a racial lynching of Justice Oscar Moorman."

Nevertheless, some legal scholars feel that Senator Powers is just echoing the politics of her close alliance to President Ramsey and the Republican party line.

The past histories of confirmations have always been threaded with practical political maneuverings. Therefore, despite the apparent emptiness of the rape assertion at this stage, issues filled with such combustibility of forcible sex and race could enter the fabric of Moorman's hearing and explode at the slightest spark. Perhaps the appearance of a possible mystery victim from England could be that flashpoint. If so, then the resulting explosion from the materialization of such a woman who would put a face and some substance to the rape allegation would be tremendous. And it undoubtedly would derail the confirmation hearing of Justice Moorman and almost certainly destroy his judicial career. The possibility of such an appearance also may well land him in an English prison. The fall from such a height in the judicial world would be unprecedented in modern times.

This is Kim Jaret reporting for CNN News.

How did the reporter for this story know that Quinn sent two investigators to London? Obviously Quinn's reports to the Senate Judiciary Committee members were being leaked to the media. Not a surprising development on the savage political battlefield of Washington.

More troubling to Moorman was the effect that this date rape story was having in Moorman's own home. Naturally Vince Bianco's wife had already called Debby. Even before this story, Debby was drinking more . . . and more. Moorman felt his wife was not handling the present pressure very well at all. He feared the attack on him was sure to get more personal—perhaps identifying him as a possible rapist.

God, what have I done? What have I set in motion? Why didn't I keep my mouth shut about Judge Temple? Well, it's too late. Quinn told me his investigators in London were going to see Judge Morgana Temple today. I know I was drunk that night when I went to her flat. But that doesn't excuse what I may have done to Morgana. But Debby's the immediate problem now. Can she live with any more bad news like this?

❖

The second Internet news story added more unwanted weight to the mental load Moorman was carrying that day:

CNN.com—*Breaking News (Internet)—Financial News Update*

WASHINGTON, D.C., MONDAY, DECEMBER 15, 2008—As the markets opened this morning, there was a report that a major New York City investment company would predict shortly that the Carpa Pharmaceuticals Corporation will lose their patent lawsuit next month in the Supreme Court. The Court loss will undoubtedly result in lower earnings in the coming year for Carpa, the drug giant. According to the analysis done by Soma Investment Company, Carpa's income projections were based in large part on speculation that the Supreme Court would most likely overturn the United States Court of Appeals for the Federal Circuit's shaky decision that denied Carpa almost a three-year extension on its patent rights for the popular drug Varakain, a major pain reliever for arthritis. The Soma Investment analysis took the opposite view and indicated that certain legal experts have predicted a Carpa loss in the Supreme Court case. The report also hinted that Soma's experts were privy to rumors from a source inside the Supreme Court. The bottom line of the analysis was a prediction that the likely loss of the patent exclusivity would result in a potential revenue deficit of at least four billion dollars for Carpa in the world market.

The Director of Public Relations from Carpa's global headquarters in Richmond offered no comment on the projected analysis by the investment company other than saying, "The matter is in litigation and it would be inappropriate to speculate on the outcome of a case pending in the Supreme Court."

The big board on the NYSE in apparent reaction to this news has already seen a significant drop of Carpa's stock from $26.80 to $23.95 as of 12 P.M. (EST).

When Justice Moorman read this second CNN News report and, later, the full online analysis done by the New York investment firm, he was both surprised and concerned.

If he hadn't been in such a troubled mood, he would have been mildly amused while reading the news report on his computer at the Supreme Court because he knew that the statement of the possible outcome in the Court was completely wrong. But he was also shocked at the amount of money involved.

I had no idea that the Carpa patent decision was worth that much.

On the outcome of the Court's decision, he had little doubt.

From casual lunch conversations over the last week, Moorman was certain that at least four of the justices were definitely voting with him—and, therefore, Carpa would surely win the case. With only eight sitting justices, a 5–3 decision would overrule the U.S. Court of Appeals (Federal Circuit) decision and win the case for Carpa. The big drug company would then be legally entitled under the view of Moorman (and of the four justices who had told him that they would join him) to enjoy three more years on its lucrative patent for its popular painkiller and, as it appears from the CNN News report, earn billions more in profits.

Yet the financial report's speculation about the case worried him. Naturally this pending case was very important to Carpa, the largest employer in Virginia and a well-known supporter of Irma Powers, its Senator from Virginia. But in a more sinister vein, he thought back on Senator Powers' seemingly oblique question about the pending Carpa case while she was conducting her interview of him to be nominated as the Chief Justice.

Now that he thought about it, the very fact that the patent question was asked by Senator Powers during that "drive around the Mall" meeting before she committed herself to call the President and ask for his nomination underscored to Moorman the power of the drug giant. It apparently could reach into the U.S. Senate and maybe the White House to influence presidential appointments. The question about his patent position proved to Moorman that Carpa, at a minimum, was wired into Senator Powers' office. Now on the eve of his hearings, Moorman wondered if his present judicial nomination was based on his race or his politics—normal factors he would expect in Washington and political nominations—*or* was it his past patent-friendly legal positions and their impact on the extremely valuable Carpa case in his Court that had led to Senator Powers' unexpectedly strong influence on the president's nomination?

Damn, I'm probably getting the Presidential nomination for the Center Seat because a drug company wanted to make more money. Many times in Washington when clever people scraped and peeled away the glittering crust of Senate politics and Presidential action they found but often couldn't prove the DNA of a green substance beneath—money.

Suddenly Moorman suspected strongly that he was part of a very big game. This appointment wasn't about Moorman and his abilities; it was really about his pro-patent voting record.

The power of Carpa was amazing. If Carpa could get a U.S. President and the Senate to give him the Chief Justice position on the Supreme Court, what else could they do?

Oscar Moorman didn't like being used.

Maybe I should recuse myself from the Carpa case next month? It would be clear to anyone who studies this situation that Powers is known to be a big booster of Carpa—a large corporation in her state—and her support is key to my confirmation. That's an unhealthy connection for me. Moreover, if it ever comes out that the only substantive question she asked me before she endorsed me for the Center Seat was about my pro-patent position. Well, this doesn't look good. It will look like I sold my vote on the Carpa case to get the confirmation.

Moorman knew that a Federal judge can take himself off a case without any reason . . . any reason at all.

And I have a reason—an important one to me. I won't be used or even let the situation look like I've been used to become Chief Justice. . . . Let justice be done to Carpa without my vote!

So when Moorman got to his chambers that morning, the first thing he did was to write out a short memorandum and send a copy to each justice and one for the Clerk of the Court. In the cover note to the Clerk of the Court, he ordered that when the Clerk's Office mails out the notice of recusal to the counsel in the case according to the Court's Rules, the Clerk's Office should also send a courtesy copy of his note to the Special Counsel, Judge Tim Quinn.

I want it known on the record that I will not be sitting on the Carpa case before the Senate votes on my confirmation. Quinn can make sure it is brought to the Senate's attention before the full Senate vote.

Chambers of Justice Oscar D. Moorman

U.S. Supreme Court

One First Street, N.E.

Washington, D. C. 20543

Memorandum for the File

December 15, 2008

Re: *Carpa Pharmaceuticals Corporation v. Logan Drug Enterprises,*
    No. 07- 561

I recuse myself on this case effective immediately.

/s/
Oscar D. Moorman
Justice

Within thirty minutes of receiving the hand-delivered memo of recusal from Moorman, Justice Vincent Bianco walked over to Moorman's chambers.

"Hi, O. I just saw that you recused yourself on the Carpa case.
That's a surprise, since you're the only justice with patent experience.
What's up? Why did you disqualify yourself from a case where we
need you?"

"You don't want to know, buddy. I just thought I should in light
of some things going on."

Bianco asked, "Like what?"

Moorman looked annoyed at the follow-up question and answered in an even tone. "Once when I had just joined the U.S. Court
of Appeals, I received a letter from some young political guy in the
White House gently reminding me that one of the litigants, a corporation, was a heavy contributor to the Republican party. I wasn't going to let the letter affect my judgment, but I showed it to another
judge on the same panel and told her I was going to disqualify myself,
because if I ruled for the corporation and the letter was ever made
public, it would look like I was repaying a favor to the White House
for getting my judgeship. Well, the other judge said I was right and
that she was going to disqualify herself as well, because she had been
appointed by the same President. So two different judges had to be
assigned to sit on that case. . . . Bottom line, Vince, I shouldn't tell
you the reason."

Bianco was persistent and remembered Moorman telling him about
the drive-around interview of Senator Powers before she obviously

pushed President Ramsey to nominate Moorman for the Center Seat. "I bet it has something to do with Powers asking about your pro-patent positions. Was that the reason?"

Moorman stiffened and replied with a tight face, "I'm not telling you, Vince."

Bianco smiled and said, "You just did. By the way, O, did I ever tell you to stay out of poker games."

Bianco shifted off the obviously sensitive subject and stayed to chat about another court case. After a few minutes, he left to return to his own chambers.

As he walked down the gleaming tall white marble corridor to his office, he thought about what to do with the information he had just learned. Recusals were usually not made public until the day of oral argument on a case. Now only the other members of the Court and the Clerk knew that a justice had disqualified himself from a case.

I wonder who I could leak this information to to benefit me.

Bianco concluded that the information about Moorman no longer being a force in the Carpa case was worthless now that President Ramsey had given the nomination to Moorman.

He was wrong. Leaking Moorman's recusal to the public at this time would have greatly weakened Senator Powers' desire to push for Moorman's confirmation and possibly could have saved Judge Temple's life.

❖ 62 ❖

SEATED IN REGGIE'S JAG DOWN THE STREET FROM THE
Old Bailey in London, Dagnar was being quizzed by Reggie, "What
happened? Did Judge Temple give a statement to the investigators?
Where to now, Gov?"

Dagnar ignored the grating cockney voice of Reggie. His quick
mind was racing.

*The woman Justice Moorman raped obviously isn't talking to the
Senate investigators now . . . but she might later. Perhaps after pressure
is applied from someone in the Senate—the Democrats will pull out all
stops to keep President Ramsey from getting such a major lame-duck
appointment. So it came down to Carpa and Dagnar to do a blocking
move. Judge Temple has to die. And die now—quickly, quietly, and accidentally. A death that won't cause any ripples for the Moorman nomination.*

So much to do. With an internal bone-cold attitude, Dagnar's
mind began to plan—a list of priorities and time lines for the im-
pending "accident" of Judge Temple.

"Reggie, first take me to the Dorchester Hotel on Park Lane. I'll
check in, take a shower, and then we'll swing by and take a look at
Temple's house. I'll leave you there to observe when she comes home.
In the meantime, I'll take a cab to Carpa's london headquarters and
rejoin you, later before I visit her at home. Now, before we go, what
data you have found out about Judge Temple?"

"Well, Mr. Dagnar, I have done some research on her schedule
and she has an official dinner tonight. Probably won't be home

before ten tonight. That is, unless she comes home to change before dinner."

Dagnar's mouth fell open.

"Yes, that's right. You mentioned that before. You can tell that from your Scotland Yard computer?"

"Sure, Governor. Our MPs can track all the social functions of the high-ranking officials day-to-day. Important information it is. Who's going where and all."

Dagnar motioned with his hand to Reggie to give him the open laptop that Reggie had used to get the private data on Judge Temple. Dagnar was soon reviewing the private government files on Judge Temple. Details on her financial records and personal data on her life, the security system of her home. Information on Temple was the key to Dagnar's planning. The more, the better.

Having Reggie—a liaison officer with Parliament—being able, without any trace, to tap into the British governmental database listing personal details on Judge Temple was invaluable . . . or at least, well worth the fifty-thousand-euro bonus. Reggie, as irritating as he was, had already justified the offering of the bonus, by allowing Dagnar to bring in his special equipment without any customs officer looking in any bags at Heathrow this morning . . . and now being able to get personal info on Judge Temple. Well, Reggie was a great Carpa asset. Dagnar's recruitment of Reggie a few years ago was paying off big time.

As they drove through the traffic toward the hotel, Dagnar was using the time to make notes in a small leather notebook from the screen information of Reggie's wireless laptop.

Christ, Reggie has found a gold mine of info on Temple—home and vacation home addresses, car registration, her judicial and official social calendar for this week, the latest financial reporting form for Her Majesty's Court Service, which includes her bank account number and the number of her credit card . . . dynamite stuff I can use to plan the "accident."

Dagnar, with a twisted grin on his face, was controlling his glee from

Reggie. And Dagnar was obviously intent in his work copying data from Judge Temple's personnel and court files; however, Reggie, being a gregarious type, couldn't keep himself from talking while he drove.

"Why are you going to see her tonight?" asked the too curious Reggie, who, Dagnar noticed, had an irritating and dangerous habit of speaking without thinking.

He's being paid well to do what I ask without question . . . this fat fucker is starting to become dangerous with his questions. Dangerous for him.

"I . . . I plan to talk to her and perhaps offer her some money to keep quiet about her little sexual romp with Justice Moorman," replied Dagnar in a pleasant even-voiced lie, without showing any resentment about the question . . . and his having to answer it.

Dagnar saw the lie's reaction on Reggie. The Scotland Yard man was not one to conceal his emotions. Dagnar's answer obviously troubled Reggie, whose winkled forehead seemed to signal that he was mulling it over as he drove through the heavy traffic. They were now in Mayfair, still headed west toward Hyde Park, a short distance from the five-star Dorchester Hotel, which was situated on one and a half acres directly opposite the park. It has almost two hundred individually de-signed rooms as well as fifty-three suites. Most of its well-decorated suites had a view of Hyde Park. And Dagnar was in one of the suites on the top floor. Some say the Dorchester occupies one of the most expen-sive pieces of property in the world—and has room rates that reflect it.

As the car turned onto Park Lane within sight of the Dorchester, a comment bubbled out of Reggie's mouth. Although Reggie had clearly bought the lie, he couldn't stop himself from giving advice. "Governor, I'm sure you being a gentleman with high contacts and wide experience in dealing with top-ranking government officials and all—but I really don't think a judge at the Old Bailey would take any money to keep quiet on something like reporting a rape or what-ever. Not bloody likely in my view. Those twelve or so Bailey judges are really special—the cream of the crop, so they say. No, sir, I don't think they would take any hush money. I believe that on something important, Judge Temple won't be silenced about this date rape that's been in the papers. I just don't think it's a good idea to offer money to a judge like Temple . . . not a good idea at all."

"Everybody has a price," snorted Dagnar.

Or I can take her life, he added silently.

FROM THE TEN-STORY GLASS AND STEEL MODERN Carpa building on the Southern bank of the Thames River, Dagnar was staring out the large rain-streaked windows of an executive-floor office on the top floor, with its magnificent view of the Thames and Tower Bridge. Although many drug companies had moved their research laboratories to the tax-benefit haven of Ireland, Carpa had remained in London, close to the leading hospitals of London, where many drug experiments were carried out.

The Carpa lab here in London was second to none in Europe. Dagnar, an expert chemist, was pleased to have the powerful capabilities of Carpa so handy in preparing for his night ahead.

Dagnar had left Reggie outside Judge Temple's home in central London after they had driven around the neighborhood to do a recon of the entrances and exits of the street where Temple lived. Dagnar left Reggie on a stakeout of her house. He had been sure to take Reggie's cell phone and his computer. All wireless traffic can be traced by GPS these days. Dagnar wanted no records showing that Reggie was making calls from the street outside Temple's house.

Now in the Carpa executive office, Dagnar allowed himself a moment of relaxation to stand up and stretch from his chair. His plan was almost finished. He had been working on computers and in the lab most of the last few hours putting together the pieces of the complex puzzle that would lead to the death of Judge Temple that night.

Using information from Reggie's Scotland Yard computer and the powerful Carpa computers, he had expertly hacked into the various databases of the British government. He had discovered a wealth of personal data on Judge Temple.

Using the Yard laptop computer, Dagnar confirmed what Reggie had told him earlier by examining Judge Temple's calendar for the week from the official schedule of the Old Bailey. Tonight's listed activity was the key piece of information. Dagnar confirmed that because of her duties as the Common Sergeant of London, she and her cohost, Sir Brian Fairmont—the Old Bailey's chief judge, officially called the Recorder of London—would be the two top-ranking British officials for the small reception and dinner in the Guildhall for the Secretary of Justice from Hong Kong. With this social obligation of being a cohost for an official dinner, Dagnar knew that she would not be returning to her home in Burlington Square until at least ten P.M.

Using Carpa's industrial access to the national health care system of England's database, Dagnar was able to review Judge Temple's medical records and to learn the prescription drugs she had received in the last few months. It was very helpful to know the items that would no doubt be present in her medicine cabinet at her home that night. Of particular interest was the knowledge that Judge Temple for years had been using a strong tranquilizer, Elavil, to prevent migraine attacks. Also Dagnar found out that she had recently been prescribed a strong painkiller, Darvocet-N100, when she had fallen and broken her wrist several weeks ago. The effect of these two drugs taken together made interesting reading when Dagnar consulted the LD-50 tables (lethal dose statistics) of a recent edition of the *Physicians' Desk Manual.*

Earlier he had used Reggie's Scotland Yard laptop, with its untraceable access code and the pin number of Reggie's Parliament employee account. Using that laptop, Dagnar was able to see Temple's financial history as revealed in sensitive court records, as well as the number of her credit card with National West Bank. Using this confidential information, Dagnar was able to hack into the bank computers and review her recent credit card purchases. Using plastic is convenient, but it does create a list of your vulnerabilities for your enemies. And although Judge Temple didn't know it, Dagnar was a terribly dangerous enemy.

Ah, the lady buys Grey Goose Vodka. Regular purchases of one-liter-size bottles on a per week basis going back several months showed that Judge Temple liked her vodka . . . maybe too well. Perhaps she was close to being a problem drinker, although her career progression indicated that she obviously kept her drinking fairly private and under control. But it's nice to know that there should be Grey Goose in her home tonight.

With information such as the above, Dagnar was able to go down several floors to use Carpa's research lab facilities to fashion a method and to put together the required tools that he hoped he could use to kill Judge Morgana Temple.

Dagnar now was satisfied that he could kill her with a plan that seemed unplanned. He had assembled all he needed that night in a boxy leather briefcase.

A perfect murder . . . but only if he handled it right.

He knew how he would kill her. However, the opportunity to be alone with her tonight in her home was the big question now. He needed to get inside her house that night and to exit leaving no trace.

That clandestine entry and exit would be a *big problem*—access to the house of a highly visible English judge living in the heart of London.

As he stared out the windows at the dark waters of the Thames, he thought about the various types of home security systems that a powerful and protected member of the judicial arm of the British Government would have.

Who would know of the specific protections Judge Temple would have at her home? Dagnar questioned himself in his creative mind.

And then it hit him.

Fucking-A! I have an inside pipeline—the Scotland Yard computer.

Since Scotland Yard was the key protector of London, the Yard would have to know about the active CCTV cameras around the vicinity of her house. It also might have information about an official's security systems.

Quickly Dagnar opened the Scotland Yard computer and, using Reggie's untraceable access code, began trolling through the Yard's vast data banks for the site listing the CCTV cameras. Later he switched over to security data for top-ranking officials. Soon he knew the exact system that Judge Temple was using in her home.

Damn, it's all here! Including the ability to view the coverage of each camera. And the fucking security system Temple is using for her home. No motion sensors, just door and window metallic contacts. Because she has a cat, she doesn't use motion sensors. Great stuff.

TIM QUINN WAS STUCK IN THE USUAL TRAFFIC JAM over the Fourteenth Street Bridge into Washington when his cell phone chirped loudly. He scanned the display on the phone and smiled when he saw the readout indicating it was Vicky Hauser calling from London.

Must have been a damn short interview with Judge Morgana Temple. I hope it went Moorman's way. I like the man. Moorman would make a great Chief Justice. He's proven himself on the battlefield not in some D.C. lobbying firm. Probably the first real leader the Court will have in its ranks in a century.

He clicked on the mobile phone and listened carefully as Vicky concisely relayed the details of her talk with Judge Morgana Temple. She went through the events of the entire night as related by Temple.

"Great work, Vicky. Now you and Bill are sure that this is the real story?"

"Tim, Temple was very convincing to me; and Bill was watching her all the time for signs of deception. We're both solid on this—she's telling the truth about her night with Justice Moorman. No date rape . . . and no sex."

"Well, this is good news. I'll get out a report to the Committee by early afternoon clearing Justice Moorman of any hint of date rape. God, Vicky, you and Bill are quite the team. If we couldn't clear up this issue quickly, the hearing most likely would have been postponed and Moorman's nomination would have died in the political jungle of Washington. Now, both of you get back to D.C. on the first plane out of London. I need you here."

And I miss you, added Quinn silently as he clicked off the phone.

E-MAIL	(Committee Senator—Eyes Only)
FROM	TIM QUINN, SPECIAL COUNSEL
DATE	MONDAY, DECEMBER 15, 2008
TO	MEMBERS OF U.S. SENATE JUDICIARY COMMITTEE
SUBJECT	CONFIDENTIAL—REPORT TO THE JUDICIARY COMMITTEE #4

With regard to the media reports about a rumored date rape by Justice Moorman in England some years ago, I wish to inform the Committee that my Deputy, Ms. Victoria Hauser, has interviewed the alleged date rape victim today in London. From the clear and unambiguous statement given to Ms. Hauser, it is apparent that there was neither a sexual assault nor even consensual sex between Justice Moorman and the Englishwoman who was the female subject of the rumor. According to the purported victim, Justice Moorman did visit her at her home pursuant to her invitation, but he did not have sex with her nor touch her in any inappropriate manner. She also mentioned that she has the highest respect for Justice Moorman and does not plan to relate any facts of her social evening with Justice Moorman to anyone. It should be noted that at the time of this incident, the woman was a practicing well-respected barrister over thirty-five years of age and single. Justice Moorman was also unmarried at the time of the visit to her home. The Englishwoman was adamant that absolutely no embarrassing conduct took place during this private social encounter.

When quizzed by Ms. Hauser as to the possibility of Justice Moorman having a sexual experience with another woman that could form the basis of any charge of "date rape" during the time period of the conference, the Englishwoman opined that such a possibility was highly unlikely. Her opinion was based on her direct observation of Moorman as one of the three official conference escorts from Gray's Inn of Court. In her opinion, Justice Moorman had no opportunity to be alone with any other woman due to the extremely busy schedule during the conference at Gray's Inn and the related social activities and dinners.

The Englishwoman was judged a very credible witness by Ms. Hauser, an experienced prosecutor, and by Mr. Sharkey, a leading FBI deception detection expert, who both observed and heard the woman's statement.

A further point—the Englishwoman has communicated to Ms. Hauser a request that her identity be protected, and I concur. There is no reason to make her a victim of unfounded rumors in the media, since she was never a victim of any assault. Real rape victims are routinely granted anonymous status in many instances, and I believe the same should be true with this unusual situation of a possibly politically or racially manufactured report of rape.

Based on this investigation, I consider that there is no credence to the recent news reports and the originating source, the English blog site that started the rumor that a forcible sexual assault upon an English barrister by Justice Moorman occurred during a legal conference in London. In my opinion and that of the investigating team of Ms. Hauser and Special Agent Sharkey, there is absolutely no evidence of misconduct by Justice Moorman during the Gray's Inn conference. Therefore, I conclude that the source document—the English blog report which was attached to my prior report (Report to the Judiciary Committee #3) on this subject—to be false and misleading.

Accordingly in my view, the rumor of rape against Justice Moorman has no basis in law or fact and I see no obstacle to the Committee proceeding to promptly consider the nomination of Justice Moorman forthwith. I also see no need for this Committee to postpone the scheduled start of the Moorman confirmation hearing on December 17, 2008.

If any member of the Committee has any questions regarding this report, I am available to discuss this matter with that Senator. In addition, once Ms. Hauser and Special Agent Sharkey return from England tomorrow, I will make them available to answer any details of this report.

Timothy R. Quinn
Special Counsel
U.S. Senate Judiciary Committee

Immediately following Quinn's official act of transmitting his report by e-mail to the Senators on the Committee, Quinn wondered whether he should leak at least the conclusion to an anxious man who no doubt was waiting for the outcome of the London interview.

Specifically, knowing that Moorman was worried about the interview of Judge Temple, Quinn debated with himself whether he should notify Justice Moorman of the encouraging news from London—the fact that Judge Temple apparently would deny any date rape charge.

Before he made his final decision to notify Justice Moorman, Tim thought back to the report of the investigation he had just put his name on. Was he right in ending the investigation at this stage based on one interview? Thinking about whether there really was a rape charge that could be proved, Quinn knew that he was correct. The alleged victim had given a solid "no" to the alleged charge. That was the ball game—no rape case could be brought given the statement Temple gave to Vicky.

The "why" bothered him, and he came up with two possibilities. Both were practical: First, Judge Temple refused to confirm that she had been raped (even if it were true) in order to protect her immediate aspirations of becoming a justice on the Royal Court of Appeal. The second and more likely possibility (and one Vicky and Sharkey seem to accept as true) was that there *really* had been no rape—Judge Temple's version of getting Moorman drunk to avoid sex was so strange and unusual that it was very believable. Moorman was most likely unable to perform the act of rape due to intoxication. Tim reasoned that the "water and vodka—no sex" scenario was probably the truth here. But who knew what really happened? "What could be proved" and "what happened" were often two separate things.

On whether he would notify Moorman, Tim's conclusion was more clear-cut.

The guy must be going through hell wondering whether he should have given me Judge Temple's name in the first place. He deserves to know.

So thirty minutes after Tim Quinn sent his Report to The Judiciary Committee via e-mail to all the Senators on the Committee, he dialed the private cell phone of Justice Oscar Moorman.

"Oscar Moorman here," came the crisp answer on the phone.

"Your Honor, it's Tim Quinn. I have news from England. Can you talk on a landline?" For Quinn, old habits of not wanting to talk on insecure cell phones died hard.

"Yes, Tim. I'm at the Court. I have your direct number at the Senate. I'll call you back on the lima-lima. . . . Can you tell me? . . . Is it good news from London?"

Oscar Moorman's use of the words "lima-lima" for a landline telephone triggered an equally military response from Quinn.

"Affirmative, Your Honor. Good news," replied Tim. For Quinn, the shared Vietnam experience of Moorman and Quinn made military talk comfortable between them.

Justice Moorman called Quinn back within thirty seconds. Moorman's voice was clearly anxious.

So Quinn wasted no words with this man he was increasingly growing to understand . . . and like.

"Oscar, no rape . . . or even sex . . . is the firm statement Vicky Hauser got from Judge T. And furthermore T will not go public with any statement that you visited her flat that night. She is in the running to become a member of the Royal Court of Appeal and is unlikely to want anything made public about having spent a night with you. By the way, you were drinking vodka that night and she was fixing herself water as a nightcap. So that is why you don't remember much. My report's conclusion is 'no date rape.' Naturally, I can't send you the Report that I made to the Committee. Wish I could, but you know it's attorney-client material as well as work product from a confidential Senate investigation. Nevertheless I thought you deserved to hear the good news. I have recommended that this date rape thing is a false issue and that the hearing should go forward. Also I will not release Judge T's name so there should be no play from this issue at the hearing. Like I said, I wish I could send you my report, but I feel it would be a breach of my attorney-client relation-ship with the Committee."

There was a long silence on the other end of the phone line. Then a quiet reply from the Justice. "Tim, it's not necessary for you to send the Report. My wife at home probably already has it. Her father, the Sena-tor, gets all your reports from Senator Powers immediately. He faxes them to Debby at our home fax—Powers does Senator Sloane this fa-vor no doubt looking forward to cashing in on it later when she runs for President. If she doesn't win, she'll still be a Senator and any favor she does for Debby's father goes into her Senate favor bank."

"Roger all, O. The leaking doesn't surprise me," replied Quinn.

WITHIN SEVERAL HOURS OF THE QUINN REPORT HITTING the government computer screens of the Senate Judiciary Committee members, copies had been sent out all around Washington . . . and farther. The effect of the Report was the apparent deflation of the "date rape" balloon the Democratic opposition counted on to float over the confirmation hearings and use to bomb Moorman. The Re-port successfully demolished the planned "rape" smear during the hearings. The reaction was mixed, but three individuals had strong emotions triggered by the Report that they expressed in telephone conversations.

⬦

The first conversation was based on jealousy and fueled by alcohol. It was between Justice Oscar Moorman and his wife, Debby. She called

O's chambers at the Supreme Court about noon on that Monday, the day the Report went out to the Committee members.

Debby's voice over the phone was hysterical and disjointed. She was upset by the Report. Moorman tried to calm her down.

"Debby, please slow down and think. The Report is actually very good. It proves what I told you was true . . . that I didn't remember having sex. And now it's certain that I didn't. The Englishwoman said so to the investigators," Oscar Moorman said in a soothing voice.

His wife was slurring her words and was obviously drunk. "Your English slut is covering up for you, the almighty Supreme Court Justice. I know you fucked her. I have the Report in my hand. Daddy faxed it to me. It says you went to her home for a 'private social encounter.' Christ, do you think I'm stupid! I know you screwed her. Hell, you're probably still fucking her . . . and other women around D.C. I just finished talking to Lucy Bianco and she agrees with me that once a womanizer always a womanizer. How can I ever trust you?"

Christ, of all her friends to call she calls Lucy Bianco—Justice Bianco's uptight "born-again" wife.

"No, Baby. It's been only you. You're the only one I've slept with since I met you. I love you." Moorman could tell he was going to lose the phone argument. When she was drunk and jealous, he could never reason with her until the drugs and drink wore off.

"I'm leaving the courthouse right now. We don't have Court today so I'm coming home. Why don't you lie down in bed until I get home. . . . I'm leaving now. I love you, baby. You're the only one for me. The only one I'll ever make love to the rest of my life. Please go to sleep until I get home. I love you, Debby baby."

✦

The second conversation occurred later in the day, and it was based on pure racial hatred. It was between the Alabama billionaire and Senator Dalton (D-Ala.), the Minority Leader of the U.S. Senate.

"Did you get that Quinn Report from your attorney?" Senator Dalton inquired cautiously.

Long ago, a confidential communication pipeline was set up by Dalton and the billionaire to transmit sensitive documents via the Washington law firm of the billionaire. Neither e-mail nor fax was ever used. An attorney from the firm, when called, traveled over to the Senate offices of Dalton to receive whatever papers Senator Dalton wanted passed to the billionaire.

Dalton was afraid the fallout from the failed "date rape" smear would fall on him. The billionaire had a terrible temper to match his rude manners.

A thick Southern drawl answered, "Yeah, got it from those shyster overpaid D.C. lawyers I use. The Report was damn interesting reading. Downright pity the English thing didn't work. The English press is a bunch of pussies. My people over there were very close to getting the name. That was a very good lead in the Report about the lady barrister being one of three on the escort committee. With a little more time we could have gotten to her. With the right financial incentive, people will sing any song. Well, that dog apparently won't hunt now and there's no time to put pressure on the bitch, moneywise or otherwise. Good thing I have two backup plans for our boy!"

Relieved but still wary and actually afraid of the answer, the Minority Leader cautiously asked in a low voice, "Should I do anything up here?"

"Nope, just keep trying to do your fucking opposition job to the confirmation. Ramsey shouldn't be able to get a fucking judicial appointment of this level through the Senate this late in his goddamn presidency. You fucking Democrats are a bunch of limp-dick screwups. Last two Democratic senators who had balls were Truman and Johnson. And they both became Presidents. Fat chance any of your fellow Senate Democratic clowns will make president! Most likely that Republican bitch Powers will become the next senator who becomes president. She has a set of big ones."

With that last blast, the phone went dead in Senator Dalton's hand. No good-bye. This was not unusual. Typically when the billionaire was through with a conversation, he just hung up. The Senator over-looked the rudeness because he was more concerned with the well-known unreasonable temper of the billionaire.

Well, at least he didn't blame me for the date rape failure, said the Senator to himself. Then he shook his head and wondered briefly what the billionaire meant by the remark about having "two backup plans." Dalton quickly decided that he *really* didn't want to know and made the senatorial decision to push the remark into the category of things that if asked about in an investigation, his response would be *"I don't recall."*

❖

The third conversation was based on fear and greed. It was the most interesting conversation because it was filled with vague terms by the two men talking. They both were clever men and knew that they must use their words carefully, because all international calls were closely monitored for key words by the listeners at the NSA—the National Security Agency, the big ears of America in the sky. The American network of spy satellites constantly monitored all international calls—and reviewed the interesting ones. The NSA's large, powerful computers down-linked audio data from the satellites and recorded all calls. Then complex software was applied to the data which searched for certain words that could help locate terrorists or threats to national security. This listening operation was on "high drive" especially now for calls to and from England, where there had been a recent bombing in London by terrorists. Dagnar knew that the big ears were on full alert, probably recording the talk between Don Fay, Carpa CEO, and his chief of security, Victor Dagnar. He wanted to be sure that the conversation wasn't pulled out of the line of calls to be discarded as "no security interest" and put in the line of "national security interest" or "terrorist-related."

"How are you, my friend? Do you recognize my voice?" started Fay.

"Busy with my project," replied an obviously irritated Dagnar, "and yes, I know you. Why are you calling now? I'm very busy with the project. I'm in the final stage."

"Yes, yes. I know. Well, I'm having second thoughts about finishing the project. I received some information in a report. Information that indicates the subject might not be talking, as we initially thought. Apparently there was no . . . ah, misdeed."

Dagnar's quick mind processed this in an instant. Not doing the Temple project would mean no bonus for him. This was not a good development, especially since he had planned so hard and was so confident that he would succeed. Also his act of terminating Judge Temple on Fay's orders would put Dagnar on the permanent "do not fire or fuck with" list at Carpa. No better job security existed than killing for your boss or company.

"Is the subject the one who was interviewed by investigators to-day?" asked Dagnar.

"Yes," answered Fay, "but it appears she won't be admitting to the activity we discussed. There's a report from London, from the inves-tigators over there, saying she won't talk and that nothing happened."

"Listen, I'm ready to . . ."

Dagnar abruptly stopped in mid-sentence because he almost said "pull the trigger here." He knew "trigger" was probably one of the ob-vious key words that would highlight the exchange for the NSA lis-teners. If the discussion were highlighted, it would be put in the long line of conversations to be examined by analysts as possibly "terror-ist-related." That would not be good. Some smart NSA geek might put things together and connect their talk timewise with what was about to happen to Judge Temple. Definitely bad for Dagnar and Carpa.

Keep this dialogue in the business context. Chose your words care-fully.

Dagnar after a pause continued. "As I said, I'm in the final phase of the project. I really should finish. Just because that woman—ah, ah . . . researcher—reported today that nothing happened in the experiment five years ago doesn't mean she won't change her mind tomorrow. You know how these sensitive things are. People say one thing and then change their mind and the truth comes out. Let me finish it. That's the best way. It's all planned . . . and there is a lot of money at stake. You told me about the four number—a number with a lot of zeros behind it for your shareholders. And you also said the board knows of that future profit potential. To make it happen, don't you need to do everything you can? I know you're calling the executive decision here, but . . . well, I wouldn't want to take *any* chance to disappoint the board . . . or the company. Trust me, I can ensure completion very quietly and soon. I assure you this will be a piece of cake and with no blowback to the company. Absolutely none. Come on, boss. Give me the green light here."

There was a long hesitation by the Carpa CEO. "All right. Finish it."

Dagnar smiled and closed with confidence, "Consider it done, boss."

WHEN DAGNAR CLICKED OFF THE CALL FROM FAY, DAG-nar cursed and turned off his company cell phone, removing the battery.

Damn, I should have turned off this telephone hours ago now that I'm in final prep. If Fay called me when I was on the stakeout near Judge Temple's home, it could be traced by inspecting the records of the cell tower in the area. That's one of the first things the police would do—check on phone calls from the area around the Judge's home— standard procedure—get a list of all completed calls in the area. That almost sure examination of calls would place my Carpa cell phone at the scene of the crime. It's lucky he caught me here at Carpa's London offices before I left for the Judge's home. More important, now once I leave the Carpa building, Fay will have lost control of the operation— he can't call it off once I've severed communications. I've got his final go-ahead. Got to get out of the building before he changes his mind.

It was seven in the evening. As Dagnar looked from the glass wall of his office at the Thames River and out across the spread-out City of London, he saw the blaze of lights crossing the bridges. Evening traffic was winding down. From the forecast on www.weather.com, he knew the night would be clear and cold. As he contemplated the mission ahead of him that night, he subconsciously reached into his inner pocket of his suit and took out a slim contoured silver flask. The bourbon was smooth to his taste as he took a deep pull. Then he shook it and frowned.

Better top this off now. It's going to be a tough night and I don't want to run out of my medicine.

Quickly he reached into the desk of the office that was reserved for him whenever he was in London and retrieved a full liter bottle of Jack Daniel's. His hands were steady as he carefully refilled the container. He never was nervous before a "dark side" job. Of course, he always drank more than usual during these jobs outside the law. He was in his prime—a truly gifted functioning alcoholic.

After he filled up his flask, Dagnar considered himself finished with his prep for the job. He and Reggie had done a visual recon of the area around Judge Temple's home once he'd checked into the Dorchester. The ground reconnaissance was uneventful and he was sure hadn't been captured on traceable CCTV tapes. Since landing in England, Dagnar cautiously had worn a dark blue plain baseball cap whenever he got into the Jag. He was always aware of hidden CCTV surveillance cameras all over London.

To prepare for this night's job, Dagnar worked hard at his office and in the Carpa labs. His research and intelligence gathering on Temple was done using the quite formidable resources of the Carpa resources in London, as supplemented by Reggie's laptop computer access to Scotland Yard's data banks. It had been very convenient to have Detective Inspector Reggie Whiteside on the Carpa payroll. The information Dagnar was able to get via the link to the Yard's computers was invaluable and saved Dagnar a lot of planning time.

For the gear he would need that night, Dagnar had transferred all the special equipment he would use to a large leather top-opening bag. To an observer it could be a physician's bag or a businessman's "Gladstone" briefcase—both of which would not look out of place in the hands of a well-dressed gentleman on a city street.

In security-conscious London, this type of upscale bag was a more proper way to carry his equipment. No backpacks or black canvas bags—those would arouse suspicion, especially since he had to remain exposed for some time in the park across the street from the judge's house, waiting for her to return from her formal dinner at the Guildhall with the Hong Kong Secretary of Justice.

Dagnar put on his heavy black Burberry trench coat, grabbed his leather bag, and opened the closed heavy soundproof door to the outer office and left to walk down the long corridor to the bank of elevators. To anyone watching he was a Carpa executive going home after a long day.

Dagnar thought back on what Reggie had said to him when he left Reggie on the Judge's street to keep an eye on her house.

Back then, in the midafternoon, Reggie had again warned him, "Governor, I still think it is a bad idea to try to bribe Judge Temple."

"You're not being paid to think," Dagnar had snapped.

Dagnar dismissed thinking about that earlier warning as he left the Carpa building and now hailed a taxi outside Carpa's walled parking lot. Dagnar's cab soon entered the stream of traffic headed for the Tower Bridge into Central London.

Dagnar was headed to link up with Reggie at the stakeout.

Dagnar and Reggie were two men whose mutual purpose that night was to silence Judge Temple from ever speaking to anyone about her evening with Justice Moorman. The only difference was the method.

Reggie thought it was to be done by a bribe paid by Dagnar.

Dagnar knew it was by murder.

What Dagnar didn't know was, Temple's silence was meaningless—not knowing that Temple had already decided to silence herself about the night with Moorman. Irony would be with the two men as they were about to silence a woman who would never talk about a rape that never happened.

Dagnar was going to kill someone to put Moorman in the Center Seat to influence a case that the Justice had already disqualified himself from sitting on.

AS THE LONDON CAB APPROACHED THE GENERAL AREA where Judge Temple resided, Dagnar got out on Oxford Street near Marks & Spencer, a giant department store. He was playing a visitor from another country on the busy walking street, a forgettable rider in a tourist area if there was a police investigation into Judge Temple's murder.

Dagnar was feeling good. Powered by a slight buzz from the bourbon and a rush of adrenaline from the anticipated event, he was proud of himself. A good preparation for a killing takes days, if not weeks. Dagnar had had less than a day in London, the target area. Nevertheless he'd done it. It was remarkable, but he was smart and resourceful and came up with what he thought was an unbeatable plan.

The initial problem he had faced was the successful covert entry into Judge Temple's home. He knew that reconnaissance of a target site can make or break any illegal operation. Dagnar had the choice to recon Temple's home by ground, by air, or by map. He did all three that afternoon.

On the ground recon, Reggie did a slow drive-by of the neighborhood where Judge Temple lived. This was accomplished on the way to Carpa's London offices from the hotel after he checked in.

On the drive-by, Dagnar made Reggie drive slowly as he closely studied the front of Temple's house. Her house was on a corner of a side street across from the park in the middle of Burlington Square. The entrance was from the side street, but the best place to wait for her was across the street at the edge of the park, where one could stand by the bus stop and pretend that they were waiting for a bus.

Yes! The way into the house will work just as I planned on the jet to London.

For the recon by air, Dagnar did a Google Earth satellite search of her residential area. The ever-cautious Carpa security chief wisely never focused directly on the actual house of Judge Temple in case Google kept data search records. Instead with the satellite search, he looked for entrances and exits from the general neighborhood.

Besides, it was not necessary to look at her house from above. He already had decided how he was going to get inside the house and the drive-by showed him where he would wait for Temple and how Reggie would help with the stakeout.

Leaving nothing to chance, Dagnar did a map search of the area by using the Scotland Yard computer, paying special attention to the placement of the public CCTV video cameras in the area and their coverage. There was only one CCTV camera that concerned him—it had the coverage north from Oxford Street, the street hit recently by the bombing, up a side street toward the square Judge Temple lived on. That camera had to be dealt with, since the twenty-power scope on the 360-degree surveillance camera might catch a glimpse of Dagnar waiting in the park across from Temple's home—his stakeout position. That camera was dangerous and had to be taken out because it would show Dagnar's approach to the front door of Temple's house.

Dagnar devised an ingenious way to disable it without making the London police suspicious.

Judge Temple lived in a three-story row corner house on Burlington Square. Burlington Square was a quiet residential area just two blocks from Oxford Street, the busy shopping street of Mayfair in central London.

Dagnar walked up Oxford Street, and soon he approached the side street with the CCTV camera looking up to Burlington Square and to Temple's corner house two short blocks up. Naturally he walked past the side street and turned into an alley a hundred feet up, slipping out of coverage of the dangerous CCTV camera. When he came out of the alley on the street parallel to Oxford Street, he doubled back and reached into his bag, grabbed what looked like a flashlight, tugging once again on the blue baseball cap he was wearing to lower the bill closer to his eyebrows.

Then Dagnar confidently walked with his distinctive limp up to the corner. There were no pedestrians in the area. When he reached the corner, Dagnar thrust the flashlight device around the corner and pointed it at an electrical transformer high on a pole midway up the side street toward Oxford. He pushed a button on the device and the transformer burst briefly into sparks, and one half of the homes and four-story apartment buildings went dark. The power was out for the block on one side of the street.

Seeing the results of the power outage, Dagnar again extended the device around the corner and aimed it directly at the critical CCTV camera back on the intersection of Oxford Street and the side street, and again pushed the button on the top of the device.

There was no visible effect, but Dagnar knew that the internal circuits of the camera were fried, and any surveillance coverage looking up to Burlington Square was lost until they were fixed. Reggie had told Dagnar earlier it normally takes eight to twelve hours to repair any malfunctioning camera. To a camera repair crew, their examination of the camera insides would most likely conclude that the nearby power surge from the electrical transformer had burned out the guts of the camera. Such an outage happens from time to time. An occurrence that would raise no suspicions if Judge Temple died an accidental death.

His work knocking out CCTV coverage in the area done, Dagnar walked up the thoroughfare and slipped into Reggie's car, parked a hundred feet farther up the side street, where Reggie could watch the entrance to Judge Temple's corner house on the square. Reggie noticed Dagnar had a slight grin on his face and guessed he had knocked out the power and disabled the surveillance camera they had discussed earlier. It was the only video threat to Dagnar being observed walking up to the entrance of Judge Temple's home.

"What did you do to make the bloody lights go out down the street?"

Dagnar spoke as if in a lecture to a university class. "It's called EMP. Electromagnetic pulse. Really this flashlight-looking device is a high-energy microwave gun. It sends a pulse of high-frequency energy to the electrical transformer and creates a power surge that fries the circuits. I neutralized the camera immediately after I did the electric transformer. The repair crews for both the transformer and the CCTV camera will think it is a freak power surge that knocked both out."

"Christ, you're something!" remarked Reggie.

"You have no idea," said Dagnar.

REGGIE HAD THE CAR IDLING TO KEEP THE HEATER AND the windshield defroster on to prevent the windows from fogging up. Now that Dagnar was settled in the seat next to Reggie, he turned to the surveillance of the Judge's home.

"What's the status at Temple's house?" asked Dagnar sharply. It was close to eight o'clock.

"Nobody appears to be home. And no one came while I was here," replied Reggie. "By the way, where's my bloody cell phone?"

"I'll give it back to you later. I want no calls from this area until after I have my little talk with the Judge. You know records are kept on completed calls by cell towers in the area. . . . Well, things are looking good for me. It appears that Carpa's European CFO has a very good friend from Oxford—an English appeals court judge, and that judge knows Temple very well. Anyway, he has arranged for her to talk with me tonight," lied Dagnar.

Dagnar knew Reggie was a crooked cop, but even those sometimes could not travel too far from the line and help kill an Old Bailey judge. That was probably beyond the limits of even Reggie.

I must keep him in the dark about what I have planned for Judge Temple, thought Dagnar. *Now, before I get a lot of questions from this fucking cockney, I better put him to work.*

"Reggie, I want you to park down the road at the very corner leading up from Oxford Street. That's where she'll turn up to come home. Be on the lookout for the Judge's car, a white 2006 BMW 325i. When you see it, call me on this special cell phone. Let it ring four or five times. I won't answer, so the cell phone records won't show any call in the area of her house. It'll just alert me that she's coming up the street. . . . Also, do the same thing if you see a police car or a policeman on foot. Do you understand?"

Reggie nodded.

"By the way, here's your laptop back. I'm afraid the battery's dead. Didn't have time to recharge it. Sorry. Anyway, it was very useful to my understanding of Judge Temple and her vulnerabilities. I also talked to Carpa headquarters and my boss had some ideas. As you may have read in the papers, she is rumored to be up for an appellate judgeship. Carpa can help her on that front politically. Carpa's very connected here in the U.K. Moreover, I learned that she has a sizable credit card debt and a big mortgage on her house. So if I need to I can go the money route. . . . Well, whatever it takes. I'll find the right approach after I chat with her for a bit. Bottom line—I'm confident we'll work something out and that she'll be receptive to my offer." A further lie to cement the misleading of Reggie for the night's meeting with the Judge.

"Well, you better be off to your new position down the block. Stay alert. By the way, what did you tell your wife you were doing?"

"I told the missus that I was working late at Parliament and would spend the night in the members' dorm. They furnish the Yard with several rooms for when we work late. Just so you know, I never mentioned to my wife my business relationship and 'retirement fund' with Carpa. Too many coppers on the take have been nabbed by a wife's bragging or careless talk."

"Reggie, you're a wise man."

Then Dagnar got out and watched the Jaguar turning 180 degrees and heading down the road to take up the lookout position.

The night was clear and cold so Dagnar pulled up the collar of his thick coat and headed up toward the bus stop next to the park. He had checked the evening bus schedule, and since the stop was on a secondary route, the bus came only every forty-five minutes. A good cover for waiting across from a Judge's house.

Dagnar took off his baseball cap. He was now in the role of a local proper English businessman waiting for a bus home and needed to look the part.

Appearances were deceiving. Anyone looking at him waiting at the bus stop would think they were looking at a businessman after a late night's work, not a killer mentally rehearsing his plan to murder an English judge.

· 70 ·

white columns and brass carriage lights framing the doorway, Dagnar was well dressed and looked like a proper caller, whom the judge might very well open the door for. In case Reggie had lied or was mistaken about the judge not being home, Dagnar had a small canister in his overcoat pocket. In it was a strong incapacitating gas that he would spray in the Judge's face to stun her as he raced inside the door. He hoped he didn't have to use it, since it would vastly complicate making the Judge's death look like an accident.

After thirty seconds had passed with no response, Dagnar looked about and saw no one on the street. He reached inside his bag and removed two objects. One was a slim strip of metal he expertly slipped inside the top half of the door frame in a smooth motion like he was leaving a note tucked at the edge of the door. It was no note, but a magnetized strip that would close the electric circuit of the door's security system. Now if the door was opened, the magnetic strip would keep the door alarm from going off—the system would be fooled into thinking the door remained closed.

That done, Dagnar turned and quickly hooked a long chain with a curious black device over the metal arm of the brass carriage light next to the door. A few feet away from it, unless you looked very closely, you couldn't see the hanging black object.

Having finished with his work at the door, Dagnar pretended to ring the doorbell again and left after waiting one minute.

Now he was ready for the return of the Judge from her Guildhall dinner. Dagnar walked across the street to again play the role of waiting for a bus.

As it was cold at the bus stop, Dagnar paced to keep warm . . . and fortified himself with several deep pulls on his silver flask, looking up at the stars on the clear night.

God, I hope that bitch breaks away from the party early! It's cold.

To his relief, his cell phone in his right coat pocket started to emit a quiet ring at a quarter to ten o'clock.

She's coming . . . or it's the police.

Then he saw it, a white BMW slowing and backing up to park in front of Temple's house. Dagnar pulled out and flipped open another cell phone from his left pocket. This was a special one, a satellite one that didn't use any local cell receivers. He started to slowly walk across the street as the Judge went up the three stone stairs to the porch and began to put her key in the door.

With one hand set on the speed dial of the sat phone, Dagnar spoke loudly but firmly. "Your Honor, I have an extradition subpoena for you to look at from the American Embassy."

The Judge had the door open and turned toward Dagnar just before stepping inside her house.

It was at that moment that Dagnar pushed the speed dial and tightly closed his eyes and lowered his head while still walking toward Judge Temple. He was fifteen feet from her when the "flash bang" grenade hanging from the carriage light exploded.

There was a blinding light and a small muffled poof of noise. Dagnar, the expert chemist, had removed the "bang" part of the stun grenade. Nevertheless, the flash of light two feet from Judge Temple's eyes rocked her back and she tumbled on the hall floor of her home. She collapsed, not moving.

Time was precious now as Dagnar raced up the porch stairs, removed the keys from the lock, and entered the house, remembering to close the door before the cat bolted out. There was no worrying about that. At the flash and the falling of her mistress with a loud crash, the cat wisely shot upstairs two steps at a time.

Thank God, the security alarm never went off. The magnet strip worked. The cell phone–activated grenade worked. The plan is working!

Dagnar knew he had very little time before the Judge regained consciousness. The effect of the grenade gave him only less than a minute before Temple came around from the stun effects.

Kneeling beside the Judge, Dagnar reached into his bag and removed an eyedropper from a small bottle in one of the side pockets. He delicately pinched her nose, which made the Judge involuntarily open her mouth. With a latex gloved hand, he grabbed her tongue and lifted, squirting the contents of the eyedropper directly beneath her tongue—a point on the human body where drugs are quickly absorbed into the tissue. The liquid in her mouth that wasn't absorbed, the Judge swallowed as a reflex action when he released the pinch on her nose. It was imperative that he leave no bruises during this drug insertion operation.

Now the Judge was stunned and drugged. As a chemist he knew it would take a few minutes for her to become completely unconscious, so he started to talk soothingly to her as the stun effects wore off and the drugs kicked in.

Dagnar softly whispered, "Your Honor, there was a gas explosion from the gas carriage lamps. Please stay still. I've already called a doctor. You took a nasty fall. You shouldn't move just yet."

The Judge started to sit up. "What . . . What . . . Gas explosion . . . you say . . . ," she uttered in an already slurring voice.

"Yes, yes, Your Honor. You must wait to get your orientation. We wouldn't want you to fall down again." Dagnar's voice had a comforting quality for Judge Temple.

Dagnar was pleased that Judge Temple's eyes were blinking weakly and starting to lose focus. He had had a tough time getting the right mix for the compound he used in the eyedropper and he was very pleased to see it was working better than planned.

Temple slurred one more phrase before she passed out. "There's . . . no gas in the carriage lights. They're . . . elec—tric. . . . What's . . . happen—ing . . . ?"

As he saw her eyes close and her body go limp, Dagnar released her, and she went from a sitting position into lying on the hall floor, breathing softly and not moving.

Dagnar got up and surveyed the first floor of the Judge's house. He was aware of the living room with the TV next to the hall and could also see all the way back into the kitchen

Got to move fast. She won't last in this stage long. Decision time!

His first priority was to find out where she would die. To help with that decision, he wanted to find out where she kept her medicine—the painkiller and her antidepressant. The location of these might well determine how he would set up her death.

Dagnar searched the most likely place, the medicine cabinet of the bathroom next to the master bedroom on the second floor. There were medicines—aspirin, antacids, iodine—but not the particular potent medicines he needed to find. As he was coming out of the bathroom, he saw a flash of movement. On instinct he reached into his pocket for the canister of gas.

Damn, it's the fucking cat. Almost gave me a heart attack.

Next he searched the kitchen. Lots of people take medicine with food. No luck there.

Dagnar was getting worried. His plan called for a seeming accident using the prescription medicine she was currently taking, but he needed to set up the proper stage for his scenario using the medicine vials as props. Time was running out. He might have to improvise and make it a break-in and murder. Definitely not preferable—then there would be a second person—the killer. That would generate way too much police heat . . . and publicity. His plan was to have a rather embarrassing accidental death that would be believable, but one where would be a tendency for officials to cover up the details in order not to embarrass the English judiciary.

Nevertheless time was running out. He had to decide how this was going to go down.

Dagnar was about to panic. Then it occurred to him.

Christ, a lot of women keep their pills in their handbag.

Dagnar went to the hall where Judge Temple was unconscious, breathing in shallow gulps.

And there it was next to her—her purse. He searched through the purse and breathed a sigh of relief when he found both containers— the Darvocet-N 100 (the painkiller) and the Elavil (the tranquilizer and antidepressant) for her migraines.

Bingo. Now he knew the "how" she would die. The "where" was a choice he had to quickly make. He looked into her living room and stared at the sofa in front of the TV.

Then Dagnar smiled for the first time that night, as he went to her hall closet to get one of her other outer coats. He would use that other coat to carry her into the living room where the TV was. Using one of her coats by putting his arms through the sleeves so he was wearing it backward—as a shield—was a trick he had used before so the fibers from his clothing wouldn't be transferred to Judge Temple's clothes. *CSI*-type TV shows were like classrooms to some people— they taught the criminals about fiber analysis. Real criminals, like Dagnar, loved these shows and considered them educational—how *not* to be caught.

With the other coat on, he looked down on his victim and thought, *Come on, Dear. You are going to have a nice nightcap and then take a long, long sleep.*

Satisfied with the transportation method, his powerful arms picked her up and carried her effortlessly to the living room. He put her gently on the sofa. He took off her topcoat, straightening her evening dress. After that he brought both topcoats out to the hall closet and hung them side by side, the topcoat she'd been wearing and the one he'd used to carry her. Now fiber analysis by the crime scene techs wouldn't come up with any abnormalities on Temple's clothing from his handling of her unconscious body.

Adjusting her on the sofa in front of the TV, he checked her position.

Yes, this will do. She came home, made herself a drink, and took a few pills too many. Naughty girl! Shouldn't mix alcohol and pills. They can kill you.

Dagnar went into the kitchen, selected a glass, and found the Grey Goose in a cabinet. He poured most of the bottle down the sink and ran the water to remove traces of the vodka. Things were going well.

He brought the glass and the almost empty bottle of vodka to the living room and poured a small portion in the glass. With his latex gloves—the same type used by the London police—Dagnar put the glass in her limp right hand several times to get multiple prints. She moaned and tried to pull her right hand away as he was putting her prints on the glass.

Oh, not feeling so well, are we? Don't worry; soon you won't feel a thing.

Setting the glass on the coffee table in front of her, Dagnar took off her shoes and stepped back to make sure he had set up the right pose of a woman coming home to have a drink and to have her medicine while relaxing in front of the TV.

Perfect pose. A judge home relaxing and having her evening medicine. The picture of an accidental overdose. . . . Actually, she looks pretty sexy with her dress hiked up, revealing she was wearing a black garter belt. . . . No, no, this is a job to be done. And quickly, no time to fondle her . . . although it was tempting. These thoughts ran through his head randomly. The sex drive was taking him off the mission.

Dagnar felt himself getting hard at the thought of the garter belt and the white thighs.

Goddamn it. . . . No, there will be time for that later. Dagnar snapped himself out of those thoughts and pulled down her skirt. He was now focused—businesslike. He reached into his bag and took a surgical Nasal-Gastro tube—a very soft N-G tube—so soft it would not bruise any membranes in her nose as he gently pushed it through her nose to reach her stomach.

It was critical for there to be no bruises or abrasions for the medical examiner to find in order to show that a tube wasn't used or that the overdose wasn't poured forcibly down her throat. It had to appear that the overdose was accidentally taken and naturally entered her stomach, where its lethal effects would be absorbed into her system. Dagnar assumed that the death of a judge, even an accidental one, would be carefully examined in an autopsy.

The tube was a special Carpa product known for its smooth and efficient operation of feeding babies who had trouble swallowing. When the tube was in place with the bottom now inserted directly into her stomach, he carefully reached into his bag and got a large syringe. It was full—filled with a combination of Grey Goose vodka, Darvocet-N 100, and Elavil—the exact amount that would eventually allow Judge Temple to stop breathing . . . forever.

Dagnar attached the lethal mixture to the N-G tube and started to slowly push the plunger of the syringe.

Judge Temple would soon die of an accidental overdose.

Just like Marilyn Monroe, thought Dagnar.

Or did Monroe die accidentally? Dagnar always wondered about that one.

On Temple, he didn't wonder. He knew.

· 71 ·

INSIDE THE JUDGE'S HOUSE, ONCE JUDGE TEMPLE stopped breathing Dagnar checked her pulse.

No pulse. She's dead.

His deathwatch finished, he started to complete his exhaustive checklist of setting up the crime scene. TV turned on and tuned to the BBC late news, cat water bowl refilled, new cat food set out, car and house keys put onto the key tray on the table just inside the hall-way, and so on. On the way out of Judge Temple's house, he removed the magnetic strip and was pleased to see the alarm was not dis-turbed. He folded it up and put it in one of his large coat pockets, where he had placed his EMP "flashlight device"—tools he would use perhaps again in his next assignment for Carpa. Dagnar put the chain for the "flash bang" grenade into his laundry bag and noticed that the residue from the explosion had disappeared from the front porch due to the stiff breeze. He had made the grenade himself and encased it in thin cardboard, which would burn up during the ex-plosion to leave almost zero residue. And even that was gone from the porch.

Outside the white row house, Dagnar thought about the scene he had set up for the eventual discovery of Judge Temple, which he thought would happen tomorrow at noon when her maid service was scheduled for its usual twice-a-week cleaning.

Dagnar was very pleased with himself. A perfect murder: an acci-dental overdose using prescribed drugs and alcohol by a judge in a locked house with a security alarm turned on.

Walking down the street toward Reggie's car, Dagnar treated himself to a deep pull on his flask. After he drained the contents, he wiped his lips and realized that he was still wearing the latex gloves. He removed the gloves before he got to the car.

Wouldn't want to scare Reggie. If he saw the gloves, he would prob-ably guess that I wasn't negotiating with Judge Temple, but was mur-dering her . . . Reggie may be a pompous ass, but he's no fool.

As he slipped into the left front passenger seat of Reggie's Jaguar, he said, "Well, it pays to have friends on the bench as well as Scotland Yard. Yes. Judge Temple was very amenable to my proposal. . . . She will keep her mouth shut about her evening with Justice Moorman."

"I don't believe it. She took money to keep quiet?" asked a shocked Reggie.

"No, no, Reggie. It turned out that approach was too crude for a judge like her. You were right, my man. However, she did have her price . . . although not money. As I mentioned before, she is up for an appellate judgeship, and Carpa has some pull with the upper tiers of the British government, so that is the arrangement I offered to-night. . . . The appeal court judgeship for her silence on this matter. After some beating around the bush, she took our offer. Very reasonable lady, that Judge Temple."

Reggie was quiet and then asked, "Where to now, Mr. Dagnar?"

"Back to the hotel. My business is finished here in London. . . . You better go up Bayswater Road and cut through Hyde Park to drop me off by the Serpentine. We better not be seen together again. I can explain that since we are old friends, you picked me up at Heathrow and dropped me at the Dorchester Hotel. But to be seen coming back to the Dorchester so late tonight . . . well, it really links us too much together in one day."

"I understand. . . . But the park is very isolated this time of the night. Do you really want me to drop you in Hyde Park? Eh?"

"Yes," said Dagnar in a voice that made the decision final.

"Right. Right you are. Well, then there's a little car park near the Ring Bridge. It's a short walk to the Dorchester from the lake. That should be the place. We can park and get our . . . business done before you get out," Reggie said, without taking his eyes off the road. Then he added, "Interesting place. The car park's a very popular spot to pick up prostitutes."

"Really. Well, that's okay. Probably too cold for them tonight," replied Dagnar.

Reggie's voice was hesitant as they drove past Speakers Corner near Marble Arch at the northwest corner of Hyde Park. "Mr. Dagnar . . . about my bonus. How will I get it? A wire transfer to my Swiss bank as usual?"

"No, Reggie. I have it for you in cash, in euros actually. I'll give it to you when we park. It's down at the bottom of my bag."

"Lovely," replied a smiling Reggie Whiteside of Scotland Yard.

Soon the Jaguar pulled into the small dark car park in an open spot of the huge, well forested Hyde Park. In the distance, Dagnar saw the Ring Bridge over the north end of the Serpentine Lake right ahead and farther away, in the distance, the halogen streetlights of Park Lane, where his suite at the Dorchester was waiting for him. He wouldn't go to sleep for a few hours. He was wired . . . and sexually aroused from killing the judge.

After the car stopped, Dagnar reached into his bag. Reggie was looking around to see if there were any cars or people nearby. There were several cars at the other end of the parking lot, but here in an isolated part of the car park Reggie's car was alone.

Dagnar reached into his bag and rummaged around. He quickly found what he was looking for, and it wasn't a package of euros. His right hand closed around a black instrument called an "agency letter opener."

Some people say it was developed for the CIA. Dagnar didn't care about the origin. All he cared about was that it was a seven-and-one-half-inch nonmetallic knife with a three-and-a-half-inch blade. It was a "push knife" as opposed to a slashing-type. It was meant to surprise a victim and to penetrate for a kill—the perfect weapon for a man with Dagnar's powerful arms. He had carried this type of weapon for several years and was never stopped at any security checkpoints by metal detectors. It was made of a glass fiber–based compound called GV6H. It had a comfortable contoured grip with a thumb depression for a controlled thrust. . . . And Dagnar had used this before.

Dagnar had the knife inside a thick absorbent white towel, and all Reggie saw in the dim light coming in through the windshield was something wrapped inside a white towel.

"Here's your bonus, motherfucker!" Dagnar said as he pushed the weapon into Reggie's left side with such tremendous force that Reggie's head bounced back and hit the driver's window on the right side of the English auto.

It's almost perfect—the angle I have on Reggie. For once, I'm happy these fucking Brits drive on the wrong side of the road and have the driver's seat on the right side of the car. An easy short stab to the heart for me in this confined space.

Reggie started to yell, but Dagnar's powerful left hand was soon on his mouth.

The blade, held at a horizontal plane, scraped a rib but slid past it and plunged directly into Reggie's heart.

Reggie's bulging eyes were staring into Dagnar's.

Dagnar's strong left arm kept the squirming Reggie hard against his seat.

The white towel Dagnar was using to cut down on the transfer of fibers to Reggie's outer coat had a spreading red spot coming from the middle where the knife had entered Reggie's chest.

Reggie's arms were pinned to his sides by the lower portions of Dagnar's muscular arms. Dagnar's face was almost touching the policeman's.

"Relax, Reggie. Let yourself go. Don't fight it. It will only hurt more," said Dagnar in a calm reassuring manner, looking into the wild eyes of the dying man.

And Reggie did so . . . the last hiss of his breath escaping like a deflating balloon. He died in the strong embrace of the Carpa man and the seat belt of his car.

72

DAGNAR RESTED IN THE LEFT-SIDE PASSENGER SEAT for a few minutes and then began his calculating of the postdeath orchestration of the inside of the car. To a professional like Dagnar, the scene of the crime was a stage on which to set up the proper props to give a certain effect to the audience of the police first responders and the follow-up crime techies.

First, Dagnar stabbed Reggie several more times with the knife to create the illusion for the police crime scene techies that the knifing was done by a nonprofessional. Several of the stabs scraped and cracked ribs since he held the knife vertically like an amateur for the short jabs.

Then he got out a small laundry bag that was ventilated by holes all over. Into the bag went the knife, the bloody towel, Reggie's wallet and watch, Reggie's cell phone with the battery still detached, the Scotland Yard laptop with its hard drive history of the computer search of the judge on it, the N-G tube and syringe, the special cell phone he had given Reggie for his lookout duties, and the blue baseball cap he had been using on and off all day to defeat the ever-present London CCTV cameras. In that bag was the evidence of two murders. Evidence that needed to be disposed of—forever.

Next he examined all of Reggie's pockets and the car console and glove compartment for any notes or papers that might in any way connect him to Reggie. There were none.

On his movements in the car's interior, Dagnar had been careful ever since he initially got into Reggie's car that morning at the airport. He'd only touched the door handle. Now he wiped it very clean with his handkerchief.

After a final check, and on an impulse, Dagnar used his handkerchief to pull down Reggie's fly.

Got to satisfy the dirty minds of the police by making them think Reggie pulled into the parking lot to get a blow job. A lollipop lick gone bad. A little sex that turned into a robbery and a murder. Crime happens even to Detective Inspectors.

Before he got out of the car, Dagnar quickly looked about the deserted area around the Jag. No one in sight. Then he got out of the Jag, closed the door, and started walking with his distinctive limp to the Ring Bridge over the Serpentine Lake. Before he got to the bridge, he found a rock that weighed several pounds and fit it neatly into the nearly full laundry bag.

Near the middle of the bridge, Dagnar looked around. Not a soul in sight. Knowing it was a heavy throw, he rocked back on his rear foot so far that his face was looking up at the stars and heaved the ventilated laundry bag like a large football into the lake. By the lights on the bridge, Dagnar could see it hit the water and then drop like a bubbling stone beneath the small waves of the large lake. The laundry bag was made of durable heavy plastic and would last intact for several decades at a minimum.

All the evidence is now six feet underwater, embedded in years of silt at the bottom of the lake. No one will find it.

Dagnar confidently walked to the nearby Dorchester and went up to his suite. It had an excellent view of the Serpentine Lake and the lights of the car park near it.

Looking at the distant car park, he felt charged with a kind of electricity as if he'd just won an important game—a game that was going to be worth a fortune in his bonus to be paid now and in tenure at the company as long as Fay was CEO. Dagnar was relaxed now and moved to a mood of celebration. He got out a bottle of Jack Daniel's and poured himself a large drink in a crystal tumbler.

That bitch Temple was a nice-looking piece of ass, he thought, as he replayed his touching of her and the look of her white skin.

Before he changed and took a shower, he used the hotel phone to call a very discreet and very expensive escort service he used whenever he had time in London.

His raspy whiskey voice was plain. ". . . I want your girl to stay all night. Remember the girl must be white—very pale skin—and with short dark hair. And she should bring a black robe to change into, and tell her to wear a black garter belt . . ."

Dagnar was going to relive the portion of the night denied to him.

⬧ 73 ⬧

Washington Post (Editorial Page)
Tuesday, December 16, 2008

Justice Moorman and Common Sense

Tomorrow the United States Senate starts the Confirmation hearings of Justice Oscar Moorman to become the next Chief Justice of the U.S. Supreme Court. His nomination has been controversial on the surface only because of unsubstantiated charges of misconduct. Some people say that the attempts to smear this jurist have been born in racial hatred.

It is commonly accepted in law cases that only true evidence in the record of a trial is allowed in reaching a verdict either by a jury or by a judge. Rumor and unproven charges should play no part in the rendering of justice.

So too should this standard of judging by the record be applied by the U.S. Senate. Justice Oscar Moorman has a record of excellence carved by hard work and unselfish behavior in the service of his Country and people both here in America and in Africa. Justice Moorman has distinguished himself on the battlefield during the Vietnam War, in the high reaches of governmental service, and in the humble service as a staff medical helper in African refugee camps. Justice Moorman has a record that can be judged. Unproven charges of misconduct should not be part of the Senate's deliberations. That's only common sense.

74

"DID YOU SEE THE WASHINGTON POST THIS MORNING?" asked a cheerful Oscar Moorman to his wife, Debby, as she slowly came into the kitchen. "It's a good article on the confirmation, very supportive," added Moorman.

The stress of the pending confirmation hearing had caused Debby to drink even more. Moorman was worried that she was becoming an alcoholic. He thought that the news out of London that there was no truth to the date rape rumor would have caused her anxiety to decrease. He was wrong. Last night she drank so much he had to carry her to bed. Today she was hungover and she looked depressed—a bad sign.

"It doesn't matter what the *Post* says. Your . . . my reputation has been damaged . . . beyond repair. We'll never recover," said Debby in a despairing voice.

"No, no, Baby. We're okay. The hearings will start . . . and without any more of these attempts to smear me . . . I mean us. You and I are a team and we will get through this rough spot. I should be confirmed this week. I think I'll face only the reason why I've changed my position on affirmative action. I'll try to keep secret my reason. I'll keep it vague.—but you know the real reason. We'll be fine. Trust me. The Senate goes out for the holiday recess Friday and Senator Powers said she'll get a vote by then. Soon all this mess will be in the rearview mirror."

"I don't know, O. I worry that people will always look upon us as damaged goods from the beating you've taken in the press. Besides, how can I ever trust you to stay with me? You're handsome and do have a wandering eye. All those women before me . . . how can you just stop and love just me. . . . only me? I've seen you eye other women. Look at their butts at receptions, parties . . ."

"No, no, Baby, since I've met you I don't want any other woman. Your mind is confused with the stress. I love you . . . I want to make love to you, only you."

"O, how can I believe you?"

"You've got to trust me. I would die for you. . . . You are the best thing that happened in my life." Tears filled up in his eyes, but he didn't let them out.

Looking at her, he said, "Debby, I've got to go to the Court. I've got to leave you. I've got to get ready for tomorrow's hearing—and Marshal John Abbot just called and wants to see me on an urgent matter. . . . Please don't drink today—don't drink until I come home. We'll have a glass of wine—together before dinner and go to bed early. The hearing is tomorrow. Big day for us tomorrow, Baby."

"I love you, O. I'll be good and won't drink. I love you . . . forever."

"Me too, my sweetheart. Our love is forever. I love only you."

Then Oscar Moorman left. He got in his red Corvette and drove to Court and his appointment with the Supreme Court Marshal, John Abbot. The only other black official on the highest Court in the land.

⟡ 75 ⟡

AS MOORMAN ENTERED HIS CHAMBERS AT THE SU-preme Court, John Abbot, the Marshal, stood up.

"Sorry I'm late, John. Come in."

When the ex-SEAL entered the inner office of Justice Moorman,

Oscar Moorman was a different person. With the door shut, the two black men could drop the pretenses of protocol. Behind doors, Oscar treated John as a fellow warrior—no boundaries. Moorman knew that John Abbot was wired somewhat differently. To him, Moorman would always be a Supreme Court Justice, his superior. Nevertheless, in Moorman's office, Moorman knew that John Abbot would tell him exactly what was on his mind.

Today Abbot had some bad news for Moorman.

"Boss, I've got something to show you. It's a video from the Court's security system. As you know, last year we installed a threat assessment software system to our surveillance cameras. A company called Abraxas, a private 'hush hush' company of former CIA spooks, came up with the system that tracks suspicious activity from our video feeds around the Court building and gives a threat assessment. The system is called TrapWire."

"Yeah, John. I remember you and your team briefed all the justices on it. Good stuff. So TrapWire has detected a threat?"

"You got it, Your Honor. Let me set up this DVD player. I have three suspicious events plus something happened this morning I want to show you. That's why I called you this morning and asked to get on your calendar." John Abbot quickly placed a small DVD player on Moorman's conference table and pulled two chairs up so they could watch the video together; he paused before pushing the play button.

Moorman sat down for the show. "So the Court is under a threat?"

Abbot looked Moorman directly in the eye and said in a grim voice, "No, Boss. I . . . and a few of my people who are cleared to see this classified system think the threat is directed against you."

Moorman blew out some air and tightened his lips. Then he replied, "Okay. Let's see what you've got."

Abbot started the DVD player and provided running commentary for the video that appeared on the small screen. "This first incident happened last Friday. As you can see, a white male approximately twenty-five years old is walking by the entrance to the Court's under-ground parking lot. Look at his left hand."

"Yeah. I see he's got a cell phone in it—it's open."

"Correct. Now I'll slow the video down. See it . . . He just took a picture of the entrance. Look as he goes farther down the street—just took another picture of the exit ramp from the parking garage. Taking pictures in a suspicious manner. Definitely started TrapWire software on alert . . . Well, that's incident number one," said the Marshal.

The Marshal continued as the screen went black and another video clip started. "Incident number two was on Monday morning—the same man, only this time he's wearing a baseball hat and using sunglasses. See he's waiting on the sidewalk opposite the entrance to the parking garage. Here comes a car. After it goes inside, he leaves."

"That was my red Corvette. Well, maybe he's just a news junkie? I am up for a confirmation hearing."

Abbot continued, "Incident number three happened later on yes-terday. See your car is coming up the exit ramp from the parking lot—and there is our morning visitor again, only this time he's wear-ing a fake mustache—and he does a small wave to a motorcycle going by trailing you—probably followed you home"

Moorman shook his head and said, "Could be nothing—maybe a news organization trying to get some celebrity shots for some tabloid?"

"No, sir. We played it safe and sent the video clips to the FBI Lab at Quantico for analysis. . . . Results came back late last night. Facial recognition technology at the FBI ran the TrapWire film clips through their criminal database and came up with a name. . . . Thomas Jeffer-son Stedman, a known white supremacy nut job with a criminal record of two counts of illegal firearm possession and an assault charge. He lives . . . or rather runs a 'white power' survival camp in Idaho. Now and then he travels around the country raising money for his 'white power' movement. And here's the kicker—FBI Intel told me this morning that they picked up some very reliable intelligence that someone has put out a three-million-dollar contract on you, a racially motivated contract. Oh, one more thing—as if this is not enough to confirm a serious threat on your life. There was another incident this morning when I sent out an undercover unit to do an outer perimeter walking search of three blocks from the Court. The plainclothes unit—a man and a woman—saw Stedman outside of a Starbucks two blocks away. When they approached him and identified themselves as Supreme Court police, he bolted and escaped in a black Lincoln Town Car. There were at least two other men in the Town Car. The unit couldn't get the plates. There was mud rubbed over the rear license plates. Bottom line—sir, I think you are in danger. That's why I sent out two teams to sit on your house last night—they were located on the street up and down from your house. They pulled foot patrols around your house at thirty-minute intervals. By the way, I had you shadowed by two vehicles this morning as you drove to work. . . . Well, that's it, O. I'm fucking worried."

For one thing, Moorman was surprised at the protection level he had without even seeing it.

More important, what Abbot described worried Moorman as well. That was the first time the retired SEAL—always very strict on military protocol, called him "O." For years, Moorman had been urging him unsuccessfully to call him "O" when they were alone, but he had resisted. It shocked him to hear his first name used by Abbot. It was a signal that Abbot was highly concerned about the threat.

Moorman had checked out Abbot's record before he recommended him for the Marshal's job. He learned that John Abbot was one cool operator as a SEAL, and when Abbot was worried, you better be putting on a Kevlar vest and grabbing a gun.

"John, what do you suggest?"

"Well, Sir, to start with we should use the Court's fully armored limo, then only travel by motorcade with a minimum of three police cars, and security units should be placed outside and inside your home immediately."

Moorman got up and walked around his office. He stared out the window of his chambers, looking at the U.S. Capitol directly across the street. He was thinking of the impact such a move would have on Debby, who was pretty unstable right now with the stress of the confirmation.

After a couple of minutes, Moorman turned from the window and gave his opinion on what he wanted.

"John, I want to low-key this threat for a number of reasons. No mention of this threat outside of the security detail we use. No motorcades. I want two security units around the house 24/7 and to shadow Debby whenever she's outside. Also, if it's not too much of an imposition, maybe you could drive me to and from my house until the hearings are finished. I really don't want to use the armored limo of the Chief Justice—I wouldn't want the press or the Senate to think I felt entitled to use that perk just yet. . . . Well, this is how I want to play it for now. At least untilthe confirmation hearings are over. . . . Oh—and I'd like two handguns—one for Debby and one for me."

The ex-SEAL thought about it for a few seconds and smiled, "I don't like it, but okay. Your Honor. . . . Well, here are the guns." He pulled out a .40-cal Glock from his shoulder holster and a featherweight Smith & Wesson .38 from his ankle holster.

After putting the weapons on Moorman's desk, Abbot, with a thoughtful look on his face, added, "Your Honor, I suggest you leave your red Corvette here in the garage and I drive you home in my car—whenever you're ready."

"Thanks, my friend. Can we go to my home now? I want to show Debby how to shoot. Is there a range nearby we can use?"

"No need to travel to a range, Your Honor. You have a little land around your house—a pretty big yard and lots of trees—I think we can have her fire a few rounds behind your house into the firewood stack I saw when I made a circle around your home about three this morning."

Moorman flashed a grin. "I thought I smelled something funny this morning. . . . But seriously, John, what about the noise? The neighbors will hear our target practice."

"Nope, Your Honor, they won't hear a thing. All I'll need will be a couple of half-gallon milk cartons, some cotton, and some duct tape. . . . I can make a pretty good silencer from scratch. An old trick I learned when I worked with a firearms guy from Delta Force."

❖ 76 ❖

THE BILLIONAIRE FROM ALABAMA WAS MAD. HE WAS talking on the phone to one of his lawyers in D.C. He hated lawyers and showed it often.

"Now listen, you fucking idiot! . . . If you and your law firm want to continue to earn those eight-hundred-dollar-an-hour fees, you fucking better do *exactly* what I tell you to do. Okay, once again—I want you to go to the skating rink on the Mall next to the Smithsonian Museum of Natural History tonight at seven P.M. and give a briefcase with the million . . . in U.S. dollars—all one-hundred-dollar bills—to the man in a black cowboy hat. He'll be standing at the entrance gate to the ring. When he sees you approach him, he'll say, 'Do you have skates in there?' If he says that . . . well, then hand him the briefcase and say, 'Green light.' That's all you have to do. Do you understand?"

"Yes, sir. But still—don't you think I should have him sign a receipt before I give him the money? It's a lot of money," said the lawyer in a timid voice.

The billionaire's voice rose almost to a scream. "No, no, no. This is a business deal. A highly sensitive business deal—and this is the way I want this done. Get that through your fucking thick skull! Just do it exactly the way I said or I'll be looking for another law firm. . . . Now, when the transaction is completed tonight, send me an e-mail with only two words in it—'Deal done.' If you don't make the handoff, just e-mail me one word—'Failure.' . . . By the way, I better not get the fucking one-word e-mail."

"Yes, sir. Don't worry. I'll get this deal done for you."

"Now on the simpler task I gave you, is that done? And why do I have to ask?"

"I'm sorry, sir. I should have mentioned it. Yes, the man from the photo lab just dropped off the prints to me fifteen minutes ago and I'll take them up to Senator Dalton's Capitol Hill office right after we finish our conversation and personally hand them to Senator Dalton—Just as you ordered."

"Prints, how the fuck do you know that there are prints in the envelope? Did you open it?" The billionaire's voice rose even higher and was filled with anger.

"No, no. I didn't look inside. The envelope was marked 'Prints—do not fold' on the outside of the envelope that the photo lab man gave me. I assumed that it contained photos. I didn't open the envelope—just as you ordered." The lawyer's voice sounded apologetic and nervous—and weak like a beaten man.

The billionaire was silent for a few seconds to let the fear build in the lawyer's mind.

"Never assume anything. Just do as you are told. Get both projects done today!"

Without any further words, the billionaire hung up the phone.

Green light on both projects! That uppity Moorman thinks now that the date rape is most likely off the table, he'll have a fucking cakewalk to be Chief Justice. Well, he has a big surprise in store for him with two serious shit storms headed his way. One of them will do it. I just wish I could see his face when his world crashes. He cost me a lot of pain when he was a big shot Justice Department antitrust attorney long ago. He disapproved that merger of my first company. Cost me a shit pot of money . . . and my marriage. Now I'm going to get payback.

77

IT WAS WEDNESDAY, DECEMBER 17, 2008—THE DAY that the U.S. Senate would begin the confirmation hearings on the nomination of Oscar Moorman to be the next Chief Justice of the United States.

It was a cloudy day from the start. The sun never appeared over the hill to the east of the Moorman home. Initially, all one could see above was a charcoal gray low cloud cover with a rust-colored patch of sky marking the eastern horizon framed underneath by the almost bald hill overlooking the street of the two-story colonial-style house of Debby and Oscar Moorman. Then slowly the dull light of the cold morning increased and more of the Moormans' street became visible. D.C. weather was traditionally hard to predict, but today all the TV channels and *The Washington Post* were in rare agreement—it would be a cold and overcast day.

Moorman never liked a day without sun. He was a "sunny day" lover—his spirits were usually higher on days of plenty of sunlight— and he was disappointed that today would be a dreary day.

However, there was another reason he was in a down mood. Last night Debby had too much to drink . . . again. His worry over his confirmation hearing and the tough questions he might face was overshadowed by his concern with his wife's increasing resort to alcohol and prescription drugs. She had explained to him that the drinking and the tranquilizers were only way she was able to cope with the stress of the confirmation.

On this morning, Moorman regretted his decision to accept the nomination of President Ramsey. The only good Moorman saw in the situation was that all would be over soon. He knew that the confirmation would be voted on very quickly—the U.S. Senate was in a hurry to finish it before the Christmas recess. After this was over, no matter what the outcome, Moorman had decided that he and Debby would take a long vacation, maybe to Africa—a place far from Washington and political phoniness—a place where they would have the time to figure out together how they would face up to this dangerous trait of Debby's to escape stress through drinking and pills. Moorman was confident that their mutual strong love would allow them to confront and win this battle with the twin crutches of booze and pills.

Moorman had risen early to check on Debby. He was worried. Debby . . . and also Moorman had had a tough night.

At 3 A.M., she had gotten violently nauseous. Moorman helped her to the bathroom, Afterward, when she came back to bed, he put cold, wet hand towels on her forehead and stroked her hair until she fell into a deep sleep. Moorman didn't go to sleep for another hour or so, thinking about his wife and her addiction.

When it was six-thirty in the morning, O's alarm went off. He checked with Debby and she said she was feeling better, but had a bad headache. Moorman went downstairs to get her some toast, coffee, and aspirin—that's all she said she could eat.

He served her the light breakfast in bed with a tray.

In a sad way, she thanked him when he gave her the tray and sat by her side. When she was through with her breakfast, she told him some bad news.

"O, I feel terrible. Can I *not* go to your first-day hearing? Would it be all right for you? I just don't feel well. And I couldn't take the TV lights and the press. Everybody looking at me . . . judging me . . . and you." Her eyes were pleading. He could see she wanted to stay in the sanctuary of their home.

"Sure, Sweetheart. It's not necessary for you to be there. Stay home and rest. Would you like Lucy Bianco to come over to take care of you?"

"No, O. Honey, I'm so ashamed. She'll know I've been drinking too much. She can see those things. She's already talked to me about that. Don't worry, I'll be all right alone."

"You won't be alone. There are four Supreme Court police outside watching the house and they'll have a car blocking the entrance to the driveway. If you need anything, just let them know or call my chambers. Also I'll keep my cell phone on vibrate—even during the hearing. You can call me anytime—I'll call during the day to check up on you, like I always do. I'll worry about you, my beautiful woman."

"Don't worry. I'll be fine—and I have my gun—the one you gave me. I did okay shooting at the logs yesterday, didn't I?"

"You sure did, Baby. You're a natural. A real sharpshooter!"

Debby's eyes were heavy, but she smiled weakly at the compliment. Then her mood turned serious.

"Why am I so different sometimes? O, I get so jealous about that Englishwoman—and all the other women you dated. Sometimes I think I'm going crazy."

"Baby, you're not crazy. It's just that drinking . . . drinking with those pills seem to make you into a different person. A different Debby—one who doesn't see things the way they really are. It's just a chemical thing. You know it, Honey; the alcohol shouldn't be mixed with those pills. I realize your doctor gave you them for your stress. And that's okay, to help you. But please, just watch drinking wine when you are using them. That's all . . . and I'll help you with that. We'll get through this rough patch. It's the confirmation. Soon it will be over and we'll be just fine. . . . On other women . . . from my past . . . remember there's no need to be jealous. You're the only woman for me . . . ever since I met you. You're the one . . . the only one. I love you and will be faithful . . . forever."

The pale Debby smiled broader now, "Dear sweet O, you always say the right thing . . . just what I need. Now, in the morning, I see that this jealousy thing is not normal."

As she nestled back into her deep pillow and closed her eyes, she whispered, "Don't worry, O. I'll be fine. I'm so tired. Good luck at the hearing. Daddy told me you're going to do just great."

"OK, Baby, go on back to sleep. I'll call you at the lunch break and tell you how I'm doing."

Moorman kissed her and got his clothes to dress downstairs so he wouldn't disturb her. After dressing, he fixed his breakfast—cereal and coffee.

At seven-thirty, the Supreme Court Marshal, John Abbot, rang the doorbell. Moorman answered it within a minute. He was dressed and ready to go.

"Morning, John. Come on in. . . . What's up with the vests?"

"Good morning, Sir. . . . Your Honor, well, I've been out scrounging and I borrowed some body armor from the Secret Service—good stuff—ballistic vests with ceramic plates that will stop a 7.62 round. I got them for us for our movement to and from the Court. I've a vest for Debby as well. Just an extra precaution. You know, a little edge. . . . it's always good to bring a gun to a knife fight," remarked Abbot with light humor.

"The vests are good, John, thanks . . . but Debby won't be coming with us . . . she's not feeling well," Moorman replied with a low voice, carefully looking at Abbot for a reaction.

Moorman could see by the expression on the Marshal's face that this news was unexpected . . . and bad news.

Obviously, Abbot was enough of a Washington insider to know that not having your spouse at a Senate confirmation hearing was a big deal.

So Moorman tried to reassure Abbot. "Debby has the flu. She was vomiting last night and didn't get much sleep. I think it better if she stays home this morning. If she is feeling better, she can come to the afternoon session of the hearing."

Abbot appeared to accept the explanation. "Roger that, Sir. Your call. I'll brief the security detail outside before we leave. . . . Well, shall we saddle up and get going?"

"Okay, give me a minute to run up to see how Debby is and get my briefcase from the study."

Several minutes later, the two men, wearing the ballistic body armor vests over their suits, left the house and walked toward the vehicle Abbot had parked in the driveway.

Oscar Moorman registered his surprise.

"John, is *this* your car? I thought you had a Taurus. The one you used to drive me home last night. This is a—" Moorman abruptly stopped speaking. He didn't want to hurt his friend's feelings by expressing his thoughts about the car they were about to get into.

A grinning Marshal John Abbot was obviously enjoying the confusion of his boss.

"Yeah, it's a beauty. I don't actually own it, but I always wanted a car like this. The Mercedes dealer let me take it for a test drive. . . . Maybe I'll buy it," said Abbot in a flat voice.

Moorman furrowed his eyebrows, evaluating the explanation. He continued to walk down the brick path over to the front seat passenger side and opened the door.

When he pulled on it, Moorman instinctively knew that Abbot was bullshitting him. The door was very heavy to the touch and Moorman noticed the slight green tint of the window. The glass looked about two inches thick . . . and it was . . . that and more.

Actually the glass was exactly two and a half inches thick and the heavy door told Moorman he was getting into the most unlikely armored car he had ever seen.

The vehicle was a Mercedes ML 450 SUV. It looked new and was painted all white except for the chunky gold-colored front brush guard and the matching gold-colored rear bumpers. The tires were white-walled low profiles and had spinner hubcaps, the kind that kept spinning for a while even when stopped. On the sides of the car there were painted red and yellow flames on the rear section of the front wheel covers—a feature which highlighted the probable fact that this was a "one of a kind" car.

As Moorman settled in the front seat, he calmly said, "When I get to the Court, I better check your Court salary, John. An armored Mercedes. We're obviously paying you way too much," After a pause, Moorman said, "Seriously, John, where'd you get this vehicle?"

"OK, Your Honor. I'm not looking to buy this. It's a little too much even for me. . . . It's actually a loaner from a security company out by Dulles Airport called Triple Canopy, a tier-one group . . . all ex-Delta and Rangers. I knew that they have some nice vehicles for executive protection. And since I worked with some of the boys out there when we were in the military, I called in a favor. . . . This was the only suitable vehicle they had immediately available—a recent addition to their fleet. They bought it last week at a DEA auction of confiscated vehicles. It belonged to a drug dealer in Baltimore and was confiscated under RICO. Triple Canopy will naturally repaint it black and make the vehicle more mainstream for their corporate clients after we finish using it. . . . I figured with a group of white supremacists out to lynch us black guys we needed some wheels with added protection."

Moorman shook his head and laughed. "You SEALS are something else! Good job, John. The 'white power' good old boys surely won't be looking for me to be in this car. Well, let's get started. We're just using this to and from the Court. For the movement to the hearing today, we'll just walk the one block from the Court over to the Dirksen Senate Office Building. I don't want to pull up in front of the Senate in this rig. Remember, I'm trying to project a moderate conservative image for the hearings. This car is way over the top."

"Roger that, Sir. . . . After I brief the security on the way out of the driveway about your wife remaining behind, I'll tell you about some of the cool features of our temp wheels . . . that is besides the stylish paint job."

Abbot spent a good five minutes telling Moorman about the "run flat" tires (antiballistic wheel inserts), the V8 turbo diesel engine—less likely to catch fire than a gas-powered engine—the double wrap Kevlar- and steel-reinforced structural body of the SUV—European level B6 armor that would stop at least three consecutive rounds per square inch of 7.62mm NATO armor-piercing bullets, the defensive smoke-generating system in the rear exhaust system, the swing-up gun ports installed in the four doors, and the gun armament in holsters in the front compartment—two H&K MP5 9mm automatic assault guns. Moorman could see that Abbot was like a kid in a candy store as he rattled off the specs of the "rolling Mercedes tank" he had managed to get for the rides to and from the Court.

Both Abbott and Moorman thought they were safe in their borrowed heavy "man toy."

John Abbot asked casually as they drove down the street, "I've been wondering, Sir—well, are you worried about what kinds of questions you'll have to answer at the hearing?"

"Yeah, I'm a little worried. . . . But I'll tell you this, John. I've been doing some research on the members of the Senate Judiciary Committee and, if their questions get too personal or insulting, they might regret asking them. . . . Put it this way, I'm not going to take any shit from some of those hypocrites in the Senate. I want this job . . . for myself and for our people, but I'm not going to kiss their Senatorial white asses to get it."

"Goddamn, Your Honor. I think I'm going to enjoy this," said Abbot with a big grin as he punched on the accelerator and the turbo kicked in.

As the Mercedes SUV rolled down the street where Moorman's home was situated, three hundred yards away on the hill overlooking the Moorman house, an observer was watching the SUV using a twenty-power spotter scope. He was in a woodland camouflage ghillie suit—the type favored by Marine snipers, with green and brown rags hanging from it. Wearing it, he fit perfectly into the cover of the bushes and vegetation on the hill. He blended well and was almost invisible to someone sweeping the hill with night-vision devices if he stopped or moved slowly. The man had been waiting all night, keeping the Moorman house under surveillance. When he settled into a small dip in the hill at midnight, he had immediately seen the two unmarked police cars and had followed the foot patrol sweeps around the house during the night with a four-power night-vision scope. Although it had been a cold night, the observer was prepared with top-level cold-weather gear.

The observer was purposefully unarmed in case he was stopped by police officers or by the security detail for Justice Moorman. So all he was carrying besides his optical devices was a camera with a night lens. His role was solely that of a spotter. If he had been picked up by the outer security guarding the Moorman house, his cover story was that he was looking for deer and their hiding spots. And he had taken two shots of the plentiful deer in the area to buttress his cover story. Deer season was two months away. His story was thin, but, at first blush, believable and possible enough to escape arrest.

With Moorman on the move, now was his time to report to his superior. He'd been told to make only one call—to call when Moorman left his house.

He pulled off his battery-heated mittens and dialed a number on his cell phone.

"Hey, it's Duane. The lawn jockey just left his house. You won't fucking believe what kind of car he's in—a goddamn pimp mobile! It's a late-model white Mercedes SUV with gold trim brush guards on the front and rear bumpers. . . . And get this, it has painted flames on the sides. Do you believe it? This guy should be shot for poor taste in wheels alone. By the way, it has Virginia plates that start with the letters Y R B—that's Yankee Romeo Bravo. I couldn't get the numbers of the rest of the license due to the angle I had on my scope. FYI, both the black guy driving him and our boy are wearing what looks like the bulletproof vests that the Army wears in Iraq and Afghanistan—probably military spec body armor. So be aware of that. Better tell Ray to bring some of those 'cop killer' ammo rounds. Well, that's it. It's getting pretty light now, so I better shut down my observation post and come back to the motel to warm up."

The white supremacists that belonged to this group thought of themselves as members of a paramilitary unit and liked to talk in Army lingo and wear military spec gear, although most had never served their Country in the military. Most could talk the talk, but few walked the walk.

· 78 ·

MSNBC Broadcast—Breaking News—Justice Oscar Moorman has successful first day at confirmation hearings—solid support for the popular justice.

(Washington, D.C., Wednesday, December 17, 2008, 6:30 P.M., EST) It was a dramatic day here in Washington on the first day of the pending Chief Justice confirmation process. The hearing got off to a smooth start for Supreme Court Justice Oscar Moorman.

The nomination for Chief Justice of the United States appeared to be proceeding well for Oscar Moorman. Specifically, there were several law professors, attorneys, and leaders of civil rights group who testified in support of his confirmation. Justice Moorman's moderate centrist position in jurisprudence had garnered support from a diverse group of legal scholars. In addition, human rights organizations have been uniformly in favor of his nomination, no doubt due to his well-known public role of being an advocate for programs in Africa to help victims of Aids, including his unusual role of working during recent summers as a medical volunteer in refugee camps throughout the African continent.

The first day's hearing itself started in the typical fashion. Besides the few pro-Moorman witnesses who spoke on Moorman's qualifications for the confirmation, there was the obligatory appearance of the nominee. He was introduced to the Committee by Senator Shipiro from New York, his place of birth, and by Senator Yardly from Virginia, his residence for the past twenty-five years. Both Senators were generous in their praise of Moorman.

The nominee, once he was sworn-in, responded without any controversy throughout the initial part of the afternoon. However, there were figurative fireworks late in the afternoon when Justice Moorman was attacked by some of the expected Democratic opposition to this lame-duck nomination by the outgoing President Ramsey. It was here that Justice Moorman demonstrated the plain-speaking style of a modern-day Harry Truman.

More than the high drama of an expected political opposition attack was on display because Moorman's standing up to what some considered unfair attacks was a rare picture of coequal government in action—an instance of a Supreme Court Justice talking plainly in a straightforward manner to a Senator—his equal in the legislative branch of government. Two Senators' questions were plainly abusive, but Moorman clearly demonstrated that he was not going to be cowed by any Senator. This is not an obsequious man meekly asking for confirmation as a favor with a "by-your-leave" request for a vote of confirmation. There were direct confrontations and coequal exchanges—things rarely seen in a hearing where the nominee generally takes the opposition blows without fighting back, hoping not to lose a single vote. Clearly not the case here as you can see in the following videos. We'll cut away to the dramatic video of the hearing showing the first of two such incidents of Justice Moorman upholding the coequal status of his branch and giving as good as he was challenged—an effective counterpuncher.

(Video transcript feed follows):

SENATOR HARRIET SMYTH (D-N. MEX.): Justice Moorman, I am deeply troubled by your unexplained shift of position on affirmative action. I actually think you misled this august branch by your actions. Specifically, during your initial confirmation hearings to be confirmed as a Supreme Court Justice, you unequivocally endorsed the position of being against affirmative action. Yet less than two or so years later—the very first time an affirmative action case came before you—you changed your idea and accepted the government position of allowing affirmative action in highway contracts "set-asides." I am bothered by your obvious flip-flop in this vital area. It seemed to me that you may well have committed perjury to get on the Court in your first hearing. Can you explain to me the reason for your actions—your legal . . . and your personal reasons?

JUSTICE MOORMAN: Senator, the legal reason for my vote is explained in the opinion which I authored. . . . *If* you had read the opinion, you would know that diversity in business with the government is well justified and is consistent with the law. I will say no more on that other than this: simply, the law and my opinion had stated a proper basis for this type of action.

As to the personal reason I changed my opinion on the benefits of affirmative action. . . . Well, that reason is more complicated and private—by that I mean it is based on my life experiences in personally observing recent instances of racism, which led me to the sad conclusion that America unfortunately still needs a leveling of the playing field for minorities.

SENATOR SMYTH: Hmmph, your personal reason . . . and your life experience. Well, will you explain this flip-flop more explicitly in the context of your personal life experience? Who personally told or influenced this so-called life experience?

JUSTICE MOORMAN: With all due respect, Senator, my personal life experience and my reasons for my decisions should and shall remain private for two cogent reasons: (1) judicial independence and (2) for the principle of privacy. . . . Let me give you the same right of privacy in one of your recent actions as a U.S. Senator. My personal reasons for actions as a judge are private . . . as probably should your personal reason for flip-flopping on your vote for the oil exploration tax credit within a month of your daughter being hired as a lobbyist by the Xnopia Oil Company of Russia. The good people of New Mexico obviously trust your judgment and . . . judicial privilege and my right of privacy protect my personal reasons for my decisions. . . . If that answer is not sufficient for you, I am prepared to cite another example of your own flip-flops. . . . That is, if you are interested. Do you have any further questions on this issue, Madam Senator?

SENATOR SMYTH; Ah . . . Ah . . . no. I yield my time to the senior Senator from Massachusetts.

(End of video transcript).

    As a reporter covering Capitol Hill for several years, I have never seen such a direct and effective answer to an opposition political attack. It was also interesting to me that Justice Moorman didn't show any anger during this exchange. He processed the questions and spoke from reason and obviously very well-researched information. His replies to the Senator's question were a reaffirmation of a true belief in judicial independence and the right of privacy. The principles of judicial independence and the right of privacy, in my view, have long been eroded by politically sensitive judges in confirmation hearings—judges who are too eager to please the Senate in order to gain confirmation approval.

    Well, we can mark down Justice Moorman as a strong judge who is not going to be a crowd pleaser, but a leader for the judiciary. More to the point in this hearing, he clearly is a judge who is not going to kowtow to any Senator for a favorable vote. He will not let a Senator intrude upon his personal life or question his judicial independence.

    That exchange with Senator Smyth was not the last counter-punching episode for this principled judge. There was one more instance and a far sharper exchange—one with a racial edge—between Moorman and one of the more senior Senators on the Committee—the crusty, long-serving Senator Forrest from Louisiana—that shows this judicial nominee will not only show independence and a trait of keeping his private life private, but he will attack any objectionable question with equal and measured force.

(Video transcript feed follows):

SENATOR RUTLEDGE FORREST (D-LA.): Justice Moorman, I am concerned by these here media reports that indicate you may have sexually assaulted a white . . . I mean a local woman when you were in England on some sort of speaking tour. Is there any truth to these reports?

JUSTICE MOORMAN: All such reports are false and totally without evidence. Moreover, I find that your unsupported question at this hearing is hurtful and objectionable, Sir.

Senator, with all due respect, I might add for your consideration—you, a man who has served his state in the Senate for over fifty years. Let me add a point of personal reference. To repeat such a false accusation of assault without one iota of support is probably as objectionable to me . . . as would be a question of racial prejudice to you based on the newspaper reports in the late 1980s which indicated that you, Sir, were a member of the KKK. I recollect that charge was based on a photocopy of a membership list from the KKK Baton Rouge Chapter, which appeared in several papers at the time. . . . I'm sure you resented the accusation—which you denied as a forgery—as much as I do your question today.

Do you have any other questions, Senator?

SENATOR FORREST: You . . . you . . . (muted applause in the Senate Hearing Room).

SENATOR IRMA POWERS (R-VA.): I see the distinguished Senior

Senator's time has expired. We'll now hear from the distinguished Senator from the State of Maine, Senator Martha Ringler . . .

(End of video transcript).

As you viewers can tell, it was quite a show on Capitol Hill today as Justice Moorman finished his first day of a projected two-day hearing on his nomination. The Democrats as expected did attack Moorman. However, Moorman proved himself an unexpectedly tough counterpuncher. The KKK and Senator Forrest was old news, but the Justice used it very effectively. The statement about Senator Smyth's daughter being an oil lobbyist was sensational new information. Since she didn't deny it on the spot, I am sure the Ethics Committee will be looking into that. It could be it wasn't known generally on Capitol Hill since the daughter probably used her married name to register as a lobbyist. Having a relative as a lobbyist is not per se illegal, but Justice Moorman's use of that information today certainly took the wind from Senator Smyth's sails.

In this reporter's view, I can say that I have never seen such a candid, forceful appearance of a candidate for a Senate nomination. It was refreshing to see Justice Moorman's straightforward performance today. It was especially heartening to see how well he handled the allegations of the alleged racist-based smear campaign that started with false allegations of watching X-rated movies at a Duke Law School conference. The hearings will most likely finish tomorrow as the last three Senators on the Senate Judiciary Committee have an opportunity to question the nominee. All indications from sources indicate that the majority of the Committee will recommend to the full Senate that Justice Moorman be confirmed as the Chief Justice.

This is Alberto Perez reporting for MSNBC in Washington on Capitol Hill at the Dirksen Senate Office Building.

79

Senate Judiciary Committee, Senator Irma Powers, banged down her gavel adjourning the confirmation hearing until ten o'clock the following morning.

He felt that he had done well that day, especially in handling the smear questions from the Democratic opposition.

The Marshal, John Abbot, who was in the first row of the Senate Judiciary Committee hearing room, shook his hand and whispered, "Wow, Your Honor. You did great. Where did you get that political ammo you used?"

"My guardian angel gave it to me," a smiling Moorman said in a reply whisper.

To himself Moorman thought, *Actually it was the truth. Judge Tim Quinn had his law firm do some political "dirt" research on the opposition Senators and I found all that info in a sealed thick folder hand-delivered to my chambers this morning.*

Moorman called Debby immediately after he left the hearing room and found a spot near a window where he could get a good signal on his cell. He learned that she had watched his testimony on the TV. She said she was proud of him.

"This will all be over soon, Debby Baby. We're going to take a long trip after the January oral arguments—just you and I. Maybe we'll go to Africa. There's so much over there I want to share with you. I have to go back to the Court to catch up on things . . . also I need to get some reading material for tomorrow—lot of stuff to review. Besides, I still have to read up on the three cases the Court is hearing Friday. . . . Ah, will you be okay alone?"

Please don't have too much to drink, Baby, he thought, not wanting to lecture her about drinking.

"Oh yes, I'll be fine. And I'm not alone. Lucy Bianco came over this afternoon and we watched you on TV. It was nice having her here with me. She and I are going to order Chinese for dinner, so don't worry. I know you have to prepare for tomorrow. I love you, O, and am very proud of you."

"Thanks, Baby. Everything is looking good so far. John Abbot will drive me home. I should be there by eleven. . . . I love you and will . . . forever."

"Sweetheart, you know I love those words. Will we love each other and be together forever?"

"Count on it, Baby. See you later. I'll call you before I leave the chambers to come home."

"O, I don't want to live without you. You know that, don't you?"

Moorman's voice dropped to a whisper, "Debby Honey, don't talk like that. We have a long, long life ahead of us . . . a wonderful life full of love. We'll grow old together, my Sweetheart."

"I love you, O. You're my life. I'm sorry I talked you into going for the Chief Justice. Now I really don't care if you get it or not."

To lighten the mood, Moorman replied, "Well, I just might not get it. As you can see from the way I took off on those Senators today, I don't care either."

Debby laughed and Moorman said good-bye with an "I love you, only you."

After the call, Moorman, John Abbot, and the security detail of four Supreme Court police officers left the Dirksen Senate Office Building and walked back to the Court.

At a little before eleven o'clock that night, Abbot and Moorman pulled out of the Supreme Court garage in their white Mercedes SUV, catching a few whistles from the uniforms at the security-exit checkpoint as they drove by.

Since it was late at night, traffic on the Fourteenth Street Bridge was very light as they crossed into Virginia. John Abbot was driving and Moorman was in the front passenger seat with the reading light on, looking at the pile of papers in his lap. Before long they were on the George Washington Memorial Parkway heading north away from D.C. at fifty miles per hour, the posted speed limit. Abbot obviously knew that it wouldn't look good to get a speeding ticket when Moorman was in the middle of a Senate confirmation hearing.

The GW Memorial Parkway was noted as one of the main commuter routes out of D.C. for Virginia residents. It was a beautiful four-lane wooded highway—two lanes in each direction with a large grass median separating the north and south lanes—and followed the Potomac River, the river which separates D.C. from Virginia.

Abbot and Moorman had just gotten on the GW Memorial Parkway when a heavy Harley-Davidson pulled up even with their SUV. Abbot glanced at the rider, who was looking into the SUV. Abbot immediately punched on the accelerator and the SUV shot to seventy. The big motorcycle effortlessly accelerated and again was alongside the SUV. Abbot braked hard and the Mercedes SUV fell back to fifty. The Harley, however, shot forward and rocketed down the parkway, its red taillight growing smaller and smaller. It had to be doing ninety.

"Better turn off that reading light, Sir. I think we've just been ID'd. Hopefully just by the press, but maybe by some bad guys." Abbot spoke in a calm flat voice.

Moorman had been lost in thought reading a summary of a case he would be sitting on Friday and was confused. "What did you say, John?"

"Sir, a motorcycle came beside our vehicle and took a long look at you reading by that light. It may be nothing, but please kill the light—and you better take those MP-5s off the rack and jack a round in each of them. Take them off safe and set the selector switch to automatic. If the motorcycle man was a bad guy, we may be headed into an ambush. Most ambushes begin by a personal identification of the target . . . and that would be you. Maybe it's nothing—just an ambitious member of the press looking for a shot at the next CJ, but I've got to tell you—I've a bad feeling deep down. This motorcycle guy was way too professional the way he matched speeds and then took off. A press tracker would have dropped back to follow us."

That was sufficient warning for Moorman. He kept the light on just long enough to unhorse the two compact submachine guns from the gun rack in the center of the vehicle and ready them to fire, putting one on each of their laps—then he killed the light.

John has good instincts—good to play it safe and be ready.

Abbot kicked up the speed. The SUV soon passed Key Bridge and the turnoff for Spout Run, the last exit for two miles. The GW Memorial Parkway north at this spot is a dangerous stretch of road for an ambush. There was really no shoulder to the road here. To the right was a three-foot stone wall that prevented cars going off the steep embankment and into the Potomac River no more that five yards off the roadway. To the left was another stone wall preventing motorists from crossing the median, which was narrower here.

Just past the exit, they saw two large towing trucks partially on the side of the narrow road with their yellow top lights flashing. In front of the trucks was a dark Lincoln Town Car with its emergency lights blinking.

"Funny it takes two tow trucks for one car," remarked Moorman, thinking out loud.

"I don't like this, Sir. Can you unbuckle and take a good look to the rear?"

"Roger that, John."

As Moorman twisted around in his seat, the barrel of his MP-5 assault gun clacked against the gearbox and drew a quick rebuke from Abbot.

"Sir, *please* point your fucking gun outboard. I don't want to ruin your nomination by getting shot accidentally by you—bad press. . . . Now tell me what you see."

"The tow trucks have moved . . . they're side by side, looks like they're stopped, blocking the roadway. The Town Car is speeding up toward us. It's really hauling ass; its emergency lights are still blinking." Moorman was almost shouting now.

Abbot barked, "Turn forward and look ahead. I've got the Town Car in the rearview mirror. I need some eyes front."

"Fuck, there are two cars ahead—side by side." Abbot was going seventy again.

Soon the still blinking Town Car was tailgating the SUV and there were two heavy Town Cars blocking the way ahead. As Abbot was ten feet from the rear of the right car, the left car dropped back.

The Mercedes SUV was trapped in a "rolling roadblock"—it couldn't pass—it was stuck in the far right lane of the narrow road with a stone wall to its right.

Abbot looked beyond the four-car tight formation and saw the possible endgame of the deadly road game.

"Goddamn it. I should have seen this coming."

Three hundred yards ahead was a lighted bridge, spanning one of the creeks that fed into the Potomac. There were steel guardrails on both sides of the bridge. A pickup truck was stopped on the bridge blocking both lanes.

"They're probably going to block and decelerate us to stop our car on the bridge—that'll be the killing zone," observed Abbot with a flat voice, as if he were ordering a pizza from Domino's.

Almost as he said it the lead car started to break gradually and slow down.

At the same time, the window of the car to the left of the SUV came down. A black barrel stuck out and opened fire on the SUV.

Immediately spiderwebs appeared in the bulletproof glass, but, as advertised, no penetration.

"Well, there goes our only element of surprise—they know now we're armored," said Abbot.

"What do we do, John? Once we're stopped on the bridge, that bulletproof glass won't last forever will it?" said Moorman.

"Roger that, the glass is rated for only three rounds of 7.62mm in one place max. Looks like the gunman is using an M-16 with smaller 5.56mm rounds now. If we're stopped—and if they keep firing at the same place—there *will* be penetration, and after that we'll get rounds ricocheting around inside this Kevlar coffin, making Swiss cheese of us. Bulletproof is only a relative concept."

They were going only forty mph now, as the "rolling roadblock" was working. Abbot tried to smash his way out to the left and to the front, but the blocking cars were only inches away and the Town Cars were heavy—their drivers skilled. The left car front passenger obviously realized he was up against an armored vehicle so he smartly switched to a heavier weapon—an M-60 machine gun with 7.62 rounds. The heavier rounds striking the sides of the SUV made that fact pretty clear to Moorman.

"Talk to me, John. What do we do?" shouted Moorman above the pounding of the M-60.

"Take the wheel—drive straight. I'll do the gas and breaks. I'm going to light up the car on the left so we can get out of this shit. Ready . . . now."

Moorman unbuckled again and grabbed the wheel. Abbot lowered his driver's window three inches and poked out his MP-5. He emptied half the thirty-round mag into the passenger's door and the other into the Town Car's engine. Almost immediately, the Town Car on the left veered away from the yellow flashes of the MP-5 and started scrapping the left stone wall in a shower of sparks. At the same time, the engine started to smoke and the car decelerated abruptly, finally coming to a stop.

"I got the wheel back—now hold on. I'm going to take out the car following us," shouted Abbot as he slammed on the brakes causing the trail car to crash into the rear of the SUV. Moorman without a seat belt on crashed heavily into the front windshield, breaking off the rearview mirror.

Abbot wasn't through with his breakout maneuver.

He was now fifty feet behind the lead Town Car and he punched the turboengine hard. The lead car had slowed down, so when the

Mercedes hit the Lincoln Town Car the speed differential was at least thirty miles per hour—a jolt that sent Moorman bouncing off the dashboard.

Both the trail car and the lead car were rapidly stopping now—there was no gas for their powerful engines. The fuel cutoff, which was installed on most Town Cars to prevent engine fires, had stopped the fuel flow to the engines.

Abbot swung the SUV to the left, and in its wake were three disabled Town Cars. The road to the bridge was clear. However, there was the matter of the pickup pulled sideways across the narrow two lanes of the bridge about one hundred meters ahead. Moreover, Moorman could see in the halogen light of the bridge that there were two men standing behind the pickup—both had what appeared to be tubes with large pointed projectiles on the front of each one.

"Christ, John. They have RPGs," yelled Moorman. He could barely see out of his left eye. By instinct he patted his head and felt some warm sticky liquid on his forehead—blood from the gash over his eye when it hit the rearview mirror. It didn't seem to hurt much. There was too much going on to feel the pain.

Just as Moorman warned Abbot, there was a bright flash and a puff of smoke from one of the tubes. A sparkling object looking like a fireball came roaring toward the SUV. Abbot jerked the wheel to the right and the rocket-propelled grenade whizzed by their vehicle by inches.

Abbot shouted, "Scramble into the back and fucking hold on. We're going to smash through the truck. . . . As soon as we're past the truck, I'm going to lower the rear window. Empty your magazine at the bridge. Now listen up. This is fucking important—you've got to direct some serious firepower on that bridge. We've got to put their dicks in the fucking dirt, because we can't outrun an RPG-7. Grab an extra mag and use them both. Got it, O?"

"Got it," yelled Moorman as he climbed into the backseat.

The pickup was perpendicular across the roadway at the far end of the bridge. Abbot floored the pockmarked SUV and aimed his right front wheel at the pickup's right rear wheel. The wheels at the front of the truck would be harder to ram through because the heavy engine gave them more traction with the roadway. When the SUV hit the rear—the lighter end of the truck—the pickup swung like a hinged barroom door. As soon as they were by the truck, Abbot hit the smoke-generating switch on the dash and Moorman let loose with thirty 9mm rounds from his assault gun in several controlled bursts. He changed mags, loudly shouting, "loading" to Abbot so he would keep his eyes on the road and not turn around to see if Moorman was hit. Then after Moorman put a fresh clip in the assault gun, he lit up the bridge with another thirty. There was no RPG response. Not even small-arms fire came from the bridge.

The SUV rocketed up the traffic-empty GW Memorial Parkway toward the exit to the rear gate of the Central Intelligence Agency—it was two miles away and Moorman agreed with Abbot that it was one of the safest places to stop this wild ride. Abbot punched in "911" on his cell and reported a shooting on the GW just north of Spout Run. "There are armed and dangerous men in the disabled cars near the bridge . . ." After he alerted the 911 operator, which would start a local (Arlington, Virginia Police) and a federal (the Park Police) response, Abbot punched a speed dial for the Command Center of the U.S. Marshal Service. Once connected, he ordered the "on-call" SWAT team dispatched to protect the Moorman home and asked the duty officer of the command center to alert the CIA security force that he and Justice Moorman were headed to the Agency's back gate. Abbot gave a description of his vehicle and added, ". . . and make sure you give the CIA our vehicle description and let them know who's in it!"

When Moorman slowly climbed into the front seat, Abbot looked over and saw the blood on O's clothes.

"Are you hit?"

"Negative, just bumped my head on the rearview mirror. You should learn to drive a little smoother."

Abbot let out a loud laugh. Moorman joined in.

"Fucking good job, John!" Moorman said as the laughter subsided and he pounded Abbot's back with his hand.

"Fucking good job yourself, Judge. Not bad shooting for an old Navy man!" replied Abbot.

When the shot-up Mercedes SUV screeched to a stop in front of the CIA rear gate—a turnoff one hundred yards from the GW Memorial exit—ten guards appeared and two searchlights lit up the Mercedes.

Under the glare of the bright entrance-gate lights, Moorman, bleeding from a bad cut over his eye, and Abbot wisely exited the bullet-pocked vehicle without weapons and with their hands high in the air.

A smart move when you are pulling up at night to an installation that has standing orders to shoot at the slightest provocation.

It was a tense moment. The guards all had their guns trained on Moorman and Abbot.

Just then a tall black man in black combat fatigues, carrying a sawed-off Mossberg 12-gauge military shotgun, stepped in front of the twin searchlights and said in a deep roar, "I recognize Justice Moorman. Stand down and lower your weapons. . . . Call the duty doctor ASAP. We have a Federal Judge who is wounded."

Then the guard supervisor came forward and softly spoke. "You can lower your hands. . . . Welcome to the CIA. You guys are safe now."

Moorman turned to Abbot and, with a slight grin, remarked, "Somehow that sounds funny."

Then Abbot, Moorman, and the CIA guard all broke out in deep laughter.

✦ 80 ✦

explained what happened and reassured her that he was fine. "I'll be home soon, Honey."

Within fifteen minutes, a military doctor on call for the CIA came to the gatehouse and gave Moorman six stitches for the cut above his eye, putting a large butterfly bandage on it.

In less than an hour, Moorman was holding his Debby and whispering into her ear, "I'm fine, just fine—and we're safe now. John Abbot has arranged for increased security for us. Nobody is going to hurt us."

They went into the kitchen. Moorman was ravenously hungry and made a sandwich for himself as he told Debby about the GW Memorial Parkway ambush. He noticed a notebook on the breakfast nook table and saw that Debby was keeping a file of news stories— and all of Judge Quinn's reports to the Senate Judiciary Committee.

When she saw him page through it, she remarked, "I'm keeping a record of your confirmation. Daddy is helping by faxing me all of Quinn's reports."

"I don't know, Honey. When this is over, maybe we should try to forget about it. It's been a rough road for us."

To calm them both down, Moorman opened a bottle of white wine and changed the subject. Instead of the confirmation, they talked about their possible trip to Africa for a while.

"Baby, I know it's hard to believe, but when you are out on the African plains away from city lights, it seems that there are twice as many stars in the sky. I want you to see that with me. To share Africa with you—alone and away from Washington. It will be wonderful. . . . I love you."

"I'd like to go with you to see the beauty of it . . . and also to see what you've seen these past summers—the ugliness of the refugee camps. I want to see everything you've seen," said Debby.

That might not be such a good idea. Sometimes when he was work-ing in those medical clinics in the camps, he was moved to deep sadness by the pain he saw, especially in the eyes of the children. These places must be where God goes to cry . . . maybe we'll stay away from the camps.

"Well, let's wait until after the hearings to plan. I think tomorrow will be the last day of hearings. And I have to hear three cases on Friday—the last arguments of the calendar year. . . . Maybe we'll start our African trip planning over the weekend? . . . Honey, shall we go to bed now?"

Moorman locked up the house and called Abbot before they went up to bed. Abbot was headed home for a few hours of sleep.

In the bedroom, Moorman saw Debby was opening her medicine cabinet. When she was aware of his look, she insisted she needed two Valiums to get to sleep. He watched her take the pills and felt sad.

In Africa, we'll work on this problem.

Then he waited to hear her shallow breathing indicating she was sleeping. Only then did he allow himself to close his eyes. Moorman needed nothing more—the firefight on the parkway and the wine were enough to make him sleep like a rock.

Moorman woke before the alarm could go off at six. It was an old habit . . . or a curse. He possessed a mental alarm clock that most of the time woke him up before any alarm he set. If he knew he had to be up by 6 A.M., his eyes popped open usually at five minutes to six.

Leaving Debby asleep, he went downstairs and made coffee while looking at the morning news. The story about a wild shootout involv-ing a Supreme Court justice dominated the news on almost all sta-tions. Moorman was surprised at the depth of the known details—the three-car rolling roadblock, the shooting of the left blocking car, and the RPGs at the bridge. He knew Abbot had given a detailed version of the attack to at least three investigative teams during the long night: the Park Police, the Arlington, Virginia Police, and the FBI. It was now clear that someone was leaking the specifics . . . big time. He got his morning papers at his doorstep and saw that his parkway gunfight was the top story in both newspapers—*The Washington Post* and *The Wall Street Journal.*

The *Washington Post* front page had the best headline and captured the whole story:

RACE-DRIVEN ATTEMPT TO KILL JUSTICE MOORMAN FAILS

Well, the Post *finally got a story exactly right,* thought Moorman as he sipped his first cup of the day.

He was very interested in the details. According to both papers, there was one known death from the shootout—Thomas Jefferson Stedman, the well-known white supremacist. A bullet had pierced his neck and he bled to death in the front seat of a car stitched with holes in the right door and in the hood. Two suspects—both identified quickly as faculty members of the white power survival camp in Idaho—were arrested on the scene. The news report speculated that they possibly were left behind due to their injuries–one was wounded with a bullet through the knee and one with a broken arm and leg. The automotive wreckage on the GW Memorial Parkway had turned into a huge crime scene and the parkway was closed for over four hours.

At seven o'clock, Moorman received a call from Senator Irma Powers. After she identified herself, she asked with apparent concern, "Are you all right?"

"I'm fine."

"Oscar, the reports say you were injured. Do you feel up to appearing at the hearing today? I'm changing the hearing to eleven o'clock . . . and moving it to the Senate Caucus Room in the Russell

Senate Office Building—it's the largest room in the Senate office complex. I think it will be maxed out due to all the media play."

"I'll be there, Madam Chair."

"O, with all this happening . . . my staff thinks . . . well, this is all good for you. This makes you and your black driver real heroes . . . very good for the confirmation."

Ah, now I know where the leaking is coming from—Powers' staff members probably got the FBI reports and were dishing out the details like crazy.

Moorman didn't quite know what to say. Senator Powers obviously was looking at the GW gunfight as a tool in a political power play that could be used to get the confirmation through quickly.

What planet is she on? Abbot and I almost got killed and she thinks it is "good for you." I guess politicians have no souls . . . just polls.

Realizing that he didn't want his anger to come out, Moorman merely replied flatly, "I'm fine. I'll see you at eleven."

Then he recovered and couldn't help adding, "By the way, the African-American who was with me wasn't a driver. He's the Marshal of the Supreme Court."

Moorman hung up without waiting for a reply.

The phone had apparently awakened Debby because he heard her coming down the stairs.

After they hugged each other and kissed, she said in a soft voice, "O, I'm so glad you're alive. Last night must have been a nightmare. I'm coming to the hearing with you today. I can't be apart from you. I can't live without you. When we die, I want us to die together."

Moorman pulled back slightly, looked her in the eyes, and said, "Great, Honey. I would love to have you at the hearing today with me. And as for dying, well . . . that won't be for a very, very long time. You and I have a lot of living to do first, my sweetheart. A lot of living and loving. And with our strong love, anything is possible . . . maybe we will die together. But not yet."

He held her face in his hands. His dark hands framed the pale white face looking up at him. He was struck by the contrast in the skin color.

As he looked at her, he thought, *That's what last night was all about. It was all about skin. Killing over skin color. Madness!*

· 81 ·

THE SENATE CAUCUS ROOM IS IN THE MASSIVE Russell Senate Office Building. The room has a long pedigree and is the place of choice when there are major hearings—the Watergate hearings in the early seventies, the Senator McCarthy hearings on the communist scare in the fifties, the Truman hearings on waste in the Army in the early days of World War Two—all those historic hearings took place in this large beautiful room with its high ceiling and ornate crystal chandeliers.

By eleven o'clock the room was packed.

In the front of the room, the long green felt–covered table with nameplates and microphones for the members of the Senate Judiciary Committee was lit up with klieg lights, just like a movie set. Those powerful carbon-arc lamps gave good visibility for the TV cameras that were jammed to one side of the long hearing bench.

As Justice Oscar Moorman with his wife at his side walked down the center aisle to take his place at the witness table—a small heavy oak table set up in front of the Committee's hearing bench—something unusual happened . . . and set the tone for the hearing about to take place.

With the Senators already in their seats, looking over papers in front of them or turned sideways in whispered conversations with their legislative aides, Moorman's arrival was greeted with a hush through-out the large room . . . and then a few people got up from their seats and started clapping. Soon everybody in the room stood and ap-plauded the entrance of the black man with a heavy bandage over his left eye and his white wife. Even the Senators eventually stood. It was a stirring sight, beamed by the TV cameras to millions of people all over the globe. A magic spontaneous moment.

The Senators, very used to telling which way the political wind was blowing, immediately got the message: There was a hero among them . . . and no one better throw any mud on the hero.

The hearing could have been described as a love fest. The Sena-tors all knew that they were in the reflected light of one of the biggest stories of the year—an assassination attempt on a man who would most likely become the leader of one of the three branches of the U.S. Government. A white-power assassination that failed because the black man who was targeted personally fought back and shot his way out of the killing zone of a deadly ambush. A strong backlash against the racist attack to prevent Moorman from being the first black Chief Justice built up in the hearing room and in the media. As the GW in-cident story unfolded during the day, it became clear that a vote against Moorman would be viewed as politically incorrect . . . very politically incorrect.

Accordingly there were no political attacks on Justice Moorman or his judicial opinions this day. All the Senators took their turns praising Justice Moorman as a justice and as a role model for his work against AIDS and decrying the evilness of racial hatred.

At the end of the hearing, the Moormans were mobbed by well-wishers at the witness table. Abbot had arranged for security to pro-vide an escape route from the packed room. As Moorman and Debby exited through a side door to get away from the press and the friendly crowds, there was Judge Tim Quinn standing alone outside in the cordoned-off corridor of their escape route. Moorman went over to him and, in a friendly hug, whispered, "Thanks, Tim, for the materials yesterday. Good stuff, especially the info on the KKK."

Quinn whispered back, "The Committee is set to vote in a few minutes in closed session. You should get approval. Powers thinks she can get the recommendation to the full Senate for a confirmation vote tomorrow before the Senate recesses for the holidays."

The hug broke up and Moorman introduced Debby to his Guardian Angel.

AFTER THE HEARING, JUSTICE MOORMAN AND DEBBY rode to their Virginia home in a heavy motorcade. Abbot insisted and Moorman agreed, in part because he had Debby with him. Two D.C. motorcycles and two D.C. police cars provided the lead, and they were followed by a pair of armored Tahoe SUVs borrowed from the U.S. Secret Service. The Moormans and Abbot rode in the five-year-old armored Cadillac limo with communications gear that was reserved for the Chief Justice. The communication setup was very high tech—the latest equipment, including several telephones, one an encrypted satellite phone—a fax machine, two radios, and a TV with video conferencing. The equipment was installed to ensure that any emergency legal papers or matters could be handled by the Chief Justice. The motorcade was trailed by another borrowed armored Tahoe from the Secret Service.

Back on Capitol Hill, in a small conference area next to the Senate Caucus Room, Senator Powers immediately convened the Senate

Judiciary Committee in closed session. After a brief discussion that she forcefully led, she called for a committee vote on the nomination; the committee vote was 12-0—no dissents. Thus the Senate Judiciary Committee formally acted. The Committee would recommend to the full Senate that Justice Moorman be confirmed. The news was immediately released to the press so the committee vote could become the lead story on the major networks' evening news.

The special communication gear in the Chief Justice's limo came in handy. Shortly after the announcement of the Committee's vote to the press, one of the phones in the limo rang. Abbot, in the backseat with Moorman, answered it.

Senator Powers was on the phone.

"It's for you, Your Honor," Abbot said, and handed the phone over to Moorman. That's how Moorman found out about the Committee vote—in the limo before the motorcade reached his home. After he ended the call with Powers, he told Debby. She was ecstatic. Moorman silently said a prayer, *God, please help me do a good job.*

❖

As the media crowd was breaking down their equipment outside the entrance to the Senate Caucus Room after the media announcements that followed the Committee's vote, Tim Quinn spoke to Vicky Hauser and Bill Sharkey. "Let's go back to Dirksen and plan what's on tap for tomorrow."

They went out the staff exit one floor below and walked the block back to the Senate Judiciary Committee's offices in the Dirksen Senate Office Building.

Quinn started the meeting with a question for Sharkey. "Well, what's the news from the FBI investigation? Have you kept up?"

"Yeah, Judge. One of my pals in the Dangerous Crimes Unit told me in the late afternoon that the Bureau has rolled up almost all of the boys in on the ambush—total of eight at this time. The eight counts their dead leader, Thomas Jefferson Stedman, and the two guys left at the scene. Looks like the entire hit team came from the

Idaho survival camp and were in the D.C. area for at least a week, staying the last few days at a motel in Arlington," replied Sharkey.

'Was it a contract hit or was Moorman just the wrong color?"

"According to the couple of rednecks who are singing to get reduced jail time, they say it's a contract. Plenty of money—all cash—to finance the operation. Rented three Town Cars for the ambush. Again according to the boys talking, the money came from one source—a D.C. lawyer who represented someone who wanted Moorman taken out. The money was passed to the late Stedman somewhere in D.C. Stedman was alone when he picked up the money and didn't mention any names . . . or so the boys cooperating say. This scenario on the money fits with FBI info on Stedman. He was very secretive about funds. A real tight ass about all financial info and where he got the money for his survival camp. Well, there you have it—no clues about the source of the contract money. . . . Well, that's all the FBI knows so far."

Quinn and Vicky listened attentively to Sharkey.

When Sharkey concluded, Vicky changed the direction to the pending confirmation. "Did Senator Powers say anything about where she wants us for the Senate vote tomorrow?"

Quinn closed his eyes and grimaced. "Damn, completely forgot. Thanks, Vicky, for reminding me. . . . Yes, she wants all three of us to be waiting in the Senate Cloakroom with the files on Moorman, in case one of the senators needs to look at anything during the debate before the vote. . . . So why don't we all meet for breakfast at seven A.M.? The Senate will probably begin at nine. The Moorman vote will probably be handled in the morning. As you know, the senators are in a hurry to recess for the Christmas holidays."

"Well, Judge, if that's it. I'll head home. Looks like we're approaching the finish line with Justice Moorman."

Quinn yawned, stretched in his high-backed leather chair, and got up. "Okay, meeting adjourned. See you both at seven. Let's meet in the Senate dining room. I'll get there early and get us a table. . . . By the way, on the finish line, Bill. Remember we will have quite a bit of work to do after the confirmation—writing the final report and packing up the Moorman information for the archives. So the finish line for the three of us won't be for at least a couple of weeks. . . . But now that we're near the end, I want to say, it really has been great working with you two. Vicky and Bill, in my view, Moorman wouldn't be getting confirmed without your great work."

Vicky responded with a serious tone. "Well, let's remember this is Washington. A confirmation is not done until it's done."

THE DEMOCRATIC MINORITY LEADER OF THE SENATE and the billionaire were in a telephone fight. It was after midnight and Senator Dalton was still in his office in the Russell Senate Office Building.

The billionaire was very disappointed with the committee vote.

It was difficult for both of them to fight on the phone because of the subject matter. Both men knew they had to be careful to talk in ambiguous terms and not use any names or specific terms. But the two men did have to communicate right now, and a telephone conversation was far better than e-mail, which left a permanent record. Nevertheless, in these days of eavesdropping, legal and otherwise, one had to choose words very carefully and use metaphors and tired clichés to disguise the content of the conversation.

Even though no one could see it, Senator Dalton had a pinched face that showed his displeasure. Nevertheless, his politician voice was controlled and seemed to be very friendly. "Yes, yes, I understand what you would like me to do, but really I think that the train has left the station. And, in my opinion, his train is very popular and almost unstoppable."

"Fuck your opinion. These pictures may well stop that train. Just get them to the right people in your . . . ah . . . organization."

"That would be very difficult at this stage. Why don't you arrange for them to be leaked to the media?"

"Listen, the goddamn media is on *his* side and will closely examine these photos with a fine-tooth comb. . . . These items I had delivered to you are good, very good . . . but they are not perfect. Bottom line, under the scrutiny of a real expert, they won't float. They'll be recognized as fakes."

"Well then, it's hopeless. Our organization will eventually send them to experts as well," Senator Dalton countered, pressing the point. He really didn't want to be pulled into doing anything on Moorman now. The fight was over politically.

This guy doesn't get it. The Moorman fight is over. Continuing to try to block the nomination is fucking stupid . . . it's like paying your bar tab on the Titanic *after it hit the fucking iceberg.*

The billionaire was adamant. "Sure, I'm not an idiot. I know that your people will send them to the experts . . . but it will take hours and, while these are studied, they will have to postpone the vote. By then, your organization will already be out of session—in recess for Christmas. Then, with all of the Christmas holidays, I can think of something else to stop this guy. Just get me the time. Get the fucking vote postponed—leak those things to someone who can slow down the vote," the billionaire said with zest and enthusiasm.

Senator Dalton thought, *Great! Now anybody listening will know that the "organization" is really the Senate. Who the fuck else votes and goes into recess? Corporations don't go out of session. God, I hate pleasing this idiot. Sometimes I wonder how the fuck he made all his money.*

Giving up, Dalton said flatly, "All right, all right, I think I know where to insert . . . your things . . . into the process. I'll do my best."

84

AFTER THE CONVERSATION WITH THE BILLIONAIRE, SENator Dalton stood and went over to one of the floor-to-ceiling windows of his office suite in the Russell Senate Office Building and looked out at the light traffic on Constitution Avenue. RSOB, the oldest of the Senate office buildings, was opened in 1908, very pre–air conditioning. Once the tall windows could be opened to allow cool air in during the hot Washington weather; tonight Dalton wished he could open the window and throw out the chains that tied him to the bitter billionaire—and maybe the billionaire as well!

Why the fuck does he hate Moorman so? It had to be more than racial hatred. Although the billionaire had frequently used the "N" word in private over the years, the billionaire's diverse companies had men and women of color in their highest ranks. The reason for this vendetta had to be deeper than color.

Dalton didn't rise up the "greasy pole" to become the Minority Leader of the U.S. Senate by making mistakes. He had figured out how he would get those photos that had been handed to him by the billionaire's D.C. unethical lawyer to "someone in power"—a person who could slow down the vote based on what was in the photos.

Dalton would literally and figuratively leave no fingerprints on those photos. He intentionally only touched the outer envelope. The lawyer assured him that the inner envelope and the photos were clean—no fingerprints were on them, since ultimately they might find their way to the FBI or another investigating agency's laboratory.

Naturally he could not give the photos to one of his fellow

senators—they were all spineless political creatures who had shown their unwillingness to stop this lame-duck nomination in the face of the overwhelming support for the "heroic" Justice who was wounded in a dramatic assassination attempt.

No, he would give the photos anonymously to the one person in power who had the integrity and strong character to inform the Senate there were photos that showed current misdeeds of the "hero of the day."

Dalton would soon leave his office and walk through the underground passageway that connected the RSOB to the Dirksen building. There he would carefully slip the "fingerprint-free" inner envelope with the photos from the outer envelope and under the door of the Senate Judiciary Committee office of the Special Counsel, Judge Tim Quinn.

Quinn's strength—his integrity—would be a weakness of the system Dalton could exploit. Quinn's sense of duty would ensure that, before voting on the Moorman nomination, all the Committee members would receive damaging photos of Justice Moorman via one of Quinn's "Report to the Committee" e-mails.

Dalton counted on Quinn as one of the few people in the political jungle of Capitol Hill who would not bury dirt—he was a man of honor.

He would never know it, but Senator Dalton came close to being wrong.

· 85 ·

IT WAS A BIG DAY. THE FINAL LEG OF THE MOORMAN marathon and Tim Quinn woke up at 5 A.M. and couldn't get back to sleep. So after grabbing coffee as an eye-opener and scanning *The Washington Post*, he headed to the Dirksen building.

It was a little after six-fifteen when he entered his office and kicked a thick envelope as he turned on the lights.

The envelope had no name on it, but obviously had been slipped under the crack of his door. It felt thick. With sleepy curiosity, he ripped open the envelope and the contents—several 8" X 10" black-and-white photos—fell on the floor. There were two copies of three different shots taken with a telephoto camera with a night-vision lens. He picked up one copy of each shot.

The first photo was a very clear one of Justice Oscar Moorman at the wheel of his 2008 Corvette. Tim knew it was a new car because that evening at the University Club Moorman mentioned it to him as part of the small talk leading up to Moorman telling him about Judge Morgana Temple. The shot was large enough to show the Virginia plates on his car.

A second photo showed two very young ladies in small halter tops and very short skirts that barely covered their thighs. The ladies were on a street corner. They were standing next to the same Corvette, which was now parked at the curb next to the women. It looked like one of the ladies was bent down, talking through the passenger window. Their profession was a guess, but an observer could speculate it was prostitution.

The third shot clearly showed the purpose of the gift slipped under Quinn's door—one of the ladies, most likely a hooker, was getting into the Corvette. The photo showed the same plate as the first shot—the plate showing the car driven by Moorman.

Damn it. This is the proverbial turd in the punch bowl. Things are going so well and the Senate vote is hours away.

Tim's mind went into damage control. These photos proved nothing. No crime or evidence of wrongdoing.

Why don't I just shred them? These probably are fake. A last political or racial attempt to stop the confirmation by smearing a good man. Why don't I pretend I never got these photos?

For Tim, he had a time-out for a full minute, sitting on a fence between ethics and politics. Tim really wanted Moorman to get a pass on this smear attempt—then Tim decided what he would do.

He had to do the right thing. He stopped the mental debate and became the honest lawyer that he hoped he was. He went to his file cabinet and got some transparent folders. Then he got out his handkerchief so he wouldn't leave fingerprints on the clean copies—a complete set of the three shots was still on the floor where they'd fallen. And put the pictures in the folders—one in each. He put the folders, which had his fingerprints on them, on his desk so he could study them. And he put the folders with the photos he hadn't touched in a large manila accordion folder together with the now empty envelope—Tim had decided to send everything to the FBI lab at Quantico.

It was almost six-forty. Tim called Vicky on her cell, catching her as she was getting into her car. "Vicky, this is Tim. Something has come up. I need you at the office. Can you call Bill Sharkey and get him in here? Breakfast will have to wait."

"Sure, Tim. I'll give Bill a call. What's up?"

"We had a very strange overnight delivery. I can't discuss it on the phone. But breakfast is out. I need you and Sharkey here—in the office ASAP."

Within twenty minutes, Quinn, Vicky, and Bill Sharkey were

going over the set of photos that Tim had touched with a magnifying glass.

"Same license plate—car looks the same. Well, it's clear a pro took these—a camera with night vision, the angle and the focus—all that show it. But whether the hooker is actually getting into Moorman's car is the real question. If it's a fake, it's a very good one," commented Sharkey with the glass almost pressed into his face.

"Will the techie at the FBI lab at Quantico be able to tell it's a fake?" asked Vicky.

Sharkey shook his head. "Hard to say."

Quinn focused on the key issue for him. "We can't say it's a fake. We can't say it's real. What we must decide is whether we tell the Committee. The Senate opens in less than two hours."

"Christ, it will be hard to even get these clean ones without your prints on them to Quantico—and before the right guy at the lab—in two hours," said Sharkey.

Vicky spoke softly. "We have evidence—whether it's fake or not—we must tell the Committee before the full Senate takes up the Committee's recommendation to approve Moorman. It's our duty."

Quinn nodded and said, "Vicky's right. I'll have to tell all the Committee members. I'll have to attach the photos—I mean, they are the story here—and tell them we're getting the photos analyzed by the FBI Lab. . . . Bill, I want you to take these to Quantico ASAP. You better leave now. It's going to be a tough drive through the D.C. morning commute."

"Maybe not. I have a friend over at the air operation center of the Park Police," replied Sharkey. He hesitated a beat and added, "Judge, if you fast-track the lab for me, I might be able to borrow a chopper for the run to Quantico. . . . If you've got the juice, we may get a quick turnaround from the lab on the question of whether the 'hooker in the Corvette' shot is fake."

Quinn's head nodded approval. "I may have the juice. The FBI Director is a former Federal judge. I'll call her—those photos are important. That one of the lady getting into what looks like Moorman's car could be a real killer."

Later Quinn would remember these very words and wonder why he had said them.

<u>E-MAIL</u>	(Committee Senator—Eyes Only)
FROM	TIM QUINN, SPECIAL COUNSEL
DATE	FRIDAY, DECEMBER 19, 2008—8:05 A.M. EST
TO	MEMBERS OF U.S. SENATE JUDICIARY COMMITTEE
<u>SUBJECT</u>	<u>CONFIDENTIAL—REPORT TO THE JUDICIARY COMMITTEE #5 (3 attachments)</u>

Early this morning, my office received anonymously three photos, which have been scanned and are attached to this report. The photos, if authentic, taken as a whole present a potential story of questionable judgment for the nominee, Justice Oscar Moorman. For instance, the attached photo marked #3 could be viewed in an unfavorable light with regard to Justice Oscar Moorman and what appears to be contact with a lady whose identity is unknown at this time and who may prove to be a prostitute.

I strongly caution you that the photos have not been authenticated and, in light of past attempts to discredit the character of Justice Moorman, these photos may well prove to be yet another attempt to smear Justice Moorman. Accordingly, I have sent the photos to the FBI Laboratory at Quantico, Virginia, for photographic analysis on an expedited basis. I expect that such analysis will be completed by late morning today.

Nevertheless, I am obliged by the execution of my duty to send this unverified information immediately to you for your information and the exercise of your discretion in light of the pending vote on the Moorman nomination.

As I have said, the FBI analysis may prove that all photos are fakes. However, it may be prudent to delay the report of this Committee's recommendation that the nomination of Justice Moorman be approved by the full Senate until the analysis results are reported to me by the FBI Laboratory.

I will keep all Committee members fully and immediately informed of any developments on this issue and the results of the FBI Lab analysis.

If there are any questions on this issue or any other matter pertaining to the nomination file of Justice Moorman, I and my Deputy, Ms. Hauser, will be available to answer any questions on the Senate floor today. We will be located in the back of the Senate midway between the two cloakrooms from nine o'clock until the expected adjournment of the Senate today.

(Attachments # 1–3—scanned photos)

Timothy R. Quinn
Special Counsel
U.S. Senate Judiciary Committee

❖ 87 ❖

o'clock Friday morning, he had no idea of the threat to his nomination that had just materialized in the offices of the Senate Judiciary Committee. As are all secrets in Washington, the Quinn "Report to the Judiciary Committee" would probably be leaked across the Senate within minutes of being sent out to the committee members.

Unaware of the Quinn Report at this time, Justice Moorman was focused on the matter at hand—his day of hearing oral arguments on three cases. As he traveled in the Court limo with its muscular escort of three security vehicles and two D.C. police motorcycles to the Court, he spent the time reading over the bench memos and the parts of the records for the three cases. Abbot was in the rear of the limo with Moorman. The glass privacy shield behind the driver was raised so that Abbot and Moorman could talk without being overheard.

"Today's a big day, Your Honor."

"Let's hope so. I never thought the nomination would be this hard. Mostly for Debby."

"Listen, Sir. I know it's been tough, but God bless you for what you are doing for America. I never imagined a black man would be the head of the Court that handed down the *Dred Scott* opinion. . . . You're making history, black . . . and white history. Thank you for fighting the fight." The tough SEAL eyes were almost shining with tears that he would never let out.

Moorman saw the emotion and said nothing. He just made a fist and punched the black fist coming back to him.

Then Moorman buried his head back into the Court papers of one of the case files and kept reading until the motorcade arrived at the gleaming white marble Supreme Court thirty minutes later.

Each case was scheduled for an hour of oral argument and the hearing of the first case was to begin at nine-thirty sharp.

As usual, all the justices robed in the Court's conference room, just off the side entrance to the now vacant chambers of the Chief Justice. Before they went out into the Courtroom, they all shook hands and greeted each other.

The custom of a handshake before oral arguments was an old one and a part of the Court Moorman liked very much—it had begun in the very early 1900s at the suggestion of the Chief Justice then, Melville Weston Fuller. Fuller thought all the justices doing so before each day's oral arguments would make the Court more of a family. Moorman admired Fuller for that and hoped that he could contribute such an addition.

As Moorman worked his way through the handshakes to Vincent Bianco and shook his hand, he did so with true warmth.

"Thanks, Vince, for your friendship. . . . And your wife, Lucy, has been a blessing for Debby. Lucy has been a big help. Please thank her for me."

Vince Bianco nodded and said nothing as both men joined the line of justices filing out of the conference room in their march into the back of the Courtroom.

For Moorman, the first case seemed to go quickly. His mind naturally wandered to speculation on what would happen in the Senate. Soon, the case was over and the attorneys who argued the case packed up their papers and were seamlessly replaced by the attorneys for the next one.

The second argument was barely underway and the clock at the rear of the courtroom showed that it was ten thirty-five.

Then the most unusual thing happened.

One of Moorman's secretaries came into the Courtroom from the side section of reserved seating—something that had never happened before. She then stepped up on the dais behind the bench and walked behind the seated justices. She stopped behind the high-backed black leather chair of Justice Moorman and reached around, handing the surprised Moorman a small piece of paper.

It was a handwritten note which simply read: "Your wife is waiting on the phone. She's crying and desperately wants to speak with you *now*."

The word "now" was underlined twice.

Moorman stared at the note

With the lead attorney deep into his opening remarks at the podium, Justice Moorman looked into the eyes of his secretary. He had never seen her appear so upset. He nodded, quietly got up, and together they went through the burgundy curtains behind the Bench toward the rear exit.

As they rapidly walked down the empty marble corridor behind the Courtroom toward Moorman's chambers, the secretary said, "I'm sorry, Your Honor. I just didn't know what to do. Your wife sounded so . . . upset and said such frightening things."

"Like what?" asked Moorman, continuing his fast gait so that the secretary had to run to keep up with his long strides.

"Ah. . . . Like she was going to kill herself . . ." came the hesitant answer from the secretary, who was breathing hard from the pace.

Moorman bit his lower lip and abruptly stopped, his forehead creased in deep furrows. He thought for a split second and calmly ordered the secretary to go back to the Courtroom and get Marshal John Abbot, ". . . and have him meet me in the garage with the Chief's limo and one of those armored Tahoes—the one with the police lights on a rack on the roof. . . . Have him get both ready to roll ASAP . . . I'm going to call my wife and may be leaving to go home very soon."

The woman turned around and, with her heels clacking on the floor, ran back toward the Courtroom.

Moorman ran toward his chambers and within two minutes was alone in the inner office behind his desk talking to Debby. As he started to pick up the phone, he glanced down and saw several pink phone message slips on his desk, including two marked "Extremely Urgent"—one from Judge Quinn and one from Senator Powers. They were dated today—at nine-forty, just after the hearings in the Courtroom started.

Noting the messages, he picked up the phone and the blinking light marking his private line went to a solid light.

"Baby, what's going on? Why are you crying? . . . I don't understand."

A sobbing voice, definitely slurred, responded," You . . . son of a bitch, you've been cheating—a whore, a damn whore . . ."

"Honey, I don't know what you're talking about. Please tell me."

"God, a whore. . . . The report . . . photos . . . I'm so embarrassed . . . you bastard. . . ." Debby was incoherent, now crying in heaving gasps.

"Debby, listen carefully to me. I'm coming home right now . . . don't drink anymore. Do not take any of your pills. Lie down on the sofa. I'll be home in twenty minutes."

IT WAS NINE-FIFTEEN WHEN VICKY HAUSER FELT HER cell phone vibrate in the pocket of her navy silk suit jacket. Cell phone ringers naturally were prohibited on the floor of the U.S Senate. She glanced at the incoming number displayed and smiled. It was Sharkey's phone. She hurried over to the entrance to the Republican Cloakroom where she could take the call.

"Vicky Hauser." She said after she flipped the phone on to take the call.

"Counselor, Sharkey here. Where's the Judge?"

"About ten feet from me talking to Senator Powers here inside the cloakroom."

"Put him on. I've got good news about Moorman."

Vicky waved and caught the eye of Tim Quinn. He quickly disengaged from Powers and came to Vicky, who just said, "Sharkey," and gave Tim a thumbs-up.

Quinn said, "Talk to me, Bill. We're under the gun. Powers is pissed at me for not burying the photos. Tell me they're fake!"

Sharkey got right to the point. "The FBI Director must love you. She really lit a fire under the Lab. They already finished with the analysis and the report is being faxed to our office and to the Republican Cloakroom fax machine addressed to you. Bottom line: Photo #1 appears authentic. Photo #2 and Photo #3 have been technically altered. A license plate—the Virginia plate registered to Moorman—has been superimposed over another plate. The techies found that there was an underlap of a few millimeters that showed the existence of another license plate underneath. Moreover, the techies looking at the tire treads find that the Corvette in Photo #1 has eighteen-inch Pirelli racing tires and the Corvette in Photos #2 and #3 have eighteen-inch Goodyear Eagle F1 tires. So the treads show that there definitely are two different Corvettes."

"What tires does Moorman's car have?" said Quinn, asking the key question.

Sharkey was ready—an old pro. "I sent two Special Agents from the WFO over to the Supreme Court garage where Moorman's car is parked. He has Pirellis! The agents also called the dealer listed on the license plate holder and found out that Moorman ordered specially wide Pirelli racing tires when he bought his car last August—he drove it home with Pirellis," replied Sharkey.

"Damn, Bill. That's good news. The 'hooker in his car' photos are fakes," said Quinn with a smile on his face, and repeating the news out loud for Vicky's benefit, who was watching Tim's face closely for signs of the results. She smiled widely.

Sharkey continued. "There's more, Judge. The FBI photo people found that there were two distinctive dings in the other Corvette's right door and none in Moorman's 'vet. The agents who went to the garage confirmed that there were absolutely zero dings in Moorman's right door. . . . It's a clean sweep. The 'vet in Photos #2 and #3 is definitely not the Moorman car . . . and the FBI lab report, which incorporates the field agents' info from the examination of the Moorman car in the garage, definitely says so. That report should be waiting for you and Vicky at your location—in the Rep Cloakroom fax basket now . . . also in the fax machine in your office."

Quinn whistled and said, "Good job, Bill. A real home run! Vicky and I will tell Senator Powers and we'll distribute the FBI report to the Committee members immediately. Looks like the Senate will get to vote on the nomination this morning."

Quinn was happy for Moorman because his team had defeated another attempt to smear a good man.

After he snapped the phone shut, Vicky was standing close to him. On impulse, he hugged Vicky and kissed her on the cheek.

When he pulled away, he was struck by how good she felt . . . and smelled.

JUSTICE MOORMAN AND JOHN ABBOT WERE ALONE IN the back of the Chief Justice's limo headed north on the GW Memorial Parkway—the fastest way to the Moorman home in McLean, Virginia. The armored Tahoe with four Supreme Court police officers was in the lead and, since traffic was light, it wasn't necessary to use the roof rack flashing lights or the siren.

"Driver, could you put up the privacy glass? I need to make some phone calls."

"Yes, Your Honor." And it was done.

Moorman immediately called his home. No answer.

He tried Debby's cell and got voice mail.

"Damn it. Can't get through to Debby. John, call the security outside my home and see if my wife is still inside."

Abbot got a quick call off. He had put the security chief on speed dial.

After checking, he reported, "Sir, she's still at home."

Abbot obviously sensed there was trouble at home and, in an apparent attempt to give Moorman some privacy, said, "Sir, do you want us to stop? I can get in the front of the car. Maybe you want to be alone to make your calls?"

Oscar Moorman had both eyes closed in thought, but waved both his hands indicating a "negative" and, after a beat, said, "John, I trust you. Here's the situation. My wife called me—very upset. Someone has told her something, something bad about me—she's not herself. I think she's drunk. So I need to be with her." He hesitated to say the next thing. "John, I get no answer at home. Debby told my secretary she was going to kill herself. She has the .38. I'm scared . . . I really need to return some calls to find out what's going on."

Abbot nodded and replied, "I understand, Sir."

Moorman used one of the car phones to call Tim Quinn.

Moorman was cautious. "Tim, I got a message you called. What's going on? Any developments?"

An excited Quinn could barely contain himself. "Yes, yes. O, things couldn't be better. You probably haven't heard because it just happened. I'm on the floor of the Senate. You just got *confirmed*. The vote was 75 to 20 with 5 not voting. . . . Congratulations, Mr. Chief Justice!"

Moorman was puzzled.

Why was Debby so upset? There had to be something else. Her father, Senator Sloan, might have told her something from the Senate debate. Something negative that set her off.

"Was there a big fight before the vote? Any negative stuff said about me?"

Quinn replied, "No, nothing. Straight vote . . . wait a minute, Oscar. Were you told about my Report early this morning? Before the vote? It concerned some photos we quickly dealt with this morning. Something negative . . . that we proved was another hoax later, after my Report went out. Once we confirmed that this new stuff was false, you were confirmed."

Moorman said cautiously, "No. I heard nothing about that early Report of yours. What was in it? Was your Report . . . what was said about me?"

Quinn explained, "There were phony pictures of a hooker getting into your car. They were delivered to my office this morning. We had to inform the Committee that the FBI would investigate them. The pictures were attached to the initial Report I sent out to the committee early this morning. . . . Later the FBI proved the photos to be completely fake. The photos were technically altered. Your license plate was pasted on another Corvette to make it look like a hooker was getting into your car. The FBI Lab proved it to be a clever trick . . . computer-altered pictures. Completely discredited by the official FBI Lab report. . . . With that question removed, the Senate voted to confirm you. The commission has already been sent to the President. It's probably been signed by now and delivered to the Court—they had a Secret Service courier to get the commission document to him ASAP for his signature. The oath of office will be sent to the Court. I advise you to be sworn in immediately. The Clerk . . . or the Marshal is authorized to do it. The ceremonial swearing in can be later—in a few days."

Moorman was stunned.

That's what happened. Her father faxed the photos of a hooker to Debby. That's what probably set her off.

After asking a few more questions and hanging up with Quinn, Moorman explained the dizzying chain of events to John Abbot. Abbot focused on the positive and was very happy for Moorman.

"So it's been sorted out and now you're confirmed. That's great. Congratulations, Mr. Chief Justice."

However, Moorman was somber. He had a confrontation coming up. Debby would have to be reasoned out of the hysterical booze or pill state she was in. He had an uphill battle ahead. More and more over the last few weeks, he noticed the effect that the alcohol and drugs were having on Debby, the irritation, the combativeness, the loss of short-term memory—sometimes his Debby was gone and another one was in her body.

Within minutes, the two-vehicle convoy screeched to a halt in front of the Moorman home.

"John, please stay with the car and monitor the phones. Please keep this situation to yourself. I need to talk to Debby alone. I'll call you in after I calm her down and put her to bed to rest. . . . She just needs to sleep and then she'll be fine. When she's okay—well, you can come in and we'll have a cup of coffee then."

"Roger all. You know this info *will* stay only with me, Chief Justice."

"I know, John. I know. You're a good friend. See you in a bit." Then he turned, took a deep breath, and started for the house.

As Moorman walked up the brick walkway to the front door and disappeared into his home, John Abbot was standing in the open rear door of the limo. He heard a single phone ring behind him and then the clatter of an incoming fax from the commo panel in the limo.

John Abbot got into the limo and closed the door while he reached for the fax.

90

MARSHAL JOHN ABBOT READ THE FAX AFTER IT HAD
been printed and had fallen into the tray under the fax machine on
the communication panel in the back of the limo. It was a one-page
fax that read:

Judicial Oath (28 U.S.C. section 453)

**I (Oscar D. Moorman) do solemnly swear (or affirm) that I will
administer justice without respect to persons, and do equal right
to the poor and to the rich, and that I will faithfully and impar-
tially discharge and perform all the duties incumbent on me as
Chief Justice under the Constitution and the laws of the United
States. So help me God.**

Oath Administered by_____

Date_____

Abbot thought, *Well, the Presidential Commission for the Chief Justice
has now been signed by the President and received at the Court. The
White House moved fast.*

Abbot verified that fact by a quick call to his office. Yes, the commission had arrived.

*Now all that needs to be done for Justice Moorman is to have the Ju-
dicial Oath administered to him and he will officially become the Chief*

*Justice of the United States. I can do this for O. The quicker it's done the
better.*

◈

Abbott knew that it was customary for a justice or judge to be sworn
immediately after the Commission signed by the President arrived at
the Court. As an official authorized to give oaths, Abbot himself had
privately sworn in the last two members of the Court in his office
within hours of their signed Commissions arriving at the Court.

He also knew about ceremonial swearing-in events, which usually
occurred days later after the first oath was given. The ceremonial administration of the oath would allow time for invitations to be sent
out and receptions planned. It was then that each justice would have
a public ceremony at the White House with all the pomp of the President in attendance.

However, the administering of the first oath was the "real" one
that counted as official. As it was known around Washington, the first
oath was for "dough" and the second was for "show." That meant that
a justice or judge took office and came on the federal payroll officially at the time of the first swearing-in.

Abbot decided that when he was invited into the Moorman house
for coffee, he would suggest that he administer the oath to Moorman
immediately.

*Moorman had a long tough road to be Chief. Better to cross the fin-
ish line ASAP.*

With that in mind, Abbot folded the oath in two and stuck it in
the inner pocket of his suit jacket.

· 91 ·

WHEN OSCAR MOORMAN ENTERED THE FOYER OF HIS house, he heard Debby crying in the kitchen.

In order not to scare her, he called out, "Debby, I'm back from the Court."

The sight he saw when he entered the large kitchen made his heart sink with sadness. She was sitting at the breakfast nook table with a bottle of vodka and a glass in front of her. On the table also were three faxed copies of photos and a single sheet of typed paper.

That must be the Report Quinn said he gave to the Judiciary Committee this morning. Damn her father for sending this to her!

His wife was half dressed; she was barefooted and was wearing only a dress skirt and a bra. Her hair hadn't been combed and the black eyeliner had marked streaks down her face from the tears she had shed over this Report. When she looked up at him, her eyes had a faraway glassy look in them.

"Well, home from your other . . . girlfriends," Debby said in a slurred voice.

"Honey, let me see that report." Moorman slid into a chair opposite her across the table and grabbed up the Report and the three photos. He studied them without a word.

Then he put them down on the table and calmly said, "I talked to Judge Quinn and he said that the photos with the prostitutes are fake. A trick on the photos played by a computer. Debby, don't you understand this is another hoax . . . a phony smear?"

"Sure . . . I get it. Your Judge Quinn . . . friend is covering for you."

Debby suddenly reached over and grabbed the photo which showed a girl getting into the Corvette.

She waved it in the air and her voice was strong and hard. "This proves you've been unfaithful. And cheating on me now . . . you've only had that car for a few months. . . . You bought that damn car . . . to get women."

Then she brought the photo down and, holding the picture in front of her . . . staring at it, she whispered in a small sad voice, "Am I not enough for you? Why . . . why go to other women? Are they prettier . . . younger?"

Moorman was moved to tears. "Baby, baby, you're so wrong. You are all I want in life. I want no other woman. That photo is a lie. . . . I never had another woman since I met you. . . . Please . . ." His voice broke and he stopped talking. He lowered his head and put his hands to his forehead.

He heard Debby's chair slide back as she stood up . . . it was at that moment he noticed the small .38 caliber featherweight revolver in the waistband of her shirt.

"Debby, honey. Give me the gun. We're safe. John Abbot has the security detail outside. . . . Please give me your gun." As he said this, Moorman slowly got up and faced his wife across the small breakfast table.

She smiled with a mean face he'd never seen before. The different Debby was here. The one without reason. The one that came when she had a bad combination of drugs and alcohol. "So the big war hero is frightened of a little girl with a gun. . . . No, the gun is mine . . . you gave it to me."

Moorman reached over the table to grab it. As he did, she pulled back and now had the gun in her hand . . . pointing at Moorman.

"Come on, Debby, give me the gun. You don't need it now."

He slowly came around the table and moved where she stood. She was standing—the short barrel still pointed at Moorman. Moorman inched forward, uttering in a soothing voice, "Come on . . . please, give it to me . . ."

When he was within arm's reach, Moorman made a very quick move to snatch the gun.

To Moorman, the small gun made a large roar. Maybe it was because of the low ceilings of the country-style kitchen.

Moorman didn't feel any pain, just a punch—like a boxer had given him a sharp jab in his stomach. He thought she had missed until he looked at Debby.

Her eyes gave him an indication—the full story came when he patted his front.

His hand came away full of sticky redness. He looked at it and wiped it on his pants.

Then his legs lost their power to stand and Moorman fell to his knees.

He looked down and saw the amount of blood he was losing and knew what the outcome would be. He had seen this before—with the Marines in Vietnam.

It was then he realized what he had to do with his time left. Debby would be frightened, he had to take care of her, to reassure her . . . to forgive her.

"Debby, Baby. You have to listen to me." Moorman felt that he was drooling. He lifted his hand to his mouth. It came away red.

Debby's face was a mask of shock and remorse . . . and realization. A pump—a rush of adrenaline swept through her body and pushed away the effects of the drugs and alcohol. Debby was more alert now. She was terrifying alert.

"O, I'm sorry. Dear Jesus. It just went off. I'm so sorry."

"Don't worry, My Love. I'm going to be fine. It was a mistake . . . a mistake that I . . . I caused by reaching for it. I caused the gun to go off. It wasn't your fault . . . it was an accident."

A wave of dizziness caused Moorman to fall to his side on the kitchen floor. Debby dropped the photo and gun . . . and got down to cradle Moorman in her lap.

She was holding him and petting his hair. "I'm so sorry, sorry, sorry."

"My beautiful Debby, we know this was an accident. What's important is that you know that I love you . . . always have . . . and will be with you forever. That photo . . . it wasn't me. I would never do that. You're the one . . . the only one . . . one." Moorman was getting cold now and very sleepy. So sleepy. It was getting dark.

"Debby, I love . . . love . . ."

And then he exhaled a large breath . . . and never breathed again.

◈

Debby could hear shouts outside the front door. She knew the infinity of the reality she now occupied. She had lost her man. A long time ago, she had decided she would never have another man.

O was the one, the only one.

She would go with him. That was her decision.

Debby was peaceful as she brushed the hair out of her eyes. She reached over and picked up the gun. She didn't want to hurt her face so she put the barrel inside of her bra and pulled the trigger as she heard the kicks on the front door and the splinter of wood.

The bullet traveled the short distance and split her heart, which was already broken.

◈

John Abbot came through the door first with his Glock extended in firing position. He saw through the hallway into the kitchen. A foot was visible. Proceeding forward cautiously, he entered the kitchen and saw the two lovers in the middle of the floor.

"Clear," he shouted.

Debby was holding Moorman in her lap and her head rested against his. It was as if they fell asleep together. There was a widening pool of blood . . . so much blood beneath the bodies of the couple. The blood was touching the false photo of infidelity. Soon the photo would be covered with the blood of both lovers.

Abbot heard the feet stomping around the house and the men's shouts of "clear" room by room as the house was checked for intruders. He rushed to check the pulse on the necks of Moorman and his wife . . . gently and with care to confirm by touch what his eyes had told him.

◈

Supreme Court Marshal John Abbot's face was stone as he went alone into the study as others were shouting for 911 and ambulances. He had made a decision.

He was cool and composed as he pulled out his Mont Blanc pen and the folded paper from his inner jacket pocket.

Then he did it.

He committed a perfect crime and changed the history of the Nation.

He calmly signed and dated the Judicial Oath paper. He quickly left the study and walked to the front porch, where several Supreme Court police officers were waiting.

He ordered the security detail head to call the first responders and inform them not to risk injury in a high-speed run to the scene. "And tell them to have the medical examiner come. We have two dead bodies."

Then he told the security head to call the Clerk of the Supreme Court.

"Tell him that the Chief Justice is dead."

❖ 92 ❖

NBC Broadcast—Special Report—Chief Justice Oscar Moorman is dead.

(McLean, Virginia, Friday, December 19, 2008, 3:30 P.M., EST) It was a dramatic day here in McLean, Virginia, a suburb of Washington, D.C. I am just down the street from the home of the new Chief Justice of the United States, Oscar Moorman.

As has been reported earlier this morning, Moorman was confirmed by the United States Senate just hours ago.

We have just learned that after the President signed the Commission, Oscar Moorman was sworn in by the Marshal of the Supreme Court as the first African-American Chief Justice of the Supreme Court.

Unfortunately, we now have received official notice that he is dead. His wife, the former Deborah Sloane—daughter of Senator Sloane of Connecticut—also is dead.

Our viewers are cautioned that all the information is tentative, but we have just learned that the new Chief Justice was slain in an apparently tragic accident involving a handgun inside the Moorman home. There is speculation that Mrs. Deborah Moorman took her own life following the accidental death of her husband. I repeat, this is unconfirmed at this time.

Initial reports of a new assassination attempt on the life of the new Chief Justice similar to the widely reported attempt two days ago on a highway outside Washington have been discounted as false.

We will be keeping viewers informed of any developments on the possible causes of this tragic double death as new information surfaces. This is the second unexpected death of a Supreme Court justice in the past month. Conspiracy theorists have been outspoken in alleging that there is a plot to kill all members of the Supreme Court. Responding to public concern and as a temporary emergency measure, the President has authorized Secret Service protection for the remaining seven justices. This offer apparently has been accepted by all the justices, according to a spokesperson from the Supreme Court.

In addition, the Director of Communication for the Supreme Court has issued a statement that tentative funeral arrangements for Chief Justice Moorman and his wife have been made. According to her, preparations are being made for the Chief Justice to lie in repose in the Great Hall of the United States Supreme Court Building on December 22—this coming Monday. The public will be allowed into the Great Hall of the Supreme Court to view the closed coffin from 7 A.M. until 10 P.M. (Eastern Standard Time).

Heavy crowds are expected for the public viewing of this popular jurist.

Chief Justice Moorman and his wife will be buried with full military honors in Arlington National Cemetery on Tuesday, December 23, following a memorial service at the Old Post Chapel, Fort Myer, Virginia.

Justice Roscoe Farnsworth, the senior Justice of the Court, will fill the administrative role of the Chief Justice until there is the installation of a new one.

This is Brett Ackerman reporting for NBC News with a Special Report from Washington, D.C.

(*End of video transcript*)

93

DECEMBER 23, 2008, WAS A COLD, CLEAR, BLUSTERY day in Washington, D.C. There were long security lines at the main entrance to the military installation of Fort Myer, the Army post right next to Arlington National Cemetery.

The funeral memorial service was to begin at 11 A.M. at the Old Post Chapel. By ten-thirty, it was apparent that a mistake had been made by the funeral planners. The funeral service site would be inadequate for the crowd of mourners. Although the service was by invitation only and the list was very select, it had been assumed that many of the political invitees would not attend a funeral this close to the Christmas holidays. That assumption was proving to be wrong by the still arriving throngs of mourners. Moorman's popularity was producing a higher yield rate for the invitation list.

It was clear that there would be many more people attending the service than the two hundred capacity for the chapel. It was unfortunate that the Post Commander could not move the service to the New Post Chapel, which could take a hundred or so more. The larger chapel was under renovation and could not be used even if there was time to reroute the attendees. With the Old Post Chapel rapidly filling and reports from the gate guards reporting more cars heading onto the post for the service, the colonel as post commander did the only thing he could do—he ordered six more rows blocked off for senior VIPs—ranking judges, members of Congress, cabinet officials, and ambassadors. The first two rows had already been reserved for the Sloane family, Justice and Mrs. Bianco, and the other members of the Supreme Court. He probably was appreciative that the President and Vice President were unable to attend the funeral. The President was in Afghanistan for a pre-Christmas visit to the war zone and the Vice President was attending a Pacific Rim National Security Summit meeting in Korea. If they both had been able to attend the service, they and their required entourages would have added to an already maxed-out attendance problem for the small chapel.

Justice Vincent Bianco was scheduled to give the only eulogy in the short service. Although Senator Sloane initially wanted to speak at the service for his daughter, he was in no shape to take the stress in talking about his only child. Especially since learning that the Quinn Report and its photos—one covered in blood—were found next to the bodies, his state of mind had deteriorated to the point where he was almost incoherent with grief and guilt over faxing the Quinn Report to his daughter.

Justice Vincent Bianco and his wife, Lucy, had arrived at the Army chapel a full hour before the service. He was the first of the justices to arrive via their individual Secret Service motorcade. Bianco was basking in his key role as the only speaker at the funeral service and was shuttling back from his place in the front row to one of the two family waiting parlors off to the side of the altar. In one of the parlors was the devastated Senator Sloane with his brother and other family members who came down from Connecticut for the burial of Debby. Oscar Moorman, childless in both marriages and an only child with his parents and his ex-wife dead, had no close family attending his funeral.

At this time, just before the service, Justice Bianco was completely energized and focused. He had already attended the seven o'clock Mass at his own evangelical church near his home in Great Falls, Virginia. After attending Mass, Bianco went into the study in his home and had prayed himself to a near euphoric state. After that experience, Bianco felt infused with a holy purpose.

He was convinced that today—with God's help—he would set into motion a movement to gain a Presidential recess appointment as

Chief Justice of the Supreme Court. Since the Congress was in recess until early January 2009, the President had the power under Article Two of the U.S. Constitution to appoint Bianco to any presidential-appointed vacancy by granting a commission, which would expire at the end of the next session of Congress.

Bianco had been thinking about getting a recess appointment since the moment he heard Moorman was dead.

As a practical matter, Bianco would become Chief Justice under this recess appointment provision just by the President's act of signing a commission. It would not require any Senate hearing or confirmation and would be effective immediately—an appointment that would only last until the end of the next Congress two years from now.

Two years was fine with him. What really mattered was the goal—he would become the Chief Justice of the United States. And he would have almost two years with the help of the new Majority Leader of the Senate—Senator Dalton—to possibly get a full lifetime appointment from the new president to make his Chief Judgeship last until he died.

After his private prayer session, he felt that God had given him permission to use whatever means he could to become Chief Justice. And he was going to do whatever it took—even if it meant violating his judicial oath and breaking the law.

God had spoken to him. The end justified the means.

Bianco was willing to risk all to gain all—the Chief Judgeship.

To get the recess appointment from the President, he needed a very connected and powerful champion to advance his cause. And he had given much thought to this ever since he learned of the death of Moorman.

He knew it would be fatal for him to personally campaign for the appointment. To the political world, it could not appear that he wanted the recess appointment. It had to appear that the Chief Judgeship was offered to him in order to stabilize the Court and to relieve the public's apparent perception of a constitutional crisis on the Court due to the sudden loss of two justices. In Washington, smoke and mirrors hide ambition and crafty maneuvers. History had been replete with examples showing that high-level appointments are rarely given to people who overtly show their desire. In hypocritical Washington, no matter how desperate you are for a position, it was fatal to show it. Better to let others campaign for you.

And in Washington, no one led a campaign for a recess appointment without a sufficient motive of self-interest.

The brilliant Bianco thought he had uncovered the motive to get a powerful champion for him. His champion was a she.

And like a good judge, he had decided how to ask her so his request would be a two-way street—something for her . . . and the Chief Judgeship for him.

I know how I will win her over. I have what she wants—a motivation to make her go to the President on my behalf.

Before the service began, Justice Bianco kept a sharp eye out for his target—Senator Irma Powers, the Chair of the Senate Judiciary Committee and a rising star of the Republican party—the apparent Republican front-runner for the 2012 Presidential election.

Fifteen minutes before the service was scheduled to begin, he spotted her getting into one of the VIP pews; he rushed back and slipped into the vacant seat next to her.

"We need to talk, Irma," Bianco whispered.

Bianco knew Irma Powers fairly well. In her capacity as the Chair of the Senate Judiciary Committee, he had dealt with her many times over the years on a professional basis, since he was the justice who usually testified each year on the budget and needs of the judicial branch. Socially, he constantly saw her around Washington at many parties. In fact, last summer he had arranged for her and her husband to fly with him on a corporate jet to a law-school seminar in Florence, Italy. The trip was first class all the way—a free five-star hotel plus a generous meal allowance in Italy for a week and the corporate jet from and back to Washington gratis, since he arranged for her to teach an afternoon seminar with him one day—a very sweet deal and well within the "rubber" borders of the Senate ethics rules. From his dealings with her, he knew she was an astute politician and an extremely ambitious woman. He could see her cautiously eyeing him even now. No doubt suspecting he would ask her a favor.

"All right, Vince. Now?"

"Yes, please. It will just take a minute. Follow me."

The Old Post Chapel was filled to capacity with the side aisles jammed with standing mourners, but the military ushers made a path for the Justice and the Senator to the empty side corridor leading to the two family waiting parlors in the front of the church off to the side of the altar.

When they got to the side corridor, he said, "I've arranged to have the use of one of the family parlors."

Senator Powers stopped and countered, "Let's talk here."

"Ah, Irma. You think the parlor is bugged? Still a bit of paranoia in you, I see."

Senator Powers pinched her face in response.

"Sorry, Irma. Just a joke. Here is fine," responded Bianco, realizing he had offended her.

Then he got to the deal right away.

"I want you to persuade President Ramsey to give me a recess appointment as Chief Justice. . . . The Court has lost two justices and needs stability."

Irma Powers shifted her glance down to her shoes, shaking her head and replying without eye contact, "Too big of a favor, Vince. I know you would be a great Chief, but Ramsey is on his way out and has other priorities."

"You can convince him, Irma. . . . And the CJ position would give me the muscle to accomplish what Moorman wanted to do for one of your big Virginia corporations, Carpa Pharmaceuticals. He had lined up four votes for Carpa. Those three plus mine will ensure a Carpa victory. I'm a friend asking for a favor . . . and you know me—I pay my debts. Just think on it, Irma. That's all I ask."

The shock on Senator Powers' face was clearly visible. Her eyes grew bigger and you could hear the intake of air from her open mouth.

Bianco didn't let up. He lied—big time—without hesitation. "Yes,

Oscar Moorman told me of his effort to win the Carpa case as a favor to you. He was loyal to you. He recused himself only after he lined up the votes needed. I'm one of the votes he counted on. And if I get to be the Chief, I know I could hold all the votes for Carpa."

Powers remained speechless, staring at Bianco.

Bianco instinctively knew that he had guessed right.

So the Moorman nomination was pushed by Powers as part of her plan to get a Supreme Court win worth billions for Carpa. Everything she does is for her self-interest.

Then Bianco did a very risky thing.

He didn't wait for her to respond. He turned and walked back into the chapel. The funeral service would start in ten minutes.

Bianco thought, *No way she would answer my request now. She's too crafty a politician to ever agree in words to a deal to fix a case. She got the message. I offered her a Carpa win. If she goes to the President and gets me the appointment . . . well, that will be her answer. I've given her the motive and Ramsey's lame-duck status is perfect—by naming me Chief Justice, Ramsey would show his strength in exercising a Constitutional power and will give Irma—the probable president in the 2012 election—a favor that Ramsey can collect on many times during her years as President. The incoming Democratic President is an idiot and most likely won't be reelected if Powers runs in the next election.*

Bianco gave a wonderful eulogy. His polished words of praise for Oscar Morman, a man he described as "my best friend," and the two coffins standing side by side in front of the altar, brought many in the chapel to tears.

After the service, Bianco called Senator Dalton, the Democratic Minority Leader, and called in his chit from his earlier betrayal of his best friend.

Should make it easier for President Ramsey to act if both Irma Powers and the head Democrat both call him urging my recess appointment, thought the clever Bianco.

94

CNN Broadcast—Special Report—Justice Vincent Bianco given recess appointment as Chief Justice of the U.S. Supreme Court.

(Washington, D.C., Friday, December 26, 2008, 5:30 P.M., EST) Today at four o'clock, President Thomas Ramsey in a surprise move gave a recess appointment to Associate Justice Vincent X. Bianco as the Chief Justice of the U.S. Supreme Court. The recess appointment will be effective immediately. Under his powers pursuant to Article Two of the U.S. Constitution, the President signed a Presidential commission appointing Bianco as the Chief Justice during a recess of Congress—the appointment will last until the end of the next session of Congress, which should occur in mid-January 2011.

Vincent Bianco was immediately sworn in as Chief Justice by Justice Farnsworth in a brief private ceremony attended only by the Bianco family and selected Court staff shortly after four-thirty this afternoon when the Commission was delivered to the Supreme Court. Neither the White House Press Office nor the Supreme Court Public Information Office would take questions from the press corps after the announcement and the ceremony.

A Supreme Court spokesperson said that Chief Justice Bianco had declined to have a formal installation and reception due to the thirty-day official mourning period following the death of Chief Justice Moorman.

Chief Justice Bianco was born on January 9, 1939, in St. Louis, Missouri. He graduated from Harvard College with a B.A. degree in political science in 1966. He received his J.D. degree from Yale Law School in 1969.

After law school, Bianco was an attorney in the Washington law firm of Fyth & Victor LLP from 1969 until 1986, when he was named the Deputy Attorney General of the U.S. Justice Department. In 1988, he was appointed an Associate Justice of the U.S. Supreme Court by President Ronald Reagan.

Justice Bianco is married to the former Lucy Dora. Mrs. Bianco is the daughter of Doctor and Mrs. Dora of Ridgefield, Connecticut. The Biancos have three children.

Reached at her office on Capitol Hill to comment on the announcement, Senator Irma Powers, the current Chair of the U.S. Senate Judiciary Committee, issued a statement that stated, in part, "President Ramsey has made a wise decision to use a recess appointment to stabilize the institution of the U.S. Supreme Court, which has been rocked by the recent deaths of two Chief Justices. Chief Justice Bianco is a well-respected jurist of the highest caliber. His service on the Court to date has been extraordinary and I expect his leadership will enhance the high reputation of the Supreme Court."

The new Chief Justice is known as a moderate conservative and is considered by legal scholars as an intellectual force on the Court. Together with his good friend, the late Chief Justice Moorman, they were known as the "Center Twins" of a Court that in recent years has moved to the center of modern jurisprudence from the rightward stance of the Rehnquist Court of recent years.

This is Larry Trachtenbroit reporting from Washington, D.C., for CNN News.

(End of video transcript)

Thirty minutes after the White House press release on the recess appointment of the new chief justice, Senator Irma Powers called her husband at his law office in Richmond and said, "Jim, you can call your client and tell him to watch the news. It's done. And remind him that I had to really work the President to do it. Had to promise I would help raise money for his damn library. . . . Each of those idiots wants to outdo the last one . . . those presidential libraries have become dick-measuring contests."

"Good job. And, Irma dear, keep your eye on the ball. You did great. This win for Carpa will be very good for us."

"Goddamn it, Jim. Please think before you speak."

Then the phone went dead as it was slammed down.

I constantly have to remind him to never use clients' names on the phone. He has good looks and is an excellent politician, but he lacks common sense.

God, I don't know how I managed to get him elected Governor of Virginia for that one term.

THE TRANSCRIPT OF THE INTERVIEW IN THE LONDON pub of Vicky and Judge Morgana Temple was probably one thing in Justice Moorman's Senate confirmation file that the *National Enquirer* and other tabloids would pay big money to expose on their front pages. The content—alcohol and celebrity jealousy angle—was juicy and would give further "legs" to the Moorman accidental death/suicide story running in the media and blogging world.

Knowing that he should protect that and other sensitive papers in the Moorman files was one of the reasons Quinn was in his Senate office on Saturday, December 27.

With regard to that transcript, he had to figure out a way to protect the reputation of the good man who'd been buried in Arlington National Cemetery earlier that week. Shredding it or classifying it were two options that he was considering. No one outside of Vicky Hauser and Bill Sharkey knew a transcript existed. He would have to discuss with them what to do with the transcript. Maybe Vicky with her creative legal mind could figure a way where a Federal judge could seal the document on a temporary basis.

There was another reason that Quinn was working that weekend. A subconscious reason.

Tim Quinn was lonely and slightly depressed.

Tim Quinn tried to convince himself that he was working that weekend because he was anxious to finish up his job responsibilities at the Special Counsel's office and return to his law firm practice in D.C. But it was also a fact that he was alone. Emotionally the Moorman tragedy had hit him hard as well. So work at his office was a form of escape for Quinn.

His two grown children had come to Washington to be with him for Christmas Eve and for Christmas Day—his second Christmas since the death of his wife. However, yesterday they'd left. Anne and Paul had had to get back to their jobs and their lives—Anne in New York and Paul in Chicago.

So he decided to work the weekend and came into his Senate office to start going through files and to outline for Vicky and Bill the required final report and other tasks that had to be accomplished before the Special Counsel's Office could be officially closed.

His stint as the Special Counsel to the Senate Judiciary Committee had been an exciting challenge at first, but the death of Oscar Moorman resonated with Tim—reminding him of the death of his wife—and increased Tim's loneliness so much that he desperately wanted out of the Senate job. He reasoned that only by returning to the high tempo of his Washington law practice could he chase away—as Winston Churchill described depression—the "black dog" feeling that Quinn now had.

Besides the final report that he knew he had to do, it was a given that to close up the office properly Quinn should review the sensitive investigative documents accumulated during the confirmation process. This was one of the tasks he didn't want to delegate to his staff. He wanted to personally cull through the hundreds of confidential files accumulated during the confirmation investigation. Some of the files would be destroyed and some boxed up and sent to the U.S. Archives as the official records of the Oscar Moorman Confirmation Papers.

Reviewing the files would take many hours, and he hoped to put in a few hours today. He was especially concerned with the Vicky Hauser–Judge Temple transcript, because it had never been released to the Senators or their staffs.

Perhaps it never should. Perhaps it should be destroyed.

After he turned on the lights in his large office, he opened the locked four-drawer safe in his office. The first file he took was the file folder involving the London investigation of Vicky Hauser and Bill Sharkey. He went through the file, studying in particular the single original copy of the transcript, personally typed by Vicky per his instruction. He didn't find Judge Morgana Temple's name anywhere in the transcript nor in the whole file on the London trip taken by Vicky and Bill. There wasn't even a note or a hint suggesting that the "mystery lady" of the date rape rumor was a judge at the Old Bailey.

Good! Vicky was right in suggesting that we protect Temple's name. We got the necessary and solid information we needed to clear Moorman from the date rape smear and didn't have to disclose her name. Many victims or alleged victims have their lives destroyed by unnecessary disclosure of their names to the public or the press.

Judge Temple had done his investigative team of Vicky and Sharkey a big favor by telling them what happened the night of the alleged "date rape." It was probable that her cooperation was most likely reluctantly done at the urging of Vicky and the threat that Quinn would seek the help of her chief judge at the Old Bailey. Nevertheless,

Judge Temple had told Vicky the full story of the night with Moorman and allowed Tim's office to clear up the "date rape" rumor,
which set the stage to have the successful confirmation hearing for
Moorman proceed as scheduled.

*I bet Judge Temple is wondering whether her name will eventually
come out—especially now that Moorman is dead. Well, it might be a
good turn for me to call her and to reassure her that the files on the
date rape rumor don't contain her name. That's the least I can do for
her. . . . I wonder if she was ever named a Court of Appeal judge? Well,
I'll call her now.*

Tim knew that Judge Temple would certainly have an unlisted
number, so he decided to call her chief judge. Tim Quinn flipped
through his Rolodex to find the home number of his friend at her
court—the head judge of the Old Bailey, Sir Brian Fairmont, KCMG,
Q.C.

*Brian Fairmont will have Judge Temple's home number. Let's
see . . . it's 10 A.M. here in D.C. So it should be 3 P.M. in London.*

Brian Fairmont and Tim Quinn had hit it off from the start years
ago when they'd met at a judicial conference. And Tim had gotten to
know Brian much better when Tim visited him at his home in London several times, and one day Tim actually got to sit as an observer
judge with him for a full day at the Old Bailey.

Sir Brian Fairmont with his quick mind and dry sense of humor
was one of the stars of the English legal establishment. He was the
President of the Criminal Bar Society at age forty when he was appointed as a circuit judge and assigned to the Old Bailey. After a year
on the bench, he was detailed for six months to the British Governor
of Hong Kong to help with the transition just before Hong Kong was
turned over by the British to the People's Republic of China. Brian
had done such a magnificent job helping with writing the new Constitution of Hong Kong that the Queen knighted him by appointing him
as a Knight Commander of the Order of St. Michael and St. George.
That honor entitled him to be addressed as Sir Brian Fairmont and to

have the initials "KCMG" follow his name, indicating his status as an English Knight.

When he stayed at Brian's home, Quinn learned that the Order of St. Michael and St George actually had three levels: the lowest—Companion (CMG), the middle—Knight Commander (KCMG), and the highest—Grand Commander (GCMG). The abbreviations are humorously referred to as "Call me God" (CMG), "Kindly Call Me God" (KCMG), and "God Calls Me God" (GCMG). Consequently, Tim began calling Brian "God" in private conversations—much to Brian's annoyance.

They were good friends. Tim was sure Brian would give him Judge Morgana Temple's home phone number.

Fairmont answered on the second ring, "Brian Fairmont here."

"Is this God? It's one of your sinners, Tim Quinn, calling from Washington. Done any miracles lately?"

"Tim Quinn! I've told you to stop calling me that. . . . Bloody Yank, someday you will be struck by lighting as a blasphemer. . . . Seriously, Tim, it's a terrible shame about your Chief Justice Moorman. He was a good chap, I met him in New York once at a UN function. He was very impressive. I'd heard that you were helping on his confirmation process. High-level job and all that."

"Yes, I was helping in the Senate confirmation of Moorman. Well, it was a big tragedy for us all. He would have done a great job as Chief Justice . . . by the way, I need the home number of an English judge—Judge Temple. Do you have it? I need to pass on something to her . . . something personal and important."

A long silence passed as Tim listened on the phone. At first, he thought that they had been cut off. So he looked at the caller ID device next to the phone and saw that he was still connected.

"Brian?" Tim said. "Are you still there?"

"Yes, yes. Sorry . . . I was a little taken back. You see Judge Temple is no longer with us. She passed away earlier this past week."

Now it was time for Tim to be shocked. "Are we talking about

Judge Morgana Temple—one of your judges . . . an Old Bailey judge? A relatively young lady judge."

"Yes, Tim. Morgana Temple of the Bailey is dead . . . a very good judge. She died on Monday this past week."

Tim was confused. Much had happened in the last few days. This was another shock to his system. He needed to be certain of the date of death. He studied the small calendar on his desk.

Last Monday was the day Vicky Hauser interviewed Temple at the pub. This is too much of a coincidence!

"Brian, do you know what time she died on Monday? . . . And it was Monday, December 15, wasn't it?"

"The police told me she died somewhere between ten P.M. and midnight. And we are talking about Monday, December 15. . . . Tell me why are you asking, Tim. Is there something I should know about?'

Quinn ignored Brian Fairmont's question and asked in a solemn voice, "How did she die?"

The answer came back quickly, "Accidental overdose of vodka and prescription medication. The police were quite sure about that. Quite sure. . . . Autopsy came back with no signs of anything but an accident."

Quinn hesitated for a beat and replied, "Well, I'm not sure, but the timing is very odd. . . . I think there is a chance Judge Temple was murdered."

Sir Brian said in a serious voice, "Really. Strange, I thought so myself at the time. . . . Well, you better tell me what you know, so we can sort this out."

❖ 96 ❖

As soon as he hung up the phone after a long discussion with Sir Brian Fairmont, Quinn called Vicky Hauser and Bill Sharkey into the office for a meeting.

A witness—a witness Quinn had asked to be interviewed—in a Congressional investigation—was dead within hours of talking to Vicky Hauser in that London pub. Judge Fairmont and Quinn agreed that the timing of the death was highly suspicious.

And accidental death by alcohol and pills became more so to Quinn when Judge Fairmont explained several things to him. First, the night of her death, Temple drank no alcohol—had only water—when she and Fairmont cohosted a dinner for a visiting Hong Kong official. At the dinner, Temple told Fairmont that she was not drinking alcohol because she was on pain medication for her still healing broken right wrist.

The second odd thing about Temple's death as observed by Fairmont was that at the dinner, she told him that she was glad she was left-handed since it hurt her to use her right hand. Fairmont was shocked by the police report, which said she was drinking straight vodka from a glass with fingerprints from only her right hand on the glass.

Moreover at the dinner, Fairmont disclosed to Temple that she had won the appellate judgeship and needed to go to Parliament for an early breakfast with the Lord Chancellor the next morning to receive her appointment papers.

As Judge Fairmont concluded his talk with Tim in a summary statement: "She was overjoyed to hear the judgeship news in a private moment just before she left the dinner, but nevertheless she steadfastly declined alcohol when I offered her a toast with a small glass of champagne before she left to go home. Accordingly, I find it hard to believe that such a careful lady like Morgana at the very peak of a huge victory would then go home and drink an excess of vodka while chasing down pain pills. Quite out of bloody character. She was a very careful and responsible judge. I still find it hard to believe that the reported 'accident' was an accident."

Moreover, in a curious footnote, Fairmont told Quinn that in the police report he saw, there was a mention of an accidental power surge that occurred just before 10 P.M., which disabled the Oxford Street CCTV camera that covered the entrance to her house on Burlington Square. That camera was one of the newer powerful ones (twenty power with night vision)—at the intersection of Oxford Street and the street where Temple's home was—a short two blocks from Oxford Street—a key spot in the terrorist watch area.

All these odd things led Fairmont to believe that Temple's death was not an accident.

Yet, on the other side of the police reasoning on the cause of death was the hard fact that the police found the body the next morning in her locked house with the security alarm still on. The autopsy also indicated that the drinking and ingestion of pills was not forced. The coroner was quite skilled and looked for indications of forced ingestion. He found none.

Quinn had called Vicky and Bill because he needed help in figuring all this out. He needed to share this information from Fairmont with Vicky and Bill and to discuss the developing strong possibility that Judge Morgana Temple was murdered.

Tim knew from the Duke X-rated movie incident and from the now discredited date rape rumor that someone was willing to falsely smear Justice Moorman in order to prevent him from being confirmed. Now Tim was faced with the opposite motive—the emerging suspicion that it was possible that someone wanted to get Moorman confirmed so badly that they had murdered Judge Temple to prevent her from giving testimony about being raped—a development that surely would have destroyed Moorman's chances to be confirmed.

✦

Tim Quinn, Vicky Hauser, and Bill Sharkey were soon seated at the conference table in Tim's office and Tim filled in Vicky and Bill on the various aspects of the Temple death as related by Judge Fairmont. In addition he shared his inability to reconcile the timing of the Vicky interview and Temple's death—the suspicion he shared with Fairmont.

After Tim's briefing on the case from his and Fairmont's perspective, he opened the discussion to get the views from his team.

"Vicky, what if someone thought that Temple would say she was raped by Moorman? I know that when I sent you to England I thought that maybe Moorman did it. Might someone—someone who desperately wanted Moorman to be CJ—kill Temple to keep her from saying she was raped?" asked Quinn.

Vicky nodded her head and said, "Sure. Killing Temple would prevent her from destroying Moorman's bid to be CJ. But the two real questions remain: *was she murdered? . . . and why?*"

Quinn gave his opinion firmly, "Both Judge Fairmont and I think she was murdered. His observations at the dinner all point to the fact that Temple didn't accidentally kill herself. Moreover, Fairmont agreed with me that the fact Temple was the mystery lady in the date rape allegation was a sufficient motive to kill her by someone who didn't want that fact to come out . . . someone who desperately wanted to ensure Moorman became the Chief Justice. . . . Having said that, Fairmont and I are both baffled by the physical evidence that points only to an accidental death."

Then Quinn went on and asked out loud, "Who would kill to get Moorman as Chief Justice?"

Vicky just shook her head and replied, "I can't see a murder, if this is what it is, that is racially or politically motivated. That leaves money as a motive. But what litigant in the Supreme Court would kill for Moorman to be CJ?"

Bill Sharkey, the old FBI Special Agent, finally spoke.

"Your Honor, here's my take on all this: a smart careful lady who, the same night she's notified she's won an appellate judgeship, accidentally kills herself within hours after she is interviewed in a major Congressional investigation. She does this in a house covered by a CCTV camera, which is disabled by an accidental power surge. By itself, the disabling of the camera while that part of London is on alert from the recent terrorist attack on Oxford Street is too coincidental for me. Bottom line—that string of coincidences is just too much for an old street agent like me to swallow. I think we need to gear up an investigation. Judge Temple was a witness in a Congressional investigation and 18 United States Code Section 1512 says that if she was murdered to prevent her testimony, it is a Federal crime punishable by the death penalty. Give me the word and I'll call the FBI office in the U.S. embassy in London and get all of Scotland Yard's reports so we can start finding out the truth about her death."

"Well, I guess Bill's right. Too much smoke here. We'd better start looking for the fire. I'd better call Senator Powers and inform her that we're not closing up shop just yet. I'm authorizing an investigation into the death of Temple—that's within my power as Special Counsel and I don't need Power's approval. What do you say, Vicky?"

"Well, Judge Temple was a cooperating witness. If she was murdered, it's our duty to go after whoever did it. I will say one thing. . . . Powers already doesn't like you, Tim. With you initiating an international investigation without her permission, you're going to make a big enemy and possibly be fired."

"One of my personality flaws—I seem to accumulate enemies without really trying. On firing me—I guess I'll paraphrase Rhett Butler in *Gone with the Wind*—frankly, Irma, I don't give a damn," said the grinning Quinn.

97

SENATOR IRMA POWERS HAD JUST FINISHED A LATE lunch in her large townhouse on Capitol Hill.

This afternoon she was going to treat herself and go to an exclusive day spa in Georgetown for a facial, a hair cut, and a herb massage. There would be no charge. She was going to use coupons from a book given to her as a Christmas gift from one of the immigration lobby firms. Naturally the high-value coupons—far in excess of the Senate gift rules—were in someone else's name, so there was nothing to report on her annual Senate ethics form—completely untraceable.

Some of the lobbyists give very thoughtful gifts, the Senator said to herself.

As she was dressing, the phone rang. It was Judge Tim Quinn calling.

With a trace of annoyance, she said, "Judge Quinn, how can I help you?"

"Senator, the Senate Judiciary Committee has a problem, and since you are still the Chair and I remain Special Counsel until the new session of Congress convenes next month, I wanted to make you aware of it."

"Why, I thought your term of office had expired with the end of the confirmation hearings of Chief Justice Moorman."

"No, the letter appointment signed by you expressly states the term as ending with the closing of the present Congressional session," replied Quinn.

'Well, whatever. What's the problem that you have to call me on a Saturday?"

"One of the Committee's witnesses appears to have been murdered. The lady involved in the date rape rumor. The woman Ms. Vicky Hauser interviewed in London. I'm starting a Committee investigation to investigate the possible murder."

All of a sudden, when the implications registered in her quick mind, Irma Powers had to sit down. She was dizzy and started to hyperventilate.

Good God, this can't be happening. . . . I'm the one who told Carpa that there was a woman in London who was going to be interviewed with regard to the date rape allegation. I gave Carpa the information to follow that Hauser woman to the witness. . . . Christ, I thought Don Fay would just pay off the slut with hush money . . . never kill her. God, if it gets out that I gave Carpa the information to trace the barrister . . . well, I'm finished.

"Why . . . we don't have jurisdiction. You don't have the power to initiate an investigation," argued Powers weakly.

"Senator, I thought you were a smart lady. You *really* should read the Senate Rules on the powers of a Special Counsel. I do have the power to start an investigation on my own and I am doing so. As a courtesy, I am informing you as the Chair of the Committee."

"Well, I forbid any investigation. . . . And I want you to resign as Special Counsel at once."

"No, Senator. I'm not going to make it easy on you. You'll have to fire me. And if you do, you won't stop the investigation . . . I'll just refer this matter to the Department of Justice for an FBI investigation. You know there's a Federal statute making it a Federal crime to kill a Congressional witness—the punishment carries a possible death penalty."

"Very well, Quinn. You are hereby terminated effective immediately. I'll have a letter delivered to your office stating so this afternoon," screamed the Senator.

After a pause, Powers added, "I should never have hired you. You judges are way . . . too . . . too independent."

"Funny, I thought that's what the Constitution wanted us to be," shot back Quinn before Irma Powers slammed the phone down.

VICKY HAUSER AND BILL SHARKEY WERE IN QUINN'S OF-fice hearing only one side of the conversation . . . that is, until Senator Powers screamed at Quinn near the end.

When Tim Quinn put down the phone and shrugged his shoulders, Vicky was the first to speak.

"Let me guess—she fired you. Boy, Tim, I bet you don't even get a letter of recommendation."

"Well, that's the end of my public service. I guess I'll have to go back to my firm and start earning the big bucks again."

"Will you make a noisy withdrawal? Tell people why you quit?" asked Vicky with concern.

"No, I'll go quietly. I wouldn't want to compromise the Justice Department and FBI investigation. Vicky, I want you and Bill to go back to DOJ and the FBI and do the investigation. I'm going to write a letter to the Assistant Attorney General of the Criminal Division requesting that an investigation of Judge Temple's possible murder be started under the Obstruction of Justice statute pertaining to Congressional witnesses," said Quinn in a serious tone.

Bill Sharkey chimed in, "Good, Judge. If you sign that letter releasing Vicky and me from the detail to your staff, we can probably get to be part of the investigation. This kind of case would normally be assigned to Vicky's section at Justice, the Public Integrity Section."

Quinn nodded agreement. "Sure, will do. You two will be good to have on the case with your prior knowledge. Bill, I'm going to write a memo of chain of custody and give you the 'Hauser–Judge Temple transcript' so it will be part of the FBI file."

Vicky got up and walked over to the tall windows looking out on Constitution Avenue. She stood briefly with her back to Sharkey and Quinn.

After staring out the window, she suddenly turned and said, "This has been an interesting roller-coaster ride, and I agree now is the time for Bill and me to return to DOJ, but do you two really think we can solve this case?"

"What do you mean, Vicky? There are signs all over the place that Temple was murdered for some reason related to the Moorman confirmation. Both Judge Fairmont and I agree on this," replied Quinn.

"Tim, I don't doubt your instincts. You are probably right. But there are plenty of crimes where we *know* who did it, but we don't have *evidence* to make the case. I'm sorry to say this, but I believe this is one of those cases." Vicky spoke with more than a hint of defeat written in her face.

Bill Sharkey added to the pessimistic view of the case. "Vicky may be right, Judge. Think about it. You told us yourself that the body was found in a locked house with the security system on. Scotland Yard is good, very good—and they apparently have closed the case as an accidental overdose. The ME, alerted to the possibility of foul play, probably did a very complete autopsy and concluded the same. The only CCTV camera in the area was out of commission. . . . Lots of dead-ends here. I just don't know how we at the Bureau have a better chance to solve the case than Scotland Yard."

"Listen, gang. I have a feeling that something may come up to help you. Just get the investigation going," said Quinn with his usual upbeat approach to almost everything.

"What possibly could come up to change the state of the available evidence?" challenged Vicky.

"I'm going to call in a favor from an old friend of mine—an ex-SAS man who served with me as an exchange officer in the Army Ranger School when I was an instructor there . . . a long time ago."

Vicky shook her head and observed, "You've got quite an unusual network."

"So I've been told," said Quinn with a smile.

THE BRITISH EMBASSY IN WASHINGTON, D.C., IS LOcated on a stretch of Massachusetts Avenue called appropriately Embassy Row, because a large number of embassies are situated on that street.

The Ambassador's Residence was built in 1929 to resemble an English country manor. The home is attached to the Embassy's Chancery, where most of the 250 diplomats and 600 staffers work—one of the largest embassies in America. It is said that the British Ambassador enjoys one of the shortest commutes in Washington. His office is thirty-one paces from his bedroom.

The current Ambassador was Sir Graham McKenzie, KCMG, DSO, MC—a retired Major General, who had served as the Deputy Commander of the 22nd Special Air Services (SAS) regiment. Although usually the Ambassador to the United States is a post reserved for a career diplomat, McKenzie had been selected to serve because of his counterterrorism expertise during the global war on terror. By happenstance, Tim Quinn had a long and close friendship with

McKenzie dating back to their joint service at the Army Ranger School during the Vietnam War.

It was no surprise that when Tim Quinn called that Saturday afternoon asking to see the Ambassador immediately, his request was granted, and he was given parking space inside the Embassy gates. Although Tim knew quite a few of the ambassadors in Washington on a personal basis, due to the fact that his law firm was one of the sponsors of the Annual Ambassadors' Ball, a major charity event, he was glad that he had a special relationship with the present British Ambassador. He really needed to call in a big chit and McKenzie was in a position to deliver.

As Quinn pulled into the access side street of the Embassy at 3100 Massachusetts Avenue and waited for the gate to open, he realized that if he failed to get the Ambassador's support for the unusual request he had in mind . . . well, there would be little chance to solve the mystery of Judge Temple's death. All or nothing—no Plan B.

Quinn was greeted at his car by one of the Ambassador's secretaries and taken to a high-ceilinged living room in the residence. When Ambassador McKenzie, a muscular barrel-chested man with a shaven head, swept into the room in less than a minute, the secretary quickly disappeared as the two men exchanged bear hugs.

"How are they hanging, Your Excellency?" asked Tim.

"You bloody Yanks are so vulgar, no wonder we left America."

"You Limeys didn't leave. We threw you out," retorted Tim.

The two men suddenly quit the horseplay and turned serious.

"How have you been, Tim? This is the second Christmas since Katy passed away, isn't it?" The Ambassador put the question to Tim in a quiet voice.

"Yes, it is. God, I miss her," Tim answered and then pinched his lips. Then he added, "How is your wonderful Ann?"

"She's fine. She and the kids are up in New York City spending my Army pension on the post-Christmas sales."

"Graham, I have something I want you to do. It's a bit unusual, and may put you out on a limb, but it's like your SAS regiment's motto—Who Dares Wins."

"I'm listening, buddy. I know you wouldn't ask me to do anything you wouldn't do yourself."

Tim began to tell the Ambassador the story of Vicky Hauser's interview of Judge Morgana Temple at a pub on Monday, December 15. He also told him the suspicious details of her death. Then Tim turned to the real purpose of his visit.

"Graham, when that suicide bomb went off on Oxford Street a couple of weeks ago, do you remember that President Ramsey telephoned your PM and told him that the U.S.A. would make available substantial U.S. intelligence assets to prevent further terrorist attacks."

"I sure do. Bloody al-Qaeda cowards. The attack will be two weeks ago tomorrow."

'Now, I'm making an educated guess that the President ordered the repositioning of one of our spy satellites to keep watch over Central London. As you know, the attacks usually come in clusters. . . . My point is that the NRO, the National Reconnaissance Office, which operates all our spy satellites—the intelligence agency that I was the General Counsel of back in the 1980s—well, I think that the NRO probably has videotapes showing the activity in the area of Judge Temple's home near Oxford Street for the night of December 15, the night of Judge Temple's death—and on those tapes—if Temple was murdered—is a video of her killer, entering and leaving her home."

The Ambassador held up both hands in mock defense. "Now, Tim, you're not going to ask me to request the U.S. Secretary of State to get the NRO to release that tape to Scotland Yard so they can solve a bloody murder, are you? Christ, I'd have to go to my boss—the Minister of Foreign Affairs—to get approval. Jesus, Tim—a highly classified intelligence video. You know the national security field— intelligence needs trump crime needs, always."

"Yes, I know that mantra, but this is special. For Christ's sake,

Graham! Temple was an English Old Bailey Judge . . . and it looks like that satellite intelligence tape might be the only bullet we have to solve the case."

The British Ambassador smiled a tight grin, "You know, you're going to ruin my new career, Tim. . . . So you need the NRO bullet. . . . Well, bloody hell, I'll try to get it for you. Use it well—as the snipers say—one shot, one kill. I guess I'll bypass asking for permission from the Minister of Foreign Affairs—he'll only deny my request. I'll just call directly to the President. He'll assume I already got permission from my government. Besides, he owes me. I'm getting him an honorary degree from Oxford this spring."

✦ 100 ✦

CNN.com—Breaking News (Internet)—Large patent case argued in U.S. Supreme Court.

WASHINGTON, D.C., MONDAY, JANUARY 5, 2009—The Supreme Court heard a landmark patent case worth billions this morning. In, *Carpa Pharmaceuticals Company v. Logan Drug Enterprises*, No. 07-561, the Court heard oral arguments on whether Carpa, the drug giant, was entitled to three more years of patent protection for its popular drug Varakain, a popular pain reliever for arthritis.

Some observers of the Supreme Court argument stated that, based on the volley of questions from the new Chief Justice, Vincent Bianco, it appeared that the Court would most likely overturn the United States Court of Appeals for the Federal Circuit's close 2–1 decision that denied Carpa an almost three-year extension on its patent rights for the drug. In a dramatic series of questions, Bianco quoted verbatim from a decision of the late Chief Justice Oscar Moorman. That Moorman decision is considered propatent and could be the key to a victory for Carpa. What was interesting was that Justice Bianco had dissented from the majority opinion of Justice Moorman in the very case he cited—which is viewed in judicial circles as an extremely odd occurrence. However, this apparent unusual shift of position by Chief Justice Bianco bodes well for Carpa in this important case.

Wall Street is closely watching this case. If Carpa wins, it will not only ensure a projected profit stream of at least four billion dollars, but Carpa stock is expected to surge on the news of a victory at the Court.

The Supreme Court is expected to hand down a decision before its annual recess in early June.

✦ 101 ✦

"TIM, I'VE BEEN TRYING TO REACH YOU. . . . WHERE ARE you? Your office wouldn't tell me." Vicky Hauser was excited and talking very quickly. His memory let Quinn almost visualize her when she sounded this way. She would be smiling and her face would be slightly flushed.

"Ah . . . I'm just coming out of a meeting. I had a client meeting in McLean, Virginia . . . am walking to my car now and just checking my messages. Your voice mail came up as I turned on my phone. What's happening, Vicky? Your message sounded happy, but no details."

"Yes, yes—I'm really happy and excited. Bill and I have been in conversations and receiving data from London. You know—that English favor you asked for actually worked. . . . This morning I was called from London and Bill and I have been working nonstop on it. We have solid information—that person in Europe—the one named T—apparently was murdered. . . . And Scotland Yard has actually ID'd the killer. . . . Ah . . . We can't talk on the phone. Can you come to my office? I can't wait to share the news. Tim, it's all due to you. You're amazing."

"Well, it's about time you started appreciating me. . . . Seriously, I'll come right now. I should be at Justice in twenty minutes. Can you get me parking in the DOJ courtyard?"

Tim punched off his cell after he gave Vicky his auto license and car make and she confirmed that he would have a spot in the inner courtyard of the huge Justice Department on Pennsylvania Avenue across the street from the equally massive FBI building.

Tim picked up his step and quickly walked to his car in the VIP outdoor parking lot of the wooded CIA complex in McLean. He had just come from a one-hour meeting with the CIA general counsel and his client—a small government contractor who was currently doing some extremely sensitive communication work with the Agency. Tim was the official "outside" monitor on the CIA contract and periodically reviewed the operations of the contractor. He was coming from the quarterly review with the CIA general counsel to verify to the GC that the contractor was performing its work well within the restrictive laws that controlled privacy within the United States—an increasingly difficult task of balancing U.S. Constitutional safeguards while eavesdropping without a search warrant on some suspected terrorists—some legal residents of the United States.

Tim had been energized by the excitement of Vicky's voice and had to watch the speed limit as he raced down the GW Memorial Parkway to cross the Fourteenth Street Bridge.

Great! It sounds like Graham McKenzie somehow got the NRO satellite video for Scotland Yard! . . . Damn, it appears I was right in thinking that following the London bombing, the United States would divert an "overwatch" U.S. spy satellite of the National Reconnaissance Office to keep a watch on Central London—that spy bird must have picked up something to solve the suspicious death of Judge Temple—as we used to say at the NRO—the Eye in the Sky sees all!

Soon Quinn was processed through the DOJ security gate at the Ninth Street entrance and had pulled into a visitor's slot in the large circle of the DOJ courtyard. As he was locking his car, a young woman approached him and introduced herself as an attorney in Vicky's unit, the Public Integrity Section. She led him into the Attorney General's private entrance in the southeast corner of the courtyard. On the elevator ride to the sixth floor, the attorney said that Vicky and Bill Sharkey were waiting in a conference room in the Justice Command Center complex. She efficiently signed in Quinn at the Command Center security desk and asked if he had any electronic devices. Tim gave up his cell phone and BlackBerry before he stepped through the metal detector. One of the guards took his electronic gear and gave him a receipt for them—the same procedure he had just experienced at the CIA. Obviously, no electronic devices were allowed in the DOJ Command Center either. When the attorney brought him to the door of the conference room deep inside the complex, his escort excused herself and left with the explanation, "I'm not cleared for this operation of Ms. Hauser's. She and Special Agent Sharkey are inside the conference room," motioning with her hand as she turned to leave.

As soon as Quinn entered the conference room, he saw Bill and Vicky at the end of a long table looking at video images on a large screen. Both had big smiles on their faces when they turned to see who had entered.

Bill Sharkey was quick to acknowledge Quinn, coming up to greet him with a firm handshake. "Judge, thanks to you, the British Ambassador came through. We have been chatting for the last two hours with the two Scotland Yard investigators assigned to the Judge Temple case—it's a murder case now—a double murder. They have been sending encrypted video clips of the NRO tapes showing a break-in at Temple's house and what appears to be a murder of a London policeman . . . all this because of you going to the Ambassador." Sharkey gave Quinn a thumbs-up sign after he delivered that short summary.

When Bill was finished with his welcome, Vicky came up close to Tim and threw her arms around him with a congratulatory hug that lasted a few seconds too long for the office setting. Tim could smell her—she smelled of fresh soap and roses. . . . And she felt soft and warm as she pressed against him.

God, it's been over a year since I've felt a woman's body, thought Quinn.

As they broke the hug, one of Tim's hands dropped and inadvertently brushed her firm bottom. The touch was electric.

That woman still moves me.

Tim felt himself blush. Vicky looked flushed as well and hurried to fill in the pause with words.

"Well, we've been looking at some of the video feeds the Scotland Yard boys have been sending. They've got some dynamite stuff."

"O.K., fill me in on what's happened," asked Quinn as he recovered from the moment of touching Vicky and thinking of the time long ago when Vicky and Tim lived together at Columbia Law.

Vicky briefed Quinn quickly on the amazing progress of the Judge Temple investigation—in less than a week the British ambassador had gotten the President to release the relevant NRO satellite video from the area around Judge Temple's home to Scotland Yard—and that the results of the photo interpretations of the NRO tape led Scotland Yard to open a murder investigation and to the cooperation of an unusual team—FBI, Scotland Yard, DOJ, and the London Crown Prosecution Service.

"We've formed a team—an international five-person joint task force—two Detective Inspectors from the Yard, a prosecutor from the Crown Prosecution Office, Ms. Hauser, and me. Since you were the referring official from the Senate Judiciary Committee, and because you're a past General Counsel of the NRO and know the world of satellite imagery, the Attorney General cleared you to be an adviser to our team," said Bill Sharkey.

"And the Brits are really moving out on this investigation. They are preparing extradition papers for the killer."

Tim Quinn nodded and responded, "Well, first perhaps you better bring me up to speed on what the NRO gave the Brits. Let's take this step by step."

Sharkey gave a brief summary. "The NRO tape shows that a man entered Judge Temple's home when she arrived late at night. The man stayed in the house twenty minutes and then left with a policeman in a car. It also appears that the man who was inside Temple's home killed the policeman later in Hyde Park. It's all on a very clear tape provided by an overhead U.S. spy satellite."

"Come, Tim. Bill and I will show you. You should see the tape first. Bill and I have been through it several times during our conference call with Scotland Yard." Vicky motioned for Tim to sit at the head of the table nearest the screen. When Tim was seated with Vicky at his side, Vicky punched in some keys on her laptop, the computer projector hummed, and the video show started for Quinn.

Before he sat down, Sharkey turned down the lights of the conference room using a dimmer switch on the wall.

Quinn was about to see a show that he would remember for the rest of his life.

The first video clip appearing on the screen was a high-altitude shot of central London. Quinn was watching the screen intently and adjusting to the greenish tint of the night-vision television video feed from the satellite.

Suddenly the video zoomed in on a small area.

"As you can see, this first zoom shot is of Burlington Square, where Judge Temple's home is located. . . . Here's her home."

Sharkey used a red laser pointer to indicate Temple's corner row house.

Sharkey continued, "The zoom to this area was triggered by an unexplained EMP pulse received by one of the satellite sensors from a

suspicious activity a block away. The recorded electromagnetic pulse—
equivalent to one from a small tactical nuclear bomb—knocked out an
electric transformer, cutting power to a full block of stores and resi-
dences, and then a few seconds later a second EMP shot fried the
CCTV camera on an intersection of Oxford Street, two short blocks
from Temple's home. Well, that understandably got the satellite's and
the ground station operators' attention. So now you can see the video is
monitoring the area around the EMP bursts. . . . Look at the bus stop
up in the square—Burlington Square—right across from Temple's
home on the corner up the street from Oxford Street. See that man!
The hunched-over guy at the bus stop walking to keep warm—he's got
a distinctive limp. Remember that, he's the star of the show—now
here's the skip forward to Judge Temple's arrival at her home."

It was eerie for Tim to sit there and watch the overhead images on
the screen, knowing that he was seeing the mystery of Temple's death
unfold from a camera hundreds of miles in the sky above London.

Quinn didn't need much commentary as he watched the video.
Knowing the ending of Temple's life was near, the story was in the
images now.

When a car pulled up in front of Temple's home and a woman got
out of the BMW, Sharkey merely said, "That's the Judge."

Without words, Quinn watched the limping man on the screen as
he crossed the street to say something to Judge Temple as she was
opening the door of her home. Then he turned away and obviously
used a cell phone to trigger a flash-bang grenade to stun Judge Temple.
Immediately after the flash on the screen, the man moved quickly to
Judge Temple's porch and pulled Judge Temple inside her house.

The screen remained on the empty street in front of Temple's
house. Quinn could see that the time readout in the left bottom corner was moving quickly, as were the blurs of several cars passing. He
knew that the video had been edited to speed up the time.

The video next showed the limping man coming out of the house
and moving south toward Oxford Street. When he got into a parked
car down by the intersection with Oxford Street, the video on the

screen suddenly went to split screen—night vision TV on the left side and thermal imagery of the same video on the right side.

Now it was Tim Quinn's turn to provide the commentary to the silent video.

"Good move from the ground controller of the satellite's imagery. This is typical when a subject of interest enters a covered object. The ground controller flying this bird wants to see if he can tell how many people are in the automobile. The roof is thin enough to permit thermal imagery."

On the right side of the screen, the outline of the Jaguar showed up with three hot spots—the motor obviously much brighter than the two humans in the front seat. The satellite—using both optical and thermal video—tracked the Jag as it motored from Burlington Square near the Oxford Street shopping area down Bayswater Road and turned into Hyde Park. There it stopped in an open area car park next to the Serpentine Lake.

The split-image video screen became more interesting on the right side—the thermal side—after the car stopped.

The thermal image video showed a brief merging of the two images—it looked like a prolonged embrace—and then the night-vision video showed the limping man get out of the car with a bag and walk over to the bridge at the narrow northern neck of the lake. There, in the middle of the bridge, he stopped, stepped back, and threw a bag into the lake. The optical video showed a clear vision of his face as he reached back to throw what appeared to be a heavy bag into the lake.

With Quinn and the silent Vicky and Sharkey watching the pictures on the screen, the twin video show tracked the limping man out of Hyde Park, across Park Lane, and into the covered entrance of one of London's finest hotels—the Dorchester.

After the limping man disappeared into the Dorchester, the screen showed an obvious edit as the video view cut back in a time-speeded mode to the image of the car in the park—the speeded-up video indicated that minutes reflected hours as the thermal picture of the motor of the Jag rapidly cooled and the image of the driver cooled at a slower rate—until it disappeared—and the thermal camera no longer could register human heat on the image. Looking at the video optical portion—again with the video in a fast-forward mode—the screen slowed down as it became daylight and a man on a bicycle stopped by the Jag and looked in the driver's side of the auto—the bicyclist suddenly nearly fell as he backed off and raced away. Soon there were Met police cars and an ambulance surrounding the Jag. A covered body was taken from the Jag—the twin video screen went black at that point.

The show was over.

Sharkey turned up the lights in the darkened conference room as Quinn was the first to speak, "So now we know Temple was probably murdered by that man . . . the limping man. But how?"

Vicky answered quickly. "Remember in the video when the bag was thrown into the lake. Police divers found the bag—a literal treasure trove of evidence. It was a plastic laundry bag filled with some interesting things, including a knife and a surgical tube with a syringe. The Yard is still doing tests on the tube, but they think the tube was pushed through Judge Temple's nose and that the syringe was used to put a lethal combo of vodka and prescription drugs into her stomach—it would look like an accidental overdose, very clever. . . . Evidencewise, we may be in good shape there. Although we don't know exactly what was done in the house. Scotland Yard thinks that the tube will have DNA from Temple on it—maybe small tissue scrapes on the tube as it was inserted. Hopefully the lake water didn't contaminate the tissue to prevent a DNA test. However, Temple's body was cremated, so there's no going back to look for bruising of the nose or stomach cavity from the insertion of the tube. A little setback there, but the Yard made up for this by getting multiple DNA samples from her home—hair, nail clippings, dead tissue from a shower Swedish loofah brush, and other sources of DNA—the Yard techies are really very good."

"What about the driver in the car? How was he murdered? I assume the ambulance took away a dead body from the car."

Sharkey took that question. "Yes, the driver was murdered—and we got to see it—a most unusual sight—a murder in real time with that amazing thermal imaging. The limping man obviously used a knife—most likely the one we recovered from the bag in the lake—a special one. Nonmetal with a thumb depression for a controlled stab. We got some luck there—a beautiful clear thumbprint from the killer. Thank God, the cold lake water kept the print intact—great piece of evidence there."

"Good," said Quinn, unsmiling, as he continued, "because that knife with a print is solid evidence that will probably be allowed in a court—either here in the U.S. or over in England. . . . Which brings up a problem in the case. You both realize that the spy satellite video will most likely *not* be allowed as evidence, don't you?"

Vicky replied in a somber voice, "Yes, so we've been told by Scotland Yard. The NRO released it to our prosecution team, but we understand that one of the conditions was that the classified tape would not be allowed as evidence in court—too sensitive to release such a classified and politically sensitive cassette. It shows that the United States is secretly spying on British citizens, plus it demonstrates for the terrorists the capabilities of our satellites—the British Ambassador agreed to the condition on behalf of the English Government. Still, we can use it to solve what happened."

Sharkey rapidly chimed in, "The knife with the print is good, very good. And we have other evidence—like a call from Carpa's CEO's phone to the killer's cell a few hours before the murder. And other stuff in this laundry bag that was recovered, like the dead man's wallet and watch complete with good fingerprints of the killer . . . and a laptop belonging to the dead man—its hard drive showing research on Judge Temple."

Quinn interrupted, "Good, good. But that brings me to the next major issue. Who were these guys?"

Vicky looked at Bill and said, "Let me take it, Bill." Then she turned to Quinn and said in a steady voice, "This is where it starts to get interesting—real interesting. Just as a starting point, Scotland Yard has made positive IDs of both the players in this video you just saw. The car's registration and, more important, the fingerprints of the body confirm that the driver of the Jag was a Scotland Yard Detective Inspector named Reggie Whiteside, assigned to the British Parliament as one of the liaison officers to Scotland Yard. Whiteside died from multiple stab wounds."

"What's a police detective inspector doing wrapped up in all of this?" asked Tim.

"At this stage, we don't know. Scotland Yard thinks he was on the take and they're checking on that. But—let me go on. . . . The limping man turns out to be a U.S. citizen—Victor Dagnar, the Chief of Security for Carpa Pharmaceuticals, a global drug company based in Richmond, Virginia. The Yard ID'd him from multiple sources—facial recognition from the NRO film when he showed his face skyward as he drank from a flask several times and when he leaned back to throw that bag into the Serpentine—these shots match the passport security cameras at the private jet terminal at Heathrow and his passport photo. Moreover, the security cameras at the Dorchester and the hotel records further confirmed that Dagnar was staying there on a Carpa account. In addition, when the police divers retrieved the bag thrown into the lake, one of the items inside was the knife and it had a thumbprint of Dagnar, which matched with Dagnar's thumbprint in the U.K. print database. Dagnar's prints were in the database due to Carpa's work on several classified British Army projects—drug studies. Preliminary tests show this knife that was recovered from the lake was the murder weapon."

Quinn summed up, "So an executive—the head of security of a drug company—forces his way into Judge Temple's home, using some sophisticated toys—a stun grenade set off by a cell phone triggering device and an EMP device that fries the only CCTV camera covering Temple's home—and Temple winds up dead of an overdose."

Vicky and Bill nod agreement and wait for Quinn to continue.

"Why? I don't understand why Temple was murdered. I do understand about the policeman—the policeman in the Jag obviously was an accomplice to this Dagnar—is that the name?"

Sharkey responded, "Right—Victor Dagnar. As I may have mentioned earlier, the Brits are preparing extradition papers on him as we speak."

Quinn goes on with his point. "Well, my view is that after the break-in at Temple's house, Dagnar wants to wrap up any loose ends, so he kills the policeman who was driving him. . . . But back to the real issue—why was Judge Temple killed? . . . and why was she murdered just hours after she was interviewed by you, Vicky? Why would she—an English judge—be a target of Carpa, the drug giant—with this Dagnar security man getting a call from his CEO just before he broke into Temple's house to stage her accidental overdose death?"

"I really don't know the connection. Bill and I were talking this over with the Scotland Yard people when you came in."

There was silence for a full minute as Quinn's forehead furrowed in thought.

Suddenly Quinn stood up and almost shouted, "I think I have it. I think I know why Dagnar killed Temple. But first I need to check something. Vicky, can you get me a plain vanilla computer so I can do a search? I know this laptop you've been using is an encrypted one. I bet it's so secure you can't even get Google."

✦ 102 ✦

VICKY GOT TIM QUINN ACCESS TO A COMPUTER IN A workstation in the nearby bullpen of the large DOJ Command Center. Bill and Vicky waited back at the conference room.

Within thirty minutes, Quinn came into the conference room and said, "I think I have the key to the case—it's been my view and the view of my old friend on the Federal bench in D.C., Judge Sporkin, that every case has a key which unlocks it. . . . In Temple's case, I think it's a simple one—money. Lots of it. Four billion dollars to be precise. That's what's at stake in the patent case that Carpa argued in the Supreme Court last week."

"God, that's a lot riding on one case," exclaimed Vicky in surprise.

Then Quinn continued, "A lot of money—it could break Carpa if they lost. But to move on, I've been researching Moorman's opinions—his patent opinions. It's interesting to note that he's written *all* the patent cases since he came on the Court—and his patent views would have been very, very helpful to Carpa in that case, especially if Moorman was the Chief Justice. As CJ, he could have been very influential with some of the weaker justices on a patent case—to name two: Ryland, a real dummy who I'm told is very influenced by her law clerks or another justice who lobbies her, and Justice Farnsworth, a senile old man who lives in Florida full time. Some of the stories I heard about him from one of the other justices during a drinking session at a judicial conference was that—and I swear it's true—one time he literally gave all his votes one day to the CJ when the CJ moved the date of oral arguments so Farnsworth, a real golf nut, could play in one of the pro-am golf tournaments with Tiger Woods—amazing stuff."

"You've got to be kidding," said Vicky, rolling her eyes.

"I wish I were," Quinn said in a low voice.

Then, Quinn got to the money motive. "I think Carpa wanted Moorman as Chief Justice so badly that they sent Dagnar to London to kill the 'mystery woman' in the date rape rumor. Remember, if Temple had said she *was* raped, the Moorman nomination would not only have been dead in the water, but he would probably have left the Court to stand rape charges in England—a loss of a sure vote for Carpa's four-billion-dollar case—So it's my guess that someone fingered Judge Temple . . . and someone high up in the Carpa management, maybe the CEO in his call, decided that Temple had to be killed to protect the confirmation of Moorman. We all know that many people have been killed for a lot less than four billion dollars."

Vicky challenged him, "But Moorman recused himself—he indicated that he wouldn't sit on the Carpa case."

Quinn quickly answered, "Remember, he didn't recuse himself until December 15, the day Temple was killed. On that date, Carpa thought he was still on the case. They probably didn't learn of Moorman's nonparticipation until several days later, when the official notice of recusal went out to counsel. It's interesting that Moorman had the Clerk send the notice to me, the Special Counsel of the Senate Judiciary Committee—most likely he may have figured out one of the reasons he was selected was because of his propatent positions. So he did the honorable thing and notified the Court, plus me, the Special Counsel overseeing the confirmation. He recused himself before the vote on his nomination. A class move on his part in my view. I hope I would have had the integrity to do the same thing."

A long silence followed Quinn's speech—obviously all three were digesting his points.

Sharkey broke the silence with his usual cynical candor. "Judge, to get back to the four billion—your motive theory there is so scary that it actually works for me. . . . However, I am bothered by something else here. The timing of the murder makes me think Vicky and I were followed. We must have led Carpa right to the identity of Temple as the mystery woman."

Vicky took a breath in and put her hands to her face. "My Lord . . . I think Bill's right. We led him right to her. God, we probably helped kill her!"

◆ 103 ◆

MOST CRIMINAL CASES IN AMERICA ARE DISPOSED OF by plea bargains. Unfortunately in a plea bargain, justice is seldom the driving force—factors of expediency, lack of evidence, "small fishes" willing to turn in "big fishes," overloaded case dockets, lack of prosecutors, intimidation of witnesses, political pressure, and a host of other conditions drive a case into a plea bargain.

In some cases, a plea bargain can be a Christmas dinner for a very guilty man and a sour dessert for a prosecutor.

It appeared that the Temple case was headed in that holiday direction, because right after the arrest of Victor Dagnar in Richmond, Vicky, Tim, and Bill Sharkey were in Vicky's DOJ office, finishing up a long conference call with the English prosecutor on the case. The conclusion on what to do with Dagnar's case had been decided. The call to Vicky was from James Denison, Q.C., the English senior prosecutor from the Crown Prosecution Service. Tim Quinn and Bill Sharkey had been part of the two-hour call in which Dagnar's prosecution strategy had been dissected and analyzed from front to back.

Although Dagnar didn't know it, things were beginning to look a lot like Christmas.

"I don't agree with the English position on this. But I do like Denison. He's very bright and realistic," said Vicky as she rubbed her neck, which was stiff with tension and frustration.

"Judge Fairmont says he's the best prosecutor at the Bailey," added Quinn.

Vicky summed up the outcome of the conference call with the

English prosecutor. "Well, then it looks like we'll have to turn Dagnar over to the Brits. I really can't argue against the fact that England has the better claim to prosecute him. After all he killed an English judge and a Detective Inspector from Scotland Yard—a double murder that strikes at the core of the British legal world. All we could do here in the States would be to prosecute him for only one of the murders—the Temple murder, under the Federal law for the killing of a witness. It's really a pity that the maximum penalty Dagnar can receive under British law—even for the two killings—is only fifteen years."

Quinn spoke. "Damn, we have Dagnar with a death penalty case in a Federal court in Virginia—a state in recent years that ranks number two in executions—only Texas beats Virginia. If we could use that NRO tape, we could certainly get the death penalty for Dagnar. Well, it's an academic point since we have to turn him over to England for prosecution. It's been decided at the highest levels."

Sharkey spoke with passion and suggested a plan.

"Judge, we may have to send him back to England, but—and pardon my French—that little deformed fucker doesn't know that . . . yet. His attorneys still think he'll be tried for murder first in America. So the defense lawyers have hinted to Ms. Hauser that Dagnar may have something to trade on the American charge of murdering a congressional witness to avoid the death penalty. Remember, all we have disclosed to his attorneys so far via the criminal process in filing the charges was that there was a bag of highly relevant evidence recovered in the Hyde Park lake. That was mentioned in the affidavit I filed to get the search warrant on Dagnar's home, where we found that EMP device. . . . He doesn't know about our evidence troubles with the NRO tape yet or . . . that as a matter of England's request, he's being transferred to England with its low sentencing laws . . . he and his lawyers still think he's being measured for a Virginia pine box."

"Humm . . . It wouldn't hurt to listen to what Dagnar and his attorneys can give up, since they still think the death penalty is still on the table," said Quinn with a smile.

After making that point, Quinn added another, "I bet someone in the Carpa headquarters is having trouble sleeping. Dagnar most likely was following orders. My take—no way he would do this on his own."

Sharkey observed, "If you're right, he'll be ready to turn in the big fish who ordered the hit on Temple."

Quinn made a wry reply, "The little fishes usually aren't very loyal to the big fish."

Vicky nodded her agreement to the plan and picked up the phone to call the American defense lawyer for Dagnar. "Okay, let's play a little Virginia poker."

◆ 104 ◆

DONALD FAY, THE CEO OF CARPA, MADE A BIG MISTAKE when Dagnar was arrested on Federal charges and on the English extradition request for murder charges. Fay authorized corporate funds to be spent to hire two of the very best defense lawyers for Victor Dagnar—a top Virginia defense attorney and one of the best English barristers. Fay compounded his mistake by authorizing huge retainers to be paid up front to the lawyers—thereby losing any subconscious pressure or incentive of the already paid attorneys to protect him or the corporation.

Dagnar's two defense lawyers oddly enough looked like each other to an amazing degree. Both were midsixties, slim, approximately five and a half feet tall, with wispy thinning hair and wire-rimmed glasses. Vicky promptly nicknamed them "the bookends" to Tim Quinn and Bill Sharkey because she could hardly tell them apart, except for their manner of speaking—the American spoke in a loud, booming Brooklyn accent and the British barrister spoke in an upper-class English voice so low that sometimes only dogs could hear. Vicky was sure the Brit did so to gain an advantage by forcing people to bend toward him and concentrate on what he was saying. Both were very clever and Dagnar was well served with legal counsel.

Immediately after Vicky left a message with the voice mail of the American defense lawyer about discussing a possible plea, the "book-ends" on behalf of their client immediately returned the call and asked to come to D.C. the next day to discuss a proposed plea agreement.

Vicky asked Tim Quinn and Bill Sharkey to be present at the book-ends' plea-bargain presentation in order to provide witnesses to what-ever was said and agreed upon. Vicky had learned long ago to have witnesses as well—many defense lawyers have selective memories.

An hour before the scheduled plea negotiations, Quinn and Sharkey were in Vicky's office discussing strategy prior to the meeting with Dagnar's attorneys. Arrangements had been made to bring Dag-nar from Richmond to D.C. in case a plea agreement was reached.

Vicky summed up the U.S. prosecution position before the meeting for Bill and Quinn. "The Attorney General wants this case turned over to the Brits. Orders came directly from the White House. The President has been talking with the Prime Minister of the U.K. The Brits are firm on this—the case has to go back to England soon. The U.K. wants first crack at Dagnar. Our English prosecutor, James Denison, warned me on this when I called him yesterday and said we were going to conduct preliminary plea negotiations. Denison has already agreed to quickly prosecute Dagnar with the killing of the policeman, Whiteside. That's the case with the strongest evidence—the knife, the wallet, watch . . . all the evidence from the bag in the Serpentine. And as we know Dag-nar will get fifteen years max under English law—they have abolished the death penalty decades ago."

Quinn interrupted, "What do we get?"

Vicky answered, "The only thing the British government will do for us is to allow the U.S. to file a detainer bill and extradition papers on Dagnar for the Temple killing. As soon as Dagnar finishes his fifteen-year term in an English prison, England will turn over Dagnar

to us so we can prosecute him for killing a Congressional witness under the Federal Obstruction of Justice statute that protects Congressional witnesses. . . . By the way, in England fifteen years means fifteen
years. Unlike the situation over here in America, where a thirty-year
sentence can mean release after as little as eight years in most states.
Well, that's the present plan—we get to prosecute Dagnar in Federal
court in Virginia fifteen years from now . . . and who knows, maybe
the NRO tape will be declassified by that time."

Tim, who had spent time in the intelligence world, responded,
"Don't count on it. The spy boys are still holding on to World War
Two secrets."

Sharkey asked Vicky, "What if Dagnar gives us someone high
up—like the person who ordered the hit on Temple?"

"Then everything is subject to negotiation. The higher up we go the
better it is for Dagnar. Remember Dagnar is in the dark—he thinks
he's facing the death penalty first in Virginia. He doesn't know that he's
to be turned over to the Brits for their prosecution first." After Vicky
finished with that statement, she said, "Well, I'm told Dagnar is here,
guarded by U.S. marshals, and his lawyers are probably down the hall
in the conference room. . . . Shall we find out if they have anything to
trade?"

105

VICTOR DAGNAR'S TWO LAWYERS WERE SEATED IN THE
center portion of a long table when Vicky, Bill, and Judge Quinn entered the conference room.

Vicky and her team sat directly across from Dagnar's two attorneys.

I like this—full frontal view of both attorneys. You can sometimes get good info from body language, thought Vicky, who recently had taken a full week's course in deception detection from a contractor in Virginia, taught by a former chief interrogator from the CIA.

After the introductions, Vicky started, "You know the charges . . . and Virginia's record on the death penalty, so do we have anything to talk about?"

Vicky was completely unprepared for the answer.

Dagnar's English barrister responded in his usual low voice, "We can offer solid evidence that the CEO of Carpa was the man who ordered the murder of Judge Temple . . . and we can also supply the name of a United States Senator who helped in the murder of the Judge."

I must have misheard what he said.

Vicky looked at Tim Quinn, who also looked puzzled. So she said, "Could you please repeat what you just said . . . and make it louder?"

The Brit said in his clipped English accent, "I'll come directly to the point. My client wants to stand trial in England on only one murder. If your government can make that happen, he is prepared to implicate the Carpa CEO and one United States Senator in Judge Temple's death."

Vicky rocked back in her chair. Then she responded in a sarcastic voice, "Your client is in a tight spot. I'm sure he would give up Carpa's entire board of directors, plus all the senators from three states to get such a deal. He could make up anything in an effort to save his skin. You've given me nothing. . . . It's only his word."

The reply was short, but powerful. "My client has rock-solid evidence—a tape implicating the CEO, Donald Fay, plus the Senator."

Vicky thought for a moment and replied, "Give me the tape. If it is authentic . . . *and* if your client will give a videotaped confession of the details of both murders, I'm sure we can make a deal."

The Brit looked over at the American defense counsel, who nodded.

"Lovely," said the British barrister.

The British barrister then reached in his suit pocket and took out an object. He carefully slid over to Vicky a small tape cassette, the type used in microrecorders. "I must say I like this system. In the U.K., we hardly ever do this plea bargaining thing. Wonderful saving of time."

"You can wait here. This shouldn't take long. Although the main FBI lab is in Quantico, there's a field lab across the street. I'm sure they have the capacity to quickly check out the tape. By the way, what were the circumstances of the making of the tape? I need to know."

The Brit was hesitant, so his cocounsel, the American attorney representing Dagnar, explained, "My friend is not sure about how we do things here in the States. I told him that plea negotiations are not admissible in court. . . . To answer your question, Ms. Hauser, the tape was made by Dagnar in Fay's office without Fay's knowledge. Fay apparently thought his white noise device—which your technical people will notice as background noise—would prevent any recording of his conversation. Fay was wrong. Our client is a bit of an electronic genius. He got to Fay's office before Fay arrived and disabled some of the frequencies on Fay's white noise machine. Thereby allowing Mr. Dagnar to record the ordering of the hit on Judge Temple. Dagnar thought wisely that he might need insurance at some time in the future—like now." The lawyer paused. Then he added, "The tape *is* authentic and pretty damning for Fay and the Senator. Here are audios of Donald Fay at some press and investor conferences that you can use for voice print analysis. Also, here's a test tape of Victor Dagnar we made for you. Naturally your techies can verify the audio of Fay's voice independently by going online to Carpa's Web site and getting recent audios of Fay speaking to market analysts." The attorney gave Vicky several cassettes.

Vicky replied, "Thanks. Very helpful. You both came prepared. I'll have coffee sent in. . . . And I'll order some dinner for later on. If the tape is good, I'll check with my superiors and call England. If I get the approvals, we might be able to wrap this up tonight. Your client's down the hall. If you want, I'll have you escorted to him. . . . By the way, is pizza okay for dinner?"

The Brit said, "Lovely! I love American pizza."

Vicky led Quinn and Sharkey outside and Vicky told Bill, "Please walk this over to the field lab and have it checked. What do you think about the deal?"

Quinn, mocking the Brit, replied, "Lovely."

Sharkey gave her a wide smile.

Vicky had her answer.

❖ 106 ❖

MSNBC Broadcast—Special Report—Two top executives at the drug giant Carpa arrested in murder plot—Carpa investigation also has triggered ethics probe of Virginia Senator Powers.

(Washington, D.C., Thursday, January 15, 2009, 5:48 P.M., EST) Overshadowing the preparations for next week's Inauguration of the Nation's first African-American President, Ronald T. Hunter, there is a developing story of an unusual criminal case. The dramatic aspects of this murder case sucked the air out of the media's expected fascination with the historical significance of the new administration of President-elect Hunter and his Inauguration next week.

The media attention started when the Department of Justice here in Washington officially confirmed that Donald Fay, the Chief Executive Officer, and Victor Dagnar, the Vice President for Security, of Carpa Pharmaceuticals Corporation, a Fortune 100 company, were arrested earlier this week on murder and conspiracy charges. According to papers filed in U.S. District

Court in Richmond, Virginia, the two men are charged in connection with the death of an English judge and a member of the London police force, a detective inspector from the famous Scotland Yard. The primary Federal statute cited in the court documents is 18 United States Code, Section 1512, which deals with the killing of a witness in any investigation being conducted before Congress. The statute carries a punishment up to the death penalty or imprisonment for life. That fact alone was cause for intense speculation, since it was unknown publicly that the English judge was a Congressional witness.

Then the story was fueled by reports that, according to a plea bargain, Mr. Dagnar had consented to being extradited to England for the trial of the London policeman.

In a separate aspect of the case, Mr. Fay, who was charged with ordering the murder of the English judge, has been released on a three-million-dollar bond. The case against Fay is expected to be presented before a grand jury in Richmond, Virginia, next week. The motive for both killings remains pure speculation.

Although it is a bizarre murder case, it is the other aspects of the case that are driving the intense media attention. Reliable sources say that the murder and conspiracy charges are based in part on sealed evidence of an audiotape in which the Carpa CEO ordered the killing of the judge and confesses to industrial espionage against two of its competitors, Logan Drug Enterprises and an unspecified German drug company. Logan Drug Enterprises currently has a high visibility patent case against Carpa pending in the U.S. Supreme Court. Attorneys representing Logan have refused to comment, except to say that, in light of the reports of possible industrial spying, they are studying potential legal actions against Carpa with regard to the possible theft of trade secrets and test research.

The case also turned political with the rumors that the reported audiotape, not yet made public, has also triggered a criminal investigation and a Senate ethics inquiry against Senator

Irma Powers and her husband, James Powers, a Richmond attorney and former Governor of Virginia. It is alleged that, on the tape, Senator Powers may have received unreported gifts, income, and campaign contributions from Carpa, the major private employer in Virginia. These allegations have been vigorously denied by the Press Secretary for Senator Powers. The current Chair of the Senate Judiciary Committee, Senator Powers is facing a Senate reelection next year and was considered a strong presidential candidate for the Republican party in 2012. Political analysts have commented that these allegations are having a serious effect on the future prospects of her reelection campaign for the Senate, and also on her possible presidential race in 2012.

A source inside the U.S. Senate has leaked to various members of the press that Senator Powers is also being investigated by the Senate Ethics Committee, alleging improper conduct with regards to the recess appointment of Chief Justice Vincent Bianco and a possible connection to that appointment with the Carpa case pending in the U.S. Supreme Court. According to documents filed in the U.S. Senate, Carpa is one of Senator Powers' largest campaign donors and she frequently flies on corporate jets owned by Carpa. In addition there is an allegation that Senator Powers received several unreported gifts, including the hiring of her husband's law firm for nonsubstantive work from Carpa, just before strongly pushing President Ramsey to make a recess appointment for Justice Vincent Bianco as the Chief Justice. This allegation and the apparent flip-flop of Bianco's position on patent protection terms during the Carpa oral argument last week has fueled speculation that there had been an improper quid pro quo for the Bianco recess appointment. This swirl of possible misdoings by the Senator and a Supreme Court Justice is unprecedented in recent years and reminds historians of the Justice Abe Fortas scandal of "money for possible favors" of the midtwentieth century.

All these allegations involving the Carpa case, although unsubstantiated at this time, have had a major effect on Wall

Street. Carpa's stock has dropped from $27.89 when the market opened this morning to $22.45 at the closing bell of the New York Stock Exchange.

In a related story, two of the apprehended white supremacists who attacked former Justice Moorman have implicated Trey Bishop, a wealthy businessman from Montgomery, Alabama, in the plot to kill Justice Moorman. Bishop was harmed early in his business career by an adverse merger decision handled by Moorman when he worked for the U.S. Department of Justice.

This is Kim Columbian reporting for MSNBC News with a Special Report from Washington, D.C.

(*End of video transcript*)

⟡ 107 ⟡

United States Supreme Court (*Orders List: 748 U.S.___*)
Friday, January 16, 2009

Orders in Pending Cases

07-561   *Carpa Pharmaceuticals Corporation v. Logan*
              Drug Enterprises
The *sua sponte* motion of the Court to withdraw the Writ of Certiorari to the United States Court of Appeals for the Federal Circuit has been granted. The prior grant of certiorari is withdrawn as improvidently granted. The Chief Justice took no part in the consideration or decision of this motion.

07-369   *Scott, Reginald v. The State of Missouri*

The motion of the Solicitor General for leave to participate in oral argument as amicus curiae and for divided argument is granted.

07-877   *Halloran Uniform Company v. Monsanto Chemical Company*

The motion for petition of the Writ of Certiorari to United States Court of Appeals for the Eighth Circuit is denied.

(End of Orders List)

❖ 108 ❖

United States Supreme Court
Friday, January 16, 2009, 5:50 P.M. (EST)
Press Release (Immediate Distribution)

Chief Justice Vincent X. Bianco has retired from the Supreme Court effective immediately. Personal family reasons were given for the retirement.

❖

Alone in his huge inner office, Vincent Bianco sat behind his big mahogany desk. He was somber, but certain.

The best way out of this mess is to get off the Court, reasoned Vincent Bianco.

He had always thought most problems were solved not by the

constant seeking of new information, but by reviewing the information already known.

What facts he knew were terrifying to him:

1. That Carpa's involvement with the murders in London had drawn massive media attention.
2. Senator Powers was under investigation for her conduct in doing favors for Carpa.
3. The Supreme Court case of Carpa was being pulled into the tent of media circus.
4. Senator Powers, a survivor of the highest order, would throw anyone under a bus to save herself. In an attempt to lessen her punishment, Powers could implicate him by saying he promised to deliver a favorable decision on the Capra case for the recess appointment—that was a definite possibility. The only saving fact to that scenario was that *no one heard* his proposal in the Fort Myer chapel hallway—if she raised that in an attack on him, it would be a classic standoff: "she said, he said." Moreover, Powers would only be implicating herself in bribery by confessing that Bianco's promised help on the Carpa case was why Powers helped with the recess appointment.

With the above factors in mind, Vincent Bianco knew his decision to leave the Supreme Court was the right one. It was fortunate that he had reached retirement age on the Supreme Court—seventy years old plus over twenty years on the Court. He could draw his full annual salary of $194,200 immediately if he left the Court. That full lifetime salary plus the $650,000 per annum deanship of a new Roman Catholic law school—funded by a wealthy Catholic charismatic friend—now being built in Florida outside of Orlando would be a good new direction in his life. The offer from his "born-again" multibillionaire friend, who was footing the bill for the law school, had been given to him as an option or consolation prize the day Moorman was nominated to be Chief Justice. His wealthy friend had said he would keep the offer open for one year. "Maybe God wants you to lead from the academic world now"—was the reasoning the rich man gave Bianco.

As a practical, political matter, Bianco knew his Washington history, and especially the lesson learned from the Justice Abe Fortas case in the 1960s—Fortas's resignation from the Supreme Court saved the Court from an embarrassing investigation into possible improper payments while Fortas was a sitting Supreme Court Justice. As far as Bianco was concerned, with his decision to leave the Supreme Court and with a nonvote by the Court on Carpa, the wind would be taken from any serious inquiry into the Carpa case.

Accordingly, Bianco had secretly called each of the other justices separately and told them he was resigning and counseled them that further proceedings by the Court on the Carpa case would pull the Court into a very political criminal investigation. He had suggested the withdrawal of the cert order as a measure to do just that. Wisely, one by one, each justice accepted his reasoning that the Carpa case could and should be withdrawn from the Supreme Court's calendar. All six justices agreed with his idea—that the pain to the Court was not worth the gain of deciding the patent problems of a big drug company.

Bianco looked at his watch and saw that it was just 6 P.M. on Friday. The press announcement was being distributed to the Supreme Court press corps—the "dead zone of news"—a perfect time for the press announcement on his retirement to be released—just as he had ordered it.

Satisfied with his decision, Bianco started to do his prayer preparation. His office door was locked and he was alone in his office. Bianco slowly stood up, holding out both arms, and said out loud, "Thanks to God the Almighty, I made it to be the Chief Justice of the United States."

Then he uttered over and over his personal prayer mantra, "*Solo Christo . . . Solo Christo . . .* ('Christ Alone')" and suddenly he dropped to his knees and folded his hands together in prayer.

Soon he was in rapture—speaking in tongues.

❖ 109 ❖

MSNBC.com—Business and Financial News Headlines—Breaking News (Internet)—Carpa Pharmaceuticals stock in a freefall.

WASHINGTON D.C., MONDAY, JANUARY 19, 2009, 1:30 P.M. (EST)—Just past the midway point of the trading day, Carpa stock has seen another dramatic drop today. Carpa, a traditional strong performer, was trading at $27.89 less than one week ago. Last Friday Carpa stock started a significant decline following the news that the U.S. Supreme Court has, in effect, dismissed Carpa's appeal in a key patent case worth a projected four billion in profits to be realized by the drug giant during the next three years. The court case involved a legal issue that Carpa was entitled to three more years of patent protection for its popular drug Varakain, a pain reliever for arthritis. Carpa's stock ended the trading day Friday at $19.60.

Today was another bad day for Carpa. After a short early morning rally by some institutional investors, Carpa stock dropped to $7.38 by mid-day. At that point, the New York Stock Exchange, upon request by Carpa officials, suspended trading in Carpa stock.

Today's stock drop for the troubled drug company is attributed to reports that over the weekend the Carpa Board of Directors fired its CEO, Donald Fay, and its Vice President for Security, Victor Dagnar. Both men have been implicated in a double murder in London. In addition, the Carpa General Counsel, Jay Watsworth, has announced his immediate retirement. There were also unconfirmed reports that a competitor, Logan Drug Enterprises, will file a civil action against Carpa, charging industrial espionage and seeking damages for the theft of trade secrets and research test results with regard to its rival antacid product.

❖ 110 ❖

CNN.com—Breaking News (Internet)—New president nominates three to U.S. Supreme Court.

WASHINGTON D.C., WEDNESDAY, JANUARY 21, 2009, AT 11:30 A.M. (EST)—President Ronald T. Hunter hit the ground running and, on his first morning in the Oval Office, showed unusually prompt and decisive action in sending the nominations of three noted jurists to fill the vacancies on the Supreme Court. Legal experts had predicted a long and very political selection process, but President Hunter, a former state court judge, obviously had made this nomination action a top priority of his new administration's promised focus on law enforcement.

Nominated to the position of Chief Justice of the United States was Judge Roberta Ferson of Los Angeles. She is a Federal Judge on the United States Court of Appeals for the Ninth Circuit. If confirmed, Judge Ferson would be the first African-American woman to serve on the high court.

Also nominated was Judge Alberto Moro of Tampa, Florida.

Judge Moro sits on the U.S. Court of Appeals for the Eleventh Circuit. Judge Moro, if confirmed, would be the first Hispanic Supreme Court justice.

The third nomination was that of Judge Homer Rosemont of Montgomery, Alabama. Judge Rosemont is a Senior Judge on the U.S. District Court in Montgomery. Judge Rosemont is an African-American.

During his campaign, President Hunter had promised that he would strive to establish a merit-based Federal judiciary. In that context, it is interesting to note that all three nominated judges were listed in the *Legal Times* weekly newspaper's recent ranking of the top fifty judges in America—an annual list based on merit and conducted by a well-respected survey firm that polled litigants, lawyers, and judges. To make that list, a judge had to be good . . . very good. This factor in the selection of these judges highlights President Hunter's campaign promise to pick Federal judges on the basis of merit alone. Underscoring that point, it is telling that, although political parties are a major factor in judicial selection, Judges Rosemont and Moro were appointees of Republican presidents (Reagan had appointed Rosemont and George W. Bush had selected Moro as a Federal Judge). Judge Ferson was placed on the Federal bench by President Clinton, but before her selection, she had served as a career trial attorney in the Justice Department with no party affiliation.

Contacted immediately after these major nominations, the Presidents of both the American Bar Association and the Federal Bar Association have expressed support for all three nominations.

✧ 111 ✧

MSNBC transcript of Hardball *for the evening of January 23, 2009.*

MATTHEWS: Good evening. It has been an amazing week for the newly inaugurated President Hunter and his three nominations for the Supreme Court. Hunter's obvious interest in making these appointments a top priority was in evidence since his inauguration was on Tuesday and on Wednesday morning he moved swiftly to heal the constitutional crisis at the Supreme Court by sending the three names to the Senate for confirmation. As the Nation knows, in the last two months there has been an unprecedented leadership crisis at the high Court—the Court has lost three chief justices in those months. First, a young fit Chief Justice William Simmons died of a brain aneurysm during a session of the Court. Then, after a racially charged confirmation fight, the first African-American Chief Justice, Oscar Moorman, was confirmed—only to be killed hours later in an accidental handgun discharge by his wife, who then committed suicide—extremely tragic circumstances. Then in a truly inexplicable incident, the next chief justice, appointed via a recess appointment by President Ramsey, Vincent Bianco, unexpectedly resigned under rumors of a possible connection with influence in a large patent case pending before the high Court. Wow, there couldn't be more drama at the Supreme Court if Washington flipped roles with Hollywood!

To examine the situation at the Supreme Court, we have in our studio in Washington two well-respected judicial experts— retired Federal Judge Stan Sporkin and Tim Quinn, a former Federal Court of Appeals Judge and the former Special Counsel to the Senate Judiciary Committee for the Moorman confirmation. Our first topic is the Supreme Court—the impact of the triple change-over at the Court and the tragic story of Chief Justice Oscar Moorman and his wife.

I'm Chris Matthews and let's play *Hardball!*

MATTHEWS: First let's go to Judge Stanley Sporkin, a retired federal judge. Judge Sporkin, welcome to *Hardball,* and what can you tell us about the effect of the recent losses on the Supreme Court? Can the present Court function properly with three vacancies?

SPORKIN: Good evening, Chris. Listen, the Supreme Court can handle the present situation. There have always been unexpected losses of justices. It's a strong Court with able justices. Remember, the original Supreme Court only had six justices from 1789 until the early 1800s, when the number of justices was raised to seven. Eventually the number of justices rose to nine. Yes, Chris, the Court can function quite well with six justices until President Hunter's nominations are confirmed.

MATTHEWS: Yes. But this is very unusual, three losses in two months?

SPORKIN: Sure, it's unusual, but it's just compacted history. What happened in two months could have happened in two years. Our Constitution is prepared to handle deaths and departures from the Court according to an established process. I really don't know why people are saying we're in a constitutional crisis. You'll find that this Court can function and decide cases with the present six justices. If there's a three-to-three tie, then the Court Rules provide that the lower court's decision is affirmed. . . . No, this Court is not in any crisis. It's just in a sad time, in which unexpected deaths took two very fine justices and another decided that it was time to move on to another phase in his life. On that point, I wish Chief Justice Bianco well in his new role as the dean of a law school being built—a real challenge.

MATTHEWS: Judge, okay, so there's no crisis. Let's talk about the Moorman tragedy.

SPORKIN: What's to say? Oscar Moorman was a very fine judge and that accident was beyond tragic. The judiciary lost a good man. I didn't know Moorman that well. I think Judge Quinn would be a better source to talk about Chief Justice Moorman.

MATTHEWS: Fair enough. Judge Quinn, I know you were the Special Counsel to the Senate Judiciary Committee during the Moorman confirmation as Chief Justice. What is your view of the process? Was he treated fairly during the confirmation?

QUINN: The process worked. The Senate Judiciary Committee members did their job under the Constitution in an exemplary fashion. And Oscar Moorman was confirmed in almost record time. . . . But, as everyone knows, it was a confirmation marred by an assassination attempt that is now accepted as racially based. In addition, and unfortunately, Moorman was the subject of three separate smear attacks to his reputation. Attacks which the committee dealt with fairly and swiftly. However, the last false attack based on doctored photos, as you know, probably was what triggered Mrs. Moorman's stress, and led to the fatal accident that took the life of Chief Justice Moorman and to his wife's suicide. A real tragedy. Moorman would have been a great leader of the judicial branch.

MATTHEWS: Now there are reports in the press that the nomination of Moorman and the recess appointment of Justice Bianco are both tied to the growing scandal involving Carpa, the big drug company. Any hint of that in your investigation involving the confirmation of Moorman?

QUINN: Absolutely none. In fact, *when* there was a hint in the press that Moorman may have been nominated as Chief Justice due to his propatent positions, Oscar Moorman did the right thing—he recused himself from voting on the Carpa case . . . and notified the Senate Judiciary Committee and the public of that fact *before* the confirmation vote. In my view, that act was a courageous and honorable thing for a judge to do. Chief Justice Moorman wanted to become Chief Justice in the proper way. . . . Moorman was an honest man.

SPORKIN: Chris, let me chime in here on that point in support of Judge Quinn. My friends in the judiciary . . . to a person all think that Moorman was tops—ethically and as a judge. America has lost a great judge. Shalom, Chief Justice Moorman.

MATTHEWS: Well, I'm no judge, but let me vote with you both on Moorman and make it—three to zero. Unanimous decision—Chief Justice Oscar Moorman was a fine judge and our Nation has suffered a huge loss with his passing . . . thank you both, Judges Sporkin and Quinn, for joining us to play *Hardball.* Now, we'll move to a commercial break, and when we return, we'll take on our second topic of the night. The recent face-off between China and Taiwan over trade issues.

This is Chris Matthews. Keep watching as we continue to play *Hardball.*

✦

As Tim Quinn left the downtown D.C. MSNBC station that hosted *Hardball,* in the lobby he heard a news flash—Justice Bianco had been found dead of an apparent stroke. Tim watched the TV monitor for a few minutes and then he stepped outside into the cold winter weather of a January night, turned up the collar of his trench coat, and started walking north on First Street toward the Dubliner Pub, where he was going to meet Vicky Hauser for dinner.

Quinn's thoughts turned to his inner conflict of his spur of the moment call to Vicky to meet him after the TV show—he still loved his dead wife and missed her terribly every day since the car accident over one year ago that robbed him of growing old with her—his Katy. Yet he was about to meet Vicky . . . a love from his law school days and a woman who moved him as he worked with her on the Moorman confirmation.

Should he love again? Could he take the pain of losing again?

Suddenly he thought of Oscar and Debby Moorman—victims of their own love. Now that the pieces of their last few minutes were being discovered, he worried that true love—which he saw in Oscar and Debby—could often be self-destructive.

Then he turned off the fear—as he had learned to do in Vietnam—and thought of doing the right thing.

Life was short and very unpredictable.

He should meet Vicky and follow his heart.